I0719175

# A Question of Balance

## Justice #1

## SUZAN HARDEN

A QUESTION OF BALANCE
Justice #1

This is a work of fiction. All characters, organizations and events in this novel are products of the author's imagination and are not to be construed as real. Any resemblance to persons, living or dead, is entirely coincidental.

Copyright © 2016 by Suzan Harden
Ingramspark Special Edition: June 2019
All Rights Reserved.
ISBN: 978-1-938745-58-4
Published by Angry Sheep Publishing
Findlay, Ohio

Cover Design by For the Muse Design
Interior Design by QA Productions

www.suzanharden.com

## BY SUZAN HARDEN

(Each series is in suggested reading order)

### Bloodlines

*Blood Magick*
*Zombie Love*
*Zombie Confidential*
*Zombie Wedding*
*Amish, Vamps & Thieves*
*Blood Sacrifice*
*Love, War & a Bulldog*
*Zombie Goddess*
*Ravaged*
*Sacrificed*
*Reality Bites* (Coming Soon)
*Ghouls in the Grocery* (Coming Soon)
*Resurrected* (Coming Soon)

### Seasons of Magick

*Spring*
*Summer*
*Autumn*
*Winter*

### Justice

*Sword and Sorceress 28* ("Justice")
*Sword and Sorceress 30* ("Diplomacy in the Dark")
*Justice: The Beginning*
*A Question of Balance*
*A Modicum of Truth*
*A Matter of Death* (Coming Soon)
*A Touch of Mother* (Coming Soon)

### 888-555-HERO

*Hero De Facto*
*Hero Ad Hoc*
*Hero De Novo*

### Miscellaneous

*Sword and Sorceress 31* ("Pig-Headed")
*Sword and Sorceress 32* ("Unexpected")

*To Judge Cynthia Crowe and Author Anthea Sharp,*
*two ladies who don't realize how much they've taught me.*

# Prologue

*Two thousand years ago, every kingdom and tribe had their own names for the gods. These kingdoms and tribes battled over their gods, not realizing the different names were a construct of the inadequacies of human languages, when in fact, they spoke of the same entities.*

*She Whose Task Is Balance knew both past and future. She realized the danger such differences brought. Mortals destroyed each other, weakening not just themselves but the gods as well, because without their united worship, the gods withered. And far greater dangers lay beyond the world of gods and men.*

*She called Her priests and priestesses to Her on the shores of the Middle Sea. She bade them to sit at a round stone table. These servants of Balance were sorely afraid, for as She circled the table, Her form changed to that of each of Her Names, but always holding Her scales. When She reached the one empty chair, She was dressed in black robes, Her face hidden in a deep cowl. She drew a silver sword from nothingness and thrust it into the table. She then hung Her scales from the pommel of the quivering steel.*

*When She spoke, those who gathered trembled. And when She warned they had a thousand years to prepare for an invasion by beings from outside of reality, they shook violently. But they listened and spread Her Word.*

*The priesthoods of the other gods listened and prepared, for even their own deities attended when Balance deigned to speak. The rulers and people of the kingdoms and tribes listened and prepared. Knowledge was shared, and as a result all the lands grew and were prosperous. So wealthy the lands became over that thousand years, many, including those sworn to Balance, began to doubt Her Word.*

*Then the demons came.*

*Darkness fell across the world. First came the seduction of the demon's power, then the blood of mortals drenched the soil. Men and women pled with Balance to take pity on their plight. Seeing Her scales so weighted against them, She and her Sisters and Brothers took the field in all Their Glory.*

*It took another thousand years, but together, gods and men drove the demons back to their own dark realm. Or so men thought.*

*Balance warned them to be ever vigilant, but once again, mortals forgot because their lives are so short compared to the gods.*

*And the demons waited . . .*

— The Fifth Book of Balance, Verses I thru X

# *Chapter 1*

Since it was Rest Day, I was still in my bedclothes and breaking my fast when Duke Marco's messenger arrived. Setting aside the rich cinnamon bread, I glared at both the nervous young man and my personal assistant Sivan. "Tell me, is there a chance His Grace, his lady wife or his retainers might let me finish one morning meal in peace?"

"When the stars fall from the skies, Justice?" Humor edged Sivan's response.

My displeasure settled on the messenger. His bright scarlet face and hands quivered.

I smiled sweetly, but the boy wasn't comforted by my demeanor. My appearance discomfited nearly everyone the first time they saw me, my lover being the sole exception. "What is so important that your master could not wait for a reasonable time, like *after* Second Morning?"

"My apologies, L-Lady Justice. Duke Marco respectfully requests your presence. A-a body was found in one of the keep's wine barrels." His voice cracked on the last syllable.

Orrin was the third largest city in Issura and had the second largest seaport. While crime wasn't rampant, the city's main problem was disorderly conduct from sailors on shore leave. Or it was until I was assigned as the resident justice last summer. Even then, I was rarely called to investigate normal offenses like theft or smuggling, which the Orrin magistrate and his peacekeepers handled quite ably. It was for inconvenient things like this.

I shoved my plate away, wiped my mouth with my napkin and stood. "Thank you so very much for destroying my appetite."

The boy whimpered. From his voice and his manner, he was the highest ranking page available. No matter if he had heard the rumors many times over, my red eyes had made more than a few grown men wet their smallclothes.

"Run across the street, and request a priest from Light to accompany me."

"Y-yes, ma'am." He fled as if I'd summon demons to eat his scrawny hide. Sivan didn't bother to hide her laughter any longer.

"You did that on purpose," I accused. According to the gossip I overheard on my way to the temple kitchen one evening, my nickname was the Red Justice. So far, no one had the effrontery to call me that to my face.

Sivan folded her hands primly in front of her. "He said he was instructed to only deliver the message to you, m'lady. Far be it for me to interfere with his duty."

I stalked over to the wardrobe in the corner of my private chamber. Inside were several sets of formal cloaks. To any one else, they looked identical, the black of the Temple of Balance from hood to ankle. But for me, I could still see the blood stains on all of them.

Various laundresses' best efforts not withstanding.

Out of some sense of perversity, I chose the set that still carried the stains of the sorcerer Samael, a distant member of the royal family whom I'd illegally executed to save Duke Marco.

And the world.

Once I'd donned leggings, boots and a silk undershirt, I tied on my robes, pulled up the hood, and added my sword to the ensemble. In the half year since Marco's parents had been found guilty of treason due to their conspiracy with Samael DiRoy, little incidents had been occurring. Small challenges to the duke's authority. Carefully crafted insults.

It didn't help that he'd married a commoner who'd been conceived during the Spring Rituals, though the Lady Katarina was a healer of no mean skill.

So far, the young man had been holding his own. But a body found on his estate would only escalate the problems with the nobility, even if the young lord and his retinue were innocent. Nothing like a good scandal to stir the masses.

I reached the stables to find High Brother Luc, chief priest of Orrin's Temple of Light, already mounted, waiting for me with two of his wardens. Cold raindrops trickled dark purple tracks down his cloak.

I had to hide my delight that he came. "Brother, please don't bother on such an ugly day. Either of your junior priests would do in this circumstance. Surely as the head of your temple, you have more important duties."

"Considering where the body was found, it seemed that our best truthspeller should accompany you, Justice." Amusement flavored his tone. Now that we were both permanently assigned to Orrin, we went through this dance of words every time we met in public since we could not often meet privately without arousing suspicions.

By the Twelve, I missed sleeping with him.

I inclined my head. "Thank you for your assistance, Brother."

Little Bear, one of my own wardens, moved to assist me on my horse. I glared at him, my foul mood spilling over once again.

Luc muffled his laugh, and the warden had the grace to say sheepishly, "My apologies, Justice. I forgot."

Reining in my temper, I said, "I understand, but this behavior must stop."

"Before she knocks someone's teeth out," Luc added. Like Sivan earlier, he didn't bother hiding his laughter.

"Yes, m'lady." Little Bear bowed and turned to his own horse.

It was habit on the warden's part, I knew. Every priestess in my order was blind.

Every single one except me.

The wardens and clerks acted as the justice's eyes. None of the staff at Orrin knew what to do with a sighted justice. Not that I saw the world as they saw it, but I had vision enough I wasn't helpless by any means.

I climbed on my precious Nassa and patted her neck. "Shall we discover what's troubling Duke DiMara today?"

Luc snorted. "I'd say it was his ruined wine."

I couldn't be angry with the page for spreading unnecessary gossip. Luc could charm the knowledge out of anyone without the need of a truthspell.

We guided our mounts through the postern gate, down the alley that separated my goddess's temple from that of Mother, and up Temple Street, the main thoroughfare of the city. The business district gave way to small shops and eateries. Orrin was rich enough that the streets were cobblestoned, but the winter rains kept most of the citizens indoors despite the absence of mud.

Small homes appeared between the merchant buildings. Gradually the shops disappeared, and the houses grew larger as we climbed the bluffs on the north side of the bay.

The DiMara estate overlooked the city and harbor, an imposing stone enclave that still bore signs of its original purpose as a fortress. A guardsman swung open the ornate wrought iron gate, a show of the family's wealth, as we approached. The duke's family controlled a majority of the Orrin harbor trade, and those ships they didn't own outright, they had invested in over the years.

Two stableboys took our horses while the guardsman led us on foot to a warehouse on the left. The dry interior was welcome after our short, wet ride.

Orrin's magistrate, Malven DiCook, was not.

"'Bout time his lordship's pet priestess got here." He coughed and spat on the floor, close enough to me to be thoroughly disgusting but intentionally missing my boot. Duke Marco wasn't the only one dealing with insults and challenges to authority, but the ones aimed at me weren't so carefully crafted.

If I had the evidence Malven was involved in the former lord and lady's treason, I'd behead the bastard without blinking. But I didn't, which meant I had to tread lightly around the duly elected city magistrate.

And tolerate the sickly sweet odor of the damn licorice-scented dye he used to disguise the effects of age in his hair and beard.

He hooked his thumbs in his belt and rocked back on his heels. "His lordship wouldn't let me examine the body until you arrived."

I brushed back the hood of my cloak and stepped closer. Being a tall woman was handy at times. I met the magistrate's glare before he turned his attention toward the floor. Sometimes, my idiotic attempt to give myself sight came in handy for unnerving my antagonist.

He muttered the Cantish word for "freak."

"No," I answered in the same language. "I was chosen by the Goddess. If you have an issue with her selection, I'm sure the Reverend Mother could arrange an audience for you." I didn't add my personal opinion of his hygiene habits.

He jerked and shuffled a step backward. I didn't know whether it was due to my knowledge of Cantish or my not-so-subtle threat. Nor did I wish to probe his thoughts to find out. Mucking out Duke Marco's horse stalls would be a far more pleasant task.

Luc's amusement at the magistrate's reaction tickled my mind, but he said nothing.

"This way m'lady." The guardsman beckoned us to follow. He marched for the opening that yawned in the floor of the storage room.

Luc faced our wardens. "Two up. Two down with us." Without a word, one of his and Little Bear moved to positions where they could watch both the main door, the passage to the underground storage rooms, and each other's backs.

Marco's guardsman lit an oil lamp and led our retinue and the magistrate down the wide wooden ramp. The air was terribly dry for such a miserable, wet day. Small bowls sat in alcoves along the wall. The bone salt in them absorbed the moisture in the air to prevent mold and rot.

At the bottom of the ramp, my desiccated airways itched from both the mineral and the sawdust coating the floor. Despite the sweet scent of mountain pine, another sickly smell met me. The guardsman gestured to the wide double doorway to our right.

I strode past the guardsmen to find Duke Marco, his wife and sister, his steward, and another household servant on one side. Facing them were three of the city's peacekeepers. A wine barrel stood upright between the two sets of observers. The tension in the wine room was more suffocating than the odor of death.

"You and your household seem rather intent on disturbing my morning meals, Your Grace." I nodded to the women. "Lady Katarina, Lady Alessa."

"Truly, I would prefer not to." Marco's grim humor matched mine. "However, the circumstances warranted your curious mind."

"Would it make you more comfortable if I provided you a knife to threaten someone with, Justice Anthea?" Lady Katarina offered with the same amusement as her husband. She rested a bright red hand over her prominent stomach.

Sometimes, the odd eyesight I'd given myself let me see things that others couldn't. Like the rise in the lady's body temperature. Knowing she was with child before she did had been entertaining.

An odd sort of friendship had sprung between Lady Katarina and myself over the last six months. Probably because we were both products of the Temple of Love's Spring Rituals. Definitely because I had saved her and her husband's lives from his deranged mother and the demons her pet sorcerer had summoned.

"That will be unnecessary, m'lady," I replied and brushed the pommel of my sword at my shoulder. "I've learned to carry bigger weapons when you two are involved."

"If you're going to do nothing but joke with His Grace, maybe you should leave." The magistrate's irritation felt like steel scraped across slate.

I turned my gaze on DiCook. "I didn't realize you had been named the Reverend Mother of Balance."

"Your predecessor had a sense of decorum in these matters," he shot back.

Sometimes, I wondered if the elderly justice who held the temple seat here before me was willfully, as well as literally blind. But that wasn't fair. None of the priest or priestesses of the eleven other temples detected so much as a whiff of trouble with Marco's parents before it was too late.

Unless I'd totally misread their allegiances.

I had gotten lucky, and I knew it. Otherwise, we'd be neck-deep in another demon war now.

"Really, Sir Magistrate? In reviewing her records, I did not come across any accounts of bodies in wine barrels. Care to enlighten me?"

He muttered another obscenity under his breath, but otherwise remained silent.

The duke and his party wisely said nothing as well while I crossed to the source of the odor and peered inside. I couldn't distinguish much in the deep green mass because the body had cooled to the same temperature as the liquid it floated in, so I inhaled deeply.

I looked up at Luc who had joined me. "He or she didn't loose their bowels in there."

"She," he corrected. At my quizzical expression, he added, "Too much hair floating at the top of the barrel."

"Could be Pagonian." I shrugged. Both men and women of Issura's neighbor to the north only cut their locks during a period of family grieving.

Luc shook his head. "No. Hair's too pale even soaked in dark red wine."

I sighed. "I suppose I should examine the timeline before we pull whoever it is out of the barrel."

Luc grunted and looked over his shoulder. "Duke Marco, when was this barrel brought onto your estate?"

The nobleman's sister Alessa was the one who answered. "Three days ago, High Brother."

"Was the wine seal intact?" I asked.

The three nobles looked at the steward who turned to the man beside him who nervously shuffled his feet before he answered. "The wax weren't broken, m'lady, but the winery stamp weren't there neither." He shrugged. "We git 'em that way sometimes, usually in the summer. The tops melt."

"But this is the middle of winter," I said softly.

"During winter cleaning, the lads at the winery set the barrels outside in the sun," the steward volunteered. "The air temperature is cold enough to keep the wine fresh, but the direct light softens the wax."

"Sounds reasonable," Luc said.

Luc turned back to me. *We can always confirm with the priests at Vintner.* Out loud, he said, "With her being dead, I won't be able to track her."

I grinned at him. "Afraid the Wilding priests might show you up?"

DiCook stomped over to the barrel. "If you two are finished making light of someone's murder, maybe you'll get around to finding the culprit."

"Murder? Who said anything about murder?" I couldn't resist needling the magistrate.

His face turned a brilliant scarlet. "So this poor woman decided to take a swim in a barrel of his lordship's wine?"

"We cannot assume anything at this point." My Luc, ever the voice of reason. "What do you need, Anthea?" His question was for the benefit of everyone else in the room.

"Just some quiet," I murmured. I pulled off my gloves and settled cross-legged on the cold flagstone floor. With one hand on the barrel and one on a shard of decorative onyx embedded next to the slate, I concentrated.

The stone quivered beneath my palm, eager to tell its story. It paid more attention to the vagaries of the mobile beings than its slate brothers.

I tugged the strings of time with the stone's assistance, unwinding back to four days ago. Luc and the rest would see transparent figures moving faster than usual. I could only see gray ghosts drifting around and through the colored figures of the living in the storage room. Two phantom men rolled a barrel out of the room.

"Hold." Luc's baritone rumbled through the air.

I paused the release of the time thread.

"Names," he demanded.

"That's William and me," squeaked the retainer standing with the steward.

"Name," Luc snapped.

"Bartholomew, m'lord," the retainer squeaked again.

"I told them to bring up a barrel of the local rosé for dinner the night before the delivery," the steward offered.

"Luc," I said through gritted teeth.

"My apologies. Continue." At least he actually sounded sorry, but I don't think he truly understood the strain of what I was doing.

I let the string of time the onyx showed me slide forward. Several ghostly men rolled barrels down the ramp.

"Who are the three with Bartholomew?" Luc asked.

"The man on the barrel with him is Julian, one of the Duke's retainers," the steward answered. "The other two are the vineyard's transporters."

"Do you know them?"

The steward shook his head. "Rubio and his son normally bring the Orrin shipments. These two said Rubio had hurt his back, and they'd been hired to deliver the barrels."

"Names," Luc snapped again.

"Th-they didn't give their names." A green sheen of sweat appeared at the steward's hairline. "Their paperwork had the vineyard's seal."

Luc folded his arms. "Where did the shipment come from?"

"The Pana Valley," Lady Alessa and the steward answered at the same time.

"Lord Aleister DiGrove's estate," the duke's sister added.

Luc's concern matched my own. If this turned out to be a power play within the nobility, things could turn very ugly very fast.

I let the rest of the timeline slide through my grip. But once the barrel in question was stored, it remained in place until Bartholomew and the man he named as William tapped it this morning.

"Well, that wasn't a damn bit helpful," Luc murmured.

I thanked the onyx before I shook the feeling back into my fingers and rose to my feet. "Let's drain the barrel and get her out."

"Shame about the wine." Luc stepped out of the way.

I could hear DiCook's teeth grind, but he kept silent.

The steward and Bartholomew set buckets under the tap to drain the ruined red while the guardsman went off to fetch an old blanket. Once a sufficient amount had been removed that we wouldn't flood the cellar if we accidentally tipped it, Luc and I peered in the barrel once more.

I pulled my gloves back on. "Ready?"

"We can do it if her ladyship can't."

I didn't have to look at DiCook to hear the sneer in his voice. "My thanks, Magistrate, but I can't have you or your men vomit on the body and contaminate it." I hooked my arm under one of the corpse's shoulders. "Ready?"

Luc grabbed the other shoulder. Together, Luc and I lifted the deceased out of the barrel. She was heavier than she should have been, her skin having absorbed a great deal of wine. On the shores of the Peaceful Sea, one couldn't help seeing their share of drowning victims. We carefully settled the nude body on the blanket.

I brushed the soaked locks away from the face. A sharp gasp came from Lady Katarina. I looked at noblewoman. "You recognize her?"

She stepped closer. "The face is distorted but—" She gave a sharp nod. "Sister Gretchen from the Temple of Love. She was my playmate when we were children."

I could feel Luc watching me, which was understandable. For the six months since my assignment to Orrin, I'd managed to avoid the chief priestess of the Temple of Love, but I couldn't any longer.

With one of her people dead, I was going to have to face my mother.

# Chapter 2

My breakfast twisted in my stomach and not from the gruesome discovery in Duke Marco's wine cellar.

Luc checked the barrel and the buckets. "You were correct. No hint of bowel contents. She was dead before she was put in the barrel." He knelt next to the body. "There's bruising along her neck." He reached out, his hands matching bruises I could not see, but the rest did. "She was strangled."

Now that the dead priestess was out of the wine, slight temperature variances registered with my odd sight. My attention was drawn to the area between her legs.

Like all of the priestesses of Love, her body hair was shorn, but that wasn't what concerned me. "Luc."

He examined the slashes in the flesh. His voice was grim when he said, "That was not caused by rough loveplay."

I inclined my head in the magistrate's direction.

Luc rose to his feet. "Let's get the official questioning of everyone present out of the way. If you don't mind, Magistrate . . ."

"You can start with whoever on earth you wish," DiCook snapped.

"I mean, I will question you first." Luc grinned.

"Me? You have the audacity—"

"You were the one who said she was murdered, Magistrate." I glared at the idiot. Part of me hoped he was involved. "In front of witnesses, I might add, before the brother and I pulled her body from the barrel. You have the right to decline questioning, but I suggest you allow Brother Luc to clear you now." I smiled. "If you are innocent."

"How do I know you're not incriminating me to remove me from my position?" A barely controlled tremor shook his voice.

I climbed to my feet. "I have no reason to, and in case your brilliant powers of deduction have missed the obvious, both the crown and the temples are keeping a very close eye on events in Orrin after last summer."

"You should have been executed for what you did last summer," he spat.

"Yes, I should have been," I said dryly. "Again, if you have a dispute with the Reverend Mother of Balance, I suggest you take it up with her."

His face turned a red so dark it bordered on purple. At least, he understood his position was as precarious as my own. He turned to Luc. "Very well. Ask your questions."

"Thank you for your cooperation, Magistrate." That was Luc, ever the epitome of tact. "Is there another room I may use, Your Grace?"

"The granary is on the other side of the ramp. It will be more comfortable than the cold rooms." Marco's voice was smooth, but I had a feeling he'd just as soon shove DiCook into one of the meat or vegetable lockers and leave him there until he died of a chill.

As Luc's warden followed him and the magistrate, I turned to the female Balance warden who had accompanied us. One day I was going to get all their names straight.

"Go upstairs. Have Little Bear ride to the Temple of Balance. I'm going to need a clerk to record statements. Then have him collect the Master Healer. I want him here to examine the corpse."

"Yes, m'lady." The woman saluted before she pivoted smartly on her heels and marched out the door.

I faced the duke's party for the next order of business. "Lady Alessa, may I impose on you for a bedsheet to cover our unfortunate sister?"

From the way she clasped her hands over her mouth and the yellowish color of her skin, I thought she would be sick. She shook herself out of her shock and said, "Of course, Justice." With a quick curtsy, she scurried out the door.

The three city peacekeepers stared at me, unsure of what to do with their leader not so obliquely accused of knowledge of a murder and me issuing orders.

"Have any of you three dealt with Sister Gretchen?"

"No," they chorused, but the one on my far right blushed bright orange.

I sighed. "You do realize that if you lie to me now, then admit to knowing her under Brother Luc's truthspell, things will not go well with you."

"I—I—" The peacekeeper I noticed sounded like he was choking on a harvest ham. "I have, m'lady. At the Spring Rituals three years ago."

I crossed my arms over my chest and stared at him.

"And a few times since then," he mumbled.

I sighed again. "Your wife doesn't know about the other times."

He bowed his head. "No, m'lady."

The Spring Rituals were one of the many reasons I had preferred being a circuit justice as opposed to having a permanent position in a city temple. Not because the three-day orgy of food, drink and sex itself disgusted me.

Because I wanted to be a part of it.

And justices weren't allowed.

On the other hand, any member of the priesthood of Love was required to service any person who came to their temple for succor. I wasn't sure if my mother doomed me or saved me when she sold me to the Temple of Balance as a toddler.

But the unspoken rule was that the priesthood only provided sexual release for those who were not in committed relationships. The Spring Rituals were the one exception.

I crossed to the peacekeeper. He flinched and the other two eased away from him. It almost made me feel sorry for the man.

"When was the last time you visited Sister Gretchen?"

"I-I tried to four night ago, but I was told she was indisposed. Th-the head sister offered to entertain me herself, but I went home instead." And Sister Gretchen had been dead at a minimum of three days since the barrel was unloaded in the cellar.

"So you didn't see her at all when you went to the Temple of Love?"

"No." He shook his head vehemently.

"When was the last time you saw her alive?"

He bowed his head and played with the edges of his cloak, plucking at the embroidery. "Winter Solstice, m'lady," he murmured.

That had been six weeks ago, but instinct said there was more to the peacekeeper's story. "And?" I prompted.

"She was alive and asleep when I left her bedchambers."

"Does your wife know about your other visits to the temple?"

"No—" He stopped himself. While I couldn't fine-tune a truthspell as well as Luc, my unusual sight could detect the change in body heat when most people lied. The peacekeeper realized how much trouble he could be in after my little confrontation with his boss. "I don't believe she does. I didn't want to hurt her feelings."

*If you didn't want to hurt her feelings, you should have gone home and made love to her instead of going to the goddess-damned temple.* But I didn't give voice to that thought.

Instead, I said, "Thank you for your cooperation, Peacekeeper . . ."

"Dante, m'lady."

"Thank you, Dante." I glared at the other two. "Anything you gentlemen care to add?"

"No," they chorused. Their skin remained yellow with flickers of orange. Nervous because of me, but not obviously hiding anything.

I circled around the body and approached the duke and his party. The acid of the wine had kept the smell of decay to a minimum. But now, the odor was starting to overpower the little room. The corpse should be disposed of soon, assuming we could solve the priestess's death before the smell overwhelmed even the cold rooms at the Temple of Death.

"How well did you know Sister Gretchen?" I said, focusing on Lady Katarina.

"We were fast friends until our thirteenth winter." Wistfulness coated her voice. "She decided to formally join the temple."

"While your mother encouraged you to find an apprenticeship," I added. Katarina's healing gift had saved my life after the demons had beaten me. Part of me was grateful, but another part cursed her. I had prayed that death from my demon-inflicted injuries would free me from the Temple of Balance.

But I never had such luck any other time I tried to escape. I didn't know why I thought the goddess would release me during that night when she kept her grip tight on me every other time.

Katarina rubbed her swollen belly. "Yes."

"Did you ever hear of problems between Gretchen and any of the other priestesses?"

The noblewoman gave a sad laugh. "Only the usual manure. Backbiting and currying the head priestess's favor."

"What about supplicants?"

Katarina sighed. "Same thing. There were always fights between the sisters over the richer patrons, and fights between the patrons when they wanted a particular priestess at the same time, but I never heard of a problem between her and a patron."

My muscles tightened. Once one of the priesthood of Love lost their looks, they were demoted to general staff positions. Oh, they could request a transfer to another temple, but few thought ahead enough to acquire skills that might be useful, and it still resulted in a demotion of sorts.

The smarter members of the Love priesthood enticed jewelry, gold and other material favors from their supplicants, hoarding their wealth so they may retire in the luxury to which they had become accustomed.

"Do you have an idea of her current supplicants besides Dante?"

Katarina's gaze flicked to the peacekeepers and back. "If you wish a formal statement, Lady Justice, may we please do this inside? Standing for such a long period is not good for the baby."

Whatever she knew, she was concerned over public knowledge of it.

"Of course." I inclined my head. "Perhaps in your audience chamber, then? I do not wish to put any more strain on the duke's heir than necessary." I smiled at Marco. "If you will inform Brother Luc of my whereabouts?"

"I would be happy to, Justice Anthea." He was having trouble containing his laughter at his wife's subterfuge. "And again, my apologies for interrupting your morning meal."

"Please try not to do it again, Your Grace." The peacekeepers took my mocking for real anger from the way the three of them jumped.

I held out my elbow for Katarina. She seemed relieved as we left the wine cellar. At the top of the ramp, the female warden stood vigil with the warden from Light. She fell in step with me, but I held up my free hand.

"Stay here. No one is to leave without Brother Luc's authorization. I'm escorting the lady to her audience chamber. Should the Master Healer arrive before I return, come fetch me."

"Yes, Justice." She saluted again.

I blew out an annoyed breath. "What's your name again?"

"Tyra, my lady." No need for an origin name. We all adopted DiBalance when we entered our goddess's service.

"I'm sorry for forgetting again, Tyra."

She shrugged. "Things have been rather chaotic since you arrived, m'lady."

I leaned close the warden. In a fake conspiratorial whisper, I said, "I blame Lady Katarina for everything."

The warden froze until the noblewoman started laughing.

Katarina backhanded my shoulder. "Really, Anthea. You are incorrigible." Behind us the Light warden snorted as he tried to stifle his own humor.

We left the startled Tyra behind and headed through the gray drizzle for the great house.

Once we shed our damp cloaks, we propped our feet in front of the fireplace, and we had been served hot tea and biscuits, Katarina dismissed the maid. She sipped her tea for a moment before she said, "Could you please ward the room?"

That simple request spoke volumes.

I set aside my cup and rose. The spell was basic enough. Every priest and priestess, no matter the temple, knew it.

Unlike Luc's nearly impenetrable wall, mine was fluid, elastic. It wouldn't stop the maid from barging into the room, but it would prevent her from hearing or harming us.

Which really made no sense, considering our personalities. A spell reflected the traits of the caster, and I would be the first to admit I was rather rigid when it came to certain matters.

I hummed under my breath as I shielded our conversation from the servants or anyone else. A tickle of energy surrounded us for an instant before the spell settled into the walls, ceiling and floor of the reception room.

I sat back down, enjoyed the delicious heat on my toes, and waited for Katarina to begin.

"Gretchen began amassing a fortune as soon as she was confirmed by the Reverend Mother of Love." She sipped her tea.

I calculated in my head. Normal studies for Love meant three years from dedication to confirmation. "And she's your age, correct?" At the noblewoman's quiet affirmation, I added, "How much could she have amassed in only four years?"

"That's what the chief priestess here in Orrin wanted to know." Katarina blew out a sharp breath. "When I refused to spy on Gretchen, the bitch spread the word I *had* spied on Gretchen."

"And Gretchen refused to speak to you after that."

"Yes."

The sad part was I knew how ambitious my birth mother was. I may have only been three winters, but I understood the price she asked for me from the contingent of Balance when they came to claim me. Mother had gotten the power she wanted, but had she desired more than the temple seat here in Orrin?

And sadly, I understood why Katarina had stayed even though my mother was making her life miserable. It would have been around the time her own mother contracted the wasting sickness.

"You had to have known that you couldn't heal your mother," I murmured. "Why did you put yourself through that?"

She swiped at her cheek. "I had to try. She barely had enough gold for her basic necessities."

I coughed to cover my own discomfiture. I was alive because of Katerina's efforts. Her mother wasn't. The failure must sting her soul. "Was there any significant patron in particular who Gretchen entertained?" I reached for my cup.

Katarina laughed, an ugly, bitter thing. Six months ago, I wouldn't have believed the sweet woman could make such a sound. "Would you believe one of them was Samael DiRoy?"

I choked. My mouthful of tea sprayed over my shirt and leggings. Once I could catch my breath, I glared at her. "You did that on purpose."

"Only to see the imperturbable Justice Anthea spit all over herself." Her humor quickly faded. "If I had known then . . ."

Samael DiRoy. The great nephew of a cousin of our current queen, which made him thirty-sixth, or was that sixty-third, in line for the throne. Traitor. Demon summoner. The main reason I had been condemned to the Justice seat in Orrin.

As the Reverend Mother had surmised, being trapped in the city of my birth was a far worse punishment for illegally executing the idiot nobleman than having my own head chopped off.

Politics didn't give a whit I had stopped a demon invasion in the process.

I took another drink of tea I actually managed to swallow. "Do you think she knew about Samael's predilection for demons?"

"I don't know about the demons." Katarina pulled her shawl tight around her shoulders. "I do know the donation Gretchen commanded. It would explain where all of his money went."

"Any interactions between her and Marco's parents?"

"Not that I know of. Lady DiMara thought the Spring Rituals were beneath her. She was—"

"A controlling shrew with a thirst for power?" I offered.

Katarina smiled. "I keep forgetting that you met her."

I snorted in disgust. "Yes, the day we were both tried." I shoved the thoughts of that dark experience aside. I had been sure I wouldn't see the sunset. Not that I could actually see one. "Anyone else of rank that she entertained on a regular basis?"

"The ambassador of Jing. The crown prince of Cant. The youngest son of the king of the Sea Peoples. An admiral of the Fire Islands. The chief priest of Light from Tandor."

I froze. "Please tell me you are joking."

"You did not learn that last from me," she countered.

The Temples of Balance and Light were the only two orders that required chastity of their members. Luc and I would be executed in a heartbeat if anyone learned of our affair.

But for a chief priest of Light to blatantly strut into any Temple of Love for worship . . .

Potential suspects in Gretchen's murder were piling up faster than fallen leaves in the winter storms.

"Do you know what she did with her tokens from these patrons?"

"The jewelry she had replicas made before she sold it. According to the gossip mill, she invested her gains. Mostly in trade ships. Some in the summer caravans heading east. She owns a few of the businesses here in the city. A couple of farms on the outskirts."

I could feel my eyebrows climb toward my scalp at Katarina's recitation. This was not a typical priestess planning for her retirement. Did my mother view her as a political rival? Had she learned something she shouldn't have from one of her patrons?

Yet, the method of Gretchen's death and her horrible wounds, not to mention where she was found, indicated something else entirely.

"Who would receive her estate in the event of her death?"

Katarina shrugged. "I have no idea. If she named someone, it would be in the temple records."

We both knew if Gretchen hadn't, her possessions would go to her temple's treasury. In other words, right into my mother's lap.

# Chapter 3

The extraordinary wait for the chief healer was due to his insistence on bringing an apprentice plus his own wagon and team of horses. Therefore, my cloak and robes were dry and my toes quite toasty by the time he arrived.

And I didn't have to send Little Bear back to the Temple of Death for additional transportation.

"Nice that one of us could get out of the cold," Luc muttered in my ear as I joined the men and Lady Alessa in the courtyard.

"It was necessary," I murmured. "Lady Katarina didn't need to be on her feet. Would you and Brother Kam be available for dinner tonight?"

*Her information was that good?* his voice whispered in my mind.

I didn't look at him as we followed the chief healer down to the wine cellar once more, but Luc's grunt indicated he caught my slight nod.

Orrin's chief healer, a man named Aaron, pushed back his hood and crouched next to the corpse. Despite the red pulsing in his knuckles and garrulous quality of his voice, he acted like a man closer to my age of thirty-one winters than a grandfather.

He flipped back the sheet Lady Alessa had brought to cover the murdered priestess. His apprentice whirled and ran out through the doorway. Everyone politely ignored the sounds of the poor youth retching onto the sawdust in the hallway.

"I believe you called me a little too late, Justice," Aaron said dryly.

It took all my will not to laugh at his black humor. "I wanted your opinion on her wounds, Master Aaron."

He stroked his mustache and short beard, a style that had become popular with men in Issura over the last few years. His countenance shifted from yellow to orange as he regarded the corpse. Good to know even he wasn't immune to the brutality perpetrated on the priestess.

"The stab wounds to her birth canal wouldn't have been sufficient to kill her." He pointed to her neck. "I agree with Brother Luc that whoever strangled her caused the actual death."

Using another barrel as a desk, the junior Balance clerk Little Bear had brought back with him, whose name I couldn't remember any more than the rest of my wardens, dutifully recorded the healer's words.

Master Aaron glanced at DiCook who stood fuming on the opposite side of the cellar. As far away from Luc as he could get while still part of the conversation. However, Aaron's next question was addressed to me. "I have a new healer in my employ. Would you mind if we take the body back to my estate and allow him a look before we deliver it to the Temple of Death?"

"Hasn't the poor woman been through enough?" the magistrate snapped.

I waved a hand toward the late priestess. "I thought you were concerned about finding whoever did this to her."

"I am. But there is decency and tradition to be observed." His tone was a bit more deflated.

"Are you saying there is something I have not done according to tradition?" My voice was as cold as the steel at my shoulder.

"No, Justice." He forced the words between his clenched jaws.

Time to change tactics with DiCook. I gave him a gracious smile. At least, I hoped it appeared gracious. "Thank you for your assistance, Magistrate, but there's nothing more either of us can do here to assist Brother Luc in questioning the rest of Duke Marco's household."

"If you don't mind, Justice, I'd like to leave my peacekeepers here to help your wardens make sure everyone is questioned." Amazing how he could turn my title into an insult.

I shrugged. "That is Brother Luc's discretion, not mine."

*Thanks*, came Luc's sarcastic reply.

I ignored him. "In the meantime, I will escort Sister Gretchen's body to Healer Aaron's for his colleagues' opinion, then to the Temple of Death."

"What about informing High Sister Gerd?"

I should have known DiCook wouldn't let this go, not that I was looking forward to dealing with my mother. "I think this type of news would best come from another priestess, don't you? I will visit with her after we've delivered Gretchen's remains to High Sister Bertrice." I tilted my head to include Luc in my next statement. "My clerk will have copies of everyone's statements to both of you within two days."

"Thank you, Justice." Luc smiled.

The magistrate said nothing. I didn't need to read his thoughts to know he was plotting some kind of mischief.

I pulled Little Bear and Tyra aside. "I need one of you to stay as an escort for the clerk. The other one will accompany me."

The two wardens looked at each other. I detected a distinctive aura of confusion.

Little Bear cleared his throat. "M'lady, your authority is paramount here."

I sighed. "Neither are going to be pleasant jobs, so I don't want either of you thinking the other got the better assignment. This is me delegating my authority."

They looked at each other. Tyra shrugged. "Rocks and sticks?"

Little Bear nodded.

Somehow, it seemed appropriate that my wardens would use a children's game to decide on their tasks.

Once we loaded the corpse onto the wagon, Little Bear and I escorted the healer's wagon down the bluffs back into the city proper. The drizzle hadn't stopped since we'd left the temple this morning. I couldn't even tell what time it might be, though my stomach insisted it was past first afternoon.

"Lady Justice, if I may?" Little Bear's voice could barely be heard over the wet clopping of the horses' hooves and the rattle of the wagon wheels.

"Yes?"

He was silent, as if reconsidering whatever he wanted to ask.

"Spit it out, Chief Warden. It's too damn miserable and wet of a day for me to even want to whip you for impertinence."

"My lady, we need some guidance at times. Your method of commanding is . . ."

"Unorthodox?" I offered.

"Quite different than Justice Penelope," he rephrased. "Balance rest her soul."

I frowned. "Are my methods that disturbing?"

"No, m'lady, it's only . . ."

I waited for a heartbeat. Two. A glance over my shoulder showed Healer Aaron in a deep discussion with his apprentice. "Why didn't any of you notify the Reverend Mother that Penelope's mental faculties were questionable at best near the end?"

He blew out a deep lungful of air. For a moment, his face was obscured in a yellowish-green cloud. The temperature was dropping quickly if I could see his breath. "We did. How did you know?"

"The change in her records over the last year before her death, as if someone was mimicking her style, but there were certain words used differently. What was the response from the Reverend Mother?"

"We never received one." His voice was tight, strained.

Rage simmered in my blood. Not at Little Bear and the rest of our brothers and sisters at our temple. The bitch had known there were problems long before she forced me into Orrin's justice seat. What kind of demon-spawned game was she playing at?

Thanks to my own crime, I was forbidden from leaving the city, else I would tear up the National Road to the main temple in the capital and demand answers. Any letter I sent regarding Penelope now would be ignored as surely as the staff's had been two years ago.

For the love of Mother, Sivan, Little Bear and the rest had been running temple business for well over a year. It was a wonder they didn't resent me. Actually, it was a wonder they didn't hate me.

I swallowed the acid at the back of my throat. "Let me think on the matter. I've ridden circuit for a decade. I'm rather used to doing everything myself. My apologies for not taking your feelings and experience into account. I didn't realize . . ."

"May I speak freely, Justice?"

I nodded, not trusting my voice.

"We don't blame you." A soft burr vibrated under his words, and what I could see of his face under his hood glowed a fierce scarlet. I wasn't the only one furious with the home temple's games. "We simply want to understand your needs. Justice Penelope never allowed us the amount of . . . autonomy that you have."

"Until she became senile, you mean."

"Yes, m'lady."

I nodded to myself. "Very well, Warden. Here's the first rule for my regime. I want honesty at all times. Discretely when the situation calls for it, but I believe you and the rest of the staff have discretion mastered."

He turned and stared at me. "Thank you, Justice."

Goddess help me, what else besides the former duke and duchess's treason had passed unnoticed in this city due to Penelope's deteriorating faculties?

Journeymen and women poured out into the rain to help us carry the late Sister Gretchen inside. On Master Healer Aaron's estate, the living quarters were in a separate building than his treatment and training rooms. Once inside, I could immediately understand why. No amount of lemon oil soap or herbs could totally disguise the odors of infection, illness and death.

Apprentices lit a multitude of lamps around the room. Between the heat from the burning wicks and the sheer amount of bodies, I soon had to squint. I pulled my hood tight around my face, but it didn't help much as the room grew warmer.

Five master healers entered. There was quite a bit of tension from them due to the presence of Little Bear and me, but their curiosity overwhelmed whatever reticence they had over a priestess and her warden observing.

The healers had fought for their independence from the Temple of Death after the last demon war a century ago. They'd formed their own guild as any other craft group would. After all this time, there were still those in the temples who thought allowing any magic of such power outside of priestly control was a mistake.

*The people in this room would never believe me if I told them I envied their freedom.*

"Where's Devin?" Aaron shouted over the general hubbub.

"Here. Now what's the fuss about?" The man who entered stood a head shorter than the chief healer. His accent was one from the eastern kingdoms of the Upper Long Continent, but indistinct enough I couldn't name which one. The metallic thread in the embroidery at his shoulders indicated he was also a master healer, but his attitude was irreverent compared to every guild leader I'd ever met.

*I immediately liked him.*

Devin's attention was drawn to the white-shrouded figure on the table. "How'd you manage to get ahold of a corpse before those vultures at the Temple?"

One of the journeymen nudged him with an elbow. Devin finally noticed Little Bear and me in the corner. "My apologies, Justice."

*He didn't sound very apologetic.*

I stepped to the table and the two journeywomen made room for me, and not from politeness. "Master Aaron says you may have insights concerning my murder victim."

"Murder victim?" Devin grunted and pushed two of the apprentices out of the way. He uncovered the corpse. "She looks like someone soaked her in a wine vat."

"She was found in a wine barrel when the servants tapped it," Aaron explained.

"Ruined a barrel of decent Pana red," I added.

Devin chuckled before he peered closely at her neck. "Strangled, but you already knew that, didn't you, Justice? Possibly a small man or a woman."

"A woman?"

He looked up at me. "Yes, those of you who have been trained in fight-ing, a tumbler, anyone with sufficient strength in the arms. The fairer sex is just as capable of murder. But you're usually more subtle about it."

Interesting observation. I was even more curious about his history.

Devin shifted and checked the wrists of the corpse. "She wasn't re-strained." He lifted the hands. "As you can see, there's quite of bit of debris under the nails."

"No, I can't." I smiled to take the sting from my words.

"Forgive me, Justice. I forgot that you were sightless."

"Oh, I can see." I flipped back my hood, though the brightness bordered on painful. "Just not the way everybody else can."

"Oh." The confident Devin seemed to search for words. "I don't suppose you would let me examine you."

"Not right now, Master Healer." I waved at the body. "I have a more pressing matter. Could the material under her nails be skin? If someone was choking the life out of me, I would be fighting back."

"I surmise so."

Excitement trilled along my skin. "Could you collect it? Master Aaron, if I may impose on you for a bottle and a stopper." Luc may not be able to trace Sister Gretchen's path, but if her assailant was still alive . . .

"Of course, Justice," Aaron answered. In moments, I had the bottle with the fingernail debris secreted in my pocket.

"Justice, if you are tracking the culprit." Devin's tone turned deadly seri-ous. "The dagger wounds to this woman's birth canal—"

"I don't need a healer to tell me I'm dealing with someone violent and not quite right in the head."

"Yes." He hesitated before he said, "With your permission, I wish to confirm that strangulation was the cause of her death."

"I don't understand, Master Healer." I pointed at the neck of the corpse. "You said that the bruising—"

"Her attacker may have choked her until she lost consciousness in or-der to stab her with the dagger." He ran his palms along the corpse's inner thighs. "No other cuts. No other marks on her. Also, notice there are no cuts on her arms or hands."

"So you're saying she was unconscious or dead when that was done to her."

"To paraphrase your statement, Justice, I wouldn't meekly let someone chop off my manhood without a fight. So yes, she was unable to fight for some reason when this was done to her."

"Do what you need to, Master Healer. You won't mind if I watch?"

He stiffened and for the first time, his cheeks and ears flared crimson. "So you can report me back to your Reverend Mother?"

"No, because your reasoning and methods fascinate me."

"I apologize, Justice. I've become quite used to the Temple of Death questioning everything I do."

I grinned. "The Healers Guild is just pissing everyone off, aren't they?"

He laughed. "Even so."

"You have nothing to fear from me, Master Healer. If anything, I am in your debt for your assistance in helping me track the bastard who did this to Sister Gretchen."

A little over a candlemark later, Little Bear and I escorted the healer's wagon down the boulevard to the Temple of Death. Almost as if the gods knew our purpose, the skies opened up, and we were thoroughly drenched upon our arrival.

I explained the situation to the records clerk, who nodded and scribbled things on his parchment I couldn't read. What the frigid rain didn't soak, the air chilled. For me, the world blurred into a morass of blue, purple and gray with occasional spots of brightness. It was one of the things I hated about winter.

"Did Sister Gretchen DiLove file a statement of last wishes?" I asked.

The Death clerk finally looked up at me. "I would have to research our library, but most of the priesthood keep copies with their own temples."

I frowned. "That is not protocol established by the reverend mothers and fathers."

He shrugged "Procedure has been rather . . . lax with your predecessor, Justice."

"I see." My voice was as cold as the nasty weather. "I suppose I need to rectify certain matters during the equinox meeting." The temples dealt with formal matters the week before the Spring Rituals, clearing the slates before the new year. This year's meeting would be entertaining to say the least.

"If we have the declaration, I'm sure High Sister Bertrice will have it sent to you."

"My thanks." I nodded to the clerk. I had no illusions I would be seeing the head priestess of the Temple of Death sooner rather than later once her people saw Sister Gretchen's remains.

I pivoted and stalked out of the deep purple marble receiving room, Little Bear on my heels.

"Home, m'lady?"

"Unfortunately, no. I have one more stop to make."

His exhalation mirrored my own feelings. In fact, I'd rather suffer the lash again than what I had to do next.

The twelve temples lined the south end of Orrin's main thoroughfare, six on one side and their counterparts facing them. The ride from Death to Love was far too short.

The torches in the courtyard flared and sizzled under the downpour. Laughter and music hummed past the expensive glass panes inset in the temples windows.

A eunuch ran up to take our reins. "Good tidings, sirs. Looking for warmth and care on this miserable winter day?"

"No," I said as I dismounted. "Please inform High Sister Gerd that Chief Justice Anthea requests an audience on a matter of utmost importance."

Stutters issued from the eunuch's mouth before he called for a groom to take our horses. His deep bow was almost humorous. He raced through the main doors.

Little Bear looked at me and gave a sad shake of his head.

"I take it Penelope didn't often call on Gerd," I whispered.

"Never," he whispered back. "They hated each other's guts."

Interesting. I would have to ask him why once we were safely ensconced back in our own abode with dry clothes and hot wine.

We entered the temple, and a priestess fluttered up, the bells of her robe tinkling. The lowest ranking priestess from her total lack of composure. "Forgive us, Justice. We hadn't expected such an august presence on the day of rest."

I crossed my arms, well aware of the stares from the worshippers and the servants in the reception area. "I don't need my ass kissed by you or any other priestess of Love. I need to speak with High Sister Gerd now." If she refused to use my formal title, I could be just as rude.

"She, um, she is, um . . ."

"If she's fucking a worshipper, just say so."

I couldn't see her face because of her veil, but the junior priestess' hands exploded with heat. "If you're willing to wait, Justice?"

"Do I have a choice?" I growled. "You do understand that there are other things in life than spreading your legs, don't you?"

She gave a little squeak of dismay before she whirled and raced off.

I turned to a different eunuch who was desperately trying to hide behind a pillar. "I don't suppose you could fetch Sister Gretchen as an alternative."

Little Bear's dismay rolled across my psyche. "Um, Lady Justice—"

I held up my hand to stop him. Thank Balance, he shut up. No doubt he feared for my sanity after dealing with a senile priestess for so long.

However, the eunuch's skin remained the same yellow with nervous splotches of orange. "I'll see if she's available, m'lady."

"Interesting," I murmured. "And what does that tell us, Chief Warden?"

His jaw shifted as he considered my question, then grinned as the pieces slid into place. The Temple of Love knew the whereabouts of its priestesses at all times. Little Bear wisely remained silent.

More bells as another priestess approached, but she was over a head taller than the previous girl. "If you'll follow me, Chief Justice. High Sister Gerd will be with you momentarily."

The deep voice. The height. *Berda.*

I dropped my arms. Now we were getting someplace. "And you are?"

"Sister Dragonfly." She bowed. "I am High Sister Gerd's second. I apologize for the inexcusable rudeness you encountered here in our Goddess's home."

My mother having a *berda* as her second made sense in a warped sort of way. Even though the men who serviced both males and females were full priestesses and wore the accoutrements of such, they were never allowed to hold a city's seat, much less become a reverend mother. Gerd would view Dragonfly as less of a threat to her power.

"It is I who should apologize, Sister Dragonfly. I would have sent a formal request for a meeting if the message I bring her weren't so important."

"I assure you I would deliver any message you need to relay, Chief Justice."

"I do not disparage your abilities as second, Sister. The matter is best dealt with myself."

"And yet, it is my understanding you requested Sister Gretchen."

"Yes, I did."

She regarded me for a moment. When I didn't add anything, she pivoted and headed across the reception area. The door she led us through opened into the back hallway.

The receiving rooms for worshipers.

Moans, grunts and laughter echoed against the wood-paneled walls. The musk of lovemaking mixed with expensive perfumes and oils. If either Dragonfly or my mother expected to discomfit me, they needed something better than sex.

After a pack of demons tried to kill me, not too much else bothered me any more.

A quick glance showed Little Bear's face had turned scarlet. I prayed he saved his desire for Sivan once we return to the temple, unlike Peacekeeper Dante. My support staff was not bound by my vows, thank the Goddess.

Dragonfly finally delivered us to an audience room. The fireplace was dark. No personal effects decorated the place. It was as heartless as the woman who ran this temple. Without a word, the *berda* closed the door behind her.

They let us stew in the cold for who knew how long since we had no sun and no candles to mark time. Little Bear maintained his silence. Good. No doubt the eunuchs or a priestess or two were watching us through spy holes.

We were both pacing to keep warm by the time Gerd deigned to join us.

"Justice Anthea, how nice of you to visit." No bells tinkled as she entered the room, nor did she bother with the traditional veil. At least, she bothered to cover her body.

I swallowed a sigh. There was a time, eons ago, when that lyrical voice brought comfort to a small girl.

Now, I recognized it for the posturing it was. "I apologize for the need for my visit. It's about Sister Gretchen."

"So you decided you would tell me about her death. Over a half day after she had been discovered at that." As she drifted past me, under the musk of her *duties* laid the scent of licorice.

"I pray that Magistrate DiCook is better in bed than he is an investigator."

She sauntered over to Little Bear. "If your warden here is better than the magistrate, you'll have my full cooperation, Justice."

"Really, Mother, he has more taste than DiCook's leftovers."

She whirled so fast I automatically reached for my dagger concealed inside my robes. "Don't call me that," she hissed. "Don't you dare call me that ever again."

Little Bear's cheeks flushed orange.

"So you do remember me. Good. I won't tell everyone in the city your birth canal has been stretched as long as you answer my questions."

Her chin lifted a notch. "You dare insult me in my own temple?"

*My* temple, not my *goddess's* temple. There a certain surety in the immutability of a corrupt human personality.

I pushed back my hood and met her glare.

Her gaze quickly dropped. "Ask your damn questions," she said, her voice sullen.

I folded my arms over my chest once again. "How long has she been missing?"

"I'm not sure. Her handmaid only mentioned her bed hadn't been slept in two nights ago." No change in the pulse beating at her throat.

"I know she's been missing at least four. Care to correct your answer?"

She flicked her hand in dismissal. "It's not unusual for some of the women to share beds. Dragonfly deals with the daily duties."

I didn't believe for an instant that Dragonfly wouldn't report every little happening and piece of gossip to her mistress. By the same token, I could definitely envision my mother hanging out the *berda* as her dupe. "Are you saying your second didn't inform you that Sister Gretchen wasn't reporting for her duties?"

"I don't remember every little thing every priestess tells me."

"I didn't ask about every priestess in your temple. I specifically asked about Dragonfly reporting Gretchen's absence," I said.

"I don't remember." Her pulse jumped. I really hadn't expected otherwise.

"I'm sure you don't."

"You can truthspell me if you'd like, Chief Justice." She spat my title like a bad piece of fish.

I could truthspell her, but I didn't have cause, just suspicions at this point. Not to mention my truthspells tended to work brutally, not with Luc's finesse.

Time to try another tack. "I would think you'd be worried about the drop in income to the temple. I understand Gretchen was one of your more popular priestesses. The loss in income—"

"I'm sure the income with be offset by her investments."

"What makes you say that?"

"She didn't have a declaration of last wishes."

"Really?" I said dryly. "You're sure about that, Sister?"

"Quite sure." She couldn't keep the purr of satisfaction out of her voice.

"You do realize your admission makes you the most likely candidate for her murder, don't you, High Sister?" I drawled out her title.

"This interview is over," she snapped.

"Fine." I started to leave, but paused in my exit. "But you better pray to your goddess that the Temple of Death has a declaration on file. Otherwise, I will return." I grinned. "And with a priest of Light."

I motioned to Little Bear, and he followed me out of the room. I could literally feel the psychic residue of my mother fuming behind me.

My warden didn't say a word until we were mounted and passed the Temple of the Child. At least, the rain had slowed back down to a drizzle. "I don't mean to pry, Lady Justice—"

"But you're going to do it anyway."

"Maybe we should have handle High Sister Gerd more gently."

"'We,' not 'you.'" I faced him. "Are you saying you'd be willing to lay with her?"

"No! Balance, no." He blew out a cleansing breath. "It's that Justice Penelope didn't take Sister Gerd's influence seriously."

"What influence?"

"Duke Marco's father was one of her regulars."

I didn't countenance gossip, but I had to ask. "Which priests or priestesses from the other temples are or were her regulars?"

Little Bear's laughter was choked. "It would be easier to give you a list of who didn't frequent her bed."

"Let me guess," I said sourly. "Besides Penelope, Brother Kam?"

He nodded. "And Sister Bertrice."

I muttered a few choice curses.

We were nearly to our own stables when he said, "I understand there's bad blood between the two of you, and I can imagine why, but as Chief Justice of Orrin, you need to rein in your resentment, m'lady. This city hasn't been balanced in a very long time, and it's something we desperately need."

"Do you presume to lecture me on my duties, Chief Warden?"

He met my gaze squarely. "You said you wanted discretion and honesty, Lady Justice."

He was right. It didn't make swallowing my pride any easier. "And you've acted appropriately as I wished, Warden. I'll keep your wise words in mind."

A deeper question bothered me. As much as I would have liked to blame my mother for Sister Gretchen's murder, my gut said she was only taking advantage of her younger rival's death. So who the hell had a reason to throttle and mutilate a priestess?

# Chapter 4

I walked across the street when bells at the Temple of Mother tolled first evening. The one grace was that the rain had stopped, but the thick, heavy air said more was on its way.

Tyra accompanied me, but she had the foresight not to take my arm. I didn't need her assistance. I could see a wagon and its team if it bore down on me. Besides, traffic on the main thoroughfare had died down for the day. Not that it had been as congested as normal between the rain and it being Rest Day. But after my encounter with my mother this afternoon, I could understand my wardens' insistence I have an escort in the city.

Goddess, I missed having Luc around from sunrise to sunrise. I could trust him to watch my back.

Was it my own stubbornness that prevented better relations with my staff? They seemed so eager to please. Or had they been so terrified I would blame them for hiding my predecessor's instability they kept me at arm's length? To be released from temple service, even as a staff member, would be the ultimate disgrace for most people.

On the other hand, I couldn't get myself disgraced no matter how hard I tried.

I was escorted to the chief priest's private dining room. It hadn't changed a bit since Luc had taken over from Kam, and I said as much to the two men who were waiting there for me.

Luc laughed. "I wish I had the time or inclination to redecorate, but Kam here has been keeping me quite busy. I think he saved his entire workload from last spring for me."

The elderly priest chuckled. "Running a temple is a young person's game."

"And cooking a fine dinner takes an experienced hand," I remarked.

"Just so, my lady." Kam took my hand and looped it around his arm. The gesture was sheer graciousness, not a suggestion that I was helpless, and he did it every time I visited the Temple of Light for dinner long before I was condemned to the Orrin Balance seat.

"And at the rate he's going, I won't fit in my smallclothes by next winter," Luc grumbled good-naturedly. To Tyra's shock, he copied Kam and took the warden's arm in his.

Even after half a year, it was odd to see Luc at the head of the chief priest's private table, instead of Kam. He kept with Kam's tradition that business was not to be discussed until after the sweets course. Tonight's specialty was mountain ice mixed with cream and flavored with honey and dried blackberries.

I licked the last bits from my spoon before I said, "You're right, Luc. You're going to end up fatter than a bear before hibernation at this rate.

"After the day we've had, I told Kam we deserved a treat." Luc dropped his own spoon into the silver bowl with a clatter. "I hope your day was more productive than mine."

"Nothing from any of the duke's household?"

"Not a damn thing." He raked his hands through his hair. "In fact, the only quirk was Lady Alessa."

I sat up straighter. "What do you mean?"

"If I didn't know better, I'd say she was fighting my truthspell, but the idea is ridiculous. According to our records, none of the DiMaras' blood have ever shown a flicker of magical ability."

"Are you sure?" I asked.

"No." Despite the official end of the meal, he speared a piece of cheese from the platter in front of him. "She was one of the last people I questioned, and I could have been fatigued and imagined it."

A shiver ran up my spine. The last thing I wanted was to drop more trouble in Marco's lap. Other than Luc, he was the only person who'd ever defended me against an attacker in every sense of the word.

I relayed what Master Healer Devin had said about Gretchen's assailant having small hands and his confirmation that throttling had been the cause of her demise. That story spilled into events at the Temple of Death, and my encounter with my mother.

Luc and I exchanged looks, old habits falling into place. He had the same feeling that we were missing a major piece of this puzzle.

"Maybe we're looking at this from the wrong angle." Kam poured more wine into his goblet.

"How so?" I asked.

"It could have been a jealous worshipper who viewed Sister Gretchen as his. When she refused to run away with him, he became enraged. If he couldn't have her, no one else could."

I turned to Tyra. "What's your analysis, Warden?"

She stammered a couple of times before she said, "I'm happy Sister Gretchen wasn't found in one of our temple's wine barrels, Justice."

Kam promptly released the neck of the second decanter he was reaching for. "Oh, my."

The same worry had plagued me, but I folded my fingers and rested my chin on them. "Why so?"

More stammering. I waited patiently, Little Bear's assessment of Penelope's behavior foremost in my mind. If I wanted the Balance staff to trust me, and vice versa, I needed to extend the courtesy of allowing Tyra to finish her thought.

"W-w-well, given that Duke Marco swore for your conduct at your t-t-trial for murder, if the body had been discovered at our temple, people would blame you without evidence, and the duke's enemies would use it against him."

She sucked in a breath and continued in a rush. "Magistrate DiCook would claim Orrin's Temple of Balance was corrupt, and full jurisdiction would fall to him until the Reverend Mother could replace you. Given his assumption of guilty until proven innocent and his lack of investigative skills, both His Grace and you would be executed." Her green lashes fluttered with her nervous energy.

"Very good, Warden. My thoughts as well. Which means someone is specifically targeting the duke for scandal—"

"Or it was still a method of killing two quail at the keep with the same arrow," Luc added.

"You believe Katarina was the secondary target, not me?" I said.

He shrugged. "She knows a lot of Gerd's secrets, and with Marco's father imprisoned for life for conspiracy, kidnapping and attempted memory alteration, Gerd doesn't have the nobility as completely under her thumb as she might like."

"And most of the local lords aren't happy with His Grace either," Tyra offered. At least, the girl no longer stuttered.

"Which brings us back to the original problem." I fished the vial out of my pocket. "I'm hoping this will help."

"What's in the bottle?" Luc asked as he took the stoppered glass from my hand. He held the vial up to the nearest oil lamp to examine the contents.

"I'm praying it is skin scrapings from Gretchen's attacker. Master Devin pointed out all her nails were packed with this substance."

Luc met my gaze. "That's assuming the wine didn't overwhelm his essence."

"Or her death didn't corrupt it." I frowned. "At this point, I'm not ruling anyone or anything out. I know it's not much to start with, but the priestesses of Love are meticulous about cleanliness. That should narrow our potential list of suspects. If Gretchen tore her attacker's skin, and he's still alive . . ."

Concern filled Luc's voice. "I'll have to do a little research for this fine of a tracking spell. Otherwise, we may end up finding the grapevines that were the source of the wine. Do you have a problem with me consulting the Wildling chief priest—"

His recitation was interrupted by Tyra's yawn, a wide, jaw-cracking one. Blood rushed to her face as she realized what she'd done. "I beg forgiveness, Brothers, Lady Justice."

"Pish," Kam said as he waved his hand. "Anthea and Luc are simply more adept at hiding their boredom while listening to an old man ramble."

"Because we've had far too much practice," I said into my cup.

"There's nothing wrong with my hearing, young lady." He waggled a finger at me.

"You were meant to hear, old man," I shot back.

Kam chuckled. "Well, it's about time you two experience the other side."

Luc leaned closer to Tyra. "It's permissible to laugh at them, Warden. I do all the time."

"You were on last night's watch, weren't you?" I said.

"Yes, m'lady."

"Go back to the temple and get some sleep."

"But I can't leave you—"

"I'll escort her home, Warden," Luc said.

Warmth filled me. It had been weeks since we'd had any time alone.

"But—" she tried one more time.

"That's a direct order, Warden." I jabbed my index finger at her. "I don't need my staff nodding off in the middle of court tomorrow morning."

She tried to hide her relief as she stood. "Thank you, m'lady. Good eventide, Brothers."

Once she left, Kam rested his chubby arms on the table service. "Anthea, be careful with Gerd. Don't take her power in this city, her wrath or her ego for granted."

"She interfered with an investigation." Damn, now I sounded like the sullen, petulant child.

"If you're expecting any type of maternal consideration—"

I snorted. "Oh, believe me, I am not."

"I'm too old and too tired to argue with a mule-headed justice." He climbed to his feet with a great deal of puffing. "Do something with her before she does something stupid, Luc. Good eventide."

For an elderly, overweight man, Kam did a remarkable job of stomping out of the dining room in a huff. The door slammed behind him, and the dishes and utensils vibrated in response.

"You're poking everyone with a stick tonight, Justice." Luc's amused tone irritated me.

"This would all be so much easier if I didn't have half the city playing idiotic games."

"That means you have to play the game better than anyone else."

"I can think of games I'd rather play." I smiled at him.

He was out of his chair and pulling me into his arms before my next heartbeat. Our lips met, and I felt as if I'd been trapped in the Salt Desert for days, and finally taking a sip of fresh, sweet water.

The kiss was far too short. Or so I thought until I realized he pressed me against the wall and my legs were wrapped around his waist.

"Goddess, I miss you," I whispered.

Luc leaned his forehead against mine. "Not as much as I miss you." His breath was warm against my skin, reminding me of all those mornings he'd woken me with sweet kisses.

His hands slid from my buttocks. "But we can't. Not here. Not now."

"When?" I hated that my single word sounded like a sob. That I sounded like a lovestruck fool.

"I don't know." He pulled my arms from his neck. "You need to go back before anyone starts rumors. We have enough trouble on our tables, my love." His words were followed by a light kiss on my neck, the tender spot where I was most sensitive.

When he stepped away, I felt as shaky as if I'd been sword training during a severe ground quake. And I wished I'd argued harder that we run away to Cant six months ago.

As I lay in bed, the thought of escaping my duties crawled through my mind long after the temple and outbuildings had quieted for the night. But amid the desire to saddle Nassa and gallop south to the border, the mutilated body of Sister Gretchen taunted me. No one deserved such a painful death. Maybe if Luc could trace who, then we would know why.

Which brought me back full circle to Luc and abandoning the temple again.

I sighed, sat up and punched at the down pillows. I still hadn't gotten used to the finery afforded my new position. Luc and I had slept on the ground more often than not as we traveled the circuit of villages and towns between Orrin's territory and the mountains. I threw myself back down on the bed.

This whole situation was ridiculous. I was fretting about things I had no control over. Without sleep, I'd be crankier than usual during court tomorrow morning.

The faint scrape of stone on stone cut my self-pity off at the knees. I froze and scanned the room through slitted eyes. My hand reached between the mattress and the bed frame for my dagger.

There. A small section of wall to the left of my wardrobe separated from the rest of the blue-green marble. The brilliant yellow of a living being appeared. It stepped through the opening and straightened. A man.

My fingers tightened around the dagger handle. Fool. I could see in the dark. He couldn't.

Despite the chill in the air, I had kicked off my blankets long before now. It was a simple matter of rolling off the bed and crouching on the icy floor.

He crept unerringly to my bedside. This was someone who knew the lay of my chambers or had been in here before. Neither boded well.

When he reached for the spot where my head would have been, I grabbed his collar and yanked. He lost his balance and landed on my mattress with a *whoof*. The tip of my dagger rested along the pulse point of his throat.

The feel of his skin and his scent registered a heartbeat before Luc said, "Is this how you greet all your lovers?"

"You scared the piss out of me," I hissed. "By our gods, what are you doing here? How did you . . ." I glanced at the opening he'd slipped through.

He chuckled. "If you put away the dagger, I'll tell you."

"I'm glad you find this amusing," I muttered, but I released him.

He rearranged himself to lie lengthwise on my mattress. I set my weapon on the lamp table and circled the room, laying wards so we wouldn't be interrupted.

When I returned to the bed, he snagged my wrist and pulled me on top of him. My body heated as his hands roamed and his arousal pressed against me.

"How?" I demanded.

"Apparently, we are not the first of our temples to have an illegal tryst."

I waited for him to continue, but it was growing more difficult to think with the things he was doing to me. Finally, I tore my mouth from his. "The secret passage?" I prompted.

"Kam was waiting in my bedchamber when I returned." His chest vibrated beneath me. "Would you believe he lectured me on taking the edge off your irritability?"

"He didn't."

"Um-hmmm . . ." Luc flipped me so I was underneath him. Little kisses followed the hem of my nightshirt upward.

"That's rather audacious of him." A disturbing thought hit me. "Wait a moment. Kam and . . . Penelope?"

Luc buried his face against my inner thigh to stifle his laughter. "Light, no. Thalia."

The legendary justice had been Penelope's predecessor. She died defending the city from a pirate attack a generation ago. Her sacrifice hadn't been in vain. The battle had broken the marauders' power across the Peaceful Sea.

"Incredible," I whispered. "I didn't realize Kam had been here that long."

"Nearly fifty years."

I wove my fingers through Luc's hair as he layered more licks and kisses along my skin. "But the tunnel?"

"Was built long before either Thalia or Kam were assigned here. They're part of the original structures. There's another tunnel between Light and Father. He believes they were escape routes during the demon wars." His breath brushed my flesh, shooting prickles all over my body. "Now will you be quiet and let me love you, or do I have to gag you?"

I sighed. "I suppose. If you must for my mental health . . ."

Thankfully, my wards blocked the rest of the temple from hearing my shrieks as Luc showed me how much he missed me.

# Chapter 5

Desperate banging on my bedchamber door roused me from a nightmare concerning Samael and his demons. I reached for Luc, but cold blankets met my outstretched fingers. My wards were gone, and the secret passage was sealed once more. I must have been half asleep when he left. I didn't remember taking down the wards.

The knocking turned thunderous.

"What?" I shouted.

Sivan burst through the door as if my dream demons chased her. "I beg forgiveness, Lady Justice. High Sister Bertrice is here, demanding she speak with you *now*."

I didn't need a scrying mirror to know what had crawled up my fellow seat's ass. Flinging blankets aside, I sat and stretched. "Escort her to my office, and bring us both breakfast. I believe she prefers that bean drink from one of the southern Mecas."

The idea of drinking something best served with ham, onions and bread turned my stomach, but a little solicitousness would go a long way to smoothing over the priestess's ruffled feathers.

"Yes, Lady Justice." Relief filled my assistant's voice. She paused at the door. "You knew she would be here."

"I asked for a favor from the Healers Guild." I shed my bedclothes. "Death has always been the most vocal over the split between the guilds and the temples. I'm surprised it took her this long to come see me."

"Do you want assistance with your hair, Justice?" she said. Apparently, I wasn't the only one with the desire to let Sister Bertrice stew for a little bit.

"Yes, please."

For all of my vaunted independence, that was the one thing I could never get right. Mirrors were as useless for me as the rest of the priestesses of Balance. While Luc and I had ridden circuit, he braided and pinned my hair for me. He insisted he wasn't going to ride into a town or village with a justice who looked like a long-haired cat with mange.

By the time I entered my office, High Sister Bertrice had worked herself into a good froth. Traditionally, each temple had its own color, but to me, everyone's robes, including mine were the same dark blue. Friction from he priestess's rapid pacing had given her robes splotchy green patches.

She whipped around to face me. "How dare you let those heathens mutilate one of the holy!"

The door clicked shut behind me. I didn't blame Sivan for escaping.

"And a pleasant morn to you as well," I replied as evenly as I could. "Would you care to break your fast with me?"

"A priestess was—"

"Murdered and violated, yes." I sat at the table the kitchen staff had brought to my office and poured my tea from the little ceramic pot. "But not by the Healers Guild. They assisted me in confirming several oddities involved in Sister Gretchen's death."

My cold logic splashed against Bertrice's fury. She collapsed in the other chair. "Do you know who did it?"

I shrugged. "There are possibilities I am pursuing, but you know I can't speculate. Any accusations would be sheer gossip at this point."

Bertrice glared at me. "I'm not a fool, Justice. The sutured incisions to the throat were made after her death."

"You are correct. Those were made yesterday at my behest. I wanted verification that strangulation was the cause of her demise. The Healers Guild found the windpipe crushed."

"Why? The bruises made that obvious."

"Not necessarily, Sister."

"What do you mean?"

I scooped scrambled eggs onto a piece of Cantish flatbread and added pepper sauce. Luc had introduced me to the concoction years ago. "We both know there are venoms, herbs and mushrooms that paralyze a body before death."

Waves of horror rolled off Bertrice. "You think she was raped with a knife while she was alive and aware?"

I folded the bread in half. "That suspicion is part of the reason I consulted with the Guild. I'm trying to narrow down the possibilities." I took a bite, and spicy heat seared my tongue.

The priestess picked up the ceramic pot at her place and took a suspicious sniff. "Brewed Meca bean tea?"

I wouldn't call the drink tea by any stretch of the imagination, but common sense said I shouldn't rattle the tenuous relationship between us. "I understand you're fond of the concoction."

She poured a cup and sipped it. No complaints, but she wasn't about to compliment my staff or my solicitousness in her foul mood. "Why would you trust the Healers Guild?"

"They have more thorough knowledge of aspects of the human body than I do. I would support anything that would help me perform my duties."

"Balance in all things." The sneer was evident in her voice.

"For every life, there is a death," I shot her own temple's motto back at her before I gentled my tone. "We're not on opposing sides in this matter, Sister."

"There was a time when temple authority was absolute." She reached for a piece of flatbread, tore off a chunk and popped it in her mouth.

"The demon war changed things. We haven't seen the end of those consequences." I took a sip of tea to cool the burning in my throat from the pepper sauce. "The situation last summer proved to me this city, this queendom even, is vulnerable if the temples, the civilians, and the nobles don't work together."

We ate silently for a few minutes before she reached into her pocket and produced a scroll. "This may help you then." She set it on the table.

"Sister Gretchen's declaration?" I placed my bread and eggs on my plate before I ran my fingers over the wax seal. The raised letters and numbers sent a chill through me.

Bertrice stared at me. "I thought you could see."

My laugh was self-deprecating. "After a fashion. My vision isn't the same as yours." I pointed at my eyes. "I still can't differentiate ink from parchment."

She tapped the scroll. "Since one of the priests from Light will have to be there when you break the seal, he can confirm the inked date for you, but according to our records, Sister Gretchen deposited her declaration with us eleven days ago."

Which was exactly what the imprinted code of Balance said. Less than a week before the priestess of Love was brutally murdered and left to pickle in a wine barrel. "You've spoken to your priest who took the declaration."

"Yes. He will be available at your convenience for official testimony." Bertrice took another drink of her pungent brew before she said, "Let me guess. Gerd told you Gretchen didn't have a declaration."

I sighed. "You know I can neither confirm nor deny anything regarding an open investigation."

Bertrice set her cup down with a sharp *clink*. "Watch your back with her, Anthea. If Thalia could have proven any of the things we suspected about her, you and I wouldn't be having this conversation."

"What do you mean?"

"You represent one of Gerd's few failures. She tried to murder you once. We could never figure out how she beat the truthspell."

"No one can defeat a truthspell. And murder? By the Twelve, what are you—"

"She took herbs and mushrooms to stop the pregnancy."

I stared at Sister Bertrice. Her words froze my soul. My mother had tried to kill me in the womb. "It's illegal to interfere with any child conceived during the Spring Rituals."

"Yes."

That single word spoke volumes. How deep my mother's ambitions went. How ruthless she could truly be. It chiseled an entirely different sculpture of her possible culpability in regards to Gretchen's murder.

"Why wasn't she punished?"

"She claimed it was the pregnancy madness."

"And she was truthspelled." I pushed my plate away, my appetite destroyed.

"Like I said, Thalia was sure Gerd hindered it. Somehow."

"That's not possible." I was repeating myself, but I couldn't seem to stop. Luc had the same suspicion when he questioned Lady Alessa yesterday.

"Under normal circumstances, I would agree."

I sipped my tea, attempting to find some equilibrium, before I said, "Why are you telling me this now?"

Bertrice leaned forward. "Because if Kam, Thalia or I could have proven she did it deliberately, she would not be a problem today. Because I have a vested interest in keeping you alive, Anthea."

"Why?"

"Because I used to be a healer. I burned out my power saving your life." She relaxed back in her chair.

Her admission was more shocking than all of her revelations put together. It explained her animosity toward the Healers Guild. They had broken from the Temple of Death during Justice Thalia's term. Without Bertrice's gift, she was of no use to the Guild.

I cleared my throat. "Why did you enter Death's service?"

She shrugged. "I'd be nothing more than a maid if I had stayed with the guild. The high brother at the time took pity on me and sponsored my admission to the order. I rather suspect Justice Thalia put in a good word with him."

"Can anyone verify your story concerning . . . the incident where you lost your healing abilities?"

"Gerd." A smirk floated along Bertrice's voice, but her next name carried sadness. "High Brother Kam is the only other one alive who remembers the incident."

Kam. He'd known me as a child. Why hadn't he ever said anything? Was the knowledge buried so deep in me that what I thought was instinctual trust was actually a memory?

Bertrice blew out a deep breath. "I don't suppose you could arrange an audience between Master Healer Aaron and myself."

The abrupt change of topic startled me. "Why do you need me to do it?"

"Because if I seek it of my own volition, I'm a traitor to my temple, and I'll be reported to the Reverend Mother of Death. If you *force* me to meet with him during the course of your duties while investigating the murder of a priestess from another temple . . ."

Goddess, how I loathed politics. But Bertrice's suggestion made sense. "Perhaps. Tomorrow after the midday meal?"

"That would be acceptable." She climbed to her feet. "Thank you for your hospitality, Justice."

I stood as well. "Thank you for bringing Sister Gretchen's statement of her last wishes to my attention. And Sister?"

She paused as she reached for my office door.

"Thank you for . . ." I couldn't quite get the words past the lump in my throat. Bertrice had sacrificed everything that made her unique to save me.

She nodded but said nothing.

After Bertrice had departed, I picked up the statement. While I had time to summon a priest from the Temple of Light, my gut said whatever was in the document would take far longer than the two candlemarks I had before court started at Second Morning. I crossed my office. Laying my hand on the spot in the marble behind my desk chair, I spoke the words of the unlocking spell for my safe hole, and placed the statement inside the block. Only a priestess of my own Temple could access the special hiding place.

Taking the accursed document across the street this afternoon would give me the excuse I needed to question Kam about my mother. And my own past.

Thank Balance, I didn't have any capital cases that morning. As it was, I could barely keep my attention on the trivial matters before me. Especially the damn runaway horse that had cracked a cobbler's sign.

Or they seemed trivial after the shocks Sister Bertrice had delivered at my breakfast table.

Once the day's cases were heard, I gave instructions to my head clerk Donella to invite the healers and Sister Bertrice for a meeting here. She gave me an odd look but nodded before I raced across the room to catch the young priest who'd been my truthspeller today.

"Brother . . . could you wait a moment?" Death take me, I couldn't keep my own staff's names straight, much less Luc's, though the other junior priest Jeremy was inextricably linked with another demon incident. Therefore, this one was Not-Jeremy in my head.

The junior priest paused in collecting his things. "Yes, Lady Justice?"

"I have a declaration of last wishes."

"I'd be happy to witness, m'lady." Goddess help the boy, he actually sounded happy. And when did I start thinking of the juniors as green children?

"Trust me, you don't want this one sitting on your shoulders. Is Brother Luc available?" I knew damn well he wasn't. He'd said he wouldn't be able to get to the tracking spell research until after the midday meal.

"No, m'lady. Are you sure I can't help? I assure you I'm fully versed in the protocols."

I pulled him away from the crowd still filing out of the courtroom. "Is Brother Kam available? This regards the priestess that was murdered. If what I suspect is in the declaration, there are going to be some very unhappy people. I'm not allowing you to ruin your career at your temple over a potential political mess."

"I see." A little relief mixed with his disappointment. "Yes, I believe Brother Kam is available. May I escort you to the Temple of Light, or shall I bring him here?"

I laughed. "Are you seriously suggesting that Brother Kam interrupt his midday meal?"

"What was I thinking?" the junior priest said, his voice a mix of rueful humor and mock horror.

It took me a moment to retrieve the declaration. It took me more than a moment to convince Little Bear I didn't need a warden to accompany us if the brother of Light was with me. I was only walking across the street with another priest. If I didn't know better, I would think we were all seeing conspiracies under every slab and cobblestone of the city.

The young brother led me to the private dining room, where sure enough, Kam was plowing through a chicken pie. "Mat, go fetch the Lady Justice a pie and some more wine for both of us."

Kam dabbed his mouth as my escort rushed off. "Now, what can I possibly do for you today, my lovely Anthea?"

I pulled the scroll from my pocket and laid it on the table. "Sister Gretchen's declaration."

He reached for his goblet and took a long swallow of wine. "So you're painting a target on the old man?"

I smiled despite my own anxiety. "No. I want a seat to be my witness. Gretchen made a point of leaving this with the Temple of Death instead of her own." I held up my hand when Kam opened his mouth. "Sister Bertrice's staff made me aware of the irregularities concerning last declarations. But since Luc's unavailable . . ."

He glared at me. Kam actually glared at me. "Luc is the current seat, and approaching him is proper protocol. No to mention, I'm technically retired and no longer considered an active priest."

"But you are a retired seat. And if you didn't want to stay here, you could have gone to the monastery in the Pana Valley and drowned yourself in one of their vats."

"That's cruel, m'lady. Besides—" He leaned closer. "Their gastronomic efforts are sorely lacking after the years I spent training our cook here."

He'd continue evading my questions if I didn't cut to my point. "Why are you so afraid of Gerd? I'm the one she tried to kill in the womb."

There was no sound. No movement. For a brief instant, I wondered if Kam had died in his chair.

He released the breath he'd been holding. "Who told you?" He waved a hand. "Never mind. That was a foolish question."

I folded my hands and leaned my elbows on the table. "You and Bertrice seem to think she'll try to finish what she started. Something that happened over thirty-one winters ago."

"Gerd's evil, Anthea. Stay away from her."

I'd heard Kam worried, jovial, and falling down drunk, but raw terror was in his voice now. "Unless she's been consorting with demons, she's still human, therefore manageable."

We fell silent when Brother Mat entered with my food and another flagon of wine. Once the door shut behind him, Kam staggered to his feet. His age was very apparent in the way he trembled as he warded the room.

He dropped into his chair as if all his energy had been spent in that little act of magic. "She didn't have pregnancy madness. We could see it in her eyes. In her mind. We knew, but we couldn't prove it." He slammed the flat of his hand on the table's surface. The dishes shivered at the release of his anger.

I folded my hand over his. His skin was wrinkled and dry as a dead leaf. His age sunk into my heart. "Do you believe Gerd could have killed and violated Gretchen?"

"Yes."

Like Bertrice this morning, the single affirmation said everything.

Except something didn't fit. I couldn't see what Gerd would gain from the manner of Gretchen's death. The money and property interests were too obvious.

It wasn't any daughterly affection that colored my viewpoint. If there was one thing about my mother, it was her ruthless efficiency. She would have learned from her first attempt at murder. Assuming I was her first attempt. If she wanted Gretchen dead, the priestess would never have been found.

Unless Tyra had been correct last night, and Gerd planned to kill two birds. Such a plan took ruthless efficiency to a new level.

However, I needed to pry Gerd out of her comfortable denial to discover what really happened the night Gretchen disappeared. I tapped the scroll against the hardwood. "If she is behind this perversity, the contents of the declaration may force her hand."

"You don't think Gretchen left her property to the Temple of Love."

I chuckled. "Of course not. Otherwise, she wouldn't have left her declaration with Bertrice's people, and Gerd would have been pounding on the doors of my temple, demanding that the seal be cracked and its contents confirmed last night." I squeezed his hand. "Why didn't you ever tell me you knew me from my childhood?"

His other hand patted mine. "I had hoped, prayed, that you didn't remember Orrin. And that you never found out what your mother had done to you. Bertrice nearly killed herself saving you, and she always felt guilty that she condemned you to the Temple of Balance."

I shook my head in confusion. "What do you mean?"

"Her power burned out before she could fully restore your health. By the time we could get another healer, it was too late. The poison had destroyed your sight."

# Chapter 6

I'd had enough revelations for one day. In my duties, I seen some of the worst depravities humans were capable of, and some of the greatest kindnesses. Nothing in my experience matched the truths I'd learned regarding my mother or the efforts to save my life. Part of me already knew the next set of revelations within the declaration wouldn't be any more comforting.

"If you don't wish to be my witness, I'll wait until Luc is finished with supervising trade negotiations." I poked at the chicken pie in front of me a few times before I shoved it aside.

Kam grunted as he laboriously climbed to his feet once again. "No. You're right. I swore my oaths, and this is too messy to leave to a junior priest. One of them would surely bollox the matter. Come." He released his wards.

I snatched the scroll and shoved it back into my pocket. We might as well deal with this pile of manure and get it over with. He extended his arm to me, a gesture of politeness as always, and I took it.

Under my hand, he trembled, and pale green sweat beaded on his forehead. "Kam, if you're not feeling well, I can wait."

"No." He patted my hand again as we shuffled down the hall to the main portion of the temple. "Just an old man's anxiety that the sins of his past have caught up with him."

"I would hardly call saving an innocent babe a sin." I chuckled. "Though it's difficult to imagine me as a babe, much less innocent."

"How do you feel about executions?"

I missed a step at his abrupt change of topic. If I hadn't been holding his arm, I would have fallen flat on my face. "Where does that question come from?"

We resumed our slow shuffling pace. I didn't think Kam was going to answer me when he said, "You remind me of Thalia. It was the one part of her duties she hated."

"I've read the stories and heard the songs. What was she really like?"

His smile was lost in the past. "Beautiful, brilliant. I know how bad my jokes are, but she'd always laugh at them. Or me. I was never sure which. Anyone who fought her thought she was sighted. She always knew what strike an opponent would use before he was in motion. I think she had a touch of precognition, though she would have denied it with her dying breath."

Grief shrouded him. "It's been twenty-five years, but I still miss her every day."

I wanted to comfort him. I didn't know how. This wasn't like ensuring Marco and Katarina's chance at happiness. I couldn't fix my own past. How could I fix Kam's?

We entered the public sanctuary. A handful of worshippers knelt before the altar. At the opposite end, a few farmers and the retinues of two traders either milled and murmured to each other or sat on the pews, bored out of their minds from the greenish tinge in their body heat. Three wardens paced through the sanctuary as a precaution. Brawls during trade conferences were rare, but that didn't rule out other means of intimidation.

I didn't envy Luc. Mediating trade negotiations were tedious enough to make me want to slit my own throat.

Kam and I claimed one of the small consultation rooms that lined the walls between the altar and the main doors. With a flick of his forefinger and a murmured word, he lit the wall sconce. The glow would shine through the thin alabaster to show the room was in use. He swiped the sweat from his forehead with his sleeve before he circled the tiny room, laying his warding.

I sat at the small table to stay out of his way. The familiar itch of magic in a tightly enclosed space prickled along my skin.

He took the seat next to me, and with a wave of his power, he lit that lamp as well. Since the priestly glows didn't emit heat as a traditional oil lamp or a torch did, I didn't need to squint against painful brightness.

Kam held out his hand. "Ready?"

I blew out a harsh breath as I took his clammy palm. "No, but let us proceed anyway. Lady of Balance, show us the will of the one who has passed through the veil."

The feeling of someone peering over my shoulder always accompanied the invocation of my goddess. Never was the impression stronger than it was right now. With a jolt, I realized this was the first time I'd done the opening of a declaration in ten years with someone other than Luc. Was that the difference?

"May the Lord of Light confirm the truth of the one who has passed Death's door," Kam answered.

Prickling energy spiraled around the edges of the parchment until they joined at the seal. The wax cracked and parted.

Any priest or priestess from any temple could bind a declaration of last wishes. According to Luc, the color symbolic of the temple colored the edges of the scroll. Only when Balance and Light opened it together was the declaration considered valid.

I asked him once what the edging looked like when the seal was released. He whispered that it was black twined around gold.

Like us in bed.

I shook my head to clear the distracting memory.

We unrolled the scroll, the ink record in front of Kam, the raised dots and lines impressed into the parchment in front of me. I ran my fingertips over the special raised code my order used. My heart skipped a beat, and I touched the name of Gretchen's heir again. I hadn't misinterpreted.

Lady Alessa DiMara.

# Chapter 7

"Father, help us," Kam swore.

I tapped my fingers against the table. "Now why would Sister Gretchen designate Lady Alessa?"

Kam stared at me. "Really, Anthea? Do I have to spell it out for you? She uses the phrase 'my beloved soulmate' in the naming."

I frowned. "But the sisters of the Temple of Love don't marry."

His exasperated sigh revealed his annoyance with me. "That doesn't mean they don't fall in love."

I leaned back in my seat. "I'm sorry. I'm having trouble wrapping my mind around the quiet, efficient Alessa with a priestess of Love."

"Sometimes, true love doesn't recognize arbitrary boundaries." The sadness in Kam's voice reminded me of my own forbidden affair. And Duke Marco had almost died because his mother couldn't deal with the fact he was in love with a veterinary apprentice.

"I wonder if this is why Lady Alessa's not married yet. The nobility gets rather prissy about such things when heirs and tradition are involved."

He slowly shook his head. "Not according to the gossip mongers. The issue is her parents' treason."

I rubbed my temples. A nasty ache was developing behind my eyes. "Unfortunately, this puts an entirely different twist to Sister Gretchen's body being found in the DiMara wine cellar."

"Surely, you don't believe—"

I held up my hand to stop him. "Right now, any conjectures are just that without evidence."

Balance must have been looking out for me. Three separate discussions over the last day melded into one.

I leaned forward again. "Both you and Bertrice mentioned that you thought Gerd had a way to circumvent a truthspell. Yesterday, Luc said when he questioned Lady Alessa, she seemed to be fighting his spell. What if the Loves have managed to develop a counter-spell?"

"You're mad," Kam spluttered.

"No." I held up an index finger. "Think about it. The order has always been privy to a great number of secrets thanks to pillow talk. What's stopping some unscrupulous group from abducting a priestess and truthspelling her?"

Kam rubbed his chin as he considered my theory. "To protect their sisterhood, they wouldn't inform any of the other temples. And definitely not share the information with any of the registered talents such as the guilds."

"But what if one priestess shared that information with her lover—"

"Who happened to be an unregistered, unknown talent," Kam finished. He frowned and tapped the parchment. "Not that the properties Gretchen has left Alessa are insignificant, but the DiMara holdings outstrip those named in the declaration. That wouldn't be a motive for Alessa to kill Gretchen."

I laughed, a mirthless one. The circumstantial evidence mounted against a woman I truly liked. "Are you going senile, too? You were one of the priests presiding over the sentencing at the DiMaras' trial last summer. All their properties went to Marco and Katarina."

A treason case was the only time the high priests and priestesses of all the temples sat as judges. Normally, such cases were heard in the capital, but the demon aspect of the DiMara's situation made the Reverend Mother of Balance reluctant to risk transporting them to Standora. Their trial coincided with mine for the illegal execution of Samael DiRoy. The crowds at the joint trials had surpassed both the Spring Rituals and the last Vintner's Festival put together.

Kam's sigh at my reminder was weary. "Leaving his sisters with nothing but their brother's obligation for their bride price should they marry." He shook his head again. "Even if she were responsible, I can't see Lady Alessa being foolish enough to hide the body on the family estate."

I folded my arms over my chest. "Neither do I. And the barrel containing Gretchen's corpse was definitely on the wagon from Pana Valley. Members of the household staff and my own rewinding of the timeline verified—"

Except we hadn't seen the barrel actually removed from the wagon when I replayed the delivery. We only saw the barrel rolled down the ramp with the rest of the shipment. Someone could have easily swapped the one with Gretchen's body for one of the delivered barrels when the men were in the storage room. The different wagoners added complications to this matter. An injury to any manual laborer wasn't unusual, but the coincidence raised many concerns.

I tapped my forefinger on my cheek. "I'm going to need to question the duke's household again."

Kam frowned. "Do you want me to accompany you to the estate?"

"Would you mind terribly if I ask for two priests this time? One to truthspell Alessa while I question her, another to watch for the counterspell?"

The old priest laughed. "You'll need to ask the new chief priest for that particular favor. I doubt he'll say no to you." He winked.

I shook my head. "You're incorrigible."

He nodded toward the declaration. "What about this?"

Something nagged at the back of my mind, but for the life of me, I couldn't tell if it were the declaration, the possibility of a counter to a truthspell, or the circumstances of Sister Gretchen's brutal murder. "Place it your safe hole for now. Would you please ask Luc to read it after his other business?"

"I can accommodate your request to use our safe hole, and I'll pass on your other two requests, my dear."

I kissed the old man on the cheek before I retrieved my heavy cloak, stalked through the main doors and down the steps. My clerk Donella would have today's docket paperwork ready for me to proof and sign. And maybe I'd have a little time to research a possible counter to a truthspell in our temple library.

The street teemed with traffic today since the rain had stopped for the last few hours. I checked for oncoming wagons and carriages before my foot descended from the last marble step onto the cobblestone. A horse and rider raced around the corner of the cross street between Light and Thief. He leaned farther in his saddle than the corner warranted at the speed he traveled. Almost as if he was trying to snatch at my cloak.

I jumped back, a stream of invectives on my tongue. Someone snagged my arm as I stumbled against the step behind me. More steeds poured out of the cross street, all performing the same odd maneuver. I climbed another step to keep out of their reach.

I turned to my rescuer, who stepped up as well. My polite thanks died at the telltale indigo in his hand. Sidestepping the knife aimed for my gut, I head-butted the man's nose. Sticky warmth splashed my cheeks.

Instead of a shriek, he pivoted and swept my legs from under me. My hip landed on the corner of the marble step, and pain shot across my gut. His kick to my ribs forced any remaining air out of my lungs.

"Stupid bitch. You should have been as blind as your sisters," he hissed as he drove the knife toward my throat.

Chapter 8

I threw up an arm to block his blow. Fire sliced my skin as the steel pierced my glove and my silk sleeve. Far better then the main blood vessel in my neck. If I stayed on the ground though, I was definitely dead.

My boot shot toward his crotch. He shifted to avoid my kick, and the momentum allowed me to shove him while I rolled the other way.

Directly into the path of more oncoming horses.

I curled into a tight ball, arms over my head to protect me from the multitude of sharp hooves. My body rang from the vibrations and pain of my injuries.

As suddenly as they appeared, the pack of riders and steeds were gone. I leapt to my feet, right hand already drawing the sword at my back. But my knife-wielding assailant had disappeared as well.

I whirled around to find wardens pouring from both the temple of Light and Balance. Little Bear must have been standing at the doors, watching for my return.

"Anthea!" Luc's familiar scent washed over me. He beat the wardens to me by a couple of paces.

He caught himself. "Are you all right, Lady Justice?" He reached for the blood on my face, but I shoved his hand away.

"No. Don't." A vicious smile twisted my lips. "We spilt each other's blood."

Luc's smile was just as feral. "We have him."

Or so we thought. But like everything else in this damnable day, the gods seemed to be laughing at our efforts, including the two we were personally sworn to.

We left our team of wardens to watch the possible exits at a decrepit inn near the docks. The tracking spell failed as we reached the room it indicated. Luc kicked in the door. Inside was my attacker's still warm body, bloody nose and all, in the tiny, third-story room lodging. The scent of bitter almonds told us what type of poison he used. A quick search gave no clue of his identity, which in itself spoke of his origins.

Luc raked his hands through his hair. "There hasn't been an attempt in Issura by the Assassins Guild since—"

"The reign of the Twin Queens before the last demon invasion." I blew out an exasperated breath. "That was nearly two hundred years ago. The question becomes why me?"

His voice whispered in my mind. *Shi Hua mentioned the Jing School of Sorcery had you at the top of their list of targets after her.*

I shivered at the memory. We didn't dare speak of the sensitive situation aloud.

Last fall, a sorcerer had hired or tricked one of Orrin's merchant captains into smuggling a demon egg into the city. That's when we discovered that the woman we thought was the Jing ambassador's concubine was in fact a priestess of Light and acted as Ambassador Quan's bodyguard. She and I had met a few times since then to exchange information that benefited both of our nations.

*No.* I shook my head. *The Jing Imperial Guard and their wardens raided the school. Anyone who survived was put to death.*

*Unless they hired and paid for the Assassins Guild's service before the raid.*

Again, I shook my head. "That was months ago. It doesn't fit the current situation. There must be another reason."

"You believe the attempt is due to you investigating Gretchen's death or administering her estate?"

"That makes no sense either. We have no reason to believe my attempted assassination is connected with Sister Gretchen's death."

Luc snorted, his disgust evident. "I don't believe in coincidences."

I sheathed my sword. "Whichever priest of Light witnessed the opening would know her last wishes also."

"Which is why I assigned a warden to watch Kam before we headed here."

I stared at Luc. "Let's assume for a moment you are correct, and there's a connection. Who knew the contents of Gretchen's declaration? She deliberately filed it with the Temple of Death so Gerd wouldn't know."

Luc shrugged. "Everyone at Death?"

"If one of their members is involved, why not switch scrolls? For that matter, why not lose it?"

Luc grunted. "Too many safeguards. The entire temple would have to be involved in the conspiracy." He crouched next to the body and lifted its hand. "What did Master Devin say about a man with small hands?"

I knelt and held my gloved hand against the corpse's. His palm was wider, but my fingers were longer. "I suppose it's possible, but no assassin is going to waste precious escape time to mutilate their target."

"Unless whoever hired him gave him specific instructions."

I let the hand drop and climbed to my feet. "Now, we've officially jumped into wild hare territory."

Luc rose as well. "I haven't had a chance to research a separation and tracking spell for the scrapings Master Devin provided you. Do you want me to do that while you have a talk with Lady Alessa?"

I shook my head. "No, I want you and another priest there when she's truthspelled during this little interview."

"No." Luc pushed me toward the door. "I'm not involving Mat or Jeremy in this mess."

"Kam—"

"I'm not dragging him up the bluffs either." Anger coated Luc's words. "You and I can handle this. You'll be in the room this time, and you know what to look for."

Not sure if he was angry with me or the situation, I took the conciliatory route. "You're right, and the longer we wait to question Lady Alessa, the more likely something else will go wrong in this investigation. The tracking spell can be performed later." I stared at the rapidly cooling body. "If this is Gretchen's killer, your spell won't work anyway, and we're no closer to understanding why."

As we exited the room, we found Magistrate DiCook and a handful of peacekeepers pounding up the staircase of the inn.

"What in the names of the Twelve is going on here?" He spat on the landing. "None of your wardens would say a word."

When I didn't answer, his attention switched to Luc. "I am the duly elected magistrate of this city. One of you had better answer me!"

"A member of the Assassins Guild tried to murder me," I said.

"On the steps of the Lord of Light's home," Luc added.

"When?" the magistrate demanded.

"Less than a candlemark ago." I pushed past him, and he grabbed my left arm. I couldn't stop the hiss of pain. When I refused to waste time waiting for a healer, Little Bear and Tyra had threatened to hold me down while one of the brothers bandaged the ugly cut from the assassin's knife.

"Why wasn't I notified?" DiCook's lip curled into his familiar sneer.

I yanked my arm out of his grasp. "Because we were trying to catch him before he escaped."

"You let him get away?"

I wasn't sure if DiCook was more pleased that the assassin escaped or that I failed. If I gambled, I would have bet on the latter. "You could say that." I gestured toward the wide open door. "If you can get more out of him or his belongings than me, let me know."

I continued painfully down the stairs, Luc right behind me though he didn't complain the way my hip was. The joint would stiffen from the bruising if I rested now, not that I could afford the time.

The exclamations from the peacekeepers and DiCook's curse when they discovered the body beat us to the first floor.

"You really need to stop antagonizing the man, Anthea."

I smiled up at him. "When the Lord of Light's domain freezes over."

Duke Marco's face froze, his air of disappointment and despair obvious when Luc and I appeared at the gate of his estate and asked to speak with his sister. Lady Katarina graciously allowed us to use her reception room, but the fire couldn't warm me as it did yesterday.

Lady Alessa held her composure until her brother and sister-in-law left the room. The moment the door clicked shut, hot shame tinted her cheeks. "You know."

"Know what?" I said.

She sank into a chair while I sat on the stool facing her. "Please don't play with me, Lady Justice. Please, don't. You have no idea how h-hard . . ." Pale yellow tears ran down her cheeks.

Luc cursed under his breath. I knew at once he hadn't asked the right questions during his original interview of her. He hadn't conceived of the two women having a secret affair. Magic tickled my skin as he warded the room.

"You could have pulled one of us aside yesterday," I said gently. "We would have listened."

She stared at the painfully bright grate. "I couldn't. Things have been so difficult for my brother. There's been so much scandal. He tried, he really did, to find me an appropriate match. I thought if he did, I could suppress my desires . . ."

"Alessa, I need Luc to truthspell you."

She nodded though her attention never wavered from the fire.

The moment that the tingle of magic surrounded her, I said, "Tell me about the counterspell Gretchen taught you."

Her head jerked, and she stared at me, eyes wide as she realized her mistake. She winced in pain as she reached for her neck, and I seized her arms. It wasn't much of a physical struggle despite my injuries. But around the room, objects chittered from vibrations. I knew damn well it wasn't Luc or me losing control of our power.

Luc removed the chain hidden beneath the collar of her dress. Dangling from the links was a carved ruby heart. A thin line of energy hummed around the jewel. A talisman.

Alessa's face crumpled, and her sobs came loud and fierce. Her terrible grief overrode the agony of the spell. For once, I was the one patiently stroking the distraught witness's hair while Luc paced behind her chair. Underneath the noblewoman's emotion, the stones of the keep moaned in sympathetic agony.

When her weeping faded to hiccups, I released her. "Don't make me ask you again, Alessa. Otherwise, the truthspell will force you to answer me, and it will be painful."

She nodded. "Gretchen gave me the heart a year ago. When we first started . . ." Her blood pulsed as she acknowledged their affair. "She taught me the words and gestures to activate and deactivate the magic."

Alessa's pulse slowed, her voice turned numb, as she stared at her hands. "She didn't mean any harm. She was protecting me as best she could when . . . when Mother would have one of her hired sorcerers truthspell us."

My own blood ran cold. I didn't want to know the answer to the next question, but duty forced me to ask anyway. "Us? You mean you, Marco and Isabella?"

Behind Alessa, Luc stiffened. "That's how your mother found out Marco was courting Katarina, isn't it?"

"Yes." Her head bowed once more. "Ironically, Mother sending our baby sister to the capital protected her from the worst of Mother's predations. Isabella loves the university, and now she can focus on her studies without Mother breathing down her neck about seducing one of the princes."

Time to get the questioning back on track. "Alessa, did you kill Sister Gretchen of the Temple of Love?"

"No." Anger threaded through her single word. There was a hint of power behind it.

"Do you know who killed Sister Gretchen?"

"No." The fire flared, and I couldn't stop my wince at the brilliant heat. Thankfully, Alessa couldn't see my reaction with my hood in place.

"Do you know who put Sister Gretchen's body into the barrel she was found in?"

"No."

"When was the last time you saw her alive?"

"Five mornings ago. I had snuck out of the manor and met her at a hunting cabin on our lands about a candlemark's ride north. We spent the night together." Once again, her pulse jumped at revealing such intimate secrets. "We parted shortly after third night in order for me to return to my bed without arousing suspicion. She was very much alive when I rode off."

I glanced at Luc, his frown matching my own. Alessa's testimony narrowed the time for Gretchen's murder.

Turning my attention back to the noblewoman, I asked, "Why didn't your parents have you tested for magical talent?"

Her gaze met mine again. "They did when I was eleven winters. The priest of Light who supervised said I was a passive."

A passive talent could activate a spell created by an active talent, but they couldn't cast one on their own. Therefore, they weren't required to register with the temples. It explained why no one knew about Alessa's latent abilities.

Luc finally stopped pacing. He crossed to the chair on the other side of Alessa and sat. "I know you are still dealing with your lover's death, m'lady, but I would like you to come see me, say, two weeks from today for retesting." So I wasn't the only one bothered by her flashes of power. They were far more than a token ability.

I could feel her mounting panic splash against my mind. "You are not in trouble, Alessa. Either you were too young to fully manifest your talent yet, or the brother was incompetent."

"Excuse me?" Luc exclaimed in mock outrage.

Our teasing lightened Alessa's mood, and she made a burbling half-giggle, half-hiccup sound.

Luc held up the necklace. "I am going to take this for now. We need to figure out how to deal with this counterspell in order to discover Gretchen's murderer. I'll return it when you come to see me in two weeks."

"You'll remove the spell from the jewel, won't you?" she whispered.

"We have to," I said. "Technically, it's illegal." I held up my hands when the stool I sat on trembled. "I'm not charging you. You received it in good faith from another priestess." I cleared my throat. "I do need to ask you a few more questions."

She sagged in her own seat and nodded. "It's just . . . it's the only gift of hers I have."

Luc and I exchanged glances. He remained silent while I continued the questioning.

"Did anyone know that you and Gretchen were having an affair?"

"Not that I know of. As I said, we were very careful because of my mother."

"Did you receive any notes or messages that insinuated a third party knew about your affair?"

"No."

"Any oblique reference about you personally involved in a sapphic affair?"

"Not to me." She paused for a moment, but she wasn't fighting the spell. "Some lords have made derogatory comments about me to Marco, but as far as I know it was for the purpose of insult, not because they truly believed I prefer the bed of a woman."

"Do you know who Gretchen named as her heir in her declaration of last wishes?"

"Yes."

"Who?"

"Me, but a bagful of gold isn't going to replace her."

*She has no idea of the extent of Gretchen's holdings*, Luke whispered in my mind.

I inclined my head and asked the next question of the noblewoman. "When did you find out you were Gretchen's named heir?

"She told me our last night together. That she wanted to make sure I had resources if something happen to her, and my family discovered our relationship." Alessa's smile was small and sad. "She kept trying to talk me into running away with her. Cant, or the Mecas, or even the Sea Peoples' islands. When we met at the cabin, she said she could get us passage on a Jing ship."

She twisted her fingers in her lap. "I couldn't leave Marco and especially Isabella without any explanation."

"Did Gretchen ever indicate there was another reason she wanted to escape from Orrin?"

"I'd like to believe it was only our love, but I know there were problems between her and High Sister Gerd and Sister Dragonfly."

"What kind of problems?"

Alessa took a deep breath and released it. "Gerd was always accusing her of trying to usurp her authority. Dragonfly was simply jealous when Gretchen stopped sleeping with her."

I exchanged looks with Luc. Now we were getting somewhere, but neither of us said anything.

Instead, I took Alessa's hands in mine. "Your pain is mine."

Her face scrunched again at the ritual words of sympathy for the death of a loved one, but she forced back her tears. "Thank you," she whispered.

At my signal, Luc murmured the words to release his truthspell.

I squeezed Alessa's hands. "Gretchen was also Katarina's friend. She would share your grief."

"A-are you going to tell them? Marco and Katarina? About our a-affair?"

"No," I said softly. "Sharing that knowledge is not my right, but I think you are underestimating your family. About Gretchen's declaration . . ." I sucked in a deep breath. "Brother Kam and I have opened and confirmed it—"

I held up one hand at her little gasp. "I don't want to cause you any embarrassment, but I have the duty to insure Gretchen's wishes are followed. High Sister Gerd believes that no declaration exists. I'm going to have to make the public post soon to prevent her from illegally seizing your property."

"I-I don't know if I want it," Alessa murmured.

I clasped her hands again. "You have the right of refusal, of course, but right now, your grief is overriding your common sense. I would suggest confiding in your brother. Get his counsel before you make any decision."

Her eyes widened. "B-b-but the public post will cause even more scandal."

"Considering the gold equivalent of Gretchen's holdings, it will garner more noble suitors than you'll know what to do with," Luc said, dryly.

"Not to mention, Marco has already broken with noble tradition. There's no reason you cannot follow in his footsteps," I added.

Alessa nodded. "I will take your wisdom into consideration, Lady Justice, High Brother."

"If you remember anything else, come straight to us," I said. "No pages or other messengers if you want to avoid the gossip."

She nodded, but tears had started trickling down her cheeks again. Luc deactivated his wards. When we left the reception room, I closed the door behind us.

Marco stood in the hallway. By his expression, he obviously expected the worst.

I stopped before him. "Your sister isn't involved in the murder."

He sagged against the stone wall. "Thank the Twelve."

I laid my right hand on his shoulder and squeezed it in support. After all the struggle and tension with his sister, both my head and the slice on my left arm were throbbing. It was selfish of me in light of Alessa's pain, but I wanted nothing more than a hot bath and equally hot tea.

As I continued past the duke, he said, "Lady Justice—"

"I can't say anything more, Your Grace." I turned away from him before I spilled all of his sister's secrets, and I strode down the hallway.

Luc and I were nearly to the entryway when a figure stepped from behind a statue. "She didn't do it."

I remembered the voice from yesterday. "You're Bartholomew, correct?"

"Yes, m'lady."

I could remember the names of Marco's staff, but not my own. I would have kicked myself if my hip didn't ache so badly.

The man bobbed his head. "Lady Alessa, she didn't kill that priestess." His voice didn't squeak as it had yesterday when we had originally questioned him.

Behind me, Luc's irritation rippled through my psyche. "Yesterday, you told me you didn't know who killed Sister Gretchen."

"Ah don't!" Between Bartholomew's distress and Luc's growing anger, I felt as if my eyes would erupt from my head.

"Do you have an additional statement you wish to make, Bartholomew?" I said, trying to inject some calm into the situation.

"Ah just told ya. Lady Alessa didn't kill that priestess."

I wanted to believe he was a loyal DiMara retainer, but maybe he was too loyal. "And how do you know this?" I asked.

If the brilliant red heat of his face hadn't given him away, the shuffling of his feet did. "Ah-ah just know, that's all."

"If you still want a place in this household, you'd better answer the justice's question." Lady Katarina's cold steel voice came from behind Luc and me.

Unfortunately, the moment we glanced at her was the same moment Bartholomew decided to run.

# Chapter 9

Luc and I raced after Bartholomew who sped through the manor's main doors. The problem was there weren't that many places for him to go. Most of the servants were in the courtyard, accomplishing whatever tasks were necessary before the next round of winter rains.

I had to give credit to the rest of the DiMara household's presence of mind. At my shouts, a guard and a stable hand tackled him before he reached the main gate. Bartholomew would have had better luck playing cat-and-mouse in the manor itself.

Thank Balance, he wasn't the shiniest coin in the purse. My hip ached too fiercely for an extended chase.

The two men jerked Bartholomew upright and dragged him back in our direction.

I glared at the idiot as I jogged up to them. "I'll give you a choice, Bartholomew. You can come back inside with me and Brother Luc, and answer our questions. Or we'll deliver you to Magistrate DiCook." I pushed back my hood and stepped closer until our noses were a finger-length apart. "And the magistrate won't be as gentle as I will."

Bartholomew sagged between the guard and the stable hand. "I'll answer yer questions, m'lady."

*Wine cellar.*

I nodded at Luc's whisper in my mind. With the day I was having, I wasn't going to be the least bit guilty over messing with Bartholomew's head in a conventional sense.

By the time we dragged Bartholomew down to the DiMara wine cellar and tied him to a chair the guard had brought for us, Marco joined us. He pulled me aside. "Alessa told me. Katarina's with her."

I nodded. "She'll need your assistance on the financial aspects."

A bitter chuckle came from the duke. "I depend far too much on Alessa's advice than she does mine."

"Then maybe a little brotherly support?"

"Always." He inclined his head toward his bound retainer. "May I be here while you question Bartholomew?"

I frowned as I looked at him. "Are you sure? There may be things . . ."

He smiled as my voice trailed off. "It's not as if Isabella and I hadn't suspected." His expression faltered. "We did our best to protect Alessa from our mother."

I wasn't sure which of us had it worse. Having a mother who simply didn't want you, or one that only saw you as a tool to be used and discarded. "All right, but I don't want to hear a word pass from your lips."

He held his forefinger to his closed mouth.

I shooed the household guards out. Marco's steward vociferously protested, but I finally shoved him over the threshold, too. "Lock the door."

"If *anything* happens to His Grace—" he spluttered.

I slammed the cellar door in his face.

By now, Bartholomew was openly weeping. "Ah didn't kill her!"

"Silence." I circled the room, laying my wards. Luc and I had worked so long together I didn't have to say anything. He laid the truthspell on Bartholomew so quickly the retainer didn't know it was happening.

I drew my sword and planted the tip in the wood between his legs. Bartholomew squealed like a newborn pig. "If I hear one thing come out of your throat I don't like, your trial will be here and now. Do you understand?"

"Y-y-yes."

"Did you kill Sister Gretchen?"

"N-n-no."

"Did you harm Sister Gretchen?"

Bartholomew groaned and would have bent double if he weren't securely lashed to the chair.

"Stop trying to lie to me, and the pain will go away."

"Y-yes." He panted as the fire in his gut faded. I had tried to fight a truthspell before, both during my training and when I was Samael DiRoy's prisoner. I knew what he was feeling.

"Before she died?"

"Yes." Bartholomew seemed to sink inside himself. I wanted to sigh in relief. It was so much easier when the subject of my questioning gave up and simply answered.

"When?"

"Five mornings ago."

"Where?"

"Outside of Duke DiMara's hunting cabin."

A cold chill ran down my spine. "Start from the night before and tell me how you ended up at the cabin."

Bartholomew shot a furtive glance at Marco. "Ah always loved Lady Alessa. From the moment Ah saw her." He licked his lips. "B-but a noblewoman and a commoner?" He tried to shrug. "S-so when His Grace married the animal apprentice . . ."

Goddess help me, I could see where his tale was traveling. I wanted to tell him to stop, but I couldn't. We had to know what happened.

"Ah thought Ah could convince her that my love was true. That Ah would make her a good husband."

A sob tore from his throat. "Ah didn't believe the awful things people said about her. It was that priestess. She put a spell on Lady Alessa. To make her lay with the bitch instead of a proper man."

"Bartholomew," I snapped. "Did you follow Lady Alessa to the cabin six nights ago?"

"Yes," he wailed.

"Did you watch them while they made love?"

"Yes!"

King of the Wildlings take him! The bastard was actually getting aroused by the memory. The connection between his obsession and the knife wounds on Gretchen's corpse made me nauseous. I probably would have vomited if I'd bothered to eat my mid-day meal.

"Did you only watch them?"

"No."

"Did you pleasure yourself?"

"Yes." No doubt fantasizing that he was with Alessa.

I glanced over my shoulder at Marco. He remained in his original position against the wall with his arms crossed, but from the pale yellow of his fingertips, they dug into his upper arms. The rest of his exposed skin was a brilliant scarlet.

Satisfied he wasn't about to do anything stupid, I turned back to Bartholomew. "What else did you do before Lady Alessa and Sister Gretchen left the cabin?"

"Ah fell asleep shortly after they did."

"Did you do anything else while they were inside the hunting cabin?"

"No."

"What did you do when you saw them leave?"

"Ah followed the temple bitch to a nearby grove. Ah caught her as she was untying her horse. Ah told her she needed to stay away from Lady Alessa. She shouldn't be corrupting a right proper noblewoman."

"What did Sister Gretchen do?"

"She-she laughed at me. That's when Ah choked her."

"How long did you choke her?"

"Ah don't know. Ah wanted to kill her. True Ah did. But if Ah did, Ah knew Ah would be executed, so Ah threw her to the ground."

"Was she conscious?"

"Yes. Coughing and gasping something fierce, but she weren't dead. Ah told her that if Ah caught her with Lady Alessa again, Ah would kill her."

Assault on a priestess. I couldn't hand over Bartholomew's lashing over to anyone else from any of the Temples. He wouldn't survive if I did. The scars on my back itched at the thought of having to lash him myself. "What did you do to her after you threatened her?"

"Ah spat on her, and then I walked back to the manor."

"When was the last time you saw Sister Gretchen alive?"

"That morning, laying on the forest floor, before Ah turned and walked home."

I knew Luc had asked the next questions yesterday, but for thoroughness's sake I asked them again. "Did you know Sister Gretchen was dead?"

"No."

"Did you put Sister Gretchen in the wine barrel?"

"No."

"Do you know who did put Sister Gretchen in the wine barrel?"

"No."

I tilted my head, and Luc followed me to where Marco leaned against the wall. The duke's face no longer glowed scarlet. Instead, it had faded a sickly yellow-green.

"By his own admission, he did physically assault a priestess," Luc murmured.

"Yes." I eyed Marco. "He also spied on your sister in a private moment without her knowledge, Your Grace. That is also an assault."

"Do what you believe necessary, Lady Justice. He no longer has a place in my household." From the way he glared at Bartholomew, the man wouldn't survive the night if I left him here.

*And this, Lady Justice, is why you take a warden escort with you in the big city.*

If we were alone, I would have kicked Luc in the shin for his silent comment.

I sighed. "Your Grace, if we may impose on you for a wagon and a couple of your guards . . ."

Thick air and flashes of sea water boiled by lightning near the horizon said more rain was on its way. The weather matched my foul mood on the ride back to the temple district.

Whatever discussion I wanted to have with Luc concerning the investigation was thrown off the roof when we reached the stables at the Temple of Balance. Sivan, Donella and Little Bear were lying in wait for me at the back porch. Luc and the duke's household guards unloaded Marco's former retainer.

"The ambassador of Jing is in your office," Sivan started.

"Magistrate DiCook is in *my* office," Donella added.

"And by the Goddess, you are not going anywhere again without me or another warden," Little Bear shouted.

Everyone, including the cowering Bartholomew, stared at him, but Little Bear didn't alter his glower one whit.

"If you want to perform warden duties, escort this one down to a cell." I shoved Marco's ex-retainer into Little Bear's arms. "And take clay impressions of his hands so we can compare them to the marks on Sister Gretchen's corpse."

Once he marched off with our prisoner, I turned to my assistant. "Sivan, take these gentlemen to the kitchen." I waved at the duke's guardsmen. "Thanks to that piece of manure, they're going to miss their evening meal. The least I can do is make sure they have a full, warm belly and a gold coin each."

"Yes, m'lady." She curtsied and turned to lead the men inside.

"Wait. I need a pot of tea, bread and cheese brought to my office. Enough to be polite—"

"But not enough to encourage lingering." She smiled. "Yes, m'lady."

"Donella, tell the magistrate I have returned, and I will be with him shortly. Bring him a full meal." I prayed to Balance that would smooth over some feathers. I did listen to Luc once in a while.

I turned to my fellow priest.

Luc held up his hands. "I'm heading back to my own temple."

"But—"

"There's research you requested, Lady Justice. Not to mention, my own duties to attend." *And Little Bear's right. You need to trust your own wardens, instead of treating me like one.*

I cringed at his silent reprimand. "Of course, Brother. My thanks for your assistance this afternoon." *Will I see you tonight?*

*Let's see how far I get on my work.*

I swallowed my disappointment, schooled my expression and headed for my office. Though I was fairly certain why the Jing ambassador was here, I didn't bother changing into clean robes since he'd been waiting.

Two guards stood outside my office door.

Not mine.

Spears flashed down to block my way.

"You dare presume . . ." My voice sounded like a wolf who'd discovered interlopers in her den.

"Take off your hood and show us your eyes," the guard returned in an equally dangerous tone.

For half an instant, I considered drawing on the bastard, but with my luck, I'd end up as the next Reverend Mother of Balance if I killed him. I made the slightly better, though less satisfactory, choice of pushing back my hood.

The guard who spoke tried to stifle his gasp. His partner made the sign of the Dragon to ward off evil.

I sighed. "Now, may I please enter my own damn office?"

Not only did they remove their spears from my way, they edged back far enough my cloak wouldn't brush theirs.

As much as I wanted to bang and stomp, I clung to what shards of courtesy I had left and opened the door. "Please forgive my inexcusable delay, Ambassador."

The Jing diplomat wore the traditional thin moustache of his land. The tips of it grew even with his chin beard at a point a hand-span below his neck and were decorated with tiny gold beads. Gold threaded through his silk pants and jacket. From the padding and stiffness of the jacket, he wore boiled leather underneath. After we discovered his court sorcerer housed a demon within his own embassy last fall, I didn't blame him for taking extra precautions.

He rose from the same chair Sister Bertrice had occupied at our sunrise meal.

Holy Mother, had that only been this morning? It felt like an eternity. Only this time, cheese and Issuran bread replaced the Cantish bread and eggs.

Another stray thought occurred. Had my staff dragged the table to the storage room only to drag it right back? I needed to tell Sivan to just leave the damn thing in here despite the tight fit.

The ambassador and I made the requisite polite bows.

"I understand you've had an interesting day, Lady Justice."

"You could say that." I shed my outer cloak and sword. I hung them from the hook on the wall next to his cloak before I turned to face him again. "How may I assist you today, Ambassador Quan?"

His eyes widened. "Did you know you were bleeding, Lady Justice?"

I checked my arm. Sure enough, there were splotches of orange among green bandages. "So I am." I rang the bell on my desk. Of course, he wouldn't mention the unearthly color of my own eyes. Such a personal comment would violate Jing propriety.

Come to think of it, neither had his guards. They simply used my eye color to confirm my identity. I prayed they wouldn't stab Sivan in their enthusiasm.

"Surely you wish to see a healer for your wound?"

"For this trifle? After I have already kept you waiting? I wouldn't think of it." I was definitely raiding the stock of painkilling powder as soon as I could get him and DiCook out of my temple though.

A knock on my door, and Sivan entered. "Yes, m'lady?"

"Would you have some fresh bandages? My injury is disturbing the ambassador's appetite."

My ever-efficient assistant produced two rolls of cotton fabric and a jar of ointment from her voluminous apron pockets. From the looks she darted in my direction as she dealt with the reopened cut on my arm, she could barely keep control of her tongue.

As soon as the door closed behind her, the ambassador smiled. "You have an accomplished staff."

"They endeavor to keep me functional." I poured tea for both of us as Jing custom demanded. Infuriating the Orrin city officials was one thing. Not even my position as a city's chief justice would protect me from the queen if I created a diplomatic incident by insulting another country's designated representative.

"Did one of them miss a step?" He gestured with his cup toward my injury.

"My wardens would be the first to tell you the incident was my own fault for not heeding their advice." I dropped the pretense of manners. "Why are you here, Ambassador?"

He smiled again. "Since we both know you are an accomplished justice, you already know why."

I returned his smile. "Not necessarily. Either you're here to learn the status of the investigation into an acquaintance's death, or you have additional information that you believe will aid me in said investigation."

He took his time selecting a slice of bread and a hunk of cheese before he spoke again. "What I'm about to tell you cannot leave this room."

I leaned back and regarded him. "That may be next to impossible. You do realize that my own staff and members of the Temple of Light are working on this matter."

"Which priest is assisting you?" He tore off a piece of bread and popped it in his mouth.

Now why would he want to know that?

"Three of them have assisted me directly today." I chuckled. "And I have a feeling the junior-most priest was assigned to spend his evening researching a particular subject for me."

The ambassador took his dear time chewing that tiny bit of bread. "I had hoped for more discretion from you, Lady Justice."

"I can ward the room so our discussion is private. Beyond that, I have my duty and my oath to Balance and to the Crown, to see that justice is served."

He nodded sharply, as if coming to a decision. "I see I may not have a choice."

I shrugged. "There is always a choice."

He bowed at my logic. "Please ward the room."

I rose and did so. Frankly, I was a little surprised the ambassador didn't bring Shi Hua, the priestess of Light who functioned as his secret bodyguard. And the more I thought about her absence, the more worried about what the ambassador would tell me I became.

The throb in my head had surpassed the throb in my arm by the time I resumed my seat. As much as I wanted to press the ambassador, I sipped my own tea and waited.

"You've already discovered I was a frequent worshipper with Sister Gretchen."

"Yes." There was no reason to hide the knowledge. The entire city knew of his sophisticated appetites. Balance help me, he'd even propositioned me at our first meeting.

"She was obtaining a . . . favor for me."

This was going to be a very long night after all. I reached for a piece of cheese and nibbled on it.

The ambassador took a drink of his own tea. "She sent a message to me that she had acquired the favor."

"And when were you to meet her to exchange the favor?"

His gaze focused on his cup. "We would not make the actual exchange until we had left your capital and put out to sea." His eyes met mine. "She was supposed to be at the port in Standora three days ago."

My heart lurched at the timing. Gretchen had planned to head directly north after her tryst with Alessa. No doubt the priestess had hoped to convince her lover to come with her. Alessa had already confirmed Gretchen had passage on a Jing ship. And if the priestess left the duke's hunting cabin before First Morning on Third Day last week, she would have arrived in Standora well before the night's high tide on Fifth Day at the latest.

Except at that point, her body was sitting in Duke Marco's wine cellar.

"I take it she had never failed to show for an appointed rendezvous before."

"No." He set his cup back on the table, and I refilled his and mine. "The other odd thing was her request for payment."

"How so?"

"In return for the favor she acquired for me, she requested passage for two to Jing."

A sick feeling in my stomach corrupted the cheese I'd eaten. Would Gretchen still be safe if Alessa had run away with her instead of spending one last night at the cabin? Or had Alessa's guilt over abandoning her siblings saved her life?

"You do not look surprised, Lady Justice."

I released the breath I held. "No." I picked up my cup to warm my fingers. Unfortunately, the heat of the ceramic did not extend to my soul. "While I do not wish to involve myself in internal Jing affairs, I must ask what this favor was. It may have a great deal of bearing on who murdered Sister Gretchen."

The silence stretched like a spider's web until his voice sliced through the strands. "She gathered information as to the trade positions of Issura, Cant and the Sea Peoples."

"In time for the spring sailing season?"

He nodded.

Local trade negotiations had already started today under Luc's supervision. The international negotiations were scheduled for the week before the Spring Rituals. The implications were not comforting. So many ideas tangled in my mind.

Just as Gretchen's schemes had tangled her in death.

"Unfortunately, Ambassador, you've only added suspects to my list."

"I would still like to . . . acquire the favor she owed me."

I shook my head. "First of all, I could not betray my queen in such a fashion even if the favor came into my possession. You do have my assurance that it will not be used against Jing."

There was the slightest easing in his shoulders.

"However," I continued. "Whoever knew about Sister Gretchen's favor and killed her may already possess the favor and is using it against both of our nations."

His frown dipped the ends of his moustache past his beard. "That is also my concern. Perhaps her heir may find the information in her personal possessions . . ."

I shook my head. "Sister Gretchen's personal accoutrements are missing. Presumably in the possession of her murderer."

"I see." He stroked his moustache with a forefinger.

As much as I wished I could have truthspelled the bastard, trying would have landed me in a bigger diplomatic quagmire. His body temperature hadn't changed during our discussion, except for the slight warming of his fingers from the hot tea. He could be playing me for his own purposes, but why would he admit to spying on Issura to a chief justice?

"If I may, Ambassador, when was the last time you saw Sister Gretchen alive?"

He exhaled, a sorrowful sound, though I suspected it had more to do with the lost information than the death of his lover. "The last time I was in Orrin. The Winter Solstice."

Over six weeks ago, assuming he were telling me the truth.

My eyes narrowed. "When did you ask Sister Gretchen for this favor?"

He smiled over his cup. "Really, Lady Justice? I thought you were far more intelligent."

Either passing along the trade positions was an ongoing arrangement with the Love priestess, or Shi Hua had been visiting Gretchen the same way she'd been visiting me. And I already knew Shi Hua relayed all information that came into her possession to the ambassador.

Maybe it was time to play that piece. I cleared my throat. "I take it a certain member of your household has been equally unsuccessful in locating the missing favor."

Once again, he smiled over his cup, but he said nothing

I took another sip of tea, but when he remained silent, I said, "Is there anything else I may assist you with, Ambassador?"

He gave a slight shake of his head. "No, Lady Justice. You have been far more accommodating in this matter that I expected."

"More accommodating than my predecessor?"

He jerked, and his ears glowed slightly. My semi-snide question told me a little more about how bad things were getting in Orrin before Penelope died.

The ambassador set down his cup. "I see the Reverend Mother of Balance made an excellent choice in who holds the seat of Orrin." He rose. "Thank you for the tea and conversation, Lady Justice."

I swallowed the ache in my hip as I stood also. "And thank you for bringing certain things to my attention." With a word, I collapsed the wards.

After he left, I stared at the remnants of our snack. I knew I should eat more before dealing with DiCook, but it felt as if hot coals danced in my stomach.

Donella was waiting for me as I stepped out of my office. Her pinched lips and the red streaks along her neck told me what I didn't want to know. I steeled myself and followed her to the clerk's office while Little Bear escorted the ambassador and his guards out of the temple.

My only comfort was that Magistrate DiCook hadn't thrown food at the scrolls littering nearly every open space in Donella's office. In fact, he hadn't touched the beef, fresh bread and beans. He stood in the middle of the cramped space as if I'd interrupted his pacing and glowered at me.

My stomach choose that moment to growl.

"Thank you for your assistance, Donella. Why don't you retire for the night?"

Her attention flicked to the magistrate for a moment. "Shall I call a warden, m'lady?"

"That won't be necessary. Good eventide, Donella."

"And you, m'lady." She pulled the door shut behind her.

Maybe it was time to take Luc's advice and act a little more politely to DiCook. "I haven't had my evening meal yet. Would you care to join me?"

"So you can have a chance to poison me?" he snarled.

"That's Gerd's area of expertise, not mine." The words came out before I could stop them.

"Are you accusing another chief priestess of murder?" There was a certain glee in his voice.

I rubbed my aching forehead. "No, I'm not. I simply can't deal with the thought of you in bed with my mother right now."

"Mother?" He rocked back on his heels.

My tendency to blurt things out without thinking when I was exhausted worked in my favor for once. A grim smile tugged the corners of my mouth. "She gave birth to me, therefore, yes, she is my mother."

I sighed. My head throbbed, and I was too damn tired to play anymore games. "Malven, I've had a very bad day, and I don't feel like arguing with you. I've barely had anything to eat as my stomach pointed out when I walked in. If you want to know what I've learned today, come with me."

I didn't wait for his answer. I pivoted and headed for the kitchen, doing my best not to limp in the process. The smart sound of steel-shod boots followed me through the back hallways of the temple.

As usual, the kitchen was cozy and a little too bright when I walked in. And our cook was still bent over a cauldron.

"Deborah, what are you still doing up?" I scolded.

"Waitin' on you, m'lady." She hugged me, but then she hugged everyone. "Sivan told me you haven't eaten." She released me and grabbed DiCook before he had a chance to protest. "At least, ya aren't eatin' by yourself for once."

I motioned for the magistrate to follow me. I took a seat at a little table in the alcove where Deborah's kitchen girl did her prep work. The angle blocked the light radiating from the cast iron grill and the baking ovens, and a bit of the main fireplace as well. DiCook dragged a chair to the other side and sat, suspicion still lurking on his face.

Deborah set two tankards in front of us. "I heard you had an ale type of day. Did you let Sivan put my honey salve on your arm?"

"Yes, Reverend Mother," I muttered into my cup.

"Don't ya lip me, girl. Since you won't let us call a healer, someone needs to make sure that arm don't get infected." She shuffled off to dish up some dinner.

DiCook smirked. "The man you brought in give you a hard time?"

I held up the arm and pushed back my sleeve. No new bleeding, and it was starting to feel a bit better. "This was courtesy of my inept assassin."

The magistrate's smile faded. "That's why you—" He shook his head. "Your cook's right. You should have gone to a physician straight away. That blade could have been poisoned."

"Well, if it was, you wouldn't have to deal with the freak anymore." I took another gulp of the ale.

"You think that's what I want? I've been stuck between a crazy senile justice and demanding nobles since I was elected three summers ago. No support from any quarter in this city, but they blame me for everything that goes wrong. Finally get a justice that hasn't lost her marbles, and she's trying to frame me for treason." He wiped his hands over his face. "I'll be damn glad when my city service is done next year."

I tried to picture matters from DiCook's position. A bit of empathy squeezed into my heart. I'd been caught in a position I neither desired nor wanted. And unlike him, I didn't have *all* of my actions questioned.

At least, not to my face.

Deborah brought over two bowls filled with thick bean and ham porridge from the delicious aroma. She returned a moment later with a plate full of her cornbread squares, utensils and butter. "I'm heading to bed. You know where everything is, Justice."

Her interruption and departure gave me time to contemplate DiCook's words. Luc was right. I'd never considered things from his point of view.

"I'm not trying to frame you, Malven."

"Sure feels that way sometimes." He dipped a spoonful of porridge and blew on it.

I reached for a chunk of bread. "I don't know who was in the former Lady DiMara's pocket. Trust is a little hard for me to come by after one of her demons threatened to eat me."

"You sure seem to throw trust in the direction of the other temples."

I snorted as I buttered my bread. "Them least of all."

"I've never been in Gerd's bed, by the way," he said softly. "And I'm not in her pocket any other way either."

"Then why'd you go running to her yesterday?"

"The dead girl was one of hers. Thought she should know first." He dipped his spoon and took another bite of ham and beans before he added, "I thought she might actually care."

"The only thing she cares about is getting her hands on Gretchen's money. The girl had developed a sizable nest egg." The thought killed my appetite once more, but I forced myself to take a bite of bread.

"If the chief priestess is on the top of your suspect list, why'd you go up to the DiMara estate and arrest that man?"

I debated with myself for a moment of how much to tell DiCook, then I shrugged. "You might as well know since I'll have to do the public post in two days. Gretchen filed a declaration of last wishes with the Temple of Death. She named Lady Alessa as her heir." And if DiCook didn't tattle to my mother before the post went up, I would know where he really stood.

DiCook released a low whistle. "And you thought Lady Alessa might have decided to get her inheritance early?"

Again, I shrugged. "It's happened before. Brother Luc and I went to question her again. Unfortunately, we discovered one of the duke's retainers had assaulted her out of misguided affection."

Giving the magistrate some empathy was one thing. I wanted to hold Bartholomew's assault of Sister Gretchen in reserve.

DiCook winced. "His Grace may have some pretty progressive ideas, but he isn't going to tolerate someone harming his sisters." He polished off his porridge before he said, "You're sure Lady Alessa is innocent?"

"Yes."

"And this retainer . . ."

"Bartholomew. He was the one with the duke's steward yesterday morning when we were examining the body."

The magistrate nodded. "Did he rape Lady Alessa, too?"

I shook my head.

"Thank the Mother for small favors." He closed his eyes briefly before he opened them and took a drink. "Do you think he might have killed Sister Gretchen? Violated her body with a knife because Lady Alessa had spurned him? I've heard rumors that the duke's sister prefers women. If this Bartholomew was jealous of her relationship with the priestess, it would explain the wounds."

DiCook was far more clever than the credit I had been giving him.

I shook my head. "He admitted to choking the sister while he was under a truthspell, but he says she was alive when he left her."

"When was this?"

"The day before the wine shipment arrived at the DiMara estate."

"He could have been the last one to see her alive."

"He is, so far as we know." I took a long pull from my tankard.

"So where does the ambassador of Jing and the Assassins Guild fit into Sister Gretchen's death?"

I paused in taking a bite. "What do you know about the ambassador?"

"Only that he was here before me." He dabbed at his mouth and waited before he tossed his napkin on the table and said, "Once again, what does he and the Assassins Guild have to do with Sister Gretchen's death?"

"I'm not sure they do." I rose and gestured at his tankard. He passed the vessel to me, and I crossed to the small keg. "The mutilation is too personal, too inefficient, for the killer to be Guild," I said as I filled our tankards.

The magistrate couldn't let the matter go. "What about the one who killed himself when he failed to eliminate you?"

I hesitated a moment and focused on filling the tankards since I could only tell the level of the liquid by its sound. Telling DiCook about the Jing School of Sorcery's threat against me would deflect his attention from the priestess's murder. We still had nothing connecting the two incidents.

I returned to our table and set down the tankards. "I'm not sure it has anything to do with Gretchen's death. It's possible that Samael DiRoy had other nobles besides the previous duke and duchess funding his demon summoning. Nobles who are not happy that I ruined their plans. Hiring a Guild assassin isn't cheap."

DiCook took a long swallow of ale. "What about the ambassador? He was one of her regular visitors."

What could I say? I'd promised the ambassador, but my silence was just as damning. "So I've heard."

"Now you're going to withhold knowledge from me?" DiCook's scowl was back.

I sighed and resumed my seat. "If I brought in every worshipper Gretchen serviced, I'd be questioning them until the end of time."

"Yet, the ambassador made a point of a personal visit."

I rubbed my eyes. The headache grew fiercely behind my orbs. "I can't tell you, Malven. I promised my silence in return for any information he had regarding Gretchen."

"Was it worth it?" he snarled.

I could honestly tell Luc I didn't try to antagonize the magistrate. It didn't mean I wouldn't respond in kind.

"No," I snapped. "All he could tell me was Sister Gretchen made a lot of enemies in her life. Her killer could have been any one of them, including the ambassador himself." Except I couldn't imagine he would have told me about the spying if he had the information Gretchen collected for him and killed her to keep her silent. Or maybe his visit and confession came from some sort of perverse sense of Jing honor since I saved his life a few months ago. I had no doubt Quan could, and would, kill if necessary.

DiCook shoved back his chair. The wood screeched against the flagstones. "Well, thank you for such a pleasant evening." He stalked out of the kitchen.

I couldn't muster the energy to respond to his snide comment in kind.

"Well, that was an interesting turn."

I nearly jumped out of my skin. My spare dagger was out of my boot sheath and in my hand before the woman's sentence ended.

Tyra stepped from behind a stack of flour bags.

"That's a good way to get yourself killed," I said, sliding my knife back into its sheath.

She shrugged. "The chief warden thought it would be best to keep an eye on you."

"Inside my own temple?" I growled.

"Yes." Little Bear stalked into the kitchen. "He's gone."

"You've overstepped your bounds, Chief Warden." My reprimand was ruined by my yawn.

"And you're dead on your feet, Lady Justice. All in all, a target a baby assassin could hit," he responded. "You may not take today's incident seriously, but your staff does."

"You win." I held my hands up in surrender. "I'm going to bed." I paused in the doorway and turned back to Tyra. "How did you get in here without me or Malven seeing you?"

"Practice," she said shyly. "You don't see like we do. I noticed you squint in the kitchen no matter how much or how little light is in here. I figured the heat of the ovens would mask my body from you. As for the magistrate—" She shrugged. "All I had to do was stay in the shadows."

"I see." And the concept disturbed me to the core. If the Assassins Guild learned what my own warden had deduced, they could dispatch me by setting the temple on fire. "Do you really suspect DiCook would try to harm me?"

"No," Little Bear said. "At least, not on purpose. But that doesn't preclude the two of you getting into one of your arguments, and slapping at each other like little children."

I grinned. My head warden had finally made a joke. "Don't worry. I'll coldcock him if it comes to that. Good eventide."

And once again, Sivan was waiting for me in the hallway. I crossed my arms over my chest. "The crown prince doesn't get this much attention."

"No, he receives much more," she said crossly. "But he's not as insistent as you are about killing himself." She looped her arm around my uninjured one and hustled me to my bed chambers.

I blinked when I entered. There was a man under my bed. I reached for the knife inside my cloak before I realized who it was.

Luc. He held his finger to his lips and winked at me. Of course, Sivan saw nothing because of the shadows.

It was all I could do to stifle my laughter as Sivan bade me to sit while she checked the slice on my arm. The delight in Luc's presence eased my headache.

"You are fortunate the assassin didn't use poison," she muttered.

I sighed. "Everyone keeps telling me that."

She unwrapped the bandage and slathered more of Deborah's salve on. Thankfully, her hands were gentler than her words. "I brought you some pain powder as well."

"Thank you."

She looked at me suspiciously. "What are you planning?"

I blinked again, trying to maintain an innocent expression. "I'm planning to get some sleep and praying to Balance you aren't banging on my door before dawn for once."

Sivan wound a clean linen strip about my arm. "Speaking of this morning's reason for waking you, both the master physicians and Sister Bertrice have responded affirmatively to your invitation for tomorrow afternoon."

"Good," I murmured. "If I can get them to collaborate on this matter, maybe future murders won't be so fraught with clashing egos."

"Maybe it's your own ego that gets in the way."

"Sivan." I grabbed her hand. "You've been sniping at me all evening. If I didn't know better, I'd say someone switched our minds into each other's bodies."

She stared at the floor for a long time. "I'm frightened," she finally whispered.

"About?"

"If someone's put a price on your head, Justice, things are far worse in Orrin than they seem."

"Or Little Bear may be killed trying to save me?"

Shame lit her face, and the scent of it tainted the air. "I beg forgiveness. Such thoughts are incredibly selfish."

"But they're human." I gave her hand a squeeze.

She nodded and collected her things. "Good eventide, Justice." She fled out the door before the tears I suspected she dammed let loose.

Once Sivan was gone, Luc emerged from beneath my bed. Neither of us said a word until he warded the room.

"I didn't think you were coming tonight," I whispered as he pulled me close.

"There are things we need to discuss about Sister Gretchen's murder." His fingers sought the fastenings to my clothing. "But that can wait."

Much later, the Mother's bells tolled First Night. Despite the painkiller and Luc's intimate attentions, my body still ached, but in a more pleasant way.

I sighed and cuddled closer to his warmth. I told him of my encounters with Ambassador Quan and Magistrate DiCook. "After the Bartholomew fiasco this afternoon, I thought if this all turns into a midsummer romantic farce, I will be sorely disappointed."

Luc's finger drew idle circles on my unbruised hip. "And now?"

"I'm just as frightened as Sivan. We're possibly in the middle of more treason. What if the assassin and Gretchen's death are connected? What if the treason plot of Samael DiRoy and Duke Marco's parents was more extensive than the three of them?"

Luc's hand paused. "Surely, your Reverend Mother and Kam would have found out when they questioned the DiMaras?"

I propped my head on my hand so I could see his face. "What if the duke and duchess didn't know about the other conspirators? I killed Samael before he could be questioned."

Luc stroked my hair back from my face. "Is that what's bothering you? Samael? If you hadn't killed him, we would have much bigger problems than a scandal or assassins."

"But he was one of Gretchen's regulars, too," I persisted. It felt like some understanding was right at the edge of my consciousness, but I couldn't quite grasp it.

"Let's focus on the lines of inquiry that are in front of us before we start chasing unicorns. I've discovered a method for tracking the separate essences in those scrapings you brought me."

I punched him lightly in the bicep. "You mean you had poor Jeremy chase down the research."

Luc grinned. "What's the point of being the senior priest in a temple if I can't order around the rest. We can try the spell tomorrow after midday."

I shook my head. "Can't. I'm brokering a deal between the Healers Guild and the Temple of Death. Tomorrow evening?"

He blew out a frustrated breath. "All right. As long as you understand, the spell may simply point straight to your gaol if she only fought Bartholomew."

"I know, but what else do we have? Unless you think Bartholomew managed to circumvent your truthspell."

He grunted. "I doubt the man knows how to wipe his own ass." He blew out a long breath and stared at my ceiling. "Short of riding all the way to the Pana Valley winery and questioning the wagoner, which you are forbidden to do by the way, we have nothing."

I curled in the crook of Luc's shoulder once again. "We have Gerd, but questioning her is moot if a truthspell is unreliable."

"I had a chance to examine Alessa's necklace. The spell needs a physical vessel to hold it, so it remains dormant until activated. The damn thing is so subtle that anyone but the most experienced sorcerer or clergy would detect it."

"See? I told you yesterday's misstep in questioning her wasn't your fault."

"Excuse me?" His voice rumbled at my insult. "Think you can mock me at will." He tickled me until I shrieked for mercy. Thank Balance, he'd thought to ward my room so the night wardens wouldn't hear.

Once my laughter died, I asked, "Does the physical object have to be a gemstone?"

He shook his head. "Any physical object would do. For all I know, the multitude of those damn bells they wear on their robes could each have a counter. Or a whole series of different spells." Luc rubbed his chin as his irritation faded and his mind jumped on the intellectual problem. "I figured this would be an excellent project for Kam while he's sequestered."

"You said earlier you confined him to the temple. Why?"

"Because the assassin may be connected to Gretchen's death after all, and I can't chain you," Luc growled. "But dammit, I'm going to keep one of you safe."

Part of his statement made me feel warm and protected, something I'd never felt until I met him. The rest of me rebelled at the insinuation I need to be watched over like an infant. The conflict made my head ache again, so I chose to ignore both and focus on Kam. "How did he accept the news?"

"He actually seemed relieved." Luc kissed my forehead. "He did question what precautions your wardens were taking."

So much for trying to ignore my feelings. "They're spying on me," I muttered.

"This isn't the eastern territories and independent colonies where the biggest worry is the occasional brigand and the not-so-occasional jealous spouse. As city seats, we're going to have to deal with the intrigue and politics."

"What if my whole life is one big political maneuver?"

"What are you saying?"

I related Bertrice's story about my birth to Luc, and Kam's confirmation of the events. My voice was flat, dull, as I spoke. And the more words that poured from my lips, the tighter Luc's hold on me grew.

"I want her to be guilty. I want to discover she was behind Gretchen's murder. I want to feel my sword slice through her neck as she begs for mercy," I whispered.

"Vengeance won't solve anything." He held me, stroked me, trying to offer what comfort he could.

I still felt as cold as the mountain passes buried in snow this time of year. "Intellectually, I know that . . ."

"I know in the end you will do the right thing."

He didn't understand the depth of the pain, fury and hatred I'd buried in my heart the day the Reverend Mother dragged me to the capital. A stoked fire that Bertrice and Kam poured oil on without realizing it. Could I stop myself from gleefully executing my mother if I found she was even slightly connected to Gretchen's murder?

# Chapter 10

The next morning, I learned Sister Gretchen's death had become public knowledge as well as Bartholomew's arrest. The gallery was crowded with idiots hoping to see my bloody sword hung between the hands of the statue of Balance that stood behind my podium. If not from the former DiMara retainer losing his head, then at least from the hand of the street urchin caught pilfering bread from one of the establishments on Bakers Street.

I pushed back my hood and glared at the child, who couldn't have been more than ten winters. He shivered in the defendant's box. "Where are your parents?"

"Don't got none."

"Siblings?"

His little brow twisted in confusion.

"Brothers or sisters?" I amended.

"Ma little sister died of the fever last winter, same as ma parents. Don't got any others."

One more symptom of why I despised Orrin. An orphan would have been taken in, if not by his relatives, then by one of the temples or guilds in the towns and villages in my old circuit.

"'A starving man cannot be faulted for stealing food.'" I smiled at the defendant. "I suppose the old proverb is equally applicable to a boy."

The baker who'd caught the child jumped to his feet. "But, Justice, he stole. Surely you're not going to let him go!" The gallery rumbled in agreement.

"This city is based on the rule of law, not that of a mob." My magically amplified voice cracked against the marble walls of the courtroom. The spectators immediately hushed.

"And even the law needs to be tempered by mercy." I glared at the baker, and he quickly dropped his gaze. "Child help you. The fact that you want me to mutilate a starving boy in the middle of winter says quite a bit about your lack of compassion. For speaking out of turn in my court, you have a choice. A night in my gaol or a gold piece donated to the Temple of Mother."

"I-I will donate, Lady Justice."

His wife sitting next to him clasped both hands over her mouth to stop her outcry over the outrageous fine.

"When I am done hearing this matter, Warden Tyra will escort you next door. And Warden?"

The woman was already standing next to the abashed baker, who had resumed his seat. "Yes, Lady Justice?"

"Make sure you get a receipt from the sisters."

"Yes, m'lady." Her voice actually carried a hint of amusement. Good. Senses of humor developed in two wardens. Ten more to go.

My attention returned to the boy. "What is your name?"

"Nathan."

Little Bear bent close to him and whispered in his ear.

"Nathan, Lady Justice," the boy said.

"What talents are you proficient in?"

"Talents?" He gulped. "I can't sing or nuttin'. I can whistle."

The gallery tittered, Little Bear grinned, and it took all my willpower not to laugh myself. "No, Nathan. I mean skills. What kind of things did you do to help your mother and father with before they passed?"

The boy tugged at the gray shift assigned to all prisoners. I didn't blame him. The things were scratchy as a hedgehog. It was still warmer and thicker than the rags he had been wearing when he'd been brought to our temple.

"I carried wood and swept the floor for my da. He was starting to teach me how to carpenter when he took sick. 'Fore that I helped my ma carry clothes. She-she were a washer woman. Or I watched my little sister."

My decision was far easier than it should have been. I turned to Donella. "What was the cost of the bread he stole?"

"A copper, m'lady."

"Pay the baker out of our temple treasury." I focused on the boy once again. "You will pay off your damages by caring for my horse, Nassa."

"B-but I don't know nuttin' 'bout horses!" His fingers turned green from his fear. "Lady Justice," he added at Little Bear's nudge.

"You'll learn." I folded my fingers together and stared to emphasize my next point. "My assistant Sivan will find you some appropriate clothes and assign you a sleeping space. She will also take a lock of your hair. If you even think about running away before your fine is paid, I *will* find you, do you understand?"

"Y-y-yes, L-lady." He was shaking violently now.

"Good. The Orrin Court of Justice is adjourned for the day." I banged the hilt of my sword on my podium before I re-sheathed it across my back.

Little Bear passed the child to the third warden in court. He and Brother Mat from the Temple of Light approached my podium.

Interesting that I actually remembered someone's name. But then, the junior brother was astute, kept his mouth shut except when necessary, and didn't let his emotions spill. He'd have made a much better adherent to Balance than many of my sisters.

A twinge of guilt tugged my mind. If it weren't for Kam's stubborn insistence that Luc replace him as Orrin's seat of Light, Mat should have been nominated since he was Kam's second. Had the old man's own guilt over our collective pasts unduly influenced his choice?

Deep down, I knew it wasn't even a question. Not after yesterday's revelations. Luc was older and had more experience than Mat. The other priest didn't need the grief of Gretchen's murder on his head.

However, I needed to drop a hint to Luc about making things right with Mat, even though Kam's machinations weren't his fault. But then, maybe

Luc deserved a little trouble from Mat the way he stood at attention before my podium.

"Let me guess. You two are my security escort for this afternoon?" I said sourly.

Mat smiled. "Begging your pardon, Lady Justice, but I'd rather enjoy your fine company than spend my day trapped in our temple's library."

"Well, then." I clapped my hands together. "The first thing we're going to do is check on my new squire, get something to eat, and say a prayer for Brother Jeremy."

Maybe I just needed one good thing to happen after the chaos of the last three days. Nassa took to the boy, and she was a much better judge of character than many men I'd met in my decade as a justice.

Or maybe I wanted to fix one child's life after my mother had ruined mine. Here at the temple, Nathan could learn a trade and make his way in the world that had left him orphaned, homeless and starving.

I shoved my maudlin thoughts aside when Masters Aaron and Devin arrived. Moments later, Tyra escorted a robed figure into our meeting room, but when he flipped back his hood, the person definitely was not Sister Bertrice.

The physicians' skin heated when they turned to me, a blatant "we told you so" glow to their faces.

The Death priest bowed. "Forgive the subterfuge, Lady Justice, Master Healers. High Sister Bertrice respectively requests that the three of you join her at our temple."

Devin jumped to his feet. "We should have known—"

"I assure you, Master Healer, no insult is intended by our temple." The priest turned pleading eyes to me. "We've discovered something High Sister Bertrice believes has a direct bearing on your investigation, Lady Justice. She wants the master healers to independently confirm our findings." A wry smile tilted his lips. "The issues were found shortly before this meeting, and she didn't want to raise more questions by bringing Sister Gretchen's body here."

I couldn't imagine why Bertrice would resort to stealth until the priest added, "It might be a good idea to disguise the physicians as wardens as well. There are those who owe favors to the Temple of Love watching both our hall as well as yours, Lady Justice."

"In other words, High Sister Gerd has discovered I started seizing the deceased's properties this morning." Luc and I along with a team of wardens from both of our temples had started before dawn. He'd made the suggestion while we were in bed late last night.

By waking our wardens between third night and first morning, we assumed no leaks would occur as to our actions. I'd hoped to keep the matter quiet before the public posting of the declaration tomorrow morning. They weren't the first foolish things I'd ever thought in my life.

The priest tilted his head. "That is Sister Bertrice's belief as well."

I turned to the physicians, who were a bit calmer than a moment ago. "Your choice, gentlemen."

Devin shrugged and turned to Aaron. "I'm curious, but you're the guild leader in Orrin."

The chief physician smiled. "High Sister Bertrice has piqued my interest as well."

It took a few moments to borrow trousers and cloaks that would fit the two healers. My day went from unsettling to worse with my first footfall out of the temple doors.

Magistrate DiCook climbed the front steps, two peacekeepers in tow. Orange splotches already covered his face. "I have a complaint against you, Lady Justice."

I sighed. "Let me guess."

He almost seemed apologetic and lowered his voice. "I swear I did not go to her, nor did I say a word to anyone. She showed up at Government House shortly after second morning raising a holy fuss about you seizing *her* property."

Interesting. She should have called a convocation of the seats of the twelve temples of Orrin if she really believed she had a claim. Disputes between the temples were solved internally. The fact that she didn't raised all kinds of guilt signals.

"I'm already late for a meeting with High Sister Bertrice. Would you care to accompany me and my guards, Magistrate?" *Pick up the hint, you idiot.*

Maybe he wasn't so much of an idiot after all. He smiled and extended his elbow. "I would be more than happy to, Lady Justice."

I took his arm. Little Bear had already instructed the healers on how to act, so with their hoods hiding their faces, I had a heavily armed escort on the walk down the street to all appearances. Considering how my hip had stiffened overnight, leaning on DiCook was a bit of a blessing.

Bertrice's junior priest was right. The men and women Gerd hired were too obvious, even to my twisted sight. Beneath my robe, my gloved fingers tightened around the handle of my dagger. Had she been insane enough to send the assassin yesterday? It would explain the connection between Gretchen's death and the attempt on me. It would also relieve Luc's mind concerning any alleged price on my head by the dead Jing sorcerers.

I didn't relax when we entered the Temple of Death. To my dismay, the priest led us down a winding staircase, which made me even more grateful for DiCook's arm. A puff of frigid air escaped when he opened the door at the bottom.

Like the cold storage rooms of many innkeepers and the very rich, ice blocks harvested from the mountain lakes lined the walls. Sawdust was packed tightly between the blocks to insulate them from outside heat and slow their melting.

Once we were below ground, lighting for the sighted was provided by two small sorcerer's balls. The spheres didn't give off heat the way an oil lantern or a candle did for which I was grateful.

Wooden shelving lined three of the walls, but these weren't typical storage units. They were wide and long enough to hold a large man. Several of the planks held wrapped figures.

The middle of the room contained a table carved from a single slab of deep purple basalt. Lying on the table was a familiar outline under the cloth. Bertrice and another of her priests were waiting for us beside the body.

Yellow mist drifted from Bertrice's mouth. In the cold room, the vapor quickly shifted to green then indigo before it faded.

"I apologize for not sticking to our original agreement, Master Healers. Justice Anthea was very complimentary of your abilities, and, well, the three of you needed to see what my second, Brother Xander found."

The priest standing next her must be Xander. He bowed his head.

She flipped back the cloth. "No one in our temple noticed this first item until the body was bathed during funeral preparation."

Both healers bent closer to examine the corpse's neck. The magistrate released my arm and edged closer as well.

Devin straightened and grunted. "That definitely changes my original assessment."

I wrapped my arms around myself, more to retain my body warmth than discomfort over the presence of several dead people. "Would one of you care to explain to the sight-impaired justice?"

"There's a second, fainter set of bruises on the neck," Aaron said. "Here." He pointed. "Slightly above and to the right of the first bruises. They were obscured by the wine staining her neck."

"But the bottom of the second set matches the curve of the first set," Devin added. "The lighter discoloration means the bruising happened closer to her death, before the blood had a chance to pool."

"And?" I prompted.

"Two different persons strangled the poor woman." Bertrice said. She pulled the cloth further down the corpse. "Feel here." She pointed at the body's lower abdomen.

Each physician poked and prodded the area the priestess had indicated. They shared a surprised looked.

"I can't believe we missed this," Aaron muttered. He turned to me and inclined his head. "I sincerely apologize, Lady Justice."

I didn't need anyone to interpret for me this time. My headache from last night threatened to return full force.

"I don't understand," Magistrate DiCook murmured in my ear.

I whispered back, "Our possible culprit list just got extended. Gretchen was pregnant when she was murdered."

# *Chapter 11*

Quietly, our somber group exited the cold storage room and trudged back up the winding staircase. My bruised hip protested the entire way.

The priest who had fetched me and the physicians strode down another corridor, waving DiCook's two peacekeepers to follow him. They glanced uneasily at the magistrate, but he nodded his assent and they went with the priest.

Bertrice led us to a cozy parlor. Or I thought it was a parlor at first. While a fire roared in a massive grate and soft rugs covered the floor, scrolls and rare leather-bound tomes filled the floor-to-ceiling shelves along the other three walls. It was a library to envy. Bertrice rang an attendant to request hot beverages, then bade us to sit on the heavily padded benches and chairs.

The library was far cheerier than I expected for a Temple of Death. I sat with my back to the fire and pulled my hood tight. I couldn't help but notice that Little Bear and Brother Mat stood on opposite sides of the room in order to watch everyone.

Once one of the attendants brought in mulled wine and departed, everyone in the room looked at me, expectation in their manner.

The scrutiny was distinctly uncomfortable. I cleared my throat. "The point of today's meeting is to discuss a relationship between the Temple of Death and Healers Guild in assisting the Temple of Balance during our investigations."

Devin burst out laughing with Bertrice and Aaron quickly following suit. Brother Xander settled for a bemused grin.

Bertrice waved in my direction once she caught her breath. "I think we're beyond that, Anthea."

A snippet of relief raced through the ache in my head. "Well, that was the fastest dispute I've ever resolved."

"Unfortunately, our efforts are making your task harder rather than easier, Justice," Aaron said.

"No, you didn't." The flicker of reasoning in my mind that started in the cold room blossomed. "We now have a motive for the mutilation. Either Gretchen told the potential father, and he was appalled at the thought of a child—"

"Or one of her other worshippers learned of the child and was jealous it was not his seed," DiCook finished. He looked rather proud of himself, and I wasn't about to ruin it. He looked at me. "It would explain the attempt on your life. If you discover whose child Gretchen bore, it could lead you to her murderer."

Bertrice leaned forward, her attention intense. "But why is Gerd watching both you and me? Surely you've eliminated her as a potential culprit?"

I turned to DiCook and nodded.

He coughed before he began. "Sister Gerd filed a complaint this morning, stating Justice Anthea was illegally seizing her property."

Bertrice reared back, and her skin blazed with shades of salmon and scarlet. Startled gasps issued from Xander and the two physicians.

"That-that's absurd! We'll call a convocation today!" Bertrice was on her feet, ready to bolt for the door and shout for a messenger.

"Wait." When she remained on the balls of her feet, I added, "Please, wait."

When the priestess resumed her seat, I continued. "As more than one temple leader has pointed out to me, Gerd has gotten away with much over the years. If she's involved in Gretchen's death, give me the chance to collect the evidence I need to convict her."

"While I do not dispute your wisdom, Justice," Devin said. "Is it prudent to allow her to sow dissent among the various factions in the city?"

Before I could answer, DiCook spoke. "I'm with Justice Anthea. Let's give Gerd a bit of lead rope and see where she tries to go." He turned to me and grinned. "I didn't have a chance to tell you yet. The bitch also tried to bribe me this morning."

This was the first thing this afternoon that didn't surprise me. "With what?"

He shrugged. "The usual. Sex. When that didn't work, she left a bag with five gold pieces, saying there was more where that came from."

Apparently, inviting him along with me to the second examination of Gretchen's corpse ameliorated my nondisclosure of the Ambassador of Jing's purpose for his visit last night.

"Do you have it?"

He nodded and pulled a wad of scarf from his jacket pocket. "I didn't touch the coins. Something didn't seem right about them."

I carefully undid the multiple knots DiCook had tied. He hadn't taken any chances. From the energy tingling along my skin, it was a good thing he hadn't. I scanned the room. Everyone with talent felt the spell.

Even Little Bear, the only one untrained in magic besides DiCook, frowned.

Bertrice muttered an obscenity under her breath.

I just as carefully retied the scarf and placed it in my own pocket. "It's a compulsion spell."

Crimson dotted DiCook's cheeks. "To do her bidding." He wasn't even asking. It explained his change of heart from last night a little more clearly. He and I may not agree on what constitutes proper procedure, but I hadn't tried to magically manipulate him.

"Let me tease out the purpose." I grinned. "Then we'll set the trap. In the meantime, we can place some enticing bait for our little rat."

Magistrate DiCook charged out of the Temple of Death, me nipping at his heels.

"Get your arse back here right this minute! I am the duly authorized chief justice of Orrin!"

He and his peacekeepers had reached the street level, but he whirled around to face me. "For all your vaunted talents, you couldn't find a pickpocket if his hand was up your—" The rest of DiCook's obscenity was lost in the rumble of a passing freight wagon.

"I still have jurisdiction here, and I'll have you removed for dereliction of your duties!"

A rude hand gesture was his only reply before he and his startled peacekeepers marched in the direction of Government House.

I walked down the temple steps. I didn't have to emphasize my limp. My little entourage and I headed back to the Temple of Balance at a more sedate pace. We managed to reach our original meeting room before the four men started laughing.

"Really, Justice," Devin said, wiping the tears from his eyes. "Both you and the magistrate missed your callings. You would be the envy of every mummer's troupe this coming spring."

"What was funnier was that fishwife who scurried straight to the Temple of Love after witnessing the false argument," Aaron added. "She couldn't have been more obvious."

While the healers continued to chuckle, I pulled the fake document from my pocket and stared at it. I hated to admit Malven and Bertrice were right. If my mother believed I had Gretchen's declaration, and also believed it hadn't been validated by a priest from Light, she would try to steal it sooner rather than later.

Little Bear stepped closer to me. "What's wrong, Justice?"

I tapped my finger against the seal. "Yesterday's attack makes more sense. The assassin knew I'd taken Gretchen's declaration to Light for the formal opening. Under normal circumstances, I would have brought it back to Balance with me."

Except he had tried to kill me outright. And the odd behavior of the horse and riders who nearly ran me down still bothered me. Had Gerd sent them and had their real purpose been to grab the declaration from me, and the assassin sent separately by Gretchen's murderer? Or were they a mere distraction in order for the assassin to complete his task?

"Is there anything more we can do to help, Justice?" Aaron said. My obvious bad mood had completely destroyed his joviality of a moment before.

I inclined my head. "Thank you, gentlemen, for your assistance. However, it would be best if you returned to your own place of business. You've already been seen arriving here."

Devin held up a hand. "Not until we see to your injuries."

"I am fine—"

Aaron shook his head. "Like the Thief you are. Even your Reverend Mother could see the way you favor your right leg."

"We can cover by saying they were here at your bequest to examine to young Nathan," Little Bear offered.

Aaron's gaze met Little Bear's. "Nathan?"

"My new squire I acquired this morning," I said. "And I don't need any seeing to."

Devin snorted. "Of course not. Every priestess of your age limps like an old woman with gout." He latched onto my left arm.

I hissed as his thumb dug into the cut.

"So the attacker didn't just knock you to the ground." He looked at Little Bear. "Warden, if you'll be so kind as to call the justice's personal attendant."

"In the meantime, I'll examine this young Nathan." Aaron sounded far too pleased with himself. "That way we all can answer truthfully later."

This wasn't a battle I would win. Especially when Sivan and Tyra threatened to call for the rest of my wardens to carry me to my bedchambers.

In the end, I had to admit both my arm and my hip felt much better once Devin finished his work. However, I was exhausted. Healing magic takes its energy from both the injured and the spellcaster.

"You're damn lucky—" Devin started.

"That the blade wasn't poisoned," I snapped. "Thank you, Master Healer, but everyone—"

"I was going to say," he yelled to override me, then finished, "That you're damn lucky you didn't break any bones when you landed on the steps." He wiped the fragrant oil he used off his hands with a towel and lowered his voice. "But yes, the matter of a poisoned blade as well."

I rolled over on my bed and started to sit up, but he pushed me back. "No."

"I have far too much to do—"

"And you'll fall asleep on your feet if you try." He gave me a gentle smile. "Sister Gretchen's murderer will still be available for you to catch when you wake." Over his shoulder, Sivan glared at me.

This was the main reason I hated going to a healer. The worse the wound, the drowsier I felt. Considering I could barely keep my eyes open now indicated how bad the injuries had been. The dawn raids hadn't helped my energy levels either.

I sighed. "Very well then. You win." I settled back down on my mattress.

I'd lay here until Devin and Sivan left. Then I'd sneak over to the Temple of Light and check on Brother Jeremy's research. I couldn't question anyone from the Temple of Love until I found a way to block their counter to the truthspell. And I needed to talk to Alessa to find out if she knew about Gretchen's baby. Prepare the public posting for tomorrow. Review the formal charges against Bartholomew.

Death's little brother Sleep claimed me as I made my task list.

The braziers in my room glowed brightly when I awoke. My yawning and stretching abruptly ceased. Despite Devin's healing and my nap, I didn't feel totally right. What time was it? I was supposed to meet Luc for dinner, then we were going to cast the tracking spell.

"Good. You're awake." Sivan strode briskly from my bathing room. "Your water's ready."

"What hour—"

"The sun just set so you have time to clean up, but don't dwaddle in the bath."

"Yes, m'lady." I grinned while I unwound the sheet Master Devin had used for his sense of propriety. His feelings revealed he was more likely from one of the city-states north of the island of New Thenos. Their ideas concerning the Temples of Love and Vintner were unorthodox at best. I'd have to ask him about their Spring Rituals the next time we met.

When I walked to the bathing room, the tile glowed from the steam. Lime oil from Cant flavored the air. Stepping down into the heated water, I realized the pain was thoroughly gone. I sank into the bath. A hint of nausea ran on my tongue, another reason I hated healing spells, but this was worse than normal.

Running my fingers along my left arm, I felt the faint ridge of scar tissue. The worst thing that happened when Luc and I rode circuit was the occasional brawl at an alehouse or inn. Well, there was the time he surprised a polecat during our first year together while relieving himself one night at one of our regular campsites. He'd broken the little toe on his left foot, tripping over a root in his escape attempt.

But all those incidences I could count on the fingers of one hand over a decade. Goddess, why did the Reverend Mother insist on condemning me here? Punishing me this way made no sense. Not when there were plenty of justices with far more political experience.

As much as I would have liked to soak while contemplating these questions, I had a murderer to track. By the time Sivan returned, I was dressed and toweling my hair dry.

"Young Nathan has requested to see you," she said.

"Can't this wait?"

"It will only take a moment, Lady Justice." When she used my full title, she meant she was determined to get her way, but she had the grace to wait until I was dressed.

When she led him into my chambers, the boy didn't smell like a sewer anymore. Sivan must have made him bathe as well.

I smiled out of sympathy. "What can I do for you, young squire?"

"I wanted to say thank you, m'lady." His voice trembled worse than his tiny body.

"You're welcome, Nathan." When he didn't move, I said, "Was there something else you wished to talk about?"

"A-Ah was wondering if Ah could take the leftover bread from the temple here to m'friends. Mistress Deborah and Mistress Sivan said Ah needed to ask you."

I schooled my expression so not to alarm the boy with my anger. Of course, there were other orphans on the street. And it was the middle of winter.

While we didn't get the snow the eastern mountains and the territories north of Standora did, the season was by no means warm and pleasant here in Orrin.

I knelt so I could look him in the eye. He didn't shy away from me like so many adults did. "Why didn't you and your friends go to the Temple of Mother? They have food and beds for those in need."

"Th-there are stories about the things that happen there, m'lady. Some boys and girls ain't ever seen again after they go to Mother."

I didn't want to believe him, but something about his story hit me in the gut. And I'd learned long ago to trust that instinct. But I had too many other problems to deal with. Looking into the Temple of Mother would have to wait.

"I see," I murmured. "You may take the bread and whatever leftovers Deborah may have available, but—" I held up a hand. "In the morning. Sivan can take you in our cart."

"Thank you, mistress! Ah-Ah mean, Justice. L-lady Justice." He was bobbing up and down in excitement.

I stood and said softly to Sivan, "See what you can learn. Take someone with you. No insignia."

She bowed her head. "We know, and Hogarth has already volunteered, m'lady." Apparently, Little Bear pushed along my request for discretion to my staff as well the rest of the active wardens.

"Good." Deborah's husband had been a warden until age had taken its toll. Officially, he supervised the stable hands. Unofficially, he trained the current wardens. He'd knocked me flat on my buttocks during a couple of sparring sessions. He may not have the strength or speed of his prime, but the wily old man would keep Sivan and young Nathan out of trouble.

I smiled at the boy before me. "Unless there is anything else?"

He threw himself at me, his fierce hug catching me off guard. If Master Devin hadn't healed my hip, Nathan and I would have landed on the floor. Wetness penetrated my silk shirt.

Amidst his sobs, he repeated, "Yah didn't take my hand."

I had sobbed into my bedclothes like that when I'd been taken to the capital. And I'd been far younger than him. Perhaps the most miraculous thing was his willingness to help his fellows. Living on his own for the last year hadn't broken his spirit. Maybe that was the true difference between us. I'd given up on my fellow humans before I reached his age.

"Listen to me, Nathan." I knelt once again. "Stealing is wrong, but letting children starve is worse." I stroked his cheeks, wiping away the tears. "I have to go now, but you and I will have lunch together tomorrow and discuss your visit with your friends. Maybe together we can find a solution."

He nodded. Sivan led him from my bedchambers, and I donned my robes. When I stepped into the hallway, I wasn't surprised to find Tyra and another female warden waiting for me.

"Shall we ladies?"

"You did the right thing by the boy," Tyra said softly.

My gaze met hers, and the sick feeling in my gut grew worse. In Tyra's unspoken reminder, I understood. Penelope would have passed a far different verdict on Nathan.

Is the waste of human lives the reason why the Reverend Mother twisted the law to name me chief justice of a city that needed compassion rather than execute me?

I smiled at the sumptuous spread on the table in the chief priest of Light's private rooms. Luc had obviously left Kam in charge of meal selection again. Tonight though, dinner was a private affair between the three of us. My wardens joined Luc's staff in the communal dining area.

It almost felt like old times. Except for the part about discussing a pregnant priestess being strangled twice.

Kam's normal rule regarding no temple business until after dessert was thrown aside. We had too much to talk about. Maybe the old man had his rule for a reason, the way my stomach roiled as I filled in him and Luc on what the priest at the Temple of Death had discovered.

Luc groaned. "Every time I think we're getting somewhere on this matter, a new wrinkle is introduced."

I grinned. "It gets more interesting." I laid out the events concerning Di-Cook and our mock fight. "The magistrate and I have come up with a plan. We'll let Gerd believe her compulsion spell worked on him."

However, Luc didn't appear convinced. "And is he planning on laying with her?"

"That's one of the things we discussed." The roasted potatoes crusted with herbs didn't make my mouth water like they usually did, and I shoved them around on my plate. "He doesn't think she'll push the intercourse issue if she thinks the spell has taken hold of him."

"It could work," Luc mumbled around a mouthful of bread. "If nothing else, you've got her on a bribery charge—"

"Not to change the subject, but Jeremy found a reference to blocking a truthspell," Kam blurted. The old priest practically jiggled with excitement. For once, it had nothing to do with his wine consumption. "It's from one of the Banned."

A chill went through me despite the warmth of the room. The Banned were tomes of demon magic ordered to be destroyed after the demon invasions that started a thousand years before I was born. Six months ago, we discovered not all of them had been burned. "The reference or the actual spell?"

*Please don't tell me you managed to keep the book Luc seized from Duke Marco's mother.*

As soon as the thought entered my head, I pushed it aside. The queen would sprout wings before the Reverend Mother of Balance would allow a demon grimoire to be used rather than incinerated.

"Silly girl." Kam shook his head, a smile on his face. "Theodorus Luminas refers to a truthspell block in his theories on philosophy from his analysis of the Book of Chaos."

The old man reached for his cup and took a drink. Considering his penchant for gossip, especially when it was just the three of us, he toyed with our anticipation.

To my surprise, Luc broke first. "Well?"

Kam set down the goblet and dabbed at his mouth to draw out the suspense. "Theodorus didn't give the procedure for the specific counter to the block."

I slumped in my chair. "So we're right back where we started. Somehow deconstruct the talisman—"

The old man held up a finger. "Let me finish. One of our predecessors was kind enough to scribble the specifics in the margins." He pulled a small scroll out of his robes and pushed it across the table to Luc. "The book itself is with young Jeremy. I already have him drafting extra copies for the other seats in Orrin as well as for the home temples of Balance and Light."

I poked at the roasted pork on my plate. My appetite should have been ravenous after the healing earlier this afternoon. "I want to test it before we try to question anybody at Love."

Luc chuckled. "Can we get through tonight's experiment before we start on the next one?" However, he read Kam's notes aloud for my benefit.

"That's easier than I thought it would be," I murmured. Memory training would serve to cross check the dispatch before Sivan sent the spell north to the Reverend Mother.

I forked a bite into my mouth. The pork had the consistency of old shoe leather. The taste was reminiscent of a root vegetable that had been soaked in brine for too long.

What was wrong with me? I knew it wasn't the food. The cook here was excellent. Kam wouldn't allow anything than the best. Was it nothing more than my own reaction to the events of the last three days?

"Are you all right, Anthea?"

I looked up from my plate to see Kam's head cocked.

"Is the food not to your liking?" he asked

"Dinner here is excellent as always." I smiled, but my muscles felt wooden. "Devin insisted on healing my injuries from yesterday. I think I still have a bit of a magic hangover."

"Maybe we should hold off on the tracking spell tonight." Luc's concern flowed over my psyche.

I shook my head. "No. Besides, I'm not the one actually casting it."

"If you're not going to finish your meal, maybe we should get started. "

Blinking in surprise, I realized the men's platters were empty. I nodded at Luc's suggestion, and the three of us rose. I followed Luc and Kam to the center dome of their temple. The link to their god where he watched and guided their efforts.

The gilded statue dominated the middle of the chamber. His face gazed straight ahead. His sword in both hands pointed toward the sky. If both the inner and outer doors of Light and Balance were open, the statue here would stare directly at my hooded goddess in her courtroom.

My stomach rumbled uneasily as we approached the two junior priests, two Light wardens, and my own wardens waiting for us at the pedestal of the statue. The eternal lamp at the base of the pedestal was uncomfortably bright, and I tugged my hood closer to my face to block the white light.

Luc disappeared down another corridor, but quickly reappeared carrying something in a flask. "I hope you've researched this correctly, Jeremy," he teased the youngest priest of their temple.

Jeremy clasped his hands behind his back. "You're more than welcome to double-check my research, sir."

"Not this time." Luc grinned

I suppressed a smile. Luc would have checked, and I had a sneaking suspicion Mat had as well. No sense insulting the earnest young priest though.

Luc knelt before the statue and bowed his head for a moment. The younger priests followed suit. One of the Light wardens stepped forward to assist Kam, but he waved the man off.

Most of the time, Luc and I had to use quick and dirty spells while riding circuit, instead of the more formal incantations and forms. Whatever we needed to do to solve that particular problem. Which frankly, we didn't do all that much. I didn't think I'd ever seen him perform such a formal ritual to his god since we'd been assigned together a decade ago at the capital.

He lit a small brazier from the eternal flame. Thick, woody incense curled through the air. His low baritone voice chanted, more of a cadence then actual words. The other three priests joined in, the harmony of their voices blending into an intoxicating music.

Luc added the scrapings from the dead priestess's nails to the incense in the brazier. Familiar ribbons of energy danced and threaded over my skin. Too many ribbons. Too many impressions.

One ribbon shattered. Then another. The links failed because we didn't have enough or the original source was dead. There was no way to determine which was which. One of them could have been caused by flakes of Gretchen's own nails. The other broken strand might be my assailant, but logic told me not to leap to conclusions.

I made a mental note to check with Bertrice. There had to be a way to devise a spell that could track elements of the dead. Reverse the current of magic on skin, hair and nails to track trace bits clinging to an attacker.

The tempo of the men's chant became more urgent, dragging me out of my musings. There was a hint of desperation as the priests tried to latch the remaining ribbons to their living sources.

Four of the energy ribbons shot past me in the direction of the open temple doors. The remainder faded into wisps before disappearing entirely. The chanting stopped.

Luc blew out a deep breath. "I'm sorry. We couldn't solidify the others."

I held up my hand. "Don't apologize. Those are four more leads than we had before the evening meal."

The entire group trooped to the front door, those of us with talent careful not to get too close to the four separate tracks. With our luck, if we disrupted one, the rest would evaporate as well. The trails split in the middle of the thoroughfare.

As I half-expected, one ribbon arrowed straight across the street to the Temple of Balance. I sent the female warden whose name I still couldn't remember along with Brother Jeremy to make sure the ribbon led to the imprisoned Bartholomew.

For someone who was trained so thoroughly in memorization, why did I have such a hard time remembering people's names?

Two of the remaining ribbons led north, one south. North was the direction of the duke's residence. One of us would still have to confirm Lady Alessa, just as we had to confirm the former DiMara retainer sitting in my gaol.

I eyed Luc. "Rocks and sticks?"

He chuckled but nodded. Mat, one of the Light wardens, Tyra and I won the northern routes. If you could call tramping through a cold, blustery night winning.

Kam made to follow us, and I held up a hand. "No. Stay."

He pulled himself as tall as his hunched back and round belly would allow. "I am not a dog to be ordered thusly."

"No," Luc said firmly. "I've already witnessed one assassination attempt on these very steps." He pointed at the temple floor. "Stay."

"But the attack was on Anthea!" the old man blurted.

Luc crossed his arms. "Do I need to have the wardens drag you to your quarters and lock you in?"

Kam grumbled under his breath, but obeyed.

Once we were out the doors of the temple, Luc looked at me. "Whistle if you need backup." He grinned.

His joking did nothing to soothe my upset stomach, but I responded blithely anyway. "Like I need help from the city guards." If I showed a hint of illness, we wouldn't be able to stop Kam from accompanying me without embarrassing him.

"Should I get us horses, m'lady?" Tyra stared up the street. "It is a long walk to the ducal residence."

My gut twisted. I wasn't sure if it was instinct or whatever was disagreeing with it. I closed my eyes and tested the feeling. Concentrating past my physical discomfort, I sensed both of the ribbons ending much closer than the duke's estate. My original guess was wrong. If Gretchen had cleaned up after leaving Alessa, it would explain why none of the trails led to the noblewoman.

I opened my eyes and shook my head.

"No. These ribbons don't lead there." That left at least three unknown people the murdered priestess had encountered prior to her death.

I marched down the steps and headed north, Tyra, Brother Mat, and one of the Light wardens on my heels. "Our destination is closer."

The first ribbon made a hard left at Dock Street. Toward the wharves.

"Rocks and sticks?" Mat asked.

"You don't have enough seniority to make that joke, Brother," I chastised. "And for that, you can follow the trail."

"What if the ribbon goes out to sea?" he asked.

That was a distinct possibility I didn't want to think about. "If it does, then ask the harbor master which ships have left in the last seven days."

"Seven, Justice?"

"Third Day last week is the last time we know Sister Gretchen was seen alive. Today is Second Day. If that trail leads to her murderer, then odds are he left long prior to the body being discovered." I shook my head in disgust at the thought that the fiend may have escaped. "Be happy it's winter. If this had happened a few months later, your task would be far more difficult."

"Understood, m'lady." Mat pivoted smartly. He and his warden strode down the street.

Tyra and I continued up Orrin's main thoroughfare. I began to regret not saddling horses as we trod past the government and business districts. Foot traffic picked up as the more reputable inns served meals and ale to the craftsmen and women ending their day.

Sweat rolled down my spine. I shouldn't be this worn out after such a relatively short walk on a winter evening. But I also didn't want to lose the trail.

We wove between people. Those who recognized our robes gave us wide berth. Those with talent who sensed the tracking spell glanced curiously in our way before abruptly looking in another direction. Those who were too tipsy or untalented to notice went on their merry way.

At the next street, the golden ribbon veered left. The Diplomatic Corridor.

Anticipation ran up my spine. Lady Katarina had given me the list of Gretchen's regular foreign visitors. I hadn't had two breaths to check who was currently in the city other than Ambassador Quan.

If he lied to me about the last time he'd seen Gretchen alive . . .

My stomach made another queasy turn as we followed the trail. The energy ribbon led to a wooden and bronze gate of a huge mansion. Jade dragons topped the stone pillars.

The Jing ambassador's residence.

Interesting that the iron reinforcements had been replaced since my last visit. The pale blue bronze made no sense. It wasn't as durable as iron. The dragons were new additions, too.

My momentary discomfort at the probability Quan had lied to me transformed to pain. Agonizing cramps bent me over double. Vomiting followed, and soon turned to dry heaves because I'd barely touched my food at the evening meal.

"Justice?"

Without Tyra's firm grip under my arms, I would have collapsed to the cobblestones. My sight blurred into a mishmash of wild colors. "We need to follow the trail."

Or that's what I tried to say. My speech was slurred as if I was drunk.

The three sharp bursts Tyra whistled felt like silver spikes hammered into my brain.

Two peacekeepers raced up the street toward us. DiCook would be furious I didn't include him in tonight's escapade once he learned of it.

Tyra's voice barked orders. "The justice is ill. I need help carrying her to the chief physician."

Dry heaves racked my body again. I couldn't be ill. We had all eaten from the same dishes. Luc and Kam had shown no signs. I'd felt fine until . . .

The healing.

*You're lucky the knife wasn't poisoned.*

Oh, Goddess, what had Devin done to me?

"You can't take me there." I fought my own warden and the two peace-keepers. Or I tried to.

I might as well have been a calf struggling against the butcher for all the good it did. In moments, Tyra banged on the familiar painted wood.

A journeywoman opened the door. One look and she turned and yelled, "We've got another one."

The peacekeepers carried me inside. In a flurry of movement, healer apprentices were stripping off my clothes. I couldn't do anything to stop them. My body refused to obey.

Master Aaron appeared in my line of sight, his expression one of horror. "Justice?"

It took monumental effort but I forced the word between my chattering teeth. "Devin."

Aaron shook his head. "He's in worse condition than you. Your wardens brought in your assistant and squire a short while ago."

Tears trickled done my cheeks into my hair at the sheer complexity of saying a single word. "Poison."

I would have sworn I saw the mill wheel in the healer's mind rotate under the flow of his thoughts. The candle spark as he understood.

He whirled and disappeared, shouting. Then everything went black.

# Chapter 12

Surprise greeted me when I woke. Surprise that I did wake up. Warm gold wooden walls surrounded me, closer than they should be. Not blue and green marble. Not my bedchambers in the temple.

Except I couldn't remember why I thought I wouldn't awaken.

"Wh-what . . ." My throat felt as if it had been scaled raw with a fish knife. Blankets were piled on top of me, far more than needed even on Orrin's coldest nights. Dampness coated the bedsheets around me.

"Be still, m'lady. I'll call for Master Aaron." Tyra's voice. She rose from a chair by the bed.

My warden went no farther than the door and whispered to someone. Outside, wood scraped wood, then the slap of leather soles.

I wiped the cold sweat out of my eyes, but the very act of moving my hand hurt. I hadn't ached this bad when the sword master at the capital's temple had forced me through a full practice session when I was deathly ill with the winter chills.

It wasn't just Master Aaron who entered the room. On his heels was a familiar figure.

The chief priest of the Temple of the Wildling God leapt onto the footboard of the bed I lay in and crouched. His hair flared out in a nimbus of color. Even in the middle of winter, he smelled of dry autumn leaves and spring field flowers.

"Greetings, High Brother Jax." Goddess, my throat hurt saying those four simple words.

"Chief Justice Anthea." He bobbed his head. "Given your predilections for mayhem, maybe the Reverend Mother of Balance should transfer you to Sister Bertrice's temple." From his tone, he found that prospect terribly amusing.

I did not however. "Not my fault," I croaked. "Water."

Aaron had been bustling around, checking my heartbeat and my breathing. "Thirst is a good sign." He raised my head and held a cup to my lips, but half the water ran down my neck. The coolness dissolved whatever was crusted on my skin.

"Wh-what happened?" My voice sounded more like a bullfrog, which was an improvement over the nearly dead dog I sounded like a moment ago.

Aaron frowned. "What do you remember?"

"We followed a tracking spell." I waved a hand in Tyra's direction. Only then did I notice her sword was unsheathed. "I started vomiting..." The last thing I wanted to disclose was where the energy ribbon had terminated. "Everything else after that is a blur."

Aaron nodded. "When your warden and the city guards brought you here, you said two words, 'Devin' and 'poison.'"

Master Devin. "The bastard tried to poison me." I started to rise, but Aaron easily pressed me back to the herb and grass-filled mattress.

"No, he didn't. Not intentionally anyway."

"Wh—" It hurt so much to talk, but I forced my vocal cords to work anyway. "What do you mean?"

"Someone deliberately poisoned our base oil stock we use for healing." Aaron's voice was grim, frightened even.

I closed my eyes for a moment, tried to make my brain work. "Let me guess. You received your oil shipment the same day Duke Marco received his wine shipment."

Master Aaron's mouth opened and closed a few times while Jax chuckled.

"I would say her mind works just fine." The wildling priest grinned, a big toothy one. "Would you mind leaving us now that we know she will live?"

"Wait," I said as the healer turned toward the door. Bits of memory lay scattered like puzzle pieces. "When Tyra and the city guards brought me in, I remember the journeywoman said there were others poisoned."

Aaron nodded. "You and Devin got the worst of the dosage. Ironically, his healing magic saved both your lives. By all rights, you and Devin should be dead. The poisoned oil on your body was transferred to your linens, so when your assistant and squire changed your bedding—"

My heart seized. "Nathan?" I whispered.

Aaron shook his head. "We don't know yet. The boy made it through the night. He's fighting. That gives us hope."

"But your talent..." I didn't cry. I simply didn't have enough moisture left in my body. In my efforts to save him, I had condemned the child anyway.

"The poison has been removed, and we've repaired as much of the damage to his organs as we can, but the rest will be up to him."

"And Sivan?"

He smiled, a small, wan thing. "She's awake, coherent and has kept down her broth. I believe she will be fine."

I inclined my head. It was all I could do.

He patted my hand to acknowledge my gratitude and departed.

When the door closed, Jax sobered and pointedly looked at Tyra. "I would prefer to speak with you privately, Anthea."

Tyra raised her sword. "Only if you want a new wildling chief priest sooner rather than later."

"Stop. Please." Balance's scales, it even hurt to breathe. I glared at Jax. "My warden is performing her duty since there have been two attempts on my life in as many days."

I shifted my gaze to Tyra. "Don't ever threaten a chief priest or priestess without my express command. If whoever is behind this mess manages to kill me, it's a good way to have your head separated from your body."

"Yes, m'lady." She lowered her sword, but she didn't sheathe it. Her defiant expression remained fixed on the wildling priest.

Jax grinned again. "I bow to your wisdom, but I would have thought there are certain things you wish to remain private."

"What do you mean?"

"Gerd."

With his single word, I sighed. I had no doubt Little Bear had warned the rest of my wardens of the potential problems regarding my birth mother. Had one of them talked to the wrong person?

"How did you find out?" I quietly asked Jax.

Instead of answering my question, he stood, his toes balanced on the edge of the footboard. His arms swept through the air as he spoke the words of warding. His motions were beautiful, if not a little bizarre compared to my experience. Unlike the tingle of Luc's magic or the harsher buzz of mine, Jax's energy felt like the strum of a lute or sitar. It swirled and settled into the walls, floor and ceiling of the room.

He resumed his crouching position once more. "The streets hum with the gossip of Sister Gretchen's death and the rivalry between you and Gerd."

Interesting that he deliberately failed to use my mother's appropriate honorific. What had she done to infuriate him?

"Why are you here?" I croaked.

"Healer Aaron asked for my expertise. The poison laced in the healing oil is very rare. It comes from a Cantish mushroom that only grows in the high desert."

Tyra huffed in disbelief. "Mushrooms in a desert?"

"When the occasional rains come, the plants take advantage." Jax was far more patient than me. "The sands became a riot of grasses and wildflowers, but their glory is short-lived. By the second night after the rain, they are rotting, dying."

"And these mushrooms have their moment," I said. I pushed myself up on my pillows and reached for the cup beside my bed. Pain raced through my joints, but thank Balance, it meant I was alive.

Tyra sheathed her sword and rushed to my side. I hated needing her help, but I probably would have spilled a great deal more water than I drank without her assistance. And the entire exercise exhausted me.

Jax made no move to assist either of us, nor would he. The Wildling priesthood thought as the animals of the forest did. I would either live or die, and they would make no effort to swing the pendulum either way.

Except . . .

"Why are you really here, Brother Jax?"

"Brother Kam asked for my assistance through Sister Bertrice." From his tone, he found the whole matter rather amusing. "And if my aid is a thorn in the paw of she who bore you, all the better."

Tyra's body tensed next to me, but she didn't draw on Jax.

I merely sighed. "Should I even ask why you're helping me?"

"Gerd forgets that the Twelve are equal, and that civil complaints are a matter of public record. I find the Reverend Mother of Balance's appointment of you to the seat in Orrin quite . . . delicious."

My head ached at trying to follow his chain of thought. "How so?"

"Your temple is not the only one that believes in the balance of all things."

I didn't want to ask, but morbid curiosity compelled me. "How did you know I was Gerd's daughter?"

He chuckled. "The story of Justice Thalia trying to take the blind daughter of Gerd? All the Temples know that tale."

"Thalia didn't take me. Gerd sold me."

"And the Reverend Mother of Balance was the one that paid Gerd's asking price even though Justice Thalia was within her rights since you were born touched by Balance herself."

I didn't quite understand Jax's willingness to talk about my past when Kam and Bertrice had been so reluctant. Not to mention, the Wildling priest was closer to my age than theirs. He couldn't know about the events concerning Gerd's first attempt to rid herself of me.

"Why?" My voice broke. "Why would the Reverend Mother send me back here since Gerd still holds the seat of Love?" I knew I wasn't thinking quite logically, but I couldn't stop myself.

Jax shrugged. "Why does the bear torment the bee? To drive her away to get to the honey." A feral grin spread across his face. "As I said. Delicious."

"But—"

He jumped off the footboard, somersaulted in mid-air, and landed si-lently and nimbly on his feet. "We will discuss the matter more when you are strong enough to hear your truth." He silently glided out of the room.

Tyra resumed her seat by my bed. "I swear to Balance I will never under-stand the Wildlings."

Before I could agree, exhaustion reclaimed me in her arms.

When I woke the second time, Tyra was gone. The female warden who had accompanied us to the Temple of Light sat beside me, a bound book in her lap. From the lit oil lamp on the bedside table, night had fallen.

"Wh-what hour?" My mouth was dry, but my throat no longer felt at the mercy of a fishwife's knife. A scrawny stray cat clawed at the inflamed flesh instead.

The warden marked her place with a bit of ribbon and closed the vol-ume. "The Mother's bells just rang third evening, m'lady."

"I-I don't remember your name."

"Gina, m'lady." She rose, laid the book on her chair, and stretched. "And we both know you didn't forget. You never bothered to learn it."

I didn't know what to say to her chiding remark. I could have repri-manded her, but she was right. Knowing the people here in Orrin meant connecting with them, depending on them.

And I'd learned long ago not to depend on anyone. It had taken Luc two years of patience before I even spoke to him civilly.

Gina crossed to the door. Another warden stood guard outside. I couldn't catch what she said, but moments later, a journeywoman and two apprentices entered with bundles of cloth and a bucket of hot water.

"Let's see about making you more comfortable, Justice," the apprentice healer said.

I wanted to say her manner was far too jovial for my comfort, but I held my tongue. After all, the Guild members had saved my life. And Sivan. And young Nathan.

Quite simply, the woman had done nothing to earn my tongue-lashing. My anger at my incapacity wasn't her fault.

Only when they helped me out of bed did I realize I was naked. The journeywoman and Gina helped me to the second chair in the room. Though to be honest, they practically carried me.

Once I was seated, the journeywoman checked my heartbeat and my breathing. One of the apprentices sponged grime, sweat and salt from my body while the other stripped the soiled sheets and remade the bed.

"What about the others?" I said.

The journeywoman smiled. "Master Devin is in the same straits as you, m'lady. Awake but weak. Sivan was well enough to send back to the temple this afternoon."

I waited, but her omission was glaring. "And Nathan?" I whispered.

From the changes in her pulse, she considered lying to me, then thought better of it. "He stopped breathing shortly after you woke this morning. Master Aaron was able to get his lungs working again, but . . ." She held up her hands in a helpless gesture. "We simply don't know, m'lady. It is the Twelve's will now whether your squire lives or dies."

"May I see him?"

The journeywoman pursed her lips. "If you can use the chamber pot by yourself, then yes. Otherwise, you're going straight back to bed."

In the end, the journeywoman won. I couldn't manage the three steps from the chair to the bed alone, much less relieve my bladder without assistance.

Once I was settled in the bed again, the journeywoman brought me chicken broth. "If you can keep it down for two candlemarks, I'll bring you some gruel, m'lady." She patted me on the shoulder and departed.

The hot liquid actually felt good on my throat so I had no problem finishing the cup. My stomach burbled its desire for more, but I knew such a request would not be met.

Instead, I turned to Gina who had resumed her seat by my side. "What happened with the other tracking spells last night?"

"As you suspected, the trail you assigned me and Brother Jeremy led directly to the prisoner in our gaol. Brother Mat's ribbon led to the docks and out to sea. They checked with the harbor master. With the storms, only three ships have left over the last sevenday. One for Cant by one of their merchants and the other two for Standora. Of those two, one was part of Duke Marco's fleet and the other one was from Jing, but the ship from Jing returned two days ago."

The afternoon Ambassador Quan came to see me. When Sister Gretchen hadn't appeared at the rendezvous, the captain came back. If Gretchen had traded for passage to Jing, how exactly was Quan planning to get her there this time of year? Or did he plan on disposing of her once he had the trade information?

Gina cleared her throat. "I don't know if this matters, but Brother Mat said to inform you that the Sea Peoples fleet is due any day now."

The southern islanders were the only ones brave enough, or insane enough, to cross the Peaceful Sea in mid-winter. But even they weren't stupid enough to test the open ocean north of Orrin until spring. They would cross between their islands and the Mecas and work their way north. The fruits they brought to Orrin were a welcome treat in the miserable cold rains of the season.

One of their princes was a regular of Sister Gretchen's. If the youngest son of the Sea People's king had left with their fleet after the Solstice, why would his skin have been caught in Gretchen's nails weeks later? Love's obsessive behavior when it came to cleanliness rivaled the Healers Guild. It had to be someone else that left the trail out to sea.

Gretchen's body was found on the duke's estate. The dead priestess had allegedly been gathering information for Jing. Cant had been mentioned in passing since the crown prince had been one of Gretchen's regulars, but the Issuran border city of Tandor had come up far more often in the course of the investigation. Therefore, any of the three ships could have carried my potential culprit.

I realized I was jumping to conclusions as my body recovered from the poison. Not thinking straight was bad form for a justice.

Time to focus on a more immediate concern. "The Jing ambassador's ship is the only one to arrive in Orrin?"

Gina shrugged. "No, but they coast-skipped as every captain arriving would this time of year."

"And leaving as well." I sighed. Whoever Sister Gretchen was with before she died had left Orrin by sea, and with this morning's sunrise, the trail was dead.

It could have been nothing more than a seaman donating his winter bonus for a night of worship with Gretchen.

No, it had to have been her murderer with the information she had gathered for Ambassador Quan, assuming he told me the truth. Otherwise, some trace of Alessa would have been in the scrapings.

"What about Brother Luc?"

Gina became unnaturally still. "He and his warden have not returned yet, and none of the brothers of Light have heard from him."

"Not even Kam?"

She shook her head.

Queasiness that had nothing to do with my poisoning filled me. I struggled to throw off my blankets.

"Lady Justice, what do you think you are doing?" Gina rushed to the bedside and pressed me back to the mattress.

"Think about it, Warden. Brother Luc has disappeared. Two attempts on my life, and they didn't care if they killed Orrin's entire Healers Guild in their second try."

Her face shifted from yellow to a sickly green as blood drained away. "Balance help us. We must to warn the other temples." She pivoted for the door.

"No."

She halted in mid-stride and faced me, her expression incredulous as she stared at me. "But, Justice—"

"Someone is making a concerted effort to foment chaos. The last thing we do is let our culprit know we're on to them. Our first duty is to find the missing men from Light."

Understanding dawned on Gina's face. "Remove the newest seats because you're an unknown element to their plan."

"Yes. Now, help me up," I ordered.

She didn't argue with me this time. I needed her help to dress, but my panic gave me new energy. My body would make me pay for abusing it so, but I prayed my eventual collapse wouldn't be over Luc's grave.

# Chapter 13

My first battle was simply leaving the Healers Guild residence.

I discovered Little Bear guarding the door to my recovery room. He threatened to throw me back on the bed and tie me down. I told him he was relieved of his service to the temple. Gina called us both mule-headed and shoved us toward the front door.

Which was blocked by half of the Healers Guild.

Master Aaron argued until he found my sword point at his throat. Frankly, he could have knocked me and my steel down with a good sneeze.

"Do you really think your students can stand against a justice and one Balance warden?" I snapped.

"Two," Little Bear interjected.

"You are no longer employed," I argued.

Gina pushed down my sword and slid past me. "Master Healer, if the justice dies from the aftereffects of the poison, it's her own damn fault, not yours." She drew her dagger and pressed it against the artery under his jaw, her motion so fast it took me by surprise, not just the healers. "But if High Brother Luc dies because you won't let her look for him, she won't be the one who takes your head."

I could actually make out the muscle in Aaron's cheek twitching under his skin.

"Very well," he snarled and stepped away from the door.

"Thank you, Aaron," I said.

"Good hunting, Anthea." His simple statement meant more to me than he realized.

Despite my bravado, I leaned on the two wardens heavily just to make the short walk to the Temple of Light. Only to reach their temple, and have the three remaining priests fussing at me for leaving the Healers Guild as well.

I shoved back my hood and glared at them each in turn. "Brother Luc is missing. Unless you want me to clap you in chains for hindering my investigation, I suggest you help me find him."

Since the original tracking spell was gone, I asked Kam to do the next best thing. A few hairs from each man's pillow was sufficient.

By the time Gina returned with our mounts, first one, then two, energy ribbons tingled along my skin. I released my breath. They were alive.

There was a brief argument between the three priests as to who would accompany me until Brother Mat pointed out that with Luc missing, he was the senior active priest. I winced at the insult to Kam, but he seemed to handle the inconsiderate statement better than me.

Another argument broke out about which wardens would accompany Mat and me. In the end, it was only Little Bear, Gina and one of the Light wardens. For all his bluster, Mat was sensible in not depleting Light's resources until we knew for sure what Luc's situation was.

That didn't stop the fear in my belly. I worked hard to keep it from turning into a full-blown panic-induced seizure.

Thank the Goddess, Nassa was a smart, gentle creature. Otherwise, I doubted I would have remained astride her to the end of Temple Street.

Unfortunately, the ribbons didn't turn east to follow Tanner's Row. They continued on the overgrown track that used to be the coastal road until the Crown commissioned the National Road a century and a half ago.

I pulled my hood tight against the harsh glow of the torches at Death's Gate, the southernmost and least used of the city's entrances. The peacekeepers said very little, other than to verify our identities. While I doubted the magistrate had forewarned his people, their lack of questions made me wonder how often fellows of rank had left or entered the city this late at night.

I glanced at Mat as we passed under the portcullis. His emanations showed worry. Probably the same worry plaguing me. However, it was the first time I felt his emotional control slip.

"I'll take the lead," I said.

Mat reached out and grabbed my reins. Nassa whickered and sidestepped, ready to break at my signal. "That isn't wise, Justice. You were close to death less than a day ago."

"Can you see in the dark, Brother?"

He released the leather and sighed. "Don't fall off your horse."

"Don't fall off a cliff." I smiled to take the sting out of my words and nudged Nassa with my knee.

The old track was fairly wide where it traced the bluffs south of the city. It was where the bluffs turned to jagged cliffs a few leagues beyond that concerned me. If Luc or his warden's horses had spooked, all four could have found themselves dashed on the rocks at the water's edge or pulled out to sea by the riptides.

Behind my right shoulder, angry purple bruised the horizon. Another storm was rolling in from the northwest, picking up moisture from the sea to dump on us. The weather wouldn't interrupt the tracking spell, but the drenching chill would make it difficult for even me to see the old trail and keep us safely on it.

I sipped from my water skin as we rode, still terribly thirsty from the effects of the poison. I should have raided the kitchen at the Temple of Light for some fresh raised bread while Kam cast the tracking spells. That would be far easier on my stomach than the flat bread and jerky in my saddle bag.

Ironically, after a couple leagues, I felt better astride Nassa than I did when I woke this morning.

The panther in the tree ahead caught my attention first. Below a tangle of blackberry bushes, a wolf paced. A bear peered from behind another tree on the other side of the overgrown track. Beyond them, horses and riders with the metallic thread design of the Temple of Death waited in a small copse.

Waiting for us.

Now, what in the Twelve were Bertrice and Jax up to?

                    **SUZAN HARDEN**

I glanced back at Mat. *We have company.* It felt odd using silent communication with someone other than Luc. It was too intimate, like seeing a stranger without his clothing.

*Hostile?* Mat asked. His mental tone carried no emotion whatsoever.

*We'll find out.* I'd like to believe they were allies. Jax's visit with me at the Healers Guild implied he was, as did Bertrice's cooperation with the investigation into Sister Gretchen's murder. But with the Assassins Guild after me and the drama of my mother's machinations, I wasn't sure of anything at this point.

I reined to a stop several lengths from where the panther crouched in the tree. No sense making myself an easy target. "High Brother Jax, may I ask what brings you out on a night like this?"

The wolf crept from behind the bushes. I shielded my eyes from the brilliant white heat that enveloped him. When the glare died, Jax stood before me in his human form. Hair standing straight up. Naked.

Even with my strange eyesight, I could tell he had a fine form. Nor did he appear bothered by the chill winter air.

He politely inclined his head. "After the poisoning incident, I became concerned when Brother Luc did not return by midday.

One of Death's riders nudged his horse closer and pushed back his hood. Bertrice's second, Xander. "High Brother Jax and his fellows tracked the two to an abandoned manor house where the National Road swings close to the coast."

"The one Samael DiRoy was using," Jax added. "The trail for both men and horses simply stopped at the front door. Demon scent covers the area."

A chill ran through me. "Old or new?"

He shook his head, the strands of his wild hair a moment behind the motion. "We could not tell. The lore from the demon wars says that their scent contaminates the places they've been for years."

It felt as if someone or something had thrust their hand into my chest and squeezed my heart. Who had gone back to that cursed house? And why? "What about the areas outside of the manor grounds?"

Jax shook his head again. "Only the one trail of men and horses leading in. The demon scent stops in the trees and bushes bordering the estate."

"Since we had no personal effects of either man, we were on our way back to Orrin after searching the area," Xander interjected. "When the tracking spell appeared, we knew someone was on their way."

"But you didn't know if it were friend of foe?" I asked.

The young Death priest shrugged. "As Brother Jax pointed out, though he suggested it would be you or Brother Mat." He reined his horse around to head back the way they had come. "We'll accompany you. Strength in numbers and a variety of skills," he said over his shoulder.

He rode south. Jax donned his wolf form once again and trotted after Xander.

I tried to repress a shudder. I didn't want to go back to the place where Duke Marco and I were almost slaughtered by demons.

But I wasn't leaving the man I loved at a demon's mercy either.

The dark blue hulk of the abandoned manor house loomed over the dull yellow trees. When we cleared the relative warmth of the woods, I wasn't sure if the colder air around the property was part of the incoming storm or a manifestation of the demon incursion from last summer. Jax's contamination theory made sense though. If the scent was corrupted, then the relative heat visible to my sight might be as well.

The tracking spells led up the front steps and to the massive wooden doors. I tried to swallow, but my damaged throat made it nearly impossible.

I turned to Jax, who had returned to his human form. "Did you go inside?"

He looked up at me. "Only to the main hall, but the oddest part was that both the scents of the men and the horses stopped at the foot of the porch stairs. When we went inside, we found the demons', yours, the duke's, the traitor's, but nothing of Brother Luc or his warden. Nor did we discover anyone else's."

I stared at the manse again. The incident with Samael DiRoy had happened at the beginning of summer, over seven months ago. How could our scents still be there, but not Luc's or his warden's from the last day?

Unnerved, I dismounted from Nassa and led her to the front steps. She jerked at the reins. I patted her neck and whispered softly to her. She calmed, but was still skittish until I led her five paces away.

The panther shifted into a lithe woman. She padded nearer to Nassa and me. "That was interesting." Her voice was low, melodic, on the verge of a purr. "I had a similar reaction when I climbed the steps. A deep sense of unease without a true source."

I handed Nassa's reins to the Wilding priestess. "Please watch her." A temple-bred horse didn't fret at the strange odor of the shapeshifters, unlike the mounts used by the nobles and commoners. Nassa nosed the woman for a reward.

"Her treats are in the saddlebag."

The sounds of Nassa chomping on a winter apple followed me up the steps to the giant portico. I examined the area, but after a full day, any heat marks would have dissipated.

I pushed open the massive doors. The energy ribbons literally died at the threshold, but the great room was empty. If I stepped through the doorway, would I disappear as thoroughly as Luc or Kam's tracking spell had?

The more practical part of me pointed to the obvious. What if Luc and his warden hadn't entered the manor? What did they do next? The questions left one other method for finding the missing men.

I pulled off my glove and ran my fingers over the chill, bare stones of the ledge and columns of the portico, searching for one willing to tell me its tale. A younger, more vital source would have been preferable, but the grass and trees were sleeping their winter dreams.

Jax seized my arm. "This isn't wise, Anthea. You were on Death's doorstep less than a day ago." He wasn't being disrespectful by omitting my title. Fear rolled off him in waves.

"If you have a better idea, Jax, I'm willing to try it," I said softly. The disquiet I felt here made me reluctant to speak louder.

Slowly, his fingers released their grip on my wrist. "I wish by all the creatures in the forest and farm I did."

Boot heels on stone drew our attention to Mat. "I'm ready when you are, Justice." Underlying his decisiveness was a hint of unease. Whether it had been too long since he stood as witness for a justice playing with the threads of time or he was as worried about the fate of Luc as I was, he didn't say.

Which was probably for the best. If my own fear overrode my control, the results of my spell could be disastrous.

Compromised emotions was the whole reason our orders weren't allowed to form any sort of attachments, sexual or otherwise. But having someone else stand witness was disturbing in itself. I hadn't had anyone but Luc since my final days at the main temple in the capital.

I sighed and nodded. "Thank you, Brother Mat."

Several of the flagstones between the top step and the threshold were quartz-flecked granite. Tough, stubborn, reflective. They would be most difficult to work with, but they'd remember the event of the last day most accurately.

I sat cross-legged at the midway point. Jax moved off the portico and rejoined the others. The way everyone crowded close on the lawn meant I wasn't the only one picking up the disturbance of this place in the ether. I tugged off my other glove and placed my palms flat against the wickedly cold stones.

The time line fought me as I rewound it, almost as if something tethered it in place. I yanked and something shattered. Black crystals filled the air.

No, not just black. Power devoid of all warmth. Just like the demons.

And it ate the energy ribbons of the tracking spell.

I heard Mat's gasp behind me, but he didn't try to interfere. Another yank on the timeline to last night and shadows filled the grounds. I rewound a bit more until only a ghostly pair of horses and riders approached the manor, or the shadows of them did. Beside them, a pale yellow ribbon shone. Luc's original tracking spell.

"Brother Luc and Warden Gibb are riding up to the portico," Mat started his recitation of the events playing before him. All a normal part of his duties to a justice. I'd gotten used to Luc's silence unless something of note happened.

"They dismount. Brother Luc reaches for the door latch. Other riders approach from lane connecting to the National Road. Luc and Gibb turn to face them. A dozen of them." A harsh gasp. "They are dressed in the cloaks of Light."

"A city emblem?" I push the words past gritted teeth. Playing with time is difficult in the best of circumstances, but the demon power left in the manor was actively fighting me.

"No. There's not a circuit badge either." Mat continued his recitation. "Their leader pushes back his hood. White hair, hooked nose. I don't recognize him. He's speaking to Brother Luc."

"Anyone recognize him or any of the riders?" Jax asked. A chorus of negatives didn't help my concentration. Why would someone disguise themselves as priests of Light here? It was almost as if they knew Luc was coming.

I slowed the passage of the threads through my fingers to match real time. "Can any of you read their lips? Tell us what they are saying?"

"Luc asks the stranger what he's doing so far from the border." Jax's voice.

Border? The closest border was Cant to the south and was guarded by the city of Tandor. If the men were from Tandor's Temple of Light, they should have had the city's emblem on their cloaks. Or was Luc trying to catch them in a lie?

"I had business at the capital." The wilding priest who wore the form of a bear translated directly in a bass tone that matched his animal self.

"Why are you here?" Jax spoke for Luc.

"My men and I are seeking shelter for the night."

"You're less than an hour's ride from Orrin. Surely, I can offer you better beds than a decaying manor."

"Your bed is not one I would enjoy."

"Perhaps Sister Gretchen's is more to your taste." Jax's voice didn't have the same inflection as my love's, but I recognized the taunt.

Even before Mat's breath hissed, I realized Luc deliberately set off a trap. My grip on the time lines nearly slipped as my throat choked. *Luc, you foolish, glorious idiot.*

"The wardens behind the white-haired stranger draw their swords." Mat tried to maintain a neutral tone, but his voice broke with the weight of what he was witnessing. "Gibb is cut down before his weapon clears its sheath. Brother Luc tries to fight them . . ."

All I saw was a confused mass of shadows. I didn't need Mat's recitation to know how this struggle ended. If the odds were better, Luc would have stood a chance, but this many . . .

"They disarm Brother Luc and pin him to the ground. One of the men forces his mouth open and pours some liquid into it. He tries to spit it out—" Mat's strained calm doesn't match the ice cold rage I barely kept in check.

"Brother Luc is unconscious. They sling him over his horse. They bind his wrists and ankles. While three of them secure Luc, a pair of the strangers drag Gibb into the manse. The two come back outside; Gibb is not with them. The group rides toward the National Road." Silence for a moment, then Mat added, "I'm sorry, Justice. Nothing happens once the riders disappear behind the trees."

I released the threads, and time snapped back into place.

With the demonic blocking spell shattered, the two energy ribbons tingled against my skin once again. One turned back on itself and twisted down the drive to where it met the National Road. The other ribbon sputtered like a flame in a windstorm, but led straight into the manor house. Gibbs was nearby and alive.

Barely.

Mat rushed into the manor before I could stop him, Little Bear right behind him.

Jax dashed up the stairs to the portico. "Justice?"

"I'm fine," I muttered, but I needed the Wildling priest's assistance to gain my feet. Dizziness distorted my vision, and my leg muscles cramped in protest to the dehydration plaguing me. He leaned me against a column before he ran inside after Mat and Little Bear.

I took a step after them, but I would have fallen if Gina hadn't wrapped an arm around my waist. Apparently, she decided that silence was better than arguing. Instead of forcing me to sit again, she helped me shuffle after the men.

They found the injured warden lying in one of the first floor parlors. Pale blue liquid pooled on the wooden planks next to him. Shards of expensive glass laid nearby.

" . . . yelled and banged on the glass. You couldn't hear or see me. I even threw myself at the window. I couldn't pass through it anymore than I could pass through the door."

Desperation and duty had kept the man alive for a day, but I knew his fate before Jax gave me the slight shake of his head. The warden would never survive us moving him from this room, much less fetching a healer out here.

"Who were they, Gibb" Mat asked. Apparently, the young priest had kept his wits and truthspelled the warden. The magic would cut through whatever forbidden spell had been laid on him.

"Don't know who their leader was." The warden gulped for air. "But I recognized the one who stabbed me. Remar. We entered the warden academy together." His breathing grew harsher. His body demanded air, but he didn't have enough blood left to carry it. Without air, the internal fire dies.

A whisper of movement behind me. Brother Xander walked past and knelt beside the dying man.

"Did they say why they wanted Luc?" Mat kept his demeanor calm and focused, though he had to know, as we all did, that Gibb didn't have much time left.

"H-hostage."

Mat tilted his head. "Against us?"

"N-no." Gibb's voice grew fainter. His dull, accusing eyes met mine. "Against you, Justice."

With a final rattling sigh, the warden died. And all three priests turned their intense attention on me.

# Chapter 14

Brother Xander frowned. "Why would Luc be held against you?"

"We rode circuit together for a decade. We were both assigned to Orrin at the same time, but Luc's station was at Brother Kam's request while mine was a sentence by the Reverend Mother of Balance. We're colleagues, but . . ." I shrugged. There was no method this stranger could have used to discover our affair.

My heart stuttered in my chest. No method that I knew of. But I hadn't known about Love's truthspell block until three days ago. What could Luc's captor know about us? They didn't question Luc before they drugged and abducted him. The only other person who knew about us was Kam . . .

No, Kam wouldn't have told a soul. He connived too much to keep Luc and me together.

"You haven't exactly made friends in Orrin, Justice," Little Bear commented. "He's the closest thing you have to a tie other than Brother Kam, Duke Marco, and Lady Katarina."

After his parents' treason, Marco was rarely left alone. As the duke's pregnant wife, Katarina couldn't use a chamber pot without a full contingent of guards. And Luc had Kam virtually on house arrest because of the mess with Sister Gretchen's declaration. So of course, Luc was the one they abducted.

I was assuming too much again. I needed facts. These men had wanted Luc to believe they were fellow priests. That didn't mean they were. There were too many unanswered questions about both Gretchen and Gerd, and they were legitimate priestesses. For now, I would play along with the hostage game. Did the alleged priests of Light count on Gibb to survive long enough to seed doubt about me? Was that the real reason for the demon spell over the house? Freeze time to keep Gibb alive until someone found him and heard his words?

I frowned. "The real question is why does this renegade priest want to influence me? Or think he can?"

Mat glanced down at the dead warden. The priest's gloved fingers closed the eyes of his comrade. He climbed to his feet. "Unless it had something to do with Gretchen's murder. What if he's the father of her child and he has heirs by his legitimate wife? That could be sufficient reason to kill her."

"He sure as the Thief wasn't getting her properties," Xander sourly proclaimed.

Little Bear tilted his head as he regarded Gibb's body. "If Sister Gretchen's murder was an impulse, not planned, maybe he needed time for a clean escape." He regarded me. "Sowing doubt about your objectiveness, and thereby hindering the investigation into Sister Gretchen's death, would give him extra time."

"But why stick her body in a wine barrel where someone was bound to find her?" I shook my head, but that only brought about another round of light-headedness.

"Unless he had someone else dispose of her," Mat mused. "Someone who wanted the murder to be discovered."

Everything the men theorized was an assumption. I needed facts, and a half-formed idea itched at the back of my mind. I was missing something terribly important. The room swayed. Little Bear and Gina were the only reason I didn't pitch headfirst into Gibb's cooling blood.

"Enough adventure for you tonight, Lady Justice." Little Bear had the audacity to chuckle.

"No, wait." I glanced around the room wildly. Something at the edge of my exhaustion melded with my conscious mind. "The original trail Brother Luc and—" Names. Dammit, I needed to learn these people's names if they were going to sacrifice themselves in my goddess's quest for righteousness.

"And Gibb followed. The tracking spell died at daybreak, but it was still active when they arrived. Luc's unknown assailants didn't leave with anybody else but him."

Jax muttered an obscenity. "Search the manse," he ordered. "By twos. Every warden with a priest. Little Bear?"

My chief warden started to guide me to the main doors. I didn't have the strength left to even attempt to struggle.

"We need to search—" I started to protest.

"Let the rest of the lot do the heavy lifting for now," he murmured close to my ear. "If they find something, they'll let us know. Gina will keep an eye on them."

"But . . ." My argument died under his logic.

Once outside, he settled me on the steps and knelt beside me. The thump of boot steps from the searchers vibrated through the manse to the flagstones so subtly I doubted if anyone else would have noticed.

"Gibb's wound," I whispered. "How long would it take someone to die from it?"

Little Bear grunted. "Less than a day. And some of the blood should have dried on the floor in that time," he said softly. "That was a demon spell on the place, wasn't it?"

I nodded.

"Do you have a reason to suspect any of them inside are involved?" my warden whispered. Little Bear's query carried several measures of weight behind it. He shoved a water skin into my hand. I drank while I contemplated the possibilities.

Normally, I trusted Luc and Kam implicitly as I did their judgment in their order's members. Mat had transferred in when Kam's former second had been elevated as the chief priest of Light at Montero in the Pana Valley. In theory, a much better position than Orrin, but the damning barrel with Gretchen had also come from a Pana Valley winery. However, Kam had been reluctant to name Mat as his replacement. The young priest could very well resent being passed over.

Bertrice's confession regarding how she lost her healing abilities could go either way. Kam believed she had a vested interest in keeping me alive, else her sacrifice was for naught. Or, she could blame me for the loss of her power and her removal from the Healing Guild, which would explain the first assassination attempt as well as the poisoning of the Guild's oil supply. Xander's loyalty to her was undoubtable, so he'd follow her path.

Jax? Well, any of the Wildling God's priesthood was enigmatic at best. However, he was the only one who didn't seem to have an agenda in Orrin beyond his duties to Temple and Crown. And poking a bee's nest as he said.

"I don't know," I said softly.

Little Bear grunted. I handed him the water skin, and he took a swig. He swiped his mouth with the back of his glove. "First sensible thing I've heard from you in the last couple of days."

"You're making me rethink my request for sharing your opinions."

He grinned. "You released me from temple service, remember? You can't stop me from stating my opinions."

"Then I take you back just to shut you up." I grinned.

Before he answered, a shout echoed through the house, followed by the rapid stamp of boots. Priests and wardens running . . .

"I'd say they found something," Little Bear said dryly.

I counted my breaths. When I reached sixty, the bear Wildling priest stumbled out the door and rushed to side of the portico. The sounds of his heaving didn't help my own residual nausea.

The rest of the priests and wardens followed a few heartbeats later. Most of them carried the same greenish tinge to their faces and hands.

Except Jax. His skin glowed orange-red. He vaulted over the railing next to me. "Demon magic," he spat. "The man has been skinned."

My heart lurched in my chest. In the last six months, I'd encountered more violence than I had in my previous ten years as a justice. And more demons than anyone in my order had for four generations.

Since the last demon incursion. Most people believed the thousand-year war was over. Now, I wondered . . .

Without a word, Little Bear helped me to my feet. Without a discussion, the group of us crossed to the little grove where the Wildling priestess guarded the horses. The priests spread blankets and pulled out rations while the wardens fed our mounts.

Sipping water, I waited impatiently for one of them to speak. Mat stared at his jerky for a long time before he cleared his throat.

"The man we found chained in the dungeon was the same man we saw leading the group that abducted Brother Luc."

"How do you know if he was skinned?" I asked.

"Scent," Jax said sharply. "You can't change your scent."

"But when did he die?"

"Three days ago from the decay and the maggots," the bear priest answered. So the leader of the men who confronted Luc and Gibb hid his identity.

I wanted to ask how, but the answer was rather obvious. Luc's abductor had used illegal shapeshifting magic. While the Wildling God's priesthood each had an animal form as part of their allegiance to Him, transforming oneself into another human still carried the death penalty.

Luc's abductor had to have access to a demon grimoire for such forbidden magic. Only a demon spell would demand a blood sacrifice. The Light priests' tracking spell had worked because technically part of the dead man, his skin, was still alive.

A worse thought occurred. How many copies of the ancient grimoires still existed? Samael had claimed he found his in the royal library. Had someone planted it there to entice the queen's distant cousin?

Or would such a book seduce anyone who found it into using it?

I sighed. "I presume we can no longer question him?"

"This is not amusing," Jax snarled. "Whoever did this sucked the life essence from him and wears his skin as you would a cloak."

"I don't find this humorous in the least." Neither was I about to admit how close I was to breaking down from the exhaustion and fear. "Let me see what I can retrieve from—"

"No!"

I jumped at the chorus of voices, Little Bear's loudest of all.

"No offense, Lady Justice, but between the poison and rewinding

Brother Luc's timeline, you're barely upright," Brother Xander proclaimed. "I'm not about to lose you on a foolhardy attempt to investigate a corpse that appears to have a magical trap set on it. Sister Bertrice would have my head."

He looked at the piece of hard tack in his hand before he tossed it back in his food satchel. "In fact, we're leaving it here for now. I'll bring Sister Bertrice and one of the healer journeymen out in the morning."

I looked from face to face before returning to Xander. Everyone had the same disturbed demeanor. "What about Gibb?"

"We'll take him back to the temple tonight," Xander said. "His corpse is clean."

"But Luc—" I protested.

Jax rose. "My people will follow the trail your timeline spell revealed. I do not think his abductors expected anyone to shatter the demon shielding spell. Even when Mat's tracking spell dies at sunrise, there's still Luc's scent we can follow."

I opened my mouth to protest, but he held up a finger. "I swear upon my god we will take no other action without informing you and Brother Mat first."

His heat blinded me before I could shield my face. Claws scratched against the blanket, and he and his bear were gone before the spots stopped flashing in my eyes.

By the time our party, minus the two wildling priests, returned to Orrin, the roosters were crowing. And surprisingly, my appetite was ravenous.

Brother Xander and his wardens reined in at their temple. He exchanged words with Mat concerning the disposition of Gibb's remains. The wildling priestess silently returned to her own temple. Mat escorted us to Balance's rear courtyard gate before he and his man crossed the thoroughfare to get some sleep.

Both my own cook, Deborah, and the journeywoman, who had fed me chicken broth at the Healers House, were waiting for us in the stable area when we arrived.

It was embarrassing enough that Warden Gina had to ride double with me to keep me from falling out of my saddle on the way home. Even more embarrassing was Little Bear holding me upright after I'd dismounted.

Deborah and the journeywoman exchanged looks, but said nothing. I thanked the Goddess for that small favor.

They bundled me into the kitchen. Magistrate DiCook was waiting for us by the cauldron. I was too tired to summon any formality.

"Should I even ask, Malven?"

He grinned. "Oh, I'm just here to steal Gretchen's declaration and kill you."

I mulled over his statement as Little Bear helped me to the table in the kitchen girl's nook. "So she finally decided to act."

"When the poison didn't work, yes." The magistrate shrugged. "Assuming she was behind the sabotage of the healers' supplies." He shook his head. "I don't have any proof she was involved though, and no admission of guilt."

"Even if she isn't behind the poisoning, she's not one to pass up an opportunity that falls in her lap," Unfortunately, this turn of events meant vengeance wasn't driving me to frame my mother. As the magistrate had suspected she would do, Gerd had just handed me the sword with which to behead her.

DiCook stood out of the way while the journeywoman checked my breathing and heartbeat. Deborah brought over a bowl of something right as my stomach gave an atrocious growl.

The journeywoman cocked her head. "Any more vomiting? Fever? Unusual bleeding?"

"No. Just tired and hungry."

And heartsick, though I couldn't say that. Between my birth mother sending DiCook to kill me and my enemies holding my lover hostage, I was terrified. Was this how Luc felt last summer when I disappeared at the abandoned manse and he saw demons?

Except this time, it was not just a demon. I'd learned in my years on the bench that humans were far more inventive in their atrocities than anything else in the universe. A demon would simply eat you.

But I was no good to Luc if I didn't take care of myself. I reached for the bowl and spooned a bit into my mouth. Porridge sweetened with honey and dried blackberries. My stomach gurgled in delight, the only part of me not dragging with exhaustion, pain and fear. It took everything I had not to swallow the mix as fast as I could.

Malven dragged another chair over to the table and straddled it. "You still have the false declaration I can give Gerd?"

I grinned. "Of course. I told you I'd leave it on my office desk in case you came to steal it while I was out."

"I'll get it," Little Bear offered.

"Why didn't you—"

The magistrate waved a hand and laughed. "I waited on the off chance I could have some of Deborah's delicious cooking." He gave her a sad, pleading expression.

The old woman grinned and shuffled back to her cauldron.

As I started on my second bowl, Sivan came into the kitchen, wrapped in a robe, with the two scrolls in her hand. I sighed. Little Bear must have woken her.

"I've already hung up the notice that court has been cancelled for this morning," she murmured. "Unless there's any special wording you want concerning Sister Gretchen's declaration, Donella will display the public post tomorrow as you ordered."

Technically, I was a day late having it posted. If Gerd raised a fuss, I had the excuse I hadn't signed the post because I'd been poisoned. I shook my head, and the room wobbled. "No. Thank you. I'm sorry you were woken."

"It wasn't as if I were sleeping anyway." Sivan laid the first parchment in front of me, produced a bottle of ink and a quill, and dutifully pointed to the invisible spot that needed my signature. My fingers shook, and I clenched the quill between them as I wrote my name and rank.

She handed the other scroll, the fake declaration, to the magistrate before she set my empty porridge bowl on the parchment to keep it from curling while the ink dried. She tugged on my arm. "Let's get you to bed."

"There's too much to deal with, and I've already lost a day," I snapped. And immediately regretted my tone.

DiCook smacked the scroll against the palm of his other hand. "Get some rest while you can, Justice. Once I give this to Gerd, the manure will fly."

Deborah set another bowl in front of the magistrate.

"I'll delay as long as I can," he mumbled around his first spoonful of porridge.

"What are you going to tell her about failing to slit my throat?"

He swallowed and grinned. "The truth. You were surrounded by your staff the entire time I was here." The magistrate tapped the scroll more quietly. "I owe you an apology. After . . ."

Even though he obviously rethought what he was about to say, I guessed. It was the same hesitancy I had been seeing in the Balance staff since my arrival. "I don't blame you, Malven. I'm finding out more about my predecessor's actions, or lack thereof, than I care to."

"I meant—" He shrugged. "Well, thank the Father, she doesn't have your skill at questioning."

The porridge did a slow, queasy roll in my stomach as I realized he was speaking of my mother, not my predecessor. "Gerd truthspelled you?"

DiCook shook his head before he downed the rest of his bowl. "Why bother when the compulsion spell on the bribe would be just as effective?" He swung his leg around the chair and stood. "My peacekeepers and I will be ready when you need us. Just send me word. Not directly though." He strode through the doorway.

In his wake, the Mother's bells tolled first morning. The day had come far too soon. What would Gerd try next? And who had taken Luc? A worshipper under Gerd's influence, or someone hoping to trade him for the information Gretchen was attempting to smuggle out of Issura? And how did demon magic factor into the situation?

If Quan was looking for the information Gretchen possessed, had his disguised priestess of Light, Shi Hua, also done a tracking spell on the murdered woman? I'd planned to ask her when I visited the Jing embassy, but the poison had put a major wrinkle in that route.

Brother Jeremy had accompanied Luc and me on our visit to the embassy last fall when the poor ambassador had discovered his court sorcerer had smuggled a demon egg into his mansion. Maybe I should send him to talk to Shi Hua as a fellow of their order while I search for other clues concerning Luc's abductors?

My thoughts became jumbled at all the factors I needed to consider. There was another tug on my arm, and I glared up at Sivan. "I don't need to be treated like I'm incapable of caring for myself."

"I know, Anthea, but if you don't get some sleep, you'll be no good to anyone." She jammed both of her hands under my armpits and bodily lifted me from the chair.

"I'm not going to sleep." I sounded like a petulant child, but I couldn't seem to stop.

"You don't have to, but you are going to lie in your bed and close your eyes." Sivan guided me out of the kitchen and down the hallway. I would have sworn feminine titters from the kitchen staff and the journeywoman healer followed us.

"You shouldn't use my given name without my title. That's improper." My chiding slurred as she walked me into my chambers and over to my bed. I slumped down on the feathers and thick cotton padding.

"My apologies, Lady Justice." She bent over and pulled off my boots.

As she untied the lacings to my robes, I waggled an index finger at her. "I'm not drinking anything you give me either. You're not tricking me into consuming a sleeping draught."

"I wouldn't dream of it, m'lady." She pulled the robes off me and tossed them aside.

"Bedder nod," I slurred. My fingers couldn't seem to work my leggings. Sivan pulled me upright. I tottered while she peeled the leather down before she gently pushed me to sit again.

"I need shum dee 'fore I redire," I protested.

"I'll fetch a pot of tea for you, m'lady." She pulled my nightshirt over my head and placed my arms in the sleeves.

"Nod chamo-chamo-chamo—" I couldn't find the rest of the word in my increasingly fuzzy mind.

"No chamomile. I'll bring the good black tea from Jing," she murmured and swung my legs onto my bed.

Would Luc visit me tonight? The present smashed the idle wish. Luc was missing, a prisoner of an unknown person.

Tears trickled down my cheeks.

Sivan tucked blankets around me. "What's wrong, Anthea?"

Another reminder of things gone wrong. "I shorry. I 'ver thod they'd harm you or anyone elsh."

She rested a hand on my shoulder. "I'm fine, and the journeywoman said Nathan woke up in the wee hours, which is excellent news. Sleep." She extinguished the oil lantern and pulled the bed chamber door shut behind her.

I counted, waiting for her steps to fade so I could sneak through the tunnel to Light's library, but my lids grew heavy. Only then did I realize Deborah was the one who had slipped the sleeping draught into my porridge.

Banging on my bedchamber door woke me once again. I draped the feather pillow over my head in the vain hope that the noise would go away.

It did stop when someone burst through the door. I rolled off the mattress, once again my hand reaching for the knife I kept between it and the frame.

Gina watched me wave the blade in her direction, an amused air about her. "I think you've recovered sufficiently from the poison." Her amusement faded. "Donella sent me to wake you. The Temple of Mother has called a convocation." She brushed aside a couple of scrolls on my desk and set a platter full of delicious smells on the scarred wooden surface.

I blinked. Mother? What in Balance was going on now? I rose from my crouch. "When?"

"In half a candlemark." She poured a cup of tea from the scorching pot.

I stripped off my nightclothes. "What time is it?"

"Just before first morning, Justice."

I halted in mid-motion and stared at her. I had broken my fast just after first morning.

After the disastrous search for Luc and Gibb.

At my glare, Gina shrugged. "You've been asleep for a full day. The healer journeywoman has been here the entire time to keep an eye on you and Sivan."

"You mean drug me," I grumbled as I reached for clean leggings and a shirt from my wardrobe.

"Not since the porridge yesterday morning, m'lady." A hint of a smile played at the corner of her mouth, but she was intelligent enough not to let it fully blossom.

"Has there been any word from Brother Jax or Sister Bertrice?"

"The Wildling priests haven't returned." She hesitated for a moment. "Sister Bertrice sends her apologies, but her people had to salt the skinned body you found before they could move it."

Balance take whoever had murdered the man for his form. If Bertrice resorted to salt, then the demon spell couldn't be deconstructed. Or she had covered her tracks if she were part of this Balance-forsaken mess.

Or maybe the objective of my adversary was to sow chaos in my own mind so I suspected everyone.

Unaware of my internal battle, Gina continued, "She's working on identifying the man, but so far no one's come forward with information."

"Could he be from Tandor's Temple of Light?" My fingers didn't want to work. I tried to quell my irritation when Gina stepped forward to fasten the ties on my leggings.

"Brother Mat said he sent a courier to the capital with his account and a drawing of the man's features." Her deft hands made short work of the ties on my shirt as well. "He doesn't expect an answer for four days at the soonest. Now eat before you walk over to Mother. The last thing we need is you passing out in the middle of a convocation."

"Summon Little Bear and Tyra. It's time to put our plan into motion."

Gina crossed her arms. "I will not move until the Lady Justice starts to eat."

As much as I detested her chiding, she was correct. I sat at my desk and plowed through Deborah's excellent breads and sausages as my wardens arrived and filled me in on the other events I'd missed in my sound sleep.

Since whichever temple calls a convocation hosts the gathering of the chief priests and priestesses, I only had a short walk next door. Bringing two wardens with me to such a meeting would raise a major hue and cry from the other seats, but Tyra pointed out that I would have to kill her myself to stop her, and then I'd be at the mercy of another assassination attempt.

"You must have received high marks in logic class," I muttered as we trudged next door.

"The highest," she said without a hint of pride. "Which along with my weapon skills was why I was assigned to Balance."

From his odd sound, Little Bear muffled a chuckle. Though he'd gotten much less sleep than I had, it seemed more prudent to have him with me than accompany the rest of my wardens on the errand I sent them. Honestly though, I couldn't see the eunuchs at Love repelling Gina alone, much less the other wardens and peacekeepers accompanying her.

The tension was palpable when we entered the Mother's great hall. Tiny groups of clergy and attendants clung against the walls. Three tables were already set in a U-shape with four chairs on each side.

I fingered the weight of the cursed gold in my pocket. The messenger I'd sent through Bertrice had returned with a warning from DiCook that Gerd had summoned him to the convocation to testify. My gaze swept the people already here.

Speak of the demon. My birth mother glared at me before returning to her emphatic conversation with Mother Bianca. The chief priests of Vintner and Thief shot furtive glances my way as they whispered. Jax's second and Bertrice deliberately didn't acknowledge my presence though I was sure Gerd was aware of our recent contacts. Mya, the chief priestess of the Child stood alone, hugging herself to ward off the emotional wash from the rest of us. The remaining players exhibited a cultivated air of indifference.

Brother Mat approached me and my wardens. He laid his palm on my arm. *Kam and Jeremy tested the solution to the counter this morning. It works.*

*Have you distributed the spell to the other temples yet?*

He smiled. *No, but I've got the copies with me.*

Relief washed over me, and I struggled to keep my face impassive and my feelings in check. Gerd wasn't getting away with anymore lies. At least, not today.

*Any word from Jax?*

*Not yet. How do we tie Gerd to Luc's disappearance?*

Once again, I had to wonder if DiCook was correct, and she instigated the current problems rather than simply used the recent chaos to her advantage.

*Let's see how this plays out before we do anything. As the magistrate said, let's give her the rope for her own noose.* Hanging was the lowest form of execution and hadn't been performed in centuries. The eastern nations had discovered the hard way that demons fed off the energy of traitors slowly strangling to death. Yet, the analogy seemed apropos to Gerd. Especially considering how Gretchen had died.

Mat leaned closer to my ear, concern etched in his speaking voice. "Mother Bianca is going to ask where Luc is."

I was sure my own grin was more feral than Jax's as a wolf. "I'm counting on it."

The chief priest of Conflict parted from the group he conversed with and strode over to us. High Brother Han's chain mail clinked as he approached. He was a mountain of a man, easily a head taller than Mat, who stood at the same height as Luc. It meant I had to tilt my head back to see his face.

"Lady Justice, Brother." Han politely nodded. "I trust you are feeling a mite better." He sounded as if this meeting's sole purpose was his entertainment.

"Yes, thank you." Now, what exactly was he up to?

"And your squire?"

"He'll live, as will I. I'm sure that irritates some."

Han blew out a gusty breath that ruffled his full beard. "An active Assassins Guild in Issura worries me, Anthea. Better an honest enemy than a false ally."

"I agree with you on that point."

His eyes narrowed. "Whatever Gretchen's faults, she didn't deserve what was done to her."

Han's unspoken accusation hung in the air. He thought Gerd was responsible. Damn, I wanted to hug him.

"Did you know her well—"

My question was drowned when Mother Bianca rapped her distaff from her seat at the bottom of the U-shaped table. "Let us begin."

"We'll talk later," Han whispered, if his basso rumble could be called that. He winked at me before crossing to his side of the room.

Wardens and staff filed out of the room. All of them, except my two bodyguards.

Once the assemblage was seated, and my wardens failed to leave, Mother Bianca glared at me. "What is the meaning of breaking this convocation's rules, Chief Justice Anthea?"

I pushed back my hood. Time to play to my advantages. "Given there have been two assassination attempts on me this week and someone succeeded in assassinating Sister Gretchen of the Temple of Love last week, it seems prudent to follow my wardens' advice and have an escort at all times."

No murmurs of surprise from the eleven people seated at the table. The gossip network in Orrin had been working overtime.

"Do you have any way of proving your assertion? Are you sure it's not blind clumsiness?"

I smiled at her bad pun. "We found one of the assassins at the Three Doves Inn shortly after he committed suicide. You may confirm this fact with Magistrate DiCook and High Sister Bertrice if you wish."

"And where's your friend, High Brother Luc?" Bianca sneered.

I didn't answer.

Beside me, Mat stiffened at her insult in asking someone else the whereabouts of his senior. "Our High Brother was abducted three days ago while tracking Sister Gretchen's murderer. His warden was slaughtered defending him. I am the acting chief priest until he is found." The taut muscles of his body belied the calmness in his voice.

When neither Mat or I rose to her bait, Bianca turned on the Wildling priest's second. "So, where's High Brother Jax? Dead or snatched?"

"Neither," the priestess said. With her mischievous smile and sharp nose, I could definitely see her second form as a fox. "He's tracking High Brother Luc as you waste our time with your petty human squabbles."

Bianca didn't address the Wildling's accusation, but her ears and cheeks grew bright red. "Since all temple chiefs or their seconds are present—" She shot a furious look at the Balance wardens standing behind me. "We shall address the order of business."

She looked down at something on the table in front of her. "It has come to our attention that a civil complaint was filed by one temple against another with the magistrate of Orrin." She lifted her head, and her gaze swept all of us. "High Sister Gerd DiLove claims that Chief Justice Anthea DiBalance has willfully and illegally seized properties that rightfully belong to the Temple of Love."

Bianca stared at me. "What say you, Chief Justice?"

I folded my fingers together. "I will not answer civil charges in a convocation." I turned to Gerd, sitting on the opposite side of the room from me. "If my mother wishes to level accusations at me, she should do so by submitting them to a properly convened convocation."

"I said never to call me that," she screeched.

Once again, no surprise emanated from our colleagues. The matter wasn't as secret as she wished. Maybe Little Bear and the rest of my wardens also knew far more about my personal history than they let on.

Infuriated at my statement, Gerd jumped to her feet and jabbed an accusing finger in my direction. "She's a murderer, and now she's a thief."

"You agreed to her sentence on the Samael DiRoy matter last summer." That came from Jerrod, chief priest of the Temple of Father.

Gerd tossed her head, her curls flying. "I was threatened by the Reverend Mother of Balance."

I had to bite my tongue to prevent my laughter from spilling. A threat from the Reverend Mother was probably the one true thing in Gerd's list of grievances.

"You are leveling serious accusations." Despite its thin, reedy quality, Sister Mya's voice carried weight.

"Yes, I am."

"Then why didn't you call a convocation on either the alleged threat from the Reverend Mother or the equally alleged theft in the first place, Gerd?" Han's rumble dominated the huge hall.

My mother ignored the priest's logic. "I have proof of her wrongdoing." She whipped around to face Bianca. "I would like to call my witness."

"Based on what?" There was a slight buzz in the chief priestess's voice. Had she only now realized Gerd was using her? "As others, besides Justice Anthea, pointed out, you have made no formal accusation for this convocation to decide on." Bianca tapped her forefinger on the parchment lying in front of her. "This is a civil matter." Her smile showed all her teeth. "All civil matters in Orrin are heard by the chief justice."

Oh, yes, Bianca definitely realized she'd been had. Gerd's face turned a brilliant scarlet at the loss of her ally.

Not for the first time, I wondered who my father might be. I definitely didn't receive my intelligence from my mother.

Gerd lifted her chin. "I have proof the public post of Sister Gretchen's declaration is a fraud."

"And why does this concern the Temple of Love?" High Father Jerrod asked.

"If a priest or priestess doesn't leave a valid declaration of last wishes, his or her property automatically goes to their temple," Mat interjected.

Bianca frowned at my mother. "Are you claiming your temple is the heir to Sister Gretchen's property?"

"Yes." Gerd inclined her head and resumed her seat now that she thought she was getting her way.

"This is unorthodox—" Bianca began.

"She's made a charge before us," Jerrod interjected.

"Improperly!" Mya's voice grew strident. The Child's priestess was more agitated than normal in a crowd, but I wasn't sure how much was the tension in the room and how much was her own anger. I pitied the woman. Her powerful empathic gift was more of a curse than a blessing in this type of situation. She sucked in a deep breath before she said, "I move to dismiss the convocation until such time Sister Gerd petitions the temples, not the civil authorities, concerning her grievance."

"She has given every temple notice," the chief priest of the Thief noted. "Albeit, in an unorthodox manner."

"Then we should hear Love's case," Jerrod said.

I leaned forward. "Point of order, Mother."

"Yes?" Bianca didn't bother to hide her irritation.

"Sister Mya's motion has not been voted on, and Father Jerrod has not formally moved to hear Sister Gerd's charges against me."

Bianca's skin flamed so bright I wondered which would happen first—she would catch fire or a brainstorm would take her. "Fine. Those in favor of Sister Mya's motion to dismiss the convocation?"

"Until such time Sister Gerd petitions the temples," I added. Never mind a potential brainstorm in Mother's chief priestess. For an instant, I wondered if Bianca would leap over the table and beat me with her distaff.

Instead, she repeated my words through her clenched teeth. No one raised their hands, including Mat and me, which made me wonder what Mya was planning if she wasn't voting for her own motion.

Bianca's glare was as hot as the sun on my face in midsummer. "What game are you playing, Justice?"

"None, Mother. I simply want protocol to be observed since there seems to be a question of propriety the last time this august body met. Before I joined it, that is," I added.

She must have decided my poke wasn't worth the retaliation. Turning to Jerrod, she said, "Do you wish to make a proper motion, Father?"

He cleared his throat and shot a look in my direction.

Mat grasped my hand under the table. *You're getting under their skin. Like a flea. Best to keep them off balance.*

The Light priest coughed to muffle what I suspected was a bark of laughter at my bad pun.

"I move that since all temple heads are aware of Love's charge against Balance that the matter be heard and settled now." Jerrod's voice didn't sound as firm as it had a moment ago. Whatever mummer's lines he and Bianca had been given, the pages of their scripts had burned in the proverbial fire of Light. They had no control, and it unnerved them.

Balance help me, I needed to have a very long talk with my staff about what had happened under Penelope's term.

Once we found and rescued Luc.

"Those in favor?" Bianca ground out the words.

All twelve of us raised our hands.

*From their expressions and body language, it looks like an even split,* Mat whispered in my mind. Even he seemed to forget I could see those same things myself.

I gave the barest of nods. For once, I was grateful for my staff's actions. I was rested and had a full belly. In other words, no distractions while this sad, sick theater played out.

Bianca rang the tiny silver bell in front of her. At the chime, one of her attendants from outside opened the doors to the main hall.

"Bring in the witness."

The priestess repeated Bianca's request.

A moment later, Malven DiCook strode into the room. One of the Mother's wardens carried a chair to the open space between the three tables.

Bianca gestured at the chair. "If you would have a seat, Magistrate. We have a few questions for you."

"He needs to be truthspelled," Han said.

Bianca waved at Mat to proceed.

DiCook held up a finger. "One moment before we begin, Mother."

Bianca frowned. "What is it, Magistrate?"

He reached under the high collar of his formal shirt and pulled a chain of gold up and over his head. At the end of the chain dangled a single ruby carved in the shape of a heart. "You might want to confiscate this," he said with a smile.

"What is it?" Bianca's frown grew deeper.

He turned to my mother. "According to High Sister Gerd, it's a talisman that blocks the effects of a truthspell if I activate it."

A series of gasps rippled through the convocation. Gerd started to rise, but Han's huge hand clamped around her wrist. "Don't you want to stay for your witness's testimony, High Sister?"

From the bluish-green of her fingertips, he was cutting off her circulation and on the verge of breaking the bones.

At Father Jerrod's nod, Mat stood and walked over to DiCook, who handed over the talisman. Mat crossed the space to surrender the ruby and chain to Jerrod before he returned to DiCook. With the priest's soft words and a gesture, a tickle of energy radiated around the magistrate.

Father Jerrod led the questioning as DiCook related the events of the last four days, including what he knew about Gretchen's death, the attempts on me and the Healers Guild, and Gerd's attempt to bribe and ensorcel him.

"What did you do with this gold?" Jerrod asked.

"I took it to Chief Justice Anthea and asked for her advice. The magistrate's office doesn't have jurisdiction over the temples." DiCook managed to keep his tone even and factual.

I pulled the cursed gold out of my pocket and passed it around the table. The signature of Gerd's magic on the coins was unmistakable. Even more damning was the obvious compulsion spell.

There were three additional queries from Thief and Child. Bianca remained silent through the whole proceeding, probably formulating a plan to minimize the political damage to herself after giving my mother a podium for her stupidity.

"But I have the real declaration!" Gerd looked around, wildly searching for an ally after DiCook's damning testimony.

"Here?" Bianca spoke for the first time since the magistrate produced the talisman.

"Yes!" Gerd fumbled in her robe, a difficult task with one hand, but from his ugly scowl, Han wasn't inclined to release her. She finally produced the scroll, its wax seal still intact.

Han passed it to Mya, who made an expression of distaste before handing it to Jerrod. He gave it to Bianca. "This is your convocation after all."

She pursed her lips. "I'll break the seal, but only if there's a unanimous vote to override the confirmation of Light and Balance if this turns out to be Gretchen's valid declaration."

Mat and I looked at each other and back at Bianca. We both raised our right hands. The other nine priests and priestesses quickly followed suit. Bianca glared at me before she raised her own hand.

The crack of the wax sounded like a thunderclap in the silent room. Bianca unrolled the scroll and scanned the contents. It didn't take long since Bertrice and I had composed a very short message.

Bianca's body heat rose, but I wasn't sure if it was embarrassment or rage. She placed a hand over her mouth and slid the scroll to her counterpart.

Father Jerrod read the fake declaration. There was an impression of disbelief, then he roared with laughter and banged the table with his fist.

Sister Mya leaned over his arm, scanned the scroll, and snickered. "May I please be the one to read it aloud, Father?"

He scooted the parchment to her. She stood and cleared her throat. "To High Sister Gerd of the Temple of Love. You stole the wrong declaration. Yours, High Sister Bertrice of the Temple of Death and Chief Justice Anthea of the Temple of Balance."

The assembly erupted in gales of laughter. Well, everyone did except myself, my mother, and Bianca. Gerd stood there, a deer surrounded by a wolf pack, knowing there was no escape. The chief priestess of Mother covered her face with both hands. In the tumult, I couldn't tell what emotion she hid.

When the sound died, I said, "Wardens, please arrest High Sister Gerd DiLove on charges of fraud, bribery of a public official, unlawful magic, and conspiracy to commit murder."

"With pleasure," Little Bear growled.

Han released her wrist once the wardens had her secured between them. Not that Gerd fought them. She appeared to be in shock.

Silence reigned once my wardens escorted Gerd from Mother's Great Hall.

When Bianca made no move to adjourn or continue, Jerrod broke the quiet. "So the posted declaration at Balance is Gretchen's valid declaration?"

"Yes, High Father," I said.

"Do you believe Gerd is involved in Gretchen's murder?" he asked.

I shook my head. "I don't know yet."

"Then why the conspiracy to commit murder charge?" he said.

I looked at DiCook, who hadn't been dismissed and was still truthspelled. "Magistrate, please repeat your conversation with High Sister Gerd the night before last."

He explained the plot to steal the fake and slit my throat. Gasps of dismay erupted from most of the assembled seats. Everyone except Bianca.

Jerrod cleared his throat. "So what do we do about this truthspell blocker?"

I nudged Mat, and he rose to his feet. "Brother Luc discovered the blocking spell in the second day of his and Justice Anthea's investigation into Sister Gretchen's murder. We've already researched the matter." He pulled a sheaf from his cloak and started passing around copies. "This counterspell will only effect the blocker. From now on, you'll need to perform the counter, then the truthspell, to be sure."

"Until someone develops the counter to the counter to the blocker," the chief priest from Thief said wryly.

Mat shrugged. "If we get to that point, we are going to get unknown and possibly unpleasant side effects from all the intersecting power. From our research, the blocker was developed during the last demon war to hide those dealing in the forbidden magics. During our investigation into Sister

Gretchen's murder, we discovered the Temple of Love has been using it to protect their priestesses from being truthspelled over worshippers' pillow talk."

Han looked up from the parchment in front of him. "Is this spell why the poor girl was murdered?"

"Indirectly," I said. "We've determined that she was headed north on the National Road within a few hours of her death. She was also carrying sensitive information she'd learned through her duties. Unfortunately, she'd given her own talisman to a worshipper to protect that person from Samael DiRoy. We are still investigating—"

"Wait!" Mya waved a hand for me to stop. "Did the worshipper know about last summer's treason?"

"No." I shook my head. "Not directly."

Han banged his gauntlet on the tabletop. "Let's cut the horse manure, Anthea. We're talking about one of the DiMara children, aren't we?"

I sighed. "Yes. Specifically, Lady Alessa. The former Lady DiMara—" Several of the convocation members made warding signs against evil. "—did unspeakable things to her own children. To my knowledge, Sister Gretchen did her best to protect Alessa."

"And Brother Luc confiscated Lady Alessa's talisman when he discovered that she managed to lie while under his truthspell," Mat offered.

I leaned forward. "High Mother Bianca?"

She uncovered her face. Her rage was there for all to see. Gerd should be thankful she was in my custody. "Yes?"

"Are there any more questions for Gerd's witness?"

"No," she ground out.

I looked at Mat, and he released the truthspell on DiCook

I stood. "If there is no further business for the convocation to pursue, I have matters within my own temple I need to deal with."

"Aren't you afraid to cross the street by yourself?" Bianca's sneer was back. Young Nathan's comments about the missing children whispered through my mind. Had she conspired with Gerd over other matters besides discrediting me? As much as I hated to think about such possibilities, I had too many other immediate problems.

Namely, what was Gretchen really carrying that someone was willing to murder me and kidnap Luc?

And the connection to everything snapped together. Gretchen had in her possession something far more dangerous than trading positions for the spring runs. Something that if she died, Luc and I would be the first to learn of it through her last declaration. And now that secret was out about Lady Alessa being Gretchen's heir, her life was at risk as well.

Mat looked up at me, the same way Luc would. He must have felt the subtle change in my demeanor. He stood as well and stated, "I've already guaranteed Justice Anthea's safety, Mother."

"As have I," Bertrice proclaimed.

"Our claws are hers to command," Jax's second said.

"She has my sword and those of my wardens as well," Han added.

Now wasn't the time to create more trouble by confronting Bianca about the street urchins. I had bigger problems to deal with at the moment. "Thank you, ladies, gentlemen." I formally bowed and swept from the room. DiCook and Mat were on my heels as we raced out of the building and ran down the street to the Temple of Love.

And behind us, Mother Bianca still hadn't said a word.

# Chapter 15

Han and Jax's second jogged right behind us. The wardens of Light and Balance as well as a contingent of the Magistrate's peacekeepers had been prepared to raid the Temple of Love the moment Little Bear and Tyra walked out of the Mother's Great Hall with Gerd.

I had made the correct call, but not for my original reasons. Thank the Goddess, Gina had the grounds secured by the time we reached it.

She met us outside, grinning. "All clear, Lady Justice. Their wardens are used to unruly drunkards, not a real fighting force."

I glanced at Mat and DiCook. "Find Dragonfly. We'll start with her." They followed Gina inside. I started after them, but Han laid a hand on my shoulder to stop me.

"What can we do to help, Anthea?" The chief priest of Conflict enjoyed the chaos of the moment. His enthusiasm smashed unintentionally against my mental shields. Jax's second hopped from foot to foot with her own excess energy after the convocation.

Where could the two orders do the most good? The tunnel system haunted me. I wasn't sure where the other end of Love's system might come out. None of us had a chance to search the architecture designs.

"What do either of you know about the tunnel system between the temples?"

"Tunnels? What tunnels?" Han's surprise matched my original feelings.

The Wildling priestess became more enthusiastic. "They've been abandon by the humans for ages. We used to play in them as children, but the high brother before Jax's predecessor forbade any of us down there after a cave-in killed a cub."

I placed a hand on her shoulder. "We need maps of what's passable and what's not. We especially need to know if any of them exit beyond the city walls."

Han stroked his beard. "You believe that's how the assassins got in?"

"A distinct possibility. I'm fairly certain it's how they're moving around the city," I said. Even as I spoke the words, I realized the tunnels were the only way the assassin could have gotten into the Temple of Light, and behind me, without the wardens in the main chamber noticing him.

Unless some of Luc's people were traitors—

No, I needed to stop thinking in circles and focus on one problem at a time.

I turned back to the priestess. "I apologize. I've forgotten your name."

"It's Farrah, and no, you didn't." She grinned. "Balance doesn't forget anything."

"I deserve that." I smiled back. "Tap Thief and Child for additional assistance. I don't want all of one order down there at the same time."

She jogged off in the direction of the two other temples.

"Something special for me?" Han sounded especially gleeful.

"Would you please have your wardens and priests assist the city guards in watching the gates?" I said.

He frowned. "Am I mistaken, or are you expecting some sort of invasion, Lady Justice?"

"If I had more specific information, I would share it with you, Brother." Something about his question bothered me. "May I ask the reason for your query?"

Han chuckled. "Because your instructions sound like the accounts of Justice Thalia's campaign against the pirates. If Balance hadn't claimed her, she would have made an excellent strategist in my order." He held out his hand.

I clasped it in return. "I appreciate the compliment. However, I'd prefer not to die this soon."

He nodded and pivoted to cross the thoroughfare. However, Bertrice puffed to a halt beside us, and Han paused. Her warden didn't look half as winded, though he also appeared to be a third of her age.

"What do you need from us?" The priestess huffed around each word.

"Can your wardens help the peacekeepers secure the perimeter of Love? I don't want anyone slipping out." Not that I thought Gina would allow such a thing to happen, but I didn't want to hurt Bertrice's feelings by denying her offer. "Also, would you allow Brother Han to examine the two corpses your temple retrieved from DiRoy's manor?"

"I sent word the one had to be salted." She had a slight questioning note in her voice.

"Yes, I was informed." I didn't know how to explain my gut feeling. "I want him to look for something more conventional. That isn't much to go on—"

She clapped my shoulder. "Absolutely, he can take a look." Bertrice grinned at both of us. "You definitely know how to cause a scandal, Justice. We haven't had this much excitement in years." She leaned close and whispered, "If I didn't know better, I'd say you were Justice Thalia reincarnated."

I wasn't sure how to take her comparison. Too many people had mentioned the woman who formerly held my seat, and it bothered me in some indistinct way.

However, I needed to focus on the present crisis. "Right now, I'll be satisfied to learn who killed Sister Gretchen, and I'm damn well going to find out."

After waiting patiently for my conversations with the other high priests to end, Gina escorted me to Dragonfly's quarters. Mat already stood guard inside her room.

Or his. From the loose silk trousers, the raid had caught Love's second by surprise. He hadn't donned his customary cosmetics or jewelry, so he looked very much male. Well, no jewelry except the heart-shaped ruby at his throat.

"What is the meaning of this, Justice?" He didn't bother altering his voice either. He stood defiantly in the middle of his bedchamber, fists clenched by his thighs.

I crossed my arms over my chest. "Your chief priestess was just caught committing fraud in front of a convocation of the Twelve."

His entire body sagged, and he groped behind him for a bedpost. He slowly folded to sit on the bed. "It's over." He almost seemed relieved. "I told her that insane scheme of hers wouldn't work."

"It's not completely over yet. I need to question you."

"I understand," he murmured.

I held out my hand. "The talisman, please."

He opened his mouth to protest, then closed it. The rising blood in his cheeks quickly drained away. "You know."

"Yes." I waggled my fingers. "The talisman."

He unhooked the chain and dropped it and the jewel in my waiting palm.

Mat wove the counter to the block as a precaution before he performed the actual truthspell.

And I repeated the same drill I had for the last six days.

"Did you kill Sister Gretchen?"

"No."

"Do you know who did?"

"No."

"When was the last time you saw her alive?"

"The evening of Second Day last week." His voice grew rough with grief. "When she came and asked me to run away with her."

That put an interesting crimp in Gretchen's thought processes. "Why did she want to run away?"

"She was pregnant. We'd been hiding it for some time. If Gerd knew, she'd force Gretchen to . . . to . . ."

My heart spasmed. "Stop the pregnancy," I whispered. Goddess help me, my mother couldn't let well enough alone. The decision should have been Gretchen's. No one else's.

Dragonfly nodded since I hadn't actually asked a question. He swiped away the few tears that had escaped.

"Was it yours?"

He inhaled deeply, trying to compose himself. "I don't know. It could have been. We weren't always careful."

"Did you know about Gerd's plan to ensorcel Magistrate DiCook?"

"Yes, and her plan to steal the declaration from you. When the men she hired failed to take it from you the other day, that's when she decided to use the magistrate."

I didn't want to ask the next question. "Which men?"

"The ones that tried to grab you as you were leaving the Temple of Light. The one who tried to cut your throat interfered."

The riders who very nearly trampled me to death as I escaped the assassin. Why in the Twelve's names would she risk a kidnapping in broad daylight? Worry crawled up my spine. "Did you know who these men she hired were?"

"No. I never saw them. She always disguised herself and met them at an inn. She wouldn't tell me which one."

"Did she hire or barter for the assassin who tried to kill me on the steps of Light?"

He shook his head. "Not that I know of."

"Did she hire or barter for someone to poison the Healing Guild's oil supply?"

"Not that I know of."

"Why didn't you report Gerd to another temple for her schemes?"

A rueful smile tilted his lips. "She threatened to have me castrated if I failed to obey. It's the same reason I didn't leave with Gretchen at first."

Mutilation of a person's private areas again. Just like the murdered priestess. Maybe my first instincts concerning Gerd had been correct after all. "What do you mean 'at first'?"

"I tossed and turned in bed after she left, berating myself for not having the courage to leave with her. Around third night, I dressed, packed a bag and snuck out after her."

"How did you get out of the temple without being seen?"

He waved a hand toward a bare spot between a cushioned couch and a mirrored cosmetics table with a matching bench. "There's a network of tunnels beneath the temples. The main tunnel ends at an inn on the Diplomatic Corridor near the Duke's Road." Dragonfly made a wry, amused sound. "A great many of our influential worshippers come and leave this way. I bought a horse and left Orrin."

And if I wagered, I'd lay the five cursed gold pieces in my pocket that the inn in question wasn't very far from the Jing ambassador's residence. "How did you get past the city guards?"

"I bribed them."

*DiCook will be overjoyed with this news. I'll have to truthspell him to confirm he knew nothing about the matter, and he will accuse the temples of framing him again.* "Then what did you do?"

"I rode north on the National Road. Near the Trill River Bridge, I found a discarded cloak at the edge of the cobblestones. Gretchen's." Grief roughened his voice again. "I dismounted and started searching. She was never the best rider, and I feared she'd fallen off her horse and was lying injured somewhere. I found her saddlebags further on in a ditch. I searched until moonset, but I never found her or her horse."

He sniffed back more tears. "I prayed to the Goddess she had come to her senses and gone back to the temple, so I returned, but she wasn't here."

This time of the month, moonset would be after first morning. An accomplished rider could have made it past the bridge after leaving Alessa at the duke's hunting lodge before Dragonfly reached it. But it didn't answer why her belongings were left behind.

"Are you absolutely sure you did not see, meet, or speak with Sister Gretchen of Love on the National Road between Orrin and the Trill River Bridge?"

He shook under my gaze. "No, I did not. I only found her cloak and her saddlebags."

Something didn't make sense. "How did you know they were hers?"

"I recognized the embroidery on the leather of the bags. I made the cloak for her."

"Did you tell Gerd she was missing?"

He bowed his head. "Yes. I know I shouldn't have. Gerd was livid. She sent the new wardens out to fetch her back, but none of them returned with her."

"New wardens? What new wardens are you talking about?"

Dragonfly pursed his lips before answering. "Since last summer, shortly after you were named chief justice of Orrin, Gerd started replacing our wardens and staff. She had turned completely paranoid." A wry smile twisted his lips. "I didn't understand why until you came to tell her about finding Gretchen's body."

The worry at the base of my neck started breeding. Wardens being replaced on that scale would be a major topic of gossip amongst the temple staffs. I glanced at Gina, but she gave a slight shake of her head.

I returned my attention to Dragonfly. "Do you know where she's finding these wardens?"

"No. I only know they aren't from the academy, and when I asked, Gerd refused to tell me."

"Do you know who put Gretchen's body in a wine barrel?"

"No."

"Do you know who kidnapped Brother Luc of the Temple of Light?"

Dragonfly blinked, and his face yellowed. "No."

"Do you know why they would want Brother Luc?"

Dragonfly exhaled as he thought. "I suspect—" He held up a hand. "I don't know this positively, but I suspect he was taken as a hostage against you."

"Why?"

He shrugged. "Something Gerd said once about you not escaping your nature. She didn't clarify."

Despite the terror squeezing my heart, I needed to put on a good show.

I sighed. "I'm afraid her associates have taken the wrong hostage." I smiled. "Trying to kill me gets more thorough attention." I sobered. "Trying to kill a child in my household will introduce them to the business end of my sword." Another sigh. "Did you know Gerd ordered someone to kill me?"

He gasped. "No."

I glanced at Brother Mat. Like Gina in the courtyard, he gave a slight shake of his head. I hoped he was right about the likelihood of a counter to the counter to the block not existing.

Returning my attention to Dragonfly, I asked, "What did you do with Gretchen's saddlebags and cloak? I have to account for all of her property."

This time red shame flooded his cheeks and ears. "I-I kept them. I was hoping I'd see her again. Give them back."

He rose and stamped on a wooden plank next to his bed. One end popped up. Once he pried three boards free, he pulled the saddlebags and cloak from his hidden hole.

The jolt along my nerves at the sight of the saddlebags nearly undid me. The leather of the right side was pure black in my odd vision. Blotches marred the left side and the woolen cloak as if they had been contaminated by whatever was in the demon-colored bag.

I'd seen such discoloration once before, from a casket aboard a merchant ship. The one that had carried a demon egg from Jing to Orrin.

"It's best not to use magic to hide things here," Dragonfly said, handing me the items. He didn't seem affected by the contamination, but neither did he directly touch the leather.

My heart tried to pound its way out of my chest when I grasped Gretchen's belongings, clinging to parts not marred by the absolute black. "Did you go through the bags?"

"No."

I laid the saddlebags and cloak on Dragonfly's bed. My mouth grew dry at the mix of dread and anticipation, but nothing happened to me when my fingers brushed the leather. The blotchy pouch I checked had smallclothes, a small purse of gold and silver coins, and some jewelry. Real jewels that she hadn't had time to convert to paste.

The second side held only one large object from the feel. Cold penetrated my fingers through my gloves when I touched the clasp. Cold so absolute it felt as if my soul had frozen. The tome I yanked out was a familiar color. Or absence of color. Just like the demons Samael DiRoy had summoned.

"Goddess!" Gina swore. "Is that what I think it is?"

"Yes," I whispered. "It's a tome of forbidden magic."

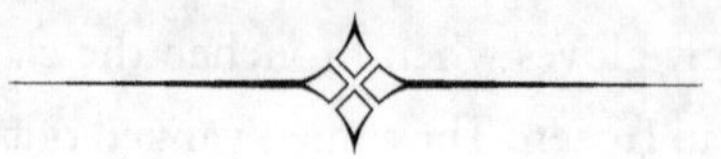

# Chapter 16

My worst nightmares had come true. I shoved the evil book back into the saddlebag. I couldn't breathe. This is what Gretchen was supposed to give Ambassador Quan. This was what my mysterious adversary thought I had when I seized Gretchen's property based on the declaration. I couldn't give something like this to either party.

Oh, Goddess, Luc was doomed.

"Justice, are you all right?" Gina asked.

"No," I ground out. "No, I'm not."

I looked up. Dragonfly was no longer beside his bed, but huddled in a corner with tears streaming down his face. Simple possession of the tome usually resulted in an automatic death sentence at the end of the trial.

"I didn't know." Sobs interrupted his words. "I swear I didn't know it was in there. I didn't look."

The electric nimbus of the truthspell still surrounded him. I strode over and crouched in front of him. "Did you know Gretchen had the book?"

"N-no." He shook his head vigorously. "She wouldn't use forbidden magic. It makes no sense. She was becoming a wealthy woman in her service here. She wouldn't—"

"Dragonfly." I grasped his hands and tried to make my tone as gentle as I could, but my own terror gibbered at the back of my mind. Shi Hua, the Jing priestess of Light, had been right last autumn. If two demon occurrences in Issura were more than a coincidence, then what on Death's door did another book of demon magic mean for us?

"Listen to me." I stroked Dragonfly's hands. "I need your help. Did anyone here at the Temple of Love have this book prior to Gretchen?"

"N-not that I knew."

This changed everything. I looked at Mat. "We need to question these new wardens first."

"Of course, Justice." His expression was grim. He knew as well as I that he'd just become the new chief priest of the Orrin Temple of Light.

I squeezed Dragonfly's hands. "I need you to write a full report for your Reverend Mother. She must know what's happening here in Orrin. Do not send it until I add the results of my investigation into Gretchen's death and my interrogation of Gerd. Understand?"

He nodded. "Yes, Justice." There was a pause as if he wanted to ask something, but he clamped his jaw shut.

"You're not charged with anything, Dragonfly. You answered under a truthspell and questioning by a chief justice that you didn't know. I'm not holding it against you."

A sad little smile curved his lips. "That's not going to stop the Reverend Mother of Love from expelling me."

I patted his hands. "Don't despair yet. This mess is not over." Except I was telling myself that as much as I was him. "I'll put in my recommendation that you stay here. If Orrin can have a sighted justice, they can certainly have a *berda* as a high sister."

Dragonfly grasped my hands and kissed the backs. He clung to my fanciful tale, which was enough for both of us. For now, anyway.

I stood, grabbed the saddlebags off the bed and slung them over my left shoulder. "Gina, stay with Sister Dragonfly for now. Luc's abductors may try to snatch her, thinking she knows more than she does."

Her curt nod said she wouldn't leave Dragonfly's side without mine or Little Bear's express order.

Mat dissipated the truthspell and followed me into the hallway. "What is your plan, Justice?"

I glanced at him. "Question these new wardens Gerd brought in."

"No, I mean . . ." He paused, and I stopped and turned back to face him.

"Kam didn't nominate me to replace him because I'm not ready. I'm still not ready. I want to get Luc back."

"That may not be possible." The agony in that admission twisted my heart even more.

"You've already given him up?" Mat stared at me, his disbelief evident. "What about creating a fake book? Like the fake declaration you and Sister Bertrice made? We use it to trade for Luc."

I sighed. I'd been doing that a lot today, but this time I wasn't acting. "Mat, the fake scroll used generic temple magic. Any priest or priestess could have created the falsified declaration. We would have to use demon magic to create a fake good enough to trick these renegades. From what little I know, and their actions over the past few days, they aren't fools." I took a step in the direction of Love's common room.

He grabbed my arm and pulled me to a halt. "So what if we trade the real book for Luc?"

I stared at him. Incredulous didn't begin to cover the emotion consuming me.

The priest released me and bowed his head. "Forgive my suggestion, m'lady. I-I just don't want to lose any more lives in this matter."

I continued down the hallway, and Mat resumed his pace at my side. "Neither do I," I said. "But if we trade this for Luc's life, he would never forgive either of us for the misery and destruction that would follow after any demons were unleashed."

We found the residents of Love in the main common room ringed with loyal wardens and peacekeepers.

DiCook marched over to me. "Brothers Jeremy and Kam have questioned about half the priestesses so far."

I closed my eyes and tried to rein in my frustrations that they started without me. "Why is Kam here?"

"Because we've already lost a quarter of our brotherhood," a too-familiar voice said.

I opened my eyes to find the elderly priest waddling in my direction.

"And it'll take Jeremy forever doing this by himself since you ran off with Mat this morning," Kam finished with a grin.

He had a point, but Dragonfly's revelations changed the puzzle of what was happening. "Who's the current head warden for Love?"

DiCook pointed to one of the men sitting on the floor. He sat with a small group apart from the rest of the male attendants. All had the metallic embroidery signifying their office as protectors of the temple. I crossed to the one the magistrate indicated while he, Mat and Kam trailed after me.

"What's your name?"

He matched my glare. "You have no right to be here, bitch."

The rudeness didn't bother me. I expected it. "I have every right when laws have been broken by your mistress."

His pulse jumped for two beats, then settled. This was someone experienced in deception, his breathing controlled.

I smiled. "But Gerd's not your true mistress, is she?"

The man surged forward. If I'd been better rested, fed, and not poisoned within the last three days, I could have avoided him easily.

Kam threw himself in front of me at the same moment DiCook jerked me backward. Sharp, honed indigo appeared in the fake warden's hand.

"Knife!"

But my warning came too late. A wet singing as the knife slashed into Kam's upraised lower arm. Instead of retreating, the elderly, rotund priest bowled into the assassin. They went down in a tangle of robes and limbs.

The fake wardens used the confusion and attacked. All of them focused on me.

No time to draw my sword. I swung the saddlebag weighted with the book. It smashed into the temple of the lead man. Mat leapt between me and the next with naked steel.

Fully half of the other retainers, both male and female, turned on the peacekeepers and Balance wardens in the room. What the assassins or I didn't expect were the Love priestesses joining the fray on our side.

Fingernails, hair pins and combs were their weapons of choice, and the women used them with brutal efficiency on eyes and exposed throats.

The fake warden, who tried to kill me first, kicked free of Kam. I swung the saddlebag again and caught him in the chin. He spun around. I caught a glimpse of the knife before he crashed to the floor. He was still. Terribly still.

As fast as the battle started, it was over.

The attendants who hadn't fought cowered next to the far wall under the watchful eyes of a few peacekeepers. DiCook and one of his men struggled to bind one of the surviving attackers. The rest were dead or dying.

Little Bear crouched next to the body of one of our wardens. His eyes met mine, and he shook his head before he covered the woman with his own cloak.

One of the Love priestesses, a woman with a mass of braids hanging down her back, looked at the others. At her nod, they all dropped whatever accessories they had been using as weapons and raised their empty hands. She turned to me. "We're not your enemy, Chief Justice. Gerd betrayed us."

A tremendous amount of anger lay in her words. I didn't want to think about the meaning behind them. What these women had suffered under the former high sister.

With the toe of my boot, I pushed my attacker onto his back. A pulse still throbbed in his neck, much too slow for the relatively minor slice in his side. His knife had glanced off the ribs, instead of penetrating his heart. He shouldn't be dying.

A sickly smile spread across the man's face. "You cannot stop us. The Temples' dominance is over." He choked, and foam bubbled out of his mouth.

*Goddess, there was poison on his knife!*

His pulse slowed and stopped, but his eyes continued staring at me.

"Kam!" I whirled around.

Mat tried to help the old priest to his feet, but his elderly muscles wouldn't cooperate.

Kam looked up at me, his expression an odd mix of amusement and sorrow. "I always wanted to go down in a good fight."

◆

I paced the Love priestesses' common room. Thief, in his guise as Fortune, must have smiled on us. The peacekeepers and the wardens only missed two of the poisoned weapons hidden on the imposters. The thought that this fight could have turned against us made me queasy. As if losing the old man wasn't bad enough.

The assassins, who hadn't died by our swords, took their own lives with hidden poison from the foam bubbling from their gaping mouths. All but the one DiCook and his peacekeepers had managed to subdue.

And now, Kam lay in Gerd's bedchamber. I would have prayed to my own goddess if I thought she would answer. There was nothing I could do to help, so I ignored everyone else waiting for word, and I paced.

After a quarter of a candlemark, Master Devin entered the common room. His expression said everything before the slight shake of his head. Cold grief rushed though the assemblage as swift as a mountain storm. I sat on a stool, before I collapsed on the floor, and bowed my head.

Devin cleared his throat. "We've made him as comfortable as we can. He's asked to speak with Justice Anthea privately."

I raised my head. "Me?"

"Yes. Don't argue with me, Anthea. He doesn't have time."

*Time.*

I wished there was a way I could control time, not just view it. Rewind to the point of the attack. Push the old fool out of harm's way.

Despite the numbness running through me, I managed to stand, then walk. Out of the common room. Down the hall. Into the chief priestess's quarters.

Kam didn't look right. His face was yellow-white with fever, instead of his usual cheerful orange. His hand atop the covers was already purplish-black. At his neck, his pulse throbbed with an obscene rhythm as his weak, old heart attempted to battle the necrosis of the poison.

Aaron rose from the chair at Kam's bedside. "I'll be outside if either of you need me." He clasped my shoulder in weak comfort as he shuffled past.

I stared at the shivering old man. I wanted to scream at him. Curse him. Shake some common sense into him

It should be me lying in a bed, dying.

Instead, I said, "You're a damned fool."

It was an awful, terrible thing to say. I knew it as soon as the words left my lips. I couldn't take them back.

Kam did the oddest thing. He laughed. He laughed so hard he started to cough and choke.

Despite my fury and sorrow, I rushed to his side and held him up. Wiped the blood-flecked phlegm from his mouth as gently as I could. Helped him sip some water when the fit passed.

I lowered him back to his pillow and adjusted the covers. Like the healers, there wasn't a thing I could do to stop the inevitable.

"You sound just like your grandmother," he said, his voice hoarse.

I patted his shoulder though he probably couldn't feel it. "I keep forgetting how long you've been here. So I assume Gerd didn't take after her mother?"

Another weak chuckle. "Light help me, Gerd and Thalia were as opposite as night and day."

I misheard him. Between my turbulent emotions and the harsh rasp of his voice, surely I had misunderstood.

He pushed aside the blankets and reached for my hand. I let him grasped it. His skin felt as dry and thin as an onion peel. And cold. So cold.

"Kept this secret for so long, but you should know." Another coughing fit took him. When it subsided, he squeezed my fingers. "You are so much like Thalia. The straight, dark hair. The high-cheekbones. The proud nose. I nearly had a heart attack the first time I saw you as an adult."

"Are-are you trying to tell me . . ." No, it couldn't be true.

"We never intended to conceive. Did everything to prevent it. But when Thalia learned she was pregnant, neither of us could even think of . . ." He sighed. "Given Gerd's behavior, I sometimes wondered if the gods cursed her because of our indiscretion."

This confession wasn't happening. And yet . . .

"But-but Mother grew up on a farm east of here. In-in the foothills." I had to deny him. I should get up and ward the room. Kam's story was a scandal waiting to explode in our faces. But I was afraid if I moved, he wouldn't finish.

That he would die before he *could* finish.

"Thalia knew a couple from when she rode the same circuit you did. We pooled our discretionary stipends to help the family with taking on an extra mouth." More coughing.

His face was white-hot with fever. He'd stopped sweating, and the cloth on his forehead was dry from its matching color.

I pulled free from his weak grasp. Wetness rolled down my cheeks as I wrung out the cloth in the bowl of cool water on his nightstand and replaced it on his forehead.

"Why didn't you stop her from entering temple service?"

"I wanted to, but Thalia pointed out we had given up the right to be her parents. Oh, your grandmother was so furious when she found out Gerd tried to end her pregnancy."

"How—" I licked my own dry lips while I helped him drink again. "How did Thalia—" I couldn't bring myself to say "grandmother" though a part of me desperately wanted to. Anything to hold onto Kam a few moments longer. "Hide her pregnancy? The way everyone watches me . . ."

"It wasn't easy. And we were very lucky it was an easy birth. Both Balance and Light were watching out for us that day."

"But her screams as the baby . . ."

"She delivered in the tunnel, my dear." He squeezed my hand again. "Once Thalia was safely in her own bed again, I took the child to the farm. The peacekeepers didn't question a junior priest on an early morning ride to the capital."

"Why didn't you tell me? You knew about me and Luc? Wh-why—" My voice broke and I found myself sobbing. I hadn't wept like this since those first weeks at the capital after I'd been sold.

"Oh, child, you know as well as I what would have happened if this became public. And you were always so rule-bound when you visited. I couldn't risk it. Even if you accepted the truth, I couldn't put you in a position where your feelings conflicted with your duty. When I figured out you and Luc were more than circuit partners, I thought, 'She's just like Thalia. She can't escape her nature.' And that's a compliment, my dear, not a condemnation."

A chill ran through me at the same words Dragonfly had quoted from Gerd, a chill similar to the one I felt from the book of forbidden magic. Had she learned who her birth parents were? Or had she known all along? Did she resent them so much that every little evil she'd done was some misguided attempt to punish them?

I choked "Then why tell me now?"

"Because I'm a selfish old man as well as a damn fool." Kam coughed up more blood before he said, "I did what I could to keep the two of you together. It's not natural for two orders to be chaste when the rest don't have to be. I wish . . ."

I carefully patted his arm, but more bruising blossomed on his fragile skin. "There's nothing to regret. What's done is done. I'm sorry I never had a chance to meet Thalia. I read about her in my classes."

"The two of you would have been close." He squeezed my hand. Or tried to. There was no strength left. His heart had worn itself out. Struggled for each beat.

"Do you want me to get Master Aaron or Master Devin?"

"There's nothing they can do for me, Anthea. Find Luc. Whoever took him will keep him alive until he gets whatever he wants from you. Then run away to Cant. It's what Thalia and I should have done the moment we learned she was pregnant."

I laughed, even as tears ran down my face. "I already tried. He wouldn't go."

"Try again," Kam whispered. He smiled, then sighed.

The beatific smile remained, but the spirit had departed.

I released my grip and placed his hand across his abdomen. The numbness I'd felt coming into this room was nothing compared to the disembodied sensation claiming me as I walked out.

In the common room, I held out my hand and Little Bear gave me the accursed saddlebags. "I need to return to our temple. Brother Mat, would you be kind enough to supervise the imprisonment of the surviving renegade so I may question him later? Also, Dragonfly is writing her report to the Reverend Mother of Love concerning today's incidents and will deliver copies to us. She is not to send it to the capital until I add our reports."

He nodded, but said nothing.

Of course, Mat already knew what I'd said to Dragonfly, but those words and the next of mine were intended to build some bridges. Balance knew we needed them. I shuffled over to the Love priestesses. I tried to meet the eyes of each of the women. "If any of you wish to add your individual statements to the main report, please feel free to do so."

The priestess who'd led the defense in the little skirmish stepped forward and bowed. "Thank you, Lady Justice."

*Kam is gone.*

I whirled and fled the temple before I started crying again. Little Bear said nothing, merely fell in step beside me. Once on the street, warmth caressed my face. The sun had pierced the gloom that had followed the storms earlier this week. From the direction of the heat, it was first afternoon. But the solar energy couldn't penetrate the ice that surrounded me.

The next thing I knew, I was in my office. I placed the saddlebags into my hiding place in the marble wall. The stone groaned in protest to the alien magic I shoved inside, but it sealed properly.

The sensation of being watched followed me to my bedchamber. I shed my formal robes and trousers for training clothes. Once I'd donned the thick cotton pants and shirt, I walked through the temple to the back courtyard.

Part of me knew I should send a messenger to the capital. Ask for another justice to hear the cases concerning the fake warden and Gerd.

I couldn't call her my mother. Not even to irritate her. Not anymore.

An ugly part of me wanted to feel my sword slice through her neck. She may not have wielded the blade that killed so many people, but her plots and schemes were the source.

I dragged a training dummy from the armory to the courtyard. A cool breeze blew from the west, harbinger of another storm. I hung the mannequin on the sparring rack. The vague feel of the sun on my back faded and the wind grew harsher and colder. I hit and kicked my silent opponent until bruises covered me and nothing was left but bits of rags, the shattered wooden frame, and a pile of sand.

My knees cracked against the cobblestones as the frigid rain started, thunder crashed, and I howled until all the dogs in the street chorused my grief.

# Chapter 17

I wasn't sure how long I knelt there. All I knew was that Tyra and Sivan came out to the courtyard after the cold rain soaked through my clothes. Neither woman said a word as they guided me back to my chambers.

A bath had already been drawn. They stripped the icy material off me. Tyra helped Sivan get me into the water, then left.

From the laurel fragrance, Sivan worked imported Aleppo soap into my sweat-and-rain-soaked hair. She was trying to comfort me, but her efforts only reminded me of what I'd lost. What I was about to lose.

Luc would never forgive me if I traded the thrice-damned book for him. Somehow Gerd had learned of the book. It was the only explanation for her replacement of Love wardens and staff.

Whoever Gerd had conspired with to obtain the book couldn't allow either Luc or me to live if I did trade the forbidden tome. And so many people had already paid with their lives to prevent anyone from getting the book even if they didn't know it. To think about trading would mock their sacrifices.

"If you allow yourself to be paralyzed, you've already let them win," Sivan said softly as she scrubbed my scalp.

"I know. I just can't feel a way out of this without more people dying."

"Aglaia's death was not your fault. Neither was Kam's."

*Aglaia. The warden whose corpse Little Bear had covered with his cloak. Gina is correct. I didn't bother to learn their names over the last six months. I treated the people here worse than I would treat Nassa.*

"You were right to be afraid," I whispered. If I spoke louder, the tears would start again.

Sivan's fingers paused. "If this is about what I said the other night—"

"No. And yes. Things *are* worse in Orrin than either of us believed. I just don't know how to make things right."

"You have already done several things right. You gave Nathan a second chance. You saved the Love priestesses from being abused by their own temple head. You protected Magistrate DiCook from mind enslavement—"

"Whereas Penelope would have hung them all on a gibbet." I couldn't stop the bitterness from welling into my words.

Sivan continued working soap through my hair. "One bad justice doesn't spoil the whole barrel, Anthea."

I snorted at her attempted levity. "Just the entire city of Orrin."

Her exhale said I was right, but she was tired of my bickering. "Tilt your head back."

I did so, and she poured a pitcher of warm water over my tresses to rinse out the soap.

*You are so much like Thalia. The straight, dark hair.* How I wish I could banish Kam's words. *Kam was my grandfather.* His admission of his and my grandmother's sins didn't change my opinion of him. After the initial shock, I was surprised how readily I took to the idea of him as family. Maybe I always had.

When Sivan finished rinsing my hair, I asked, "What would Justice Thalia have done in my place?"

She was silent for so long I turned to look at her. Finally, she shifted to sit on the tile floor. "I don't know. I'm only two winters older than you, a child when she died."

"Who would remember?"

Sivan smiled. "Deborah and Hogarth. Can you wash the rest of yourself, or do I need to bathe you like a child?"

"I think I can manage."

With a nod, she rose to leave.

"Sivan?"

She paused in the doorway and looked back.

"Thank you."

My assistant inclined her head once again. I could hear her bustling about the bedchamber, pulling out fresh clothing for me.

Sivan was correct. I couldn't let my fear paralyze me. It wasn't the first time I hated the decision I had to make.

And it wouldn't be the last unless I managed to get Luc out of this mess intact, and we fled Issura.

Once I'd donned my formal robes and eaten everything on the very full plate Sivan brought me, I sent out two messengers. By the time, I reviewed the dispatches and stamped my own reports to the capital temples of Balance, Light and Love concerning the current crisis, my guests had arrived.

I stood as Sivan escorted High Father Jerrod and Brother Mat into my office. "Thank you for responding to my request."

Jerrod sat in the chair next to the one Mat had already appropriated, and I resumed my seat as well. The father coughed discreetly. "The brother here has told me what happened after you left the convocation. I admit to a bit of surprise that you asked me to be your observer in the questioning."

I inclined my head at his acknowledgement. "Your temple was not involved in the raid on Love. Nor did it take sides during the convocation. I need a relatively objective observer of rank. It now appears that I may have to indict Gerd for conspiracy in the death of former High Brother Kam, the abduction of High Brother Luc, the two attempts on my life, not to mention the poisoning at the Healers Guild."

Jerrod relaxed against the back of his chair and stroked his beard. "While I do not mean to tell you how to perform your duties, given that Gerd is your birth mother and you are the assassins' target, should you not recuse yourself?"

I tapped the parchment on my desk. "I totally agree with your assessment, and I've started to prepare the request for another justice." I leaned forward and rested my elbows on the smooth wooden desktop. "But an answer from my Reverend Mother will take four days at the minimum, assuming no winter storms delay the couriers. I don't think High Brother Luc has four days."

"The Temple of Light cannot afford to lose another priest," Mat added. "We're down to Brother Jeremy and me, and neither of us are senior-ranked."

Jerrod grimaced. "This is a fine mess Gerd's left us with, isn't it?" He eyed me. "I trust we'll have no more shenanigans like the fake declaration of last wishes."

I shook my head. "No, High Father. With a score of dead bodies on my plate, including a priest and a priestess, I can't afford to be frivolous anymore."

After I'd reviewed all the pertinent facts with the two priests and I'd retrieved the illegal tome from my safe, the three of us and Donella headed down to the gaol. Little Bear and Tyra were already there. They hadn't found a ruby talisman on Gerd. Luc had said any object would suffice for the blocker. She could have swallowed that object or . . .

I really didn't want to think about where else she could have put it.

"I should have strangled you with your birth cord," Gerd spat when we entered her cell. She wore the standard gray shift, and her only jewelry was the spell-threaded manacles Little Bear and Gina had placed on her wrists and ankles.

Jerrod stepped closer to her. "You're not helping your cause, Sister Gerd."

"It's High Sister to you," she snarled. "And my cause? You know nothing of my cause."

"Do it," I said to Mat.

Once again, he wove the counter to the block before he laid on the truthspell. We simply couldn't take any chances, not with Luc's life at stake. The tingle of Mat's spell surrounded her.

As much as I didn't want to hear the answers from her mouth, I had to lay the foundation for her actions. The first few queries concerning her training and rank were easy. I steeled my emotions against the answers to the next questions.

"Did you become pregnant at your first Spring Ritual?"

"Yes."

"Did you try to abort the pregnancy?"

"Yes."

"Were you aware that stopping a pregnancy achieved during the Spring Rituals is illegal?"

"Yes." I didn't think her tone could become any more venomous, but it did.

"How did you try to stop the pregnancy?"

"I swallowed an herb and mushroom mixture."

"Where did you obtain this mixture?"

"I went to an herbalist."

"Why did this herbalist give you the ingredients, given the timing of your pregnancy?"

"I used magic to make it appear the baby was already dead." Gerd slapped her hands over her mouth.

I swallowed a smirk at her expression of horror. Odds were she did have a talisman secreted in a body cavity, and she believed it would protect her from my interrogation. "Is this the first time you've admitted what really happened concerning your pregnancy?"

She fought the truthspell until the fire in her belly grew too great. "Yes," she gasped.

I crossed my arms over my chest. "This will go a lot faster if you stop fighting us. Your block no longer works."

"How? How did you find out about the block?" From the ugly look she shot me, I would be dead if she weren't chained. "I know it wasn't DiCook who told you first."

"Ironically, we found out through Sister Gretchen. We also know the counter to the truthspell block. Brother Mat disbursed copies to the seats after you were arrested and removed from the convocation. The information has also been dispatched to all twelve temples at the capital."

"You bitch!" She lunged, but the chains brought her up short. "Do you have any idea of what you've done?" Her face was ugly with rage.

I gave her an equally ugly smile. "Balanced the scales. Was I the baby you tried to murder?"

"Yes." She didn't try to hide her loathing or her answers now.

"Did you lie about the reason you tried to abort the pregnancy?"

"Yes."

"Did you use the truthspell blocker?"

"Yes."

"How did you learn about the truthspell blocker?"

"I learned it from my predecessor, High Sister Elora."

"Does the rest of the Love temples know about the blocker?"

"Yes."

I reached into the satchel slung over my chair and pulled out the book of forbidden magic. "Is this the source of the truthspell blocker?"

"No." But a hint of recognition flickered in her pulse.

"Have you seen this particular book of forbidden magic before?"

"Yes."

"When?"

She fought the truthspell again, writhing until she was prostrate on the floor. "Last month."

"When specifically did you see it?"

Her loud pants filled the space between her words. "Third day of the first week."

"Where?"

Gerd screamed. I had my suspicions, but I had to know for sure. She couldn't be allowed to pass out. I waved a hand. Tyra dipped a cup into the bucket we kept for such purposes and splashed water onto Gerd's face.

She gasped and spluttered. "My temple."

Someone had to be helping her, and it wasn't Dragonfly as I originally thought. So who was it? Dammit, I hated guessing games, but I had nothing else unless I named every person currently living and working in Orrin.

I left my seat and crouched next to her. "You have a choice. Either stop fighting the spell and answer my questions fully, or I release you and spread the word that you've named Mother Bianca as one of your co-conspirators for clemency."

A shrill laugh erupted from Gerd. "So?"

So much for my attempt at bluffing. "Did you conspire with Mother Bianca to murder Gretchen?"

"No."

"What did you and Mother Bianca conspire over?"

Gerd smirked. "Getting rid of you. But it was more manipulation on my part. She's not very bright."

"I'm sure she will be happy to hear your assessment," I said dryly, resuming my place on my stool. "Given that you are a high sister, a copy of the proceedings will be available to the other seats."

Her pleased expression turned sour.

I tapped my forefinger against my chin. "Not to mention, Ambassador Quan wants Sister Gretchen's murderer to pay for her death."

"Quan has more than one toy in this city. I doubt he even let his bed grow cold. Any sympathetic story he gave you was just that, Justice." Gerd drew out my title until it become a sneering insult.

Obviously, she didn't know Gretchen's planned escape route, but she was right about Quan having no lack of bedmates. The ambassador still needed to answer for lying to me about what Gretchen was to pass to him. I thought we'd reached an accord after I'd saved his life last fall. Apparently, the sentimentality was only on my part.

"Did you conspire with Ambassador Quan of Jing to murder Sister Gretchen?"

"No," she spat.

"There's always High Brother Dav from the Temple of Light in Tandor. I'm sure he would be interested in your role concerning Gretchen's death."

Her pulse spiked. "No! Y-you wouldn't!"

That was an interesting response, and I hadn't even asked a question. It could also explain how Luc's abductors obtained the Temple of Light robes.

"Why are you afraid of Brother Dav?"

"I-I'm not." Her stammer wasn't caused by the truthspell.

"Did you conspire with Brother Dav to kill Sister Gretchen?"

"No."

"Did Brother Dav kill Sister Gretchen?"

"I-I don't know."

"Does he have a reason to kill Gretchen?"

"I don't know," she spat.

"Do you have a reason to kill Gretchen?"

"Yes!"

Before I could ask the follow-up question, she continued. "That bitch poisoned him against me. And you're adding to it!"

"Oh, my dear Sister," I purred. "The worst I can do to you is separate your aging, wrinkled head from your equally aging, wrinkled body. My guess is Dav won't be as gentle after he finds out your role in her death."

"I had nothing to do with it!"

I ignored her protest. "And after manipulating Bianca and abusing your own priestesses, no temple in Orrin will give you sanctuary. What other city would take you after they learn what you've done? And even if you manage to escape Issura, I'm sure Jing agents will be very interested in you. Ambassador Quan was quite miffed that you cheated him."

She made furtive little movements, frantically searching for an escape, even though I didn't specify what she'd swindled out of the Jing ambassador. But there were six opponents in the cell, she was manacled and her talent inhibited. I would have sworn I saw the realization of her predicament sink into her, past the aura of the truthspell. "I yield. Ask your questions."

"Did High Brother Dav of Tandor give you this book?"

"No."

"Who gave you the book?"

"A Jing noble gave it to me in return for me providing—providing—" She was fighting the spell again.

"For providing what?" I prompted.

"Children for his use." She panted.

I nearly choked on my own bile. Was that what Nathan meant about the missing street urchins? "Who was the Jing noble?"

"I never learned who it was. He remained veiled. A clerk translated." Things could get much worse if Quan was the noble involved. I heard of his odd proclivities in bed play, but the fishwives never mentioned he had interest in children.

"Do you have reason to believe the noble was Quan?"

"No."

"Why not?"

"His concubine came to my temple asking about Jing artifacts I may have come across."

Disappointment was the only name for the emotion spurred by Gerd's words. I had been stupid to trust the ambassador and Shi Hua. What game were those two playing?

"Did you tell her about the forbidden grimoire?"

"No."

"What did you do instead of turning the grimoire over to me?"

"I quietly tried to find a buyer."

"Who?"

"A merchant from Tandor."

Tandor again. "What is his or her name?" I growled.

"Ural DiSand."

"Was he buying it for himself?"

"I don't know."

"Was he acting as a broker for someone else?"

"I don't know." Sullenness was settling in. Fighting the truthspell had sapped Gerd's strength.

"What payment did you receive?"

"I didn't receive any payment."

"Why not?"

"Because that bitch Gretchen stole the grimoire!" Despite the manacles, the power inherent in Gerd's voice cracked the mortar in the floor.

"How do you know it was Gretchen?"

"I-I don't know for sure, but she'd do anything to discredit me."

"Are you sure the book was stolen?"

"Yes, it disappeared from my safe hole."

"Any priestess from your order can access their temple safe hole."

She glared at me, but said nothing because I hadn't asked a question.

I swallowed and tried again. "Can any priestess from your order access your safe hole?"

"No."

"Why not?"

"I set a curse on the safe hole to kill anyone but me." So was that part of the problem between Gerd and Gretchen? The younger woman had more magical talent than the older?

"So how did Gretchen access the safe hole if you set a curse?"

"The curse was deactivated. She and Dragonfly were the only ones talented enough to do it."

I pretended to consider Gerd's answer. Obviously, she didn't realize I'd already questioned her second. "So what makes you think it was Gretchen and not Dragonfly?"

"Because I had that sniveling *berda* under my heel. She knew what I'd do to her if she crossed me."

"Do you mean castrate her?"

"Yes," Gerd hissed. Another charge against her to add to the growing list. Would my substitute justice in this case lash Gerd for threatening a fellow priestess before she was executed for everything else?

"What were you supposed to receive for the book?" I asked, returning to her dealing in demon goods.

A vicious smile this time. "My weight in gold and your head on a platter."

# Chapter 18

I did my best not to show any emotion. Despite the animosity in her voice, her answer didn't match the facts. She hadn't delivered the book to her buyer, so why the recent attempts on my life? An assassin from the Guild didn't work for free.

"Let's go back to your previous statement. You said the book was stolen. When did you learn it was missing from the temple safe hole?"

"Two weeks ago."

About the same time Gretchen had deposited her last declaration with the Temple of Death. What had that girl been up to? Why not turn the grimoire and Gerd over to me or Luc? It would eliminate her rival. Or was Gretchen just as power hungry for demon magic as the late, unlamented Samael DiRoy had been? No, she intended to flee to Jing with at least one of the people closest to her.

But if she asked both Dragonfly and Alessa to accompany her into exile, why did she ask Quan for only two passages on the ship?

Maybe because Gretchen knew in her heart Alessa wouldn't abandon her family. Gretchen asked Dragonfly first and when she refused, then Gretchen had gone to the noblewoman.

I set aside my concerns for Alessa and Dragonfly. Gretchen was beyond my reach, but not so the woman before me. And something prodded the back of my mind concerning Gerd's reaction when I mentioned the Jing ambassador. "What did you cheat Quan out of?"

She sighed. "Gretchen was unavailable one night, so I sent a serving girl to him in return for his worship donation."

"You sent an untrained child to him?" One of the worst stories about the man popped into my mind.

Gerd sniffed. "She was the age of adulthood. He paid the going rate for a virgin, and that's what I gave him."

The urge to slap her rose behind the gorge in my throat. I clenched my hands into fists in order not to give in to the stupid impulse. I wasn't about to be lashed for striking her.

Instead, I took a deep breath and focused on the next line of questioning. "When did you start replacing your wardens and servants with outsiders?"

Gerd emitted a small grunt of pain before she said, "When I received the book." Last month. Her statement matched the other Love priestesses' accounts.

"Who were these replacements?"

"Most were mercenaries."

"Why did you hire mercenaries?"

"To keep those silly girls in line. If one of them found out that I had the book, they would have reported me."

As well they should have, but I managed not to give voice to that thought. "Were all of the replacements mercenaries?"

"No. The remainder were from the Assassins Guild."

A terrible thought occurred to me, one that added to the chill of Kam's death on my soul. "Where did the relieved wardens go?"

Gerd's coloring turned a sickly yellow-green. Her gaze dropped to her lap. "Nowhere."

It took all my will not to reach for my sword or knives. "Where are their bodies?"

"I'm not sure," she whispered. "All they would tell me is that they were disposed of."

From the corner of my vision, Father Jerrod looked like he was about to lose his dinner, but he remained silent.

"How did the mercenaries and assassins get into the city?"

"I issued work orders."

The peacekeepers wouldn't question documentation from one of the temples, but it didn't preclude the fake wardens from sneaking through the tunnel system, especially since Love used it extensively. Gerd's admission made me wish I'd included DiCook in questioning her. If nothing else to childishly taunt him for his people's failure, which was petty of me. And it wasn't the peacekeepers fault if a high sister had provided valid paperwork. I quashed the foolish need to gloat, and gathered the thread of my interrogation.

"Why did you hire members of the Assassins Guild instead of more mercenaries?"

"I didn't."

"Who did?"

"Ural DiSand."

My eyebrow rose. "Why would you give a merchant from another city control of your temple?"

"I didn't," she spat.

"Then why did you allow him to place assassins inside Love?"

From the rhythm of her pulse and her coloring, Gerd's fear shone in the dark cell. "DiSand said he'd kill me if I didn't. He insisted on it after Gretchen stole the book." She said the word "book" as if we were simply talking about a tome of history or poetry, not something one could be executed for possessing.

"Were the assassins there to search the Temple of Love for the demon grimoire?"

"Yes."

I leaned back and turned to Mat. He shivered under my gaze but remained silent. I couldn't depend on his counsel the way I could Luc or Kam's. My chest tightened in grief and fear, but I pushed them away. Someday, I would pay for my denial of my emotions, but for now, I needed a clear head.

Turning to Gerd, I continued. "What is the connection between this Ural DiSand and Brother Dav of Tandor?

"Dav would disguise himself as part of DiSand's caravan coming up from Cant."

"And why would Dav do so?"

"He used to visit me."

At the broken sadness in her voice, I almost felt sorry for her. Almost, until she added, "Or he did until he went to fuck that bitch Gretchen because I was too old for him." The vehemence in her voice could have peeled my skin off.

It took all my training to remain impassive, both from Gerd's spite and the realization of what Gretchen had foolishly done. Ironically, if she'd simply stolen the book from the high sister and delivered it straight to Ambassador Quan, she might still be alive.

"Did you kill Sister Gretchen of the Orrin Temple of Love?"

"No."

"Do you know who did?"

"No."

"Did you tell Ural DiSand that Gretchen had stolen the book?"

"No."

"Who did you tell that Gretchen had stolen the book?"

"Dragonfly and Marston."

I cocked my head. "Who is Marston?"

"The leader of the guild assassins at my temple."

I held up the sketch that Bertrice's clerk had done of the imposter who drawn his knife on me and killed Kam. "Is this him?"

"Yes."

I wanted to scream curses at the Twelve for losing a valuable prisoner. The doomed fight he and his people put up in Love made sense. They knew they couldn't escape me through conventional means. It almost made me wish I could raise the dead to question them.

Almost.

I could have sworn the grimoire whispered behind me, responding to my rage and offering to show me how to manipulate the dead. Instead, I took a deep breath to calm my anger. "Did Marston and his people search Gretchen's room?"

"Yes."

"Did they question Gretchen?"

"Yes."

"When?"

"Two weeks ago when the grimoire first went missing. Then again, Fourth Day last week."

The story became clearer. Marston and his men had to have caught the priestess between the hunting cabin and the Trill River Bridge. It explained the discarded cloak, and especially the saddlebags. "Did Gretchen use the counter to the truthspell when she was questioned?"

"Yes." So she had more than the talisman she'd given to Alessa.

"How do you know she did?"

Gerd crumpled. "Because Marston said she didn't tell them a thing, not even when they tortured her."

"How did they torture her?" I didn't want to know. Goddess knew I didn't.

Gerd swallowed hard. "They paralyzed her body and they-they—" She leaned to the side and vomited. This wasn't the truthspell, but her own horror at the events she'd set in motion.

Or maybe the realization that this Marston would have done the same to her.

Once she wiped her mouth on the shoulder of her shift, she whispered "First all the men he took raped her. Th-then their leader raped her with a knife."

The scratching of Donella's quill halted. This was the most egregious case I'd dealt with. I could only imagine what was going through the mind of my very young clerk.

And Gerd's testimony made me re-evaluate my opinion of the dead priestess.

I swallowed the bile at the back of my throat. "You said Marston was the leader of the fake wardens."

"He's in charge here, but he reports to someone else."

"Who?"

"I don't know. They were careful never to say his name in my presence."

"You also said you didn't know who killed Gretchen."

"I don't know who actually killed her. Marston didn't tell me."

"Why didn't you tell Marston about the counter to the truthspell?"

"Because I knew it was the one way I could stay alive," she whispered again.

Finally, the odd events over the last several days formed a coherent pattern. But if Gretchen had given her talisman to Alessa months ago, how did she get another one?

"Can you trigger the counter without having the talisman to carry the spell?"

Gerd sighed. "No. We know how to make new talismans. To do so is part of our initiation."

"Do any of the Love priestesses give these talismans to others?"

"Rarely, but sometimes."

"Have you ever given a talisman to someone outside of Love?"

"No."

"When did you discover Gretchen was gone?"

"Third Day last week, the day she ran away. Marston—" Gerd sucked in a deep breath and released it. "Marston visited her room to rape her again." She glanced up at me. "The normal method." Her eyes lowered. "Gretchen had started sleeping with Dragonfly to avoid him. When I went to Dragonfly's room, Gretchen wasn't there either, and Dragonfly said she hadn't seen her."

"Was Dragonfly truthspelled?"

"No, but I knew she was lying."

"Did you tell that to Marston?"

"No."

"So Marston rode after Gretchen."

Despite my statement, Gerd spoke. "Yes. After they left, I went back to question Dragonfly, but she was gone, too."

The timing fell into place. Gretchen's assignation with Alessa allowed Marston to catch up with her. She shed her cloak to buy time before she tossed the grimoire into the ditch, probably planning to come back for it.

Possibly throwing a temporary veiling spell over the saddlebags as well. Marston and his men caught her and took her someplace secluded, which was why Dragonfly only found the saddlebags and cloak along the National Road. Or he found them after Gretchen had been strangled and her veiling spell failed.

With the length of time between Marston's departure and return along with the fact that Dragonfly hadn't encountered them, Marston and his cronies probably were disposing of the body. It may have been purely an accident that the barrel she was stored in ended up at Duke Marco's estate and was tapped so close to her death.

Or Marston and his men had killed the wagoner and his partner and planted the barrel on purpose to keep me distracted while they tried to find the grimoire.

*Except there's no such thing as coincidences*, the ghost of Luc's voice whispered in my mind.

Maybe Marston and his accomplices were hoping to implicate me in the incident to get me out of the way. When that didn't work, they resorted to the more direct approach.

I leaned back on my stool. The mutilation of Gretchen's body made more sense. I'd run into men like Marston before, the ones who took what they wanted. Men who enjoyed inflicting pain and terror.

"Do you know how Gretchen died?"

"She was strangled. Marston said there were already bruises on her throat. He said the paralytic had worn off. H-he laughed about how she fought at the end." Maybe there was some sense of morality underneath Gerd's vicious veneer. She actually sounded sorry for the younger priestess.

Or maybe she feared she would share the same fate.

"Did Marston strangle Gretchen?"

"I don't know. He never actually stated that he was the one who killed her."

"Did you know about the bruises through any other person or method than Marston?"

"No."

Her answer was reassuring in that I didn't have a direct leak to Gerd from my inner circle. The assassins and the connection to Tandor still bothered me.

I cleared my throat. "Did Marston and his men come back to your temple after they found Gretchen?"

"Yes."

"When?"

"Two days after they left. When she didn't have the book with her, they—" Gerd swallowed hard. Was that a hint of remorse? "Came back to Orrin."

"What did Marston and his men do when they returned?"

Her voice was tear-filled. "They said if I didn't produce the book within a fortnight they would torture me the same way they tortured Gretchen." Of course. Nothing mattered to her but self-interest. However, the threat explained Gerd's desperation over the last few days.

I continued to question her, but she didn't know of any link between DiSand, Dav and the plot to overthrow the queen last summer. Neither did she have any knowledge of what the dying assassin meant about the end of the temples.

My back and leg muscles protested when I climbed to my feet. Mat dispersed the truthspell.

As I reached the door of the cell, Gerd said, "Don't you want to know who your real grandparents are?"

I looked at her over my shoulder. If that was her only bargaining chip, then she was truly desperate. "I already know. You can't hurt them. They're both dead."

My statement seemed to shake her. "Kam's dead?"

"Your little band of assassins masquerading as wardens made sure of it this morning."

"That wasn't—they weren't supposed to—"

"What? Kill him before he saw me die? Is that how you planned to punish your own father?"

"He threw me away like I was trash!" Sobs racked her body. For the first time, it wasn't anger or hatred that consumed me when it came to Gerd DiLove. It was pity.

"He found a couple willing to love and cherish you. He didn't sell you to the highest bidder."

Her sobbing screams became incoherent, and I walked away.

Jerrod blew out a deep breath as Little Bear locked the cell door behind us. "I'm sorry, but I have to ask, Justice. Is what Gerd said true?"

I stared at the ceiling. The truth couldn't hurt anyone but me.

"Yes." My laugh tasted as bitter as it sounded. "Brother Kam confessed moments before his death. I'm cleaning up two generations of my birth family's mistakes."

"Is Kam's lover really dead?"

I considered the situation for a moment. Did the circumstances of my mother's conception matter any more? What could the Reverend Mother of Balance or the Reverend Father of Light possibly do? And there had already been enough scandal lately that a little bit more wasn't going to change the situation. "Gerd's mother was Justice Thalia."

Jerrod stroked his beard. "That explains much."

"How so?"

He shook his head. "Nothing that matters now."

"It mattered to you at some point," I said softly.

"The rumors she spread about you and High Brother Luc. Misplaced rage at the circumstances of her birth." Jerrod patted my shoulder. "I should have known better. You have my apologies for even entertaining such a despicable tale."

"Apology accepted." I sighed. I didn't need a truthspell to know Gerd had concocted what she thought was a lie to ruin my already non-existent reputation. Weariness yanked at the fragile threads of my composure, but personal concerns needed to be set aside. "Shall we question the surviving assassin?"

The six of us trooped down the short hallway. Gina unlocked the next cell door, and muttered an oath before she rushed in. The assassin lay on the floor, his limbs oddly contorted and foam flecking his open mouth. She

reached out to check the pulse of the man, but I snatched her hand back
before she made contact with the cool body.

When she looked at me askance, I said, "Poison. He may have smeared
it on his skin. I don't need to lose anyone else."

"This is impossible," Little Bear growled. "I followed your orders, Justice. Brother Mat and I checked on him not two candlemarks ago."

"I'm afraid to ask where he hid the poison," Mat said dryly.

I would have laughed if Jerrod hadn't snapped, "That remark is highly
inappropriate, Brother."

Both Luc and Kam would have laughed at the younger priest's black humor, too. My vision swam at that thought. I blinked away the wetness and
straightened as Gina also stood. "He could have used a slower acting poison
while we were still at the Temple of Love if his duty was to ensure all of his
fellows were dead instead of captured."

Gina surreptitiously wiped the hand, with which she had been about to
touch the corpse, on her uniform trousers. "What do we do now, Justice?"

"There's one member of this perverted farce available." My old black humor resurfaced even though it would probably offend Father Jerrod, and I
smiled. "I need to have a little talk with Ambassador Quan."

# Chapter 19

This time I didn't plan a raid. I simply assigned wardens to watch and make note of who entered and left the Jing Embassy before I returned the cursed book to the safe in my office.

Maybe I didn't want anymore blood on my hands. The reality was we were rapidly running out of reliable wardens. Had any of the other temples been infiltrated? Were other wardens compromised? Were any of my own wardens part of this insanity? Was I trusting the wrong people in this Balance-forsaken city?

There was one thing I knew with certainty at the moment. Quan had lied to me about what Gretchen was supposed to deliver to him. I needed to find out who the other players were in this mummers' drama. However, the last thing I wanted was to battle both Quan's personal sorcerer, assuming he'd replaced the previous one by now, and his concubine, who was a disguised priestess of Light.

A priestess.

Of Light.

At first, the concept seemed alien. But as Luc had pointed out when I told him about Shi Hua's private visits to me, a female adherent to the god of Light was no stranger than a sighted justice.

Father Jerrod and Brother Mat insisted on accompanying me as I strode toward the courtyard where my horse waited. When I protested, Mat said, "You've made it clear you have a death wish from the first time I met you. Today is not the day. As you've pointed out, too many lives are at stake."

*Lives at stake.*

Oh Goddess! In the chaos surrounding the raid on Love, I'd forgotten I made Lady Alessa a target by having Donella post Sister Gretchen's last declaration.

I whirled to face them and held up a hand. "No."

"But—" Jerrod started.

"No," I repeated. "I can handle the ambassador. I have before. Brother, I need you to go to the duke's estate and bring Lady Alessa back here. Since she is Gretchen's rightful heir . . ."

The younger priest's color turn a sickly yellow as my meaning sunk in, and he uttered several rather inventive oaths.

However, Jerrod turned brilliant scarlet. "Whoever's truly behind this web of intrigue will think she has possession of that cursed book."

I nodded. "And outside of you two and Sister Dragonfly, only those in my temple know I have impounded it for evidence. I would appreciate your discretion for now, gentlemen."

"Of course, you have it," Jerrod exclaimed.

"Thief help you with the ambassador," Mat murmured as he clasped my hand. They quickly strode down the hall toward the main doors of the temple.

"So what is the plan, Justice?" Little Bear had become glued to my side. "An official visit to the Jing Embassy as we have before?"

"Not this time." I pivoted and aimed for the courtyard doors.

"What I don't understand is why the abductors haven't sent a demand for the book in return for Brother Luc?" Little Bear's boots stepped in rhythm with mine.

"Because the odds of them actually getting it are better if they're dealing with Lady Alessa. Or trying to ransom her to Duke Marco. Gerd spreading the rumor that Luc and I are bedmates is what got him nabbed." I glanced at the warden. "If you kidnapped a high brother based on erroneous information, what would you think the chief justice in question would do?"

"You wouldn't trade the book," he said grimly. "You'd hunt them down."

"Exactly," I replied. Except part of me considered cutting a deal. The part of me that would die when Luc did.

When we stepped outside, we discovered the storm that had started shortly after Kam's death had intensified, as if the Twelve themselves grieved for him. Hogarth waited inside the stable for us with Nassa and Little Bear's steed both saddled. Sometimes, I wondered if he had a bit of precognitive talent, though according to his record, he had none.

He clicked his tongue against his teeth as Little Bear and I mounted. "We'll have ice before morning, m'lady. I don't recommend going out tonight."

I smiled at him. "It can't be helped."

He patted my knee, which shocked me. In the time I'd known him, he'd never been inappropriate. In fact, I would have believed etiquette was his true religion. "Ya cain't bring the old man back by killing yerself, Anthea. Don't make his sacrifice a vain one."

He knew. Of course, he knew. I suspected bawdy songs that dishonored Thalia and Kam's memories were being sung in the inns even as we spoke. Probably the entire city knew and in a matter of days, so would the entire queendom. Another wave of guilt engulfed me.

"I won't." I tried to sound reassuring.

Hogarth stared at me for a moment before he pushed open the stable door, wide enough for Little Bear and me to ride out single file.

When we reached the main thoroughfare, Little Bear didn't say a word when I turned south instead of north. I'd decided to take Shi Hua's example.

The heavy rain and wind died as we made our way back to the Temple of Love. But as the drops slowed, the air grew colder. The world turned to a blur of purplish gray, marked only by the torches and lamps of the temples.

No one would question another visit to Love after this morning's raid. Gina nodded as we entered. She and a handful of wardens gleaned from the other temples would serve until the capital could assign replacements.

At some point, I needed to ask Bertrice and Jax what we could possibly do to find the murdered Love wardens.

The manner of the surviving loyal servants was subdued as we dismounted and were guided to Dragonfly's quarters. In fact, both the temple itself and the outbuildings were relatively quiet. The priestesses and attendants we passed murmured greetings.

It was odd seeing them working together to clean the mess that this morning's battle left in smeared blood and broken furniture. I wondered how much things would change under Dragonfly's leadership. If she would be allowed to stay.

When the handmaid announced us, the acting high sister of Love looked up from the huge parchment that covered the table in the center of her quarters. Jax's second, Farrah, finished scribbling something on the surface.

Dragonfly was dressed in the attire of a city matron. Come to think of it, none of the priestesses had been wearing their formal robes when we passed through the receiving area and the hallways. That was part of the reason for the quiet. Those damn bells they wore jingled constantly.

"Was there something wrong with the reports I sent you, Justice?"

"No. They were all very thorough." I frowned. "Are all of you renouncing your vows?"

She laughed, a sad, wry sound. "No, but given the circumstances, I thought it best to close the temple to official business for the next fortnight. We . . . took a vote. You saw our presentation to our Reverend Mother. We're waiting for her answer."

"I understand."

Ironically, Gerd's machinations had actually united the priestesses behind Dragonfly's nomination as the new high sister. Contrary to what Lady Katarina had told me, the *berda* had done quite a bit to ameliorate the worst of my birth mother's predations, according to the statements from the other priestesses.

And every single one of them had written a statement regarding the events under Gerd's governance. None of them flattering to her either.

I grinned. "Would you and the others be so bold if it weren't the dead of winter?"

Dragonfly smiled in return. "Probably not. But we hope to have the matter settled before the spring sailing season." And the lack of income during the temple's busiest season would cut into the order's coffers by nearly a quarter. Only the capital's temple brought in more gold.

While the possibility of the first *berda* high sister would be an interesting intellectual discussion, there were other, far deadlier matters I had to deal with.

"I need access to your tunnel."

Farrah jumped into the conversation. "We've only mapped a quarter of the suspected warren today, Lady Justice." She tapped the parchment, a map I couldn't see.

Little Bear braced his hands on the table and leaned over. "You're focusing on the outer temples first?"

"Yes." Farrah's forefinger traced lines invisible to me. "Orrin's docks are too well-guarded. Historically, our problem has been pirates since the end of the last demon war. The logical and least guarded ingress would be the tunnels from Death and Vintner coming out beyond the walls near the old coastal trail."

Her logic was impeccable. Especially if our adversary was connected somehow to last summer's treason plot.

"There's something else you need to know, Justice." From the heat rising off her skin and the quiver of her chin, she was barely keeping her rage in check.

"You found the missing Love wardens."

She nodded. "Yes. The tunnel directly into the Temple of Death ends at their cold storage for the deceased. It was bricked over some time ago, but that section is still colder than the rest of the system we've explored so far. We didn't find the bodies until we were nearly on top of them. High Sister Bertrice has one of her juniors searching their architectural records."

I sighed. "She won't find anything."

Farrah chuckled. "Given that none of our temples seem to have a record of the tunnels themselves, she's looking for unusual orders of bricks and mortar."

"That's a clever approach." I eyed Dragonfly. "Did someone from your temple—"

"Identify them? Yes, Lady Justice, I did." She hesitated. "I hope I was not out of place for telling High Sister Bertrice to start funeral preparations."

Weariness settled over me. Too much death in the last fortnight, and I hadn't seen the end yet. "No, you did the right thing."

"As I was saying," Farrah interjected. Her finger continued its path on the parchment. "Our tunnel used to come out at the sacred grove before it collapsed." While every city had a Wilding Temple and every village an altar, the God wasn't known for his urban tendencies. Therefore, a wild space outside every city's walls was dedicated to Him. "Since Vintner's tunnel opens where the beach meets the southern bluffs, we conjecture there should be another seaside exit and two more inland at the opposite end of the system."

"You've done an excellent job. I truly appreciate your efforts, Farrah," I gently interrupted. "However, I'm going to the inn that serves as Love's discreet entrance."

Her eyes did a slow blink. Whatever she wanted to ask, she thought better of it. "Very well."

Dragonfly nodded. "That section has been kept up and is quite safe, but it's a bit of a trek, Justice."

"It's . . . necessary," I replied. "And . . . might I impose on you for some of your male clothes?"

"Of course." She giggled. "We even have some in your size." With a wave, she beckoned me.

Little Bear moved to accompany us, but both Dragonfly and I held up our hands to stop him.

"I can't have you involved this time," I said.

"But, Justice—" His anger glowed on his face.

"No," I repeated. More softly, I said, "Mat and Bertrice are going to need you if I make a hash of this."

"And you don't need to know a lady's tricks," Dragonfly added.

I followed the priestess to her private bedchamber, leaving my chief warden to fume in her receiving room. She shuffled through trunks and closets while I stripped off my robes and shirt.

"I'll need to bind your breasts more tightly—" A slight gasp of horror from her had me reaching for my sword and whirling in search of an enemy.

"I am so sorry, my dear." She raised her hands to cover her mouth.

"What? Who?"

"Y-your back. I didn't know."

I slid my sword into my scabbard with a disgusted motion and tossed it back on her bed. "It's ancient history, Sister."

"I can tell." She swallowed hard. "Turn around."

I did, and she wound the cloth around my chest. Whatever the material was, it was far thicker and stronger than the silk I normally used. By the time she tied it off, my chest felt like Nassa was sitting on it.

My hope that she'd drop the subject disappeared when she traced the scars on my back. "What could you have possibly done to deserve this?"

"You haven't noticed my eyes?" The Reverend Mother let me know under no uncertain terms I would not leave the order through spell work or trickery.

Her voice deepened with her fury. "Why didn't they let a healer see you?"

I didn't want to discuss my lashing. It had been hard enough the first time Luc had seen my back. Instead, I reached for the small clothes and leggings.

"Anthea?"

I couldn't handle Dragonfly's pity. It was worse than my own rage at the Goddess. It was almost as bad as losing Luc and Kam. "I refused to let the healer touch me."

Thankfully, she let the matter go, and I finished dressing.

"Now for the final touches." She came at me with a cosmetic jar and a brush.

I automatically grabbed her wrists. "What on Balance do you think you're doing?"

Dragonfly sighed. "Your nose and gait may be masculine, but the rest of your face is too pretty for a man. Trust me, I have years of practice at this."

Once I released her, she lightly brushed a powder over my cheeks and chin. When she dusted it over my upper lip, I sneezed.

"What the demon—"

"Keep complaining, and I'll cut off your hair, too," she growled. "This will appear as stubble at first glance since I'm assuming any illusion is out of the question." She pushed me to a sitting position on her bed before she climbed on behind me. Sharp tugs and yanks on my scalp made me wonder if she were following through on her threat.

"What are you doing to me?"

"Tightening your braids. While your handmaid does a lovely job of making you look like a lady instead of a pig herder, we want your silhouette to match your clothing."

When she was done, I felt along my skull. My hair was tightly woven in a pattern close to my scalp. The braided loops or bun Sivan normally pinned it would have been an obvious bulk at the back of my head.

"All set," Dragonfly announced cheerily.

I reached for my sword, but she yanked it from my grip.

"Not set after all," she muttered.

"I'm not going out unarmed," I grumbled. "The Assassins Guild may not have gotten the word that their employer can't pay."

Dragonfly snorted. "Do you always whine like an infant? The silver and obsidian inlays mark your weapon as one from Balance." She rummaged in a different trunk, but this one held a load of familiar indigo steel. "Try this one." She held out a short curved scabbard.

When I took it, the plain leather felt lighter than my sword. Pulling the blade free was easier than I thought it would be. I took a couple of experimental swings, and the steel sang a sweet, high-pitched note.

"What is this?" I replaced the odd sword into its sheath and looped the leather through the belt for my baggy leggings.

"It's called a scimitar. The nomad tribes between Kemet and Indus use them. The story is one of their prophets invented it to kill demons."

I shuddered. My two experiences with the creatures were bad enough. "How did he keep them from changing their mass?"

"I beg your pardon?"

"Does everyone ignore my reports? Demons can change themselves from thin as air to heavier than a boulder."

Dragonfly snorted again and crossed her arms. "That information was not shared with the sisterhood. When the current madness is done, I'd like your assistance in going through Gerd's room and office. There may be other irregularities I don't know about. I'd be comforted to have a justice review everything."

"When the current madness is done." I left out the part that she assumed I would survive this madness.

She showed me the gesture and words to open the passage. "Take the right branch. The left connects to the Temple of Conflict. Keep straight. Any side tunnels you see connect to the other temples as far as I know."

Then to my utter shock, she swept me into a bear hug. "I don't know what you're planning, but be careful," she whispered in my ear.

"Thank you. Goddess be with you as well."

I ducked and entered the passage. Dragonfly sealed the entryway behind me.

If someone wasn't already terrified of tight spaces, she could definitely become so in here. This time, my height was a disadvantage. I bent over, sucked in a deep breath and shuffled forward.

The miniscule lavender light emitted by the tiny living things on the stone and earthen walls kept me from tripping over the uneven sections of the floor. I hadn't figured out what type of creature survived on the surfaces of caves and other underground spaces. I did know if I touched them, they died.

At the split, I travelled the right branch as Dragonfly instructed. My breathing sounded terribly loud in such an enclosed space. I tried not to imagine fighting a demon down here. Or giving birth as my grandmother had. Something squeaked, and I caught a glimpse of greenish fur and bright red eyes in the distance.

A rat. It whirled and fled up the tunnel.

As much as I hated to do so, I used the knowledge concerning my tiny light givers by placing a palm on the wall of the main tunnel every time I came to a side tunnel or intersection. If I had to run from Quan for some reason, I wanted a marked escape route.

A familiar itch of magic tugged me from both sides at a larger intersection, the left side being much stronger. The Temple of Balance. With a quick prayer for the souls of the tiny creatures lighting my way, I placed both hands on the wall. Good. Home was much better than racing all the way back to Love if I didn't need to.

The size of the space increased after that intersection, and I could walk erect. After a long time of no side tunnels, I realized I was traveling upward as well. A wooden door finally appeared in the gloom. No magic sealed it. I shoved the latch . . .

And stepped into an inn's common room. A very empty common room except for one person.

"Hey, there!" A girl paused in her sweeping, the broom she held nearly twice her height. From her size, she couldn't have been more than eight or nine winters. "They ain't taking worshippers tonight."

I shrugged. "Had to check," I said in as low a voice as I could manage.

The child gave me a disgusted look and resumed her task.

I thanked the Goddess for the girl's disinterest and charged out the inn's main door. Once outside, a blast of frigid air greeted me. Ice pellets stung my exposed face, and I pulled my hood tighter. The sleet wouldn't last past third morning, but it would make conditions slippery and dangerous in the meantime as Hogarth had warned. The small bit of good news was I had been on this street more than once and knew my destination.

Treading as fast as I dared, I made my way to the Jing ambassador's residence. While I had no doubt I could enter the compound by stealth and question Quan privately, I decided on a more straightforward approach, as much to test the wardens and peacekeepers watching the place as the desire not to die before this infernal investigation was completed. I rang the bell at the entrance gate.

A guard stumbled out of the guardhouse. From his mumbled words and attitude, he cursed me in his own language for making him come out in the storm before switching to the trade tongue. "Go away! We're closed for the night!"

I formally bowed. "Please inform the honorable Ambassador Quan of Jing that I'm here about the item Sister Gretchen of the Temple of Love acquired for him."

The skeptical guard appraised me. He must have decided he'd rather not risk his master's wrath. "Wait here." He stomped back into the guardhouse. Almost immediately, a youth plunged out of the door and ran for the main mansion.

The sleet pounded hard and fast enough I could feel the hits through my borrowed clothes. Except it no longer qualified as sleet from the size of the dark purple chunks now bouncing off the cobblestones.

Boot heels in rhythm drew my attention. A half-dozen men marched to the gate.

Their captain glared at me. "Show me your eyes."

If my need to speak with Quan wasn't so urgent, I'd tell the pompous ass where he could stick his spear. Instead, I pushed back my hood.

He gave a sharp nod. One of his men unlocked the narrow side gate just far enough for me to squeeze through. The guards surrounded me and marched back to the main house.

Ambassador Quan waited for us in the entry hall. Despite the late hour, he was still dressed in his formal silk court coat. His eyes narrowed as he examined me. None of the leering quality or innuendo of our first meeting months ago, or the delicate manners of our second and more recent. He said nothing, just beckoned me to follow him.

We reached a small parlor. An elderly man sat near the fire. His beard spilled into his lap, and the nails on the hand that stroked his lengthy whiskers appeared sharp as knives. Was he Quan's new sorcerer?

I had expected Quan's personal bodyguard Shi Hua to accompany the ambassador during our meeting, but the power emanating from the old man was incredible. He would be a far more dangerous opponent if manners soured.

Once inside, Quan closed the door and murmured an obvious command in the Jing language.

The elder painfully climbed to his feet and began to circle the room. The more he walked, the steadier his gait grew as if the magic he wielded took away the aches of his joints. The wards he laid had the delicacy of the finest lace caressing skin. When he was finished, the old man settled back in his chair by the fire.

The ambassador gestured for me to take the chair that faced away from the fire. As if my squinting was a dead giveaway the heat from the flames bothered my eyes.

And that position would put the old man at my back.

Tyra was correct. It wasn't difficult to deduce how my odd sight worked if one paid attention.

I positioned the proffered chair so I could keep both men within view before I claimed my seat.

The old man cackled, and a slight smile played at the edges of Quan's mouth.

"After the attempts on your life this week, I understand your precaution. How may I help you tonight, Lady Justice?"

"I thought after the events of autumn, we had come to an accord, Ambassador."

Surprisingly, his skin color remained the same, but the end of one side of his moustache twitched, sending the bead at its tip swinging. I fixed my countenance and silently counted to fifty before he replied.

"You know."

I inclined my head. "The story you told me in my office a few days ago does not assure me of your good faith. I hope you plan to rectify such an . . . error of memory."

His fingernails tapped a rhythm on the arms of his chair. Again, I counted while I waited for his reply.

"You understand both our needs to avoid scandal, Justice."

"Sometimes, scandal claims us regardless of our best intentions."

He grunted. "Yes, and much of it in Orrin swirls around you, despite your impeccable record as a justice."

"My record is hardly impeccable, Ambassador. Especially considering an altered sentence for an illegal execution landed me in my current office."

A real smile crossed his face. "Your reputation is better than you realize, Lady Justice." He sobered. "I regret I . . . misled you concerning the actual object Sister Gretchen was to retrieve for me. With so many other parties searching for it, I . . . erred in not trusting you with the facts. I had hoped to keep it an internal Jing matter."

I leaned back in my chair. "I would have been honored to assist in such a discretion. Before Sister Gretchen was murdered, that is."

Released breath wreathed his face in brilliant yellow. "I regret her loss as well. She was—" He stared into the fire, collecting his emotions. When he turned back to me, he said, "Would you care for some refreshment while we talk?"

I smiled. "As long as you leave out the poison, I would love some of your wonderful tea."

The old man cackled again, his laughter a little bizarre, and sang, "Poison is the coward's way, sword is the brave. If belief in your gods do fail, surely you shall cave."

I looked askance at Quan when his companion finished his odd tune.

The ambassador shrugged. "Forgive my father, Lady Justice. The Child has recently inflicted her curse on him."

I wasn't sure what shocked me more—that the elder was his father or that Quan sounded embarrassed. The affliction known as the Child's Curse usually affected the very old by taking away their memories, the newest ones first until the sufferer regressed to nothing more than an oversized infant. "There's no offense to forgive, good sir. I am surprised you would bring your father here. Surely your family could better care for him at home?"

"Ha!" the old man barked. "I may be going senile, my dear Red Justice, but I haven't lost all my mind."

I froze. I knew what they called me on the streets, but it was the first time someone had the audacity to say such in my presence.

"Again, I apologize." Quan rose from his chair and strode over to the fireplace. "Unfortunately, there's only my brother—"

"Half-brother!" the old man snapped. "Trying to rule the empire. He doesn't listen to me. Does a piss poor job, too, compared to your mother." A sharp nod emphasized his opinion.

Well, that bit of news unbalanced my scales.

"Let's not disturb the lady's digestion by recounting old family squabbles, Father." Quan opened a door built into the side of the fireplace and pulled out tray. The aroma of Jing tea wafted through the air as he brought it to the small table between our chairs.

"Is there something else important you wish to tell me, Ambassador?" I said as he poured.

"I believe you've already deduced my relationship to the current emperor of Jing," he replied. It explained why a priestess of Light would disguise herself as his concubine/bodyguard, too.

"I don't understand why you would take an ambassadorship instead of higher position at court." I glanced at the old man. "Unless it's to protect a family member."

Quan handed me a tiny saucer and cup. He served his father before he resumed his seat. We all sipped our tea. I impatiently waited while the ambassador collected his thoughts. Pressing him would get me nowhere.

"When the Imperial Guard and our Temple of Light raided the School of Sorcery last fall, they arrested or killed the masters. Unfortunately, a handful of apprentices escaped." He sipped again.

So he wasn't going to answer my question concerning his current position. Or he had by not acknowledging it.

However, to admit the Jing authorities failed to stop demon-dealers was tantamount to a threat of war. I needed to choose my next words carefully. "I would be interested in hearing your theories on how untrained magicians evaded the combined forces of the emperor and the temple."

"Bribes." He set his cup aside and leaned forward. "I'll be quite frank,

Anthea, and again, I ask that none of what I tell passes beyond these walls. Not until we're both ready."

His words intrigued me. After Shi Hua's revelations on her first visit, more pieces fell into place. "It's not just our queen who has nobles consorting with demons and their summoners."

"No," Quan said grimly. "It isn't."

I glanced at his father who was merrily slurping his tea and muttering to himself. "Nor do you believe the Child's Curse has affected your father."

"The School of the Dragon and the Phoenix existed long before Balance united all the nations two thousand years ago to fight the first demon invasion. Father was a master of the school during Empress Bao-Yu's rein."

"And the School of Sorcery considered them rivals?"

Quan chuckled, a bitter thing to hear. "They consider any academic thought but theirs a rival. There was much contention between the various schools over whose philosophy would reign supreme in court."

"And if philosophical argument failed, there were other methods of persuasion?"

I half-expected a ribald joke from either Quan or his father concerning my comment. Instead, their mood turned somber.

The ambassador rubbed his thumb along the side of his cup. "My mother actually had some affection for my father. Nor did he want any higher office than as the representative of the Dragon and Phoenix at the imperial court. However, the royal consort assumed otherwise."

While Quan was two decades older than Duke Marco, the same pang of sympathy hit me at the similarity. Why were children considered nothing more than pawns in their parents' power plays?

"Does the emperor believe you want a higher office?"

"No. However, as I said, his father believes otherwise, which is why my brother suggested this post."

"Horse manure," the old man muttered. Both Quan and I turned to look at him, but he ignored us and slurped more of his tea.

I took a sip of my own and nonchalantly asked, "When did you see Sister Gretchen last, Ambassador?"

He stilled, but his pulse at his throat beat a tad faster. "Your tracking spell from three nights ago pointed to this place, and you believe it was me."

I cocked my head. "I'm willing to hear an alternate explanation."

He bowed his head. "I suppose I should thank you. Or rather thank High Brother Luc. Shi Hua recognized the signature of the tracking spell. Otherwise, we may not have discovered the assassin in our own household until it was too late. Father, if you would please?"

The old man muttered under his breath, and the feathery sensation of his power faded from the walls and coalesced around him once more.

Quan rose and again motioned for me to follow him. I was afraid to learn what he'd done, but I forced my feet to follow his. He led me to the back courtyard of the manse.

A corpse sat in the middle of the dormant grass. Heat had fully leached from the body. The cold weather and lack of predators had kept it from decomposing as fast as it would in other seasons. Between its outstretched legs, blood and other things stained the base of the stake that impaled the corpse.

Someone had died a horrible way in the middle of the Embassy District, and no one had heard a thing, much less reported it. More bribery of the magistrate's peacekeepers? Or did DiCook take this one himself? Maybe he only refused to take bribes when it involved spelled gold.

Even worse, Shi Hua or Quan's father could have cast a spell to hide the screams.

My stomach threatened to heave its contents, more from the sinking feeling about both the Orrin's peacekeepers and Quan's people than the sight of the dead man, but I clamped down on my self-control. "I have no proof this was the man the tracking spell indicated."

Whatever reaction Quan expected, matter-of-factness was not it. He almost looked disappointed.

"What must I do to assuage your concerns?"

I couldn't stop the touch of vehemence in my voice. "You should have kept him alive long enough for me to verify the tracking spell."

"I will endeavor to do so in the future, Lady Justice."

A murder had been committed in the middle of my city, and I couldn't do a Goddess-damned thing about it. Under the Peaceful Sea Treaty, each embassy was considered that land's sovereign territory. "Did you get anything useful out of him before his heart stopped beating?"

He hesitated. Was it because he had and didn't want to share? Or was it the nasty tone of my voice? "No, Lady Justice. Somehow, he consumed a poison before he was brought to the yard."

"Where is the assassin from?"

"We believe he is Guild."

Just like the prisoner our wardens had managed to capture alive at the Temple of Love. I was so damn tired. This city was draining the life out of me, one giant hunk at a time. "I mean no insult, but I cannot trust anyone at this point, Ambassador. You should have let me help Shi Hua in questioning him."

"Perhaps, but the past cannot be changed." He stared at the frozen, naked figure. Ice pellets collected on the corpse. "Still, I owe you a debt for revealing a member of the Assassins Guild within my household before he could do any damage."

I didn't answer. The night's silence was broken only by the successive *plink*s of sleet hitting the bare branches of the trees.

Last fall's plot by the School of Sorcery had been aimed at removing Shi Hua from Quan's service. Given the recent attempts on my own life, my assumption she had told the truth about me being their next target seemed more like fact. Logically then, the Assassins Guild would try to deal with the priestess since her death was their original goal.

Then there was the chaos surrounding Sister Gretchen. I was running out of options for finding who was really behind her murder.

The ambassador cleared his throat. "I would ask that the book be returned so I may ensure its destruction."

I turned to regard him. "The other parties will know if you destroy the book here in Orrin. Anyone with talent in a fifty-league radius will know." Did some little part of me hold out hope? That if I didn't destroy that cursed tome right away, Jax would have a chance of finding and freeing Luc? With tonight's ice storm, I had an extra day before I would get a reply from the Reverend Mother.

Quan shrugged. "Maybe. Maybe not. What if I took it back to Jing and had it destroyed there?"

I shook my head. "I cannot take that risk. I believe I mentioned my oath and my duty to uphold the laws of Issura. Not to mention it slipped through your empire's authorities once already."

His color flared. "Your own mother failed to turn over the book as well."

Of course, he knew who originally had the grimoire. My bitter laugh rippled across the courtyard, snapping the fallen ice. "And she's in my gaol awaiting trial for her actions."

"Is it worth a child's life, Justice?" he said softly.

For once tonight, my rage escaped its leash. "Is that a threat, Ambassador, or merely blackmail?"

His exhale couldn't quite be called a sigh. "When we traced the stolen tome, the noble in question chose to immolate himself along with the children he'd poorly used."

I swore several choice words. This entire case had turned into one terrible agony of so many innocents.

Quan continued, "Only one survived. However, our healers could not restore her fully."

"Is she here?"

He nodded.

I clenched my fists. "I can't trade the book for her life."

His voice matched my grimness. "What are you planning to do, Justice? Surely, you won't trade it for High Brother Luc's life?"

No sense playing word games any longer. "I can't do that either as I'm sure he has already informed his abductors."

"I see." The ambassador folded his hands in his sleeves. "What is your intention, Justice?"

"Exactly as I told you in my office. I can't let you have it, but I won't use it against you. I will destroy it."

"No! You can't!"

We both whirled at the voice behind us, my borrowed sword drawn before I registered that it was Quan's father.

He struggled to maintain his footing on the slick flagstones as he joined us. "Po, you cannot let her do this thing. Cannot let her destroy centuries of work and study."

Fury swelled in me. "Those centuries of work and study can summon demons. According to the old tales, there are spells to summon the dead also. Do you think with anyone in command of such an army will stop on this side of the Peaceful Sea?"

"Please forgive my father's outburst, Justice." Quan wrapped an arm around the distraught man. "He's not talking about our . . . situation."

With a coating of shame, I sheathed the sword. The last few days had me jumping at ill, elderly scholars. However, the corpse a few yards away didn't help. "What exactly are you working on, good sir?"

"I am researching a way to block *any* summoning from working," the ambassador's father answered rather primly.

He couldn't be serious. To even attempt such a thing, he had to know how a summoning worked to begin with. Which meant he'd been practicing, bringing demons here. Had Quan told me another lie? Was his father the one who'd really traded the cursed tome to Gerd for the children?

And I was back to my original problem. I couldn't arrest the old man. I stood on what was technically considered Jing soil. Even if we were outside the embassy walls, the poor man obviously could barely comprehend his own actions. At best, he would be imprisoned for the rest of his life if he had summoned demons, regardless of his original intent.

I wiped both of my palms over my face. "Balance help us. Of all the idiotic—"

"May I bring the surviving girl to your temple?" Quan asked before I could say something truly insulting.

"It would be best to take her to the Healers Guild. I'll inform Master Aaron of your arrival." The forgotten idea from last night that had been teasing me since this morning popped into my consciousness. This was for

Luc, so I swallowed my pride. "May I please speak with Shi Hua before I take my leave of you?"

"She is unavailable right now, Justice." Quan guided his father to the back door. It swung open, and he handed the old man to the servants inside, his voice sharp as he issued orders to them in their native language.

I laid my hand on his arm before he followed them. He allowed the door to swing shut so our conversation was private.

"Please, Quan Po," I whispered. "I need to talk to her, priestess to priestess."

His body stiffened under my touch. "She told you."

"Yes." I let my hand drop. Such familiarity may have ruined my chances, but desperation drove me. I prayed I didn't make similar mistakes the way Gerd had in her own desperation. "I need to know who else is trying to obtain the book. The Assassins Guild doesn't work without a client."

The pattering of sleet slowed to become fat, heavy drops of rain that were a shade colder than the ice pellets.

"She doesn't know, and I honestly don't know, Anthea," Quan said, his voice equally quiet. "There's rumors of someone amassing power, both magical and conventional."

"Before one of the assassins sent to kill me died this morning, he said the temples' time of dominance was over."

He shrugged. "It could be as simple as more scholars and guilds vying for independence."

"Except you don't believe that is so," I stated.

He blew out a deep breath. The yellow cloud turned indigo and dissipated almost instantly. "Zealots rarely make sense, Lady Justice."

Before I could comment on his strange words, he added, "She tried to question our infiltrator." He inclined his head toward the corpse. "Somehow, he evaded her truthspell."

A little pang of guilt hit me, a reminder that Quan wasn't the only one with secrets. "That's one of the reasons I wished to speak with her. We discovered they have a way of blocking a truthspell."

"You should have told me—" His jaw clamped shut with an audible click.

I inclined my head toward the corpse. "As should you." I sighed. "We've both made mistakes."

"Yes," he breathed the word, as if he were deciding something. In a firmer voice, he added, "Shi Hua rode south two nights ago. She caught up with your High Brother Jax. Luc's abductors were headed toward Tandor, but they've veered east to the edge of the Valley of the Lost at her last report this morning."

The priestess was a distance-speaker of incredible range. She was probably making reports to her Reverend Father in Jing as well as the ambassador.

What really troubled me was the original direction the renegades headed. Every clue I'd stumbled across seemed to point to our southern sister-city.

"Why?"

He shrugged. "I cannot say what the High Brother's abductors plan—"

"No." I gave a sharp shake of my head. "Why did she join Jax?"

"We owe you both a debt of honor from last fall's incident." A rueful smile tilted the corners of his mouth. "A second one now for saving our lives yet again."

His gratitude left me with an uncomfortable sensation, one far worse than his intimate innuendos. So I changed the subject. "The men who took Luc could simply be trying to avoid the border patrols."

Not that we had much trouble with Cant itself the way we did with brigands who liked to hide in the eastern foothills leading into the high desert.

"She didn't believe so." Again, Quan hesitated. "I will send you any news when she makes contact at sunrise."

Considering my last visit from the Light priestess, I smiled. "Please have your messenger wait until the ice melts. I would hate for one of your people to slip off a roof and break his or her neck."

# *Chapter 20*

Once I took my leave of Quan, it took twice as long to return to the inn with the ice building on the cobblestones, but the slow pace gave me time to contemplate what I'd learned. I wasn't happy about the ambassador's actions, but I could understand the context. He tried to quietly retrieve an illegal object, and he had no love for demons or those foolish enough to summon them.

In fact, he almost seemed embarrassed that the grimoire had slipped past him when it arrived in Issura. Or maybe, he was concerned about his father's role in the matter. Whatever the reason, I couldn't push too hard, or both he and Shi Hua would no longer pass any information to me.

Last fall, Shi Hua had said I was a target of the School of Sorcery because I could see demons. Was the current trouble part of the same plot or something else altogether?

Luc's abductors had turned east. Jax said the poison used on the Healers Guild oil was from mushrooms in the high desert. Southeast from Orrin. The only pass to the desert accessible this time of year would be the one near Tandor. Neither the Cliffdwellers nor the Diné would allow strangers to roam their territories at will, but between them and Issura was the Valley of the Lost, a wasteland.

But how could Luc's abductors hide there for long? No drinkable water. No food but lizards and jumping mice.

The more I tried to tease out the main thread of all the incidents over the last two weeks, the more my head ached.

When I entered the inn, the owner sat in the common room with the girl. They both leapt to their feet at my entrance. With the terrible weather, no doubt I was their only custom tonight.

The girl's expression soured. "Oh, it's you." She plopped back down on the bench.

The innkeeper, a rotund man, placed a hand over his mouth, then cleared his throat. "Please forgive my daughter, Sister. She has not learned the ways of men and women."

I couldn't help my amusement. It was an equal mix that he'd seen through my disguise enough to tell my gender and the child's irritation at the foibles of adults. At least with my hood pulled low enough to cover my eyes, they believed I was from Love.

A chuckle escaped from my throat. "Let us hope she does not learn for many more years." I pressed a coin into his hand. "Silver for your troubles on such a blustery night."

"Good eventide to you as well, Sister." He scrambled ahead to open the hidden door for me.

I ducked into the tunnel. For the first time since Luc's initial visit, I was glad of the system. Trying to walk back to the Temple District on the surface streets was treacherous at best with the night's ice storm.

When I reached Dragonfly's entrance, I performed the spell to open the secret door. The blaze from the fireplace and the two braziers in her bedchambers nearly blinded me after the soft lavender light of the tunnels.

"Well?" Little Bear's tone was as harsh as the light. I wasn't sure how he talked his way into Dragonfly's personal quarters, and at this point, I didn't want to know.

"I'm still alive," I said dryly. "Could you please leave for a moment while I dress in my own robes?"

He grunted and stomped out of the room.

Thankfully, Dragonfly didn't ask any questions as she helped me change back into my own clothes. She tried to restore my hair to Sivan's original braid loops, but I refused.

"But, Lady Justice—"

I groaned. "It's well after first night, Sister. I've been on my feet since before first morning. Frankly, I need some rest, so please spare me any more assistance."

She backed away, her hands raised with palms toward me. "I bow to my custom's wishes."

"May I impose on you for another matter?"

"Of course."

"May we leave our horses here? Footing is treacherous because of ice on the cobblestones." With everything happening, I didn't want to leave my precious Nassa at another temple, but I wasn't about to lose her or Little Bear's mount to a broken leg.

"It would be our pleasure." Dragonfly sounded inordinately pleased. My suspicions rose, but she quelled them with her next words. "You honor me with your trust, Lady Justice. Thank you for letting me help, even in this small way."

"You are welcome."

And she swept me into another giant hug.

Little Bear wisely kept silent on the walk home. As silent as the streets. The Temple District was never this quiet, but the storm forced even the wharf rats to seek shelter from the ice.

I'd heard stories of mountain folks who nailed miniature sleigh runners to their boots and glided across frozen lakes as they harvested ice. After slipping for the fourth time, I decided the ice harvesters were lying or they were far more talented than me. Somehow, Little Bear and I reached Balance without falling.

We shook off the ice coating our cloaks before entering. But inside the main doors, Tyra greeted us with a grim voice. "Father Jerrod and Brother Mat returned with Lady Alessa several candlemarks ago. Duke Marco is with them. Your guests refuse to retire for the night until they see you."

Every muscle and sinew hurt, but I swallowed my exhaustion. Goddess knew I'd eventually pay for pushing myself this hard. "What about? I made myself clear before the priests left."

"This is something you need to see for yourself, m'lady."

Her tone sent a shiver of dread through me. I followed her to the receiving room, Little Bear still on my heels. Part of me wondered if he'd insist on commandeering a sleeping pallet and stay in my bedchambers for what little remained of the night if the priests' news were bad enough.

I didn't want to deal with Sivan the next morning if he did.

"Alessa received this," Duke Marco blurted the instant I passed through the doors. No formal greetings. But then, he and I were far past that point. He jabbed a bright orange finger at the casket sitting on the table.

Raw emotional turmoil swirled around the two priests and Lady Alessa as well. Foremost was fury from Brother Mat.

"When and who delivered it?"

"Early this evening, shortly before supper," Marco said. "The man who came to the gate was dressed as a priest of Light, so my household guard assumed it was something from Brother Luc regarding Alessa's inheritance from Sister Gretchen."

Mat flipped the lid open. Dreading what I would see, I peered in. A foot lay nestled in a swath of bloody woven cotton.

A human foot.

"I recognize the crooked toe, Justice." Mat's voice was low. Not out of concern or respect, but from barely contained rage.

So did I. No healer was necessary to confirm what I knew in my heart. He had broken his little toe of his left foot during our first year on circuit.

My hands covered my mouth. "Oh, Luc."

# Chapter 21

Bile burned the back of my throat. Why send such a gruesome message to Alessa? No magic sang from the mutilated appendage, so I poked the edge of the cut. Blood oozed, but it was as cold as the flesh.

"There were two notes with the box, m'lady." Marco handed me a slip of parchment. "I apologize for handling them. If we'd only known . . ."

The imprinted ridges of the Balance-stamped code pressed against my fingertips. "Two notes?"

"One written to me," Alessa choked out the words. "Telling me to turn over some spellbook that Gretchen had or to force you to do it by midnight tomorrow at Samael DiRoy's old estate. Otherwise, the next package I receive would be Isabella's head two days after that."

"And the second was addressed to you," Marco added.

"They're not going to risk abducting a noblewoman in the middle of the capital." I endeavored to be reassuring.

"They didn't hesitate in their assassination attempt on you on temple steps," Little Bear said.

When I couldn't muster a flicker of annoyance at my head warden's outspokenness in front of the nobles, the reality of how bad things were flooded my consciousness. The Assassins Guild probably had someone in place at the university, close to Lady Isabella. It would take two days alone to get a message to the capital to warn them, but with this storm—

Did my opponents have a distance speaker as well? Was that how they were staying several steps ahead of me? A distance speaker would be the only way for them to carry out the threat on Isabella.

Unless they had already abducted her as well.

My body choose that moment to decide it had enough abuse over the past seven days. My knees buckled. If it weren't for Tyra and Little Bear standing so close, I would have landed on the floor in an ungracious heap. They settled me on the chair Lady Alessa had vacated.

Father Jerrod reached for the wine flask. "Justice, you need—"

I held up my hand. "What I need is some food. I can't remember the last time I ate." I needed sleep, too, but the message from my adversary, the person Marston and the dead assassins reported to, demanded attention. Was my adversary another assassin, or the Guild's client who maneuvered us like chess pawns?

I was tired of being manipulated. A familiar odor wafted from the parchment as I broke the wax seal and unfolded it. Cantish hot pepper sauce. My heart jolted in my chest, but I tried to ignore the pain. It had to be a coincidence.

I closed my eyes while my fingertips read the message. It was a mirror of the one sent to Lady Alessa with the addition that Luc's head would follow three days after Isabella's. My opponents obviously weren't sure which of us had the demon grimoire.

If my adversary and his cronies didn't have a distance speaker, how by the Twelve could they be sending messages between the capital and the Valley of the Lost? Unless they had a prearranged plan. Or Luc wasn't in the Valley of the Lost anymore than Isabella was in the capital.

Three extra symbols rested after the end-message stamp. My heart leapt again, and I tried to squelch the surge of joy. Luc was the one who'd tapped out the message. That was the reason for the scent of pepper sauce, his confirmation.

We'd worked out a private system between us after the very same incident in which he'd broken his toe. The first symbol signified the color red—extreme danger, no rescue. The second was demon, which I already had discovered. The third was the symbol for his temple with a line diagonally through it.

A traitor in the Temple of Light.

My heart wanted to leap out of my throat and run for the eastern mountains. That's how the Assassins Guild had known my every move. How the survivor of the Love skirmish had died in my cell. Mat had been with me when I found the tome. He was the only one, outside of Jerrod, Gerd, Quan, and my own wardens who knew I had it. He was the only one who'd truly benefit from both Kam and Luc's deaths.

But why send their grisly message to Alessa?

Because with everything else happening, the odds were I wouldn't check some random delivery until too late. Or my staff would immediately become suspicious of a priest they didn't recognize with no crest on his cloak.

Thank Balance, Jerrod had been with the little bastard every step of the way this evening. Unless Goddess forbid, Jerrod was part of the conspiracy, too.

I silently cursed myself for not paying attention. Had Kam been suspicious of Mat? Was that the real reason he didn't recommend the younger priest's promotion? Had Jeremy conspired with Mat? Was he a threat to Orrin as well?

The Twelve only knew how much damage Mat had done because I had trusted him like I trusted Luc. Now, I had to come up with a plan to outwit him.

"Lady Justice?" Mat's voice grated along my skin. "Is everything all right?"

It took all my willpower not to draw my sword and drive it through his betraying heart. I had to play act along with his plan, so I sighed. No sense lying. He probably knew his conspirators' next moves. "The message is the same as Lady Alessa's with the addition of the promise to send Brother Luc's head three days after Lady Isabella's."

I struggled to my feet, hobbled over to the fireplace, and tossed the parchment into the flames. Luc's captors who were currently with him must not know the Balance code. No sense taking the chance of Mat seeing Luc's real message, even if he didn't know what it meant at first. The boy was too bright not to be able to decipher the hidden warning.

"We need to destroy that cursed thing," Jerrod said. "Justice Anthea is correct. Lady Isabella is protected at the university. And Brother Luc knows his duty, may the Twelve help him."

While the parchment curled beneath the flames, the seed of an idea came to me. Maybe the Goddess decided to grace me after all. I schooled my expression before I turned back to the others. "No. We're going to deliver the book tomorrow night."

# Chapter 22

The room erupted in a cacophony of denial that pounded through my head. Except Mat.

For an instant, he hesitated before adding his voice to the uproar. Trying to figure out if I bluffed or if I truly intended to carry through with the trade. No one else noticed.

Good. I might have a slim chance of succeeding. The trick will be how to keep things from Mat, and I had no guarantee Jeremy hadn't sided with him. I need to get a message to Shi Hua. That meant going back to the Jing embassy before dawn. It was a horrible state of affairs that I trusted a non-Issuran marginally more than my own countrymen.

Whether my wardens would trust me on my next step was the real question.

"Anthea!" Jerrod stalked over and grabbed my arms. "You can't. Don't make me place you under arrest."

"And what about my brother?" Alessa's sleeves and skirts shivered from her emotions. "If you do this, he shares your fate!"

Which was true. He'd vouched for my ongoing conduct at my murder trial last summer.

The duke folded his arms over his chest and glared at his sister. "If Justice Anthea deems it necessary, so be it. My wife carries my heir, and you're the best person Katarina has to help her manage the estates until he—" He paused to smile at me. "Or she is of age. You have my help, Lady Justice."

I cocked my head. "Anyone else wish to make their statement?"

Mat blew out a deep breath, as if he were truly considering which way to jump. "I'm with you, m'lady."

"I will have you arrested as well," Father Jerrod roared.

"Little Bear?"

He stepped to the older priest's side. "Which cell do you want him in?"

Relief flooded me, and my knees threatened to give out again. Jerrod stared at my warden, the shock obvious even to my sight.

"That's unnecessary. Father Jerrod is my guest, as well as Lady Alessa." Her mouth dropped open at my words, but Tyra took the hint and closed in on the noblewoman. "The guest rooms on the second floor will suffice. Brother Mat, if you'd be kind enough to seal them for me?"

"Of course." The priest bowed.

"You can't do this, Anthea!" Scarlet fury filled Jerrod's visage.

"I'm sorry, but it's for both of our benefits, Father. I need you out of my way for a day, and you can honestly report under a truthspell that I kept you prisoner."

He spluttered his outrage as Little Bear and Mat escorted him from the receiving room. Alessa wept quietly, but didn't struggle against Tyra's grip on her arm.

Once they were gone, Marco murmured, "I don't like doing that to my own sister."

"There's going to be a lot of things you don't like before tomorrow is over." Neither would I. Mat's inability to access my safe was the one saving grace of this whole mess. He needed me alive until he laid his hands on the demon grimoire.

And maybe, just maybe, I could get Luc and Isabella out of this farce alive, even if I'd just condemned Marco and myself.

The duke followed me to the kitchen, which was already uncomfortably bright with heat, but filled with the rich smell of oat porridge. Deborah finished shoving pans into one of the brick ovens in the wall of the fireplace before she turned and huffed at me.

"The morning bread ain't done yet, Justice."

"I'll take whatever excellent leftovers you have from the evening meal, madam."

Another huff, a little lighter since I had complimented her cooking. "Should'a bin here for it. Sit yerself down."

Silently accepting her rebuke, I claimed her kitchen girl's preparation table per usual. Once Marco took the stool across from me, I said. "I need to beg another favor from you, Deborah."

She placed plates of sausages and cornbread in front of both of us along with two flagons of fresh milk before her fists landed on her ample hips. "What kinda favor?"

"Could you feed Brother Mat a bowl of that delicious honey and blackberry porridge you gave me the other morning?"

She tilted her head. "How much?"

I calculated the time I needed to get to the Jing embassy and back, plus preparing to truthspell Brother Mat. "Two candlemarks' worth?"

Deborah gave a sharp nod. "Want the wardens to make sure he's comfortable?"

"A little less comfortable than Father Jerrod and Lady Alessa, please."

She shook her head and muttered a few choice words that questioned the brother's relationship with his horse. I focused on the food while she stalked over to the stairs that led to our own cold cellar.

I didn't realize how hungry I was until I was swiping the last of the sausage grease off my plate with the last bite of bread. My legs felt steadier, but exhaustion still plagued me. A nap after I questioned Mat and before tonight's insanity would have to do.

I leaned back and looked at Marco. "How do you feel about disguising yourself as a priest of Light?"

He finished chewing his mouthful and washed it down with his milk. "Considering I'm about to lose my head over whatever you're planning, I think I can handle a whipping for impersonating a priest."

"Good, because I can't guarantee either of us will come through my plan intact."

"What exactly—" He shook his head sharply. "Never mind. Don't tell me. The less I know, the less I can reveal under a truthspell."

The crackle of the main fireplace couldn't hide Little Bear's bootsteps, nor those of Brother Mat. They rounded the banked stove, muted golds and greens against the fire's brilliant reds, pinks, and whites.

"Your orders, m'lady?" Little Bear stood stiffly. He wanted to know what I planned, but had the common sense not to ask. The Reverend Mother couldn't fault my warden for following orders. If she did, I'd . . . do nothing more than haunt her if this mad strategy didn't work.

I rose and stretched. And once again, I fought the urge to run my sword through Mat for his betrayal. "I'll explain while you and Brother Mat eat."

Deborah puffed through the cold room door and slammed it shut. "It'll be just a moment for the sausages, Chief Warden, Brother. Our justice ate like a bear preparing for her winter's sleep. She also ate the rest of the corn-bread, so give me a moment to dish you up some porridge." She turned toward the cauldron slung over the fire, and a brilliant blue spot coated the corner of her apron.

The two men took our places at the little table while the duke leaned against the wall. Deborah insisted I take her stool. It galled me that a woman over twice my age was more spry than me at the moment.

She scooped two bowls of porridge. This time I caught her slight of hand. She produced a bottle from her apron. It smell like honey, but it definitely didn't come from the jar on the shelves next to the main pantry. And it had the slightest scent of poppies. If I hadn't been so tired and still recovering from the poison, I would have noticed it the other morning.

Deborah bustled over with the bowls and set them before the men. "A moment to warm the meat."

"So how are you going to rescue Brother Luc," Mat mumbled around a mouthful of porridge.

I considered what to tell him. Did I take the chance that he was a distance-speaker like Shi Hua? I needed to find out for sure before I said anything damaging he could pass on to his fellow traitors.

"The Wilding priesthood has cleared their tunnel. The Mining Guild has been delayed by the ice storm, so the passage hasn't been shored up yet."

Mat continued eating his porridge as he thought about it. "You're planning to race to that tunnel entrance and bring the unstable ceiling down on these renegades?"

I laughed, and prayed it didn't sound as fake as it felt. "I was going to have a contingent of wardens waiting down there, but your idea has merit. After you and I grab Luc, and we get the book back—"

Mat shoved the empty bowl aside, and it landed on the flagstone floor with a clatter. He looked down at it. "I shorry, Deb-d-d—" Confusion filled his tone. He bonelessly slid out of his chair and disappeared from my sight.

Little Bear peered under the table before his attention landed on me.

In turn, I glared at Deborah. "I said two candlemarks."

She chuckled. "I only gave you enough for a hair past a half candlemark. Yer body did the rest 'cause 'twas still tryin' to recover from that poison." She waved a hand. "Do what you need to. I'll make sure Little Bear puts 'im in your best cell."

"You'll make sure I do what?" Little Bear sounded more amused than vexed at the elderly cook.

I rose from her stool. "I'll be in my quarters. Since I'll be doing this truthspell by myself, I need some time to prepare."

"In for a copper, in for a gold crown." Little Bear shrugged. "But if I'm going to lose my head over this mess, I want my sausages first."

I reminded myself to turn left when I hit the junction to the main tunnel, but it wasn't necessary. My double handprint on the wall stood out like a black beacon amid the soft lavender light.

The trip to the inn didn't seem to take as long as it did previously. Maybe it was knowing the reception I'd receive this time. More likely it was the full belly and surge of adrenaline.

When I pushed open the wooden door, the inn's common room was empty, the fire banked for the night. I slipped silently across the floor, pausing once at a squeak from the floorboard. No one was roused by my noise.

I raised the bar at the main door, sending a silent prayer I wasn't putting the innkeeper and his daughter at risk by temporarily leaving the entryway unprotected. I doubted the extra wardens and peacekeepers on duty would be watching for everyday thievery. Stepping outside, I took in the tableau.

Orrin had been transformed into a world of deep amethyst crystal by the ice. My yellowish breath along with the dull oranges and golds of chimneys were the only hint of warmth in the darkest moments of the night.

This time I couldn't risk slipping on the cobblestones. Instead, I splashed through the half-frozen gutters. Sivan would have a fit about how I'd ruined my boots. Just as she would about the non-uniform cloak and leggings I borrowed from the laundry room. But the need to get my message to Shi Hua spurred me onward.

The same Jing guard answered my summons at the embassy. This time, he simply grunted before unlocking the gate and letting me onto the grounds. He guided me to the mansion himself.

Again, the formal sentinels at the main doors demanded I show my eyes before they allowed me inside. They passed me to a serving girl, who led me on a circuitous route through the huge mansion before stopping before a set of large ornate doors.

I discovered why by the sight that greeted me. Ambassador Quan closed another door behind him as he stepped into what was obviously the anteroom to his bedchambers. His normally immaculate appearance had devolved into messy blue hair and a pair of silk trousers. His chest was bare.

"Have you decided to accept my invitation, Lady Justice?" The suggestive quality was back in his voice.

"May we speak privately?" My reputation was already condemned to the demon lands and back. What was one more tidbit for the fishwives to gossip about?

He waved for the serving girl to leave. She bowed and closed the door quietly behind her.

"What constitutes the need for a second visit tonight?" Deadly seriousness coated his voice, but he remained silent while I warded the room.

"You need to warn Shi Hua the next time she makes contact. She and Jax are being led on a unicorn chase, and it's probably a trap of some kind. Whoever's behind this has infiltrated the Temple of Light as well as Love. Luc's being held somewhere closer to Orrin."

"How do you know this?"

I laid out a shortened version of the events after my return to the temple.

He crossed his arms. "The mutilation of a priest is disturbing, but you are correct. Blood that fresh does not lie. You're sure this brother is not what he seems?"

"I'll know for certain once I truthspell him, but until then, you're my only chance of warning Shi Hua."

"What about your Brother Jax?"

I hesitated for an instant.

My pause was enough for the ambassador to put the clues together. "You aren't sure if he's part of this plot." He smiled. "Am I to believe you have a certain affection for my concubine, Justice?" His inappropriate teasing was back.

"I respect anyone of the twelve orders." I smiled. "As long as they don't stab me in the back."

"Be careful, Justice." Quan had sobered again. "Don't take Brother Mat's betrayal personally. You're more likely to make a very dangerous mistake if you do."

I didn't need the ambassador's reminder, but I bowed anyway. "And your emperor is remiss in not taking advantage of your wisdom. However, I graciously accept your advice."

While it would be nice to credit the night's extra watch, I was sure the ice storm did more to deter any thieves from taking advantage of the inn's unbarred door. As I re-barred the door, I heard wood moan elsewhere in the building, but no one appeared in the main room. I avoided the creaky plank and made it through the tunnels without incident.

Maybe the Goddess was guiding me this night. When I slipped back into my quarters through the hidden door to the tunnel system, the main entrance to my private rooms was still locked and my wards intact. I checked the oil lamp on my desk. Another candlemark before Mat should be awake.

I yanked off my reeking boots. Sivan would have more than just a fit. I wrapped them and the borrowed clothing in a worn extra blanket and shoved the bundle into my privy chamber, so the smell wouldn't distract me.

Too much, that was.

I sat on my bed and unbraided Dragonfly's tight weave while I ran through the elements of a truthspell. My finesse lacked compared to Luc. The pain facet of that particular magic bothered me on more levels than I cared to admit, which was part of the reason I never quite mastered the finer aspects of the spell. To me, it was just another punishment inflicted by the temples for non-compliance.

My fingers paused in their task. Was that the reason for the contempt for the temples from my mysterious adversary? Was he forced into religious service as I was? Or punished more severely than his crime warranted?

If he hadn't been foolish, if he hadn't harmed Luc and the Love priestesses, if he hadn't killed Gretchen, I would have considered joining him. But then, there was his desire for the demon grimoire . . .

I started yanking at my hair again. Yes, my adversary was as idiotic as Samael DiRoy had been. Demons couldn't be controlled. We were nothing more than a meal to them. They'd turn against their summoner the first chance they had.

Sitting here and speculating wasn't getting me anywhere. I left my tresses loose and quickly donned my own clothing. For the first time, I knew I wouldn't feel remorse at inflicting pain through a truthspell.

Not after what Mat's compatriots did to Luc.

Magistrate DiCook surprised me by arriving at the Temple of Balance as I headed for Mat's cell.

"Isn't it rather slick to be out this late at night?" I asked when one of my wardens I couldn't name brought him to me.

"Thought you should know right away about the eye we've been keeping on the Jing embassy. It may be worth my banged up knee." He accepted the hot mug Sivan pressed into his hands.

I touched her arm as she turned to go. "Before I forget, could you please have Donella send a note to the Healers Guild? Ambassador Quan will be delivering an injured child tomorrow when the ice has melted."

Her eyebrow rose. "Now?"

I smiled. "In the morning after the ice has melted. Let Master Aaron know Balance will cover the costs."

She made a disgusted sound. "These foundlings should be Mother or Child's responsibility." When I made no comment, she bobbed her head. "Yes, m'lady."

DiCook waited until Sivan was out of earshot before he grinned. "She's right, you know. Just because Balance was the first of the Twelve, it doesn't give you control over the other temples."

"I'm not trying to—" I stopped when I realized he was actually trying to tease me. "You were saying about the watch we have on the Jing embassy?"

DiCook's humor disappeared. "The wardens on duty between third evening and first night reported a solitary man came to the embassy gate. The peacekeepers who replaced the wardens on watch said the man left a candlemark later, but came back to the embassy shortly after second night in different clothes and a different sword. The second visit was much shorter. Each time, he went back to the Green Lady Inn."

The folks assigned to watch the embassy did a better job than I expected. "How can they be sure it was the same man?"

"Same height, same thin build, same gait. The guard acted as if he were expecting the visitor the second time."

"Was that it?"

He raised his mug. "It's what they reported."

I had to tell him the truth. Despite our rocky relationship the first six months I had been posted to Orrin, DiCook had become one of the few I trusted over the last few days in this Goddess-forsaken city. "It was me."

"Both times?"

I nodded.

He muttered an obscenity. "I was hoping we had something to go on." One of his bushy eyebrows rose. "You going to tell me what you're up to?"

I hesitated. The last thing I wanted was to condemn him, also.

Red flooded his face. "I thought we were working together on this murder, Justice. If this is some temple bull—"

"Yes, it is temple-related."

He went silent, fingers drumming the side of his mug.

"And it's not. And quite frankly, with what I'm planning, anyone involved could find their heads on the business end of another justice's sword."

His finger drumming paused, and he looked at me for a long time before he said, "Well, you've been wanting to see my head roll since you arrived here, haven't you?"

I couldn't help it. My laugh came out in an unladylike series of snorts. When I calmed, I said, "This really isn't a joke. We could be executed. *You* could be executed. I'm planning to trade a demon artifact for a hostage."

"Then I'm in," he said.

"Malven—"

"You're going to need help. We already know one temple's been corrupted. I damn well know you can't rely on the others either. Justice Penelope—" He displayed the same hesitation my staff had when it came to my predecessor.

For the first time, I truly appreciated the difficult situation he'd been put in. "Was a senile fool from what I've read from her records, and Brother Kam didn't trust you because you weren't a priest. I really don't know how you managed to keep the peace in Orrin with the odds stacked so severely against you. And I do truly apologize for making the same misjudgment of your abilities."

He opened his mouth, but I held up a hand. "For that very reason, I don't want you to put your life at risk."

"I think that's my choice, m'lady. Not yours."

"You're an idiot," I said with affection.

"An idiot superior to Samael DiRoy, I pray," he mocked.

"I have a prisoner to truthspell and question." I extended my hand. "Would you care to accompany me, Magistrate DiCook?"

"I'd be delighted, Chief Justice Anthea." He wrapped my hand about his elbow. "Though may I ask why Brother Mat isn't assisting you?"

"Ah, my dear Magistrate—" I patted his arm with my free palm. "There's quite a bit of the evening's events that I haven't had a chance to inform you of yet."

My wardens had already removed Mat's clothing and manacled him to the wall by the time DiCook and I arrived. Donella waited patiently with her quill. For a brief moment, I wondered if I were wrong about my suspicions, but too much rode on my unraveling the real plot and the rest of the conspirators. If he were innocent, he would understand.

I laid the counter and the truthspell on Mat before Little Bear roused him with a cup of water splashed in his face. The traitor spluttered and tried to wipe the liquid from his eyes with his hands. He yanked at his shackles a few times before he leaned his forehead against the shoulder of the rough gray shift he wore.

"So you're the traitor behind—" But the truthspell aborted whatever falsehood he was about to spew. He bent double with the pain. Any sympathy I had evaporated.

"Are you Brother Mat?"

"No." All good-natured humor that had marked the man vanished. His deception also explained why no real emotions or thoughts leaked from him, and it added to my questions.

"Where is the real Mat?"

"Dead."

"Did you kill him?"

"Yes." Glee tainted his voice.

"When?"

"Three years ago."

"Where?"

"Off the National Road near the Trill River."

"Was this when he was on his way to accept his assignment in Orrin?"

"Yes."

"Why did you kill him?"

"To take his place."

My heart ached. The skeleton of the real Brother Mat was probably lying out there under the ice. Possibly near where Gretchen was tortured and murdered. Another connection to this insane mess. "Why did you take his place?"

"To gain a foothold in the Temple of Light."

"Was it only here in Orrin?"

"I don't know." He laughed. "You must be more specific in your questioning, Anthea." The way he drawled out my name made me want to strike him.

I sucked in a deep breath to organize my thoughts. Not asking the correct questions now could get Luc, Isabella, and Goddess knew how many more people killed. "What was your purpose in replacing Brother Mat here in Orrin?"

"To attain the seat of Light."

"Why do you want the Orrin seat of Light?"

Another sick smile. "To destroy the temples, of course." He wasn't even trying to fight the truthspell any more.

"Why do you wish to destroy the temples?"

"They are no longer needed."

"Why are they no longer needed?"

"The gods seek to limit humans. Control us. There are other ways to attain power."

"In what ways do you seek to obtain power?"

"By whatever means we can."

This dance of words had turned into a farce. He told enough of the truth to prevent the truthspell from igniting in his gut and to keep me guessing. Time to change directions.

"What is your birth name?"

He grunted. "Micah."

I wove the name into the spell, a little trick a junior priest wouldn't know, much less an imposter. There was a sharp tug on the strand of magic as the addition settled, and he grunted again in response.

"Where were you born?"

"The island of New Thenos." The eastern coast of the continent, thousands of leagues from Issura.

"When were you born?"

"Twenty-eight winters ago." So he was older than the age recorded with the Temple of Light.

A groan issued from Mat—or Micah. With my more direct questions, he began fighting my truthspell in earnest. Had he known about Love's counter spell before we did? Used it to slip past Kam's watch. I couldn't even ask the old man about the fake Mat's history. Maybe my grandfather's death wasn't so much an accident after all.

"Who do you report to outside of the Temple of Light's hierarchy?" I repeated.

"M-my master," he choked.

"What is their name?" I wouldn't release Micah. Couldn't. Too much depended on me ferreting out who was behind the recent spate of demon activity. If they were even connected. I tried to shove any thoughts of Luc or Lady Isabella from my mind, but saving them was the whole reason I was doing this.

Micah's screams echoed off the narrow stone cell, down the corridors and back, while he fought the agony of the truthspell.

"Justice, you need to stop!" DiCook had to shout to be heard over the imposter.

I kept my expression impassive and gave a sharp shake of my head. If we gave in, if *I* gave in now, Luc was lost.

In that moment, in my heart of hearts, my silent admission that I'd forsaken my duty smothered me and freed me at the same time. My vows, my honor, my life meant nothing if I had no one to fight for.

Micah's screeching halted when he passed out from the pain. I had to give him credit for his endurance. He'd lasted longer than I ever had, in training or in life.

"Kill him already, daughter dearest?" Gerd's voice didn't bounce the same way Micah's shouts of agony had. Her question was followed by a *tsk*-ing sound. "I don't think your Reverend Mother will let a second unauthorized execution go unpunished."

"You're only hoping I've gone mad, and I'll take your head before your guilt is laid bare for all at the capital to gossip over," I called back.

Then the realization hit me over the head as if the Father himself had struck me with his axe. I hadn't asked Gerd the correct questions either. She hadn't been trained to evade questioning like the Assassins Guild members committing suicide or my insane imposter of a priest and his word games. I'd totally made a farce of this whole affair by letting my resentment rule my training in logic.

Little Bear dipped the cup into the bucket to splash more water on our imposter.

"Wait." I rose from my stool.

"Justice?"

I understood his quizzical tone. Maybe I was still letting my emotions toward my birth mother get the better of me, but my gut said she knew more than she'd let on. If she'd remained silent instead of goading me, I would have missed this opportunity.

At my gesture, Little Bear dropped the cup into the bucket and unlocked the door to the cell.

I ignore the looks he, Donella, and DiCook exchanged while I strode out of one cell and down the short corridor to the one that held Gerd. Bartholomew peeked at me from his own cell, but wisely said nothing. For a brief instant, I wished all this whole mess could be as simplistic as a servant longing for someone beyond his station and doing something totally idiotic.

Gerd peered through the small barred window of her door. "So you decided to kill me after all?" But the dance of heat along her throat and cheeks belied her mocking tone.

"You've always been more attuned to your self-interest than anything else in your life," I replied. I whispered the words of the counter, then those of the truthspell.

Her eyes rounded. "You've already questioned me." A clink of metal followed her words. She raised her cuffed hands and backed away from the door. After her original questioning, her ankle manacles had been removed so she could use the bucket that served as a prisoner's privy.

But after seeing the other priestesses in fighting form, I wasn't about to enter the cell.

Since this wasn't part of her official record, I didn't mince words. "Did you start fucking Brother Mat, also known as Micah, after Brother Dav rejected you?" I snarled.

She screamed and collapsed to the stone floor, writhing in pain. It was the only answer I needed.

I stalked back to Micah's cell. Little Bear let me in and relocked the door.

"Allow me, Lady Justice," DiCook hissed.

I nodded, and he splashed water on the fake priest's face to rouse him. Down the hall, Gerd cried, "Yes! Yes!" as my imposter spluttered to consciousness.

"How long have you been—" I changed the word I was about to use. A justice cursing was unseemly. No doubt I would be issued a reprimand once the Reverend Mother read Donella's official transcript if I did. "—worshipping with Gerd?"

Red teeth shone against his greenish-yellow skin. "Long enough to know I can't trust her with anything important."

Damn him. I needed to do better questioning him than I did with some upcountry farmer. "How many winters, months, and days have you been worshipping with Sister Gerd of Orrin?"

Micah tried to fight the truthspell, but the last round must have consumed his will. "Two winters, four months. I don't know how many days." He slumped, gasping for air.

"Why did you select Gerd as an accomplice?"

He shrugged, not even trying to fight this time "She didn't have any ethical qualms about screwing a priest from Light. Once Dav decided on fresher pickings, her pride couldn't say no to a handsome younger thing like me."

"Did your master order you to seduce her into violating her vows?"

Micah laughed. "Yes, but I didn't need to seduce her into anything. She agreed quite willingly."

"I did not!" Gerd shrieked. "He said he would expose us both if I didn't do what he said!" Which was true, thanks to the spells binding them both, but it wasn't my main concern right now.

"Did you bring a Jing noble to Gerd for a favor?"

"Yes."

"Why?"

"The trading in children was additional blackmail material. If I'd known he had a demon grimoire, I would have dealt with him directly."

"Do you mean deal with him for you to acquire the grimoire?"

"Yes."

"Were you the one who found her buyer, Ural DiSand?"

"Yes."

"Is he one of your membership?"

Once again, he tried to struggle against the truthspell. "Yes," he finally said between gasps.

"Were the mercenaries and Assassins Guild members stationed at Love part of your membership?"

"Yes."

"Why didn't you steal the grimoire?"

"I couldn't access Gerd's safe. I made the mistake of trying to talk Gretchen into stealing it for me since she was Gerd's main rival at the temple."

The next to the last puzzle piece fell into place. Micah's plan had back-fired. No wonder he didn't have a problem spreading word of the counter to the truthspell block. His own people needed it because Gretchen had evaded his questions about taking the demon grimoire and its location. She'd fled with the book after Micah had questioned her. Marston and this mysterious master of theirs tortured her for its whereabouts, but she hadn't given in to the pain and horror. I had to re-evaluate my opinion of her conduct.

If only she'd come to me to begin with. But given the conduct of Gerd and Micah, I could understand why she hadn't trusted me. Now, it was too late. I had the damn book, and too many lives were at risk. All because we were human with all the species' inherent weaknesses. And to think Micah and his compatriots sought to elevate us above the gods themselves . . .

I giggled. I couldn't stop myself. Maybe it was my exhaustion. Or maybe it was the insanity of these plots and counterplots. The giggles expanded into laughter. I laughed so hard I fell off my stool.

The other four people in the cell, including my prisoner, stared at me as if I'd lost all sense. Maybe I had.

Once my laughter died to soft chuckling, I regained my seat and wiped the tears from my face. "All those machinations, and you totally failed."

Micah scowled at me, but for once, he had no mocking reply.

"Which other Temples of Light have your fellow imposters infiltrated?"

"I. Don't. Know."

"Which of the other eleven orders have your members infiltrated?"

"I. Don't. Know."

"Is Brother Dav of Tandor a member of your group?"

A slight hesitation, and a wince of pain crossed his face. "I. Don't. Know."

Once again, I'd wager Gerd's cursed gold that he'd been about to say yes, but the truthspell wouldn't let him. He may have simply wanted to send me on a wild hare chase. In an odd way though, Micah's answers made sense.

The leader of this secret rebellion against the temples was quite intelligent. He or she wouldn't want the other members to know too much about each other in case one was caught and truthspelled.

Balance help us, we were in so much trouble. Their target may only be the temples, but our destruction or discredit would leave all nations open to attack. Whether it was from demons or each other was irrelevant.

I also would wager there was a reason Micah accommodated the previous questions. A quick check of any other information I needed said there was one last question unanswered.

I leaned close to him and whispered, "What is the name of your master?"

He reared away from me before a howl tore from his throat. Part of me knew he wouldn't answer. The same part that watched with disturbing satisfaction as he screamed in agony. The part that had already surmised he would die before he'd give up the name of his leader.

The part that wasn't about to give him the ease of poison or my sword.

*This is for Gretchen and Kam, you perverted bastard.*

His pulse hammered in his neck, faster and faster. Finally, his cries and his heart halted abruptly. Poor Donella swiveled away to vomit into the privy bucket. Even the magistrate and my chief warden's faces had a blueish-green tinge.

I climbed slowly, wearily, to my feet. "At least, I don't have to clean my steel. Please have Master Aaron confirm his death before notifying Sister Bertrice."

Little Bear nodded and unlocked the cell door. The only sounds in the dungeon were Donella's dry heaves and Bartholomew weeping.

I strode down the short hallway and stopped in front of Gerd's cell. "Is there testimony you can add?"

"No." The word came out as a half-sob, half-curse. Of course not, she didn't want to tell me anything that would help me save Luc. The sad part was she had nothing left with which to bargain. I dissipated the truthspell on her.

"You're going to die for this," she shrieked as my foot hit the step.

I could have answered in kind, but I remained silent and continued climbing the stone stairs. If my questioning of the imposter formerly known as Brother Mat hadn't sealed my fate, what I was about to do would.

# *Chapter 23*

The bells of Mother rang third night as I strode to my office. I had Sivan fetch me a pot of tea before I locked the door. When I reached into my safe hole, the leather of Gretchen's saddlebags felt as chilled as the clasp to the pocket with the demon grimoire had a day ago when Dragonfly had produced the murdered priestess's belongings. I pulled them out and examined them. The leather and embroidery were no longer splotchy. The blackness had spread until the bags resembled the contaminated casket we found last fall aboard Duke Marco's merchant flagship, the *Mars Tranquilus*.

Not for the first time, I wished I hadn't followed protocol and destroyed the casket. We should have studied how the influence of a demon spread across an inanimate object. Granted the casket had held a demon egg, instead of the full-grown variety, but Quan's original sorcerer showed no such contamination on his clothing or jewels. We needed to understand how a demon's influence worked, how the School of Sorcery hid it, and how others with talent could detect it. More things I needed to add to my requests of the Reverend Mother.

I stamped a quick note for Donella on the question before I resumed my examination of the murdered priestess's belongings. It had taken roughly eleven days for the blackness to engulf Gretchen's saddlebags, assuming she placed the book in them for the first time the same night she met Alessa for their tryst. A quick check showed the gold, jewelry and clothing in the left-hand bag had developed the same initial splotches as the leather had, and they weren't even touching the grimoire directly.

Except Luc didn't have eleven days for a fake grimoire to be properly contaminated. He had less than one. Would the demon magic fight my haphazard spell? Nothing similar to this had been attempted by anyone in my order that I knew of. But then, no healer had ever tried the same stunt with my eyes I had either. I latched the clasp again and set the bags on my chair.

*Balance, please, for Luc and Isabella's sake, don't let this spell explode in my face like Jing flash powder.*

From my overflowing shelves, I took a Light bound tome I'd borrowed from Kam months ago. Donella had the junior clerk . . . I struggled to name her. Lailani! The quick joy at remembering a staff member's name warred with the pang at the memory of Kam.

Lailani had translated the old spell book into Balance code for me when I was researching demon activity. At first glance from a normally-sighted person, it could be a spell book from anywhere since the first chapter had a glossary of the basics before the author delved into his detailed research. If the tome were ruined or destroyed tonight, which was highly likely, Lailani could translate the Balance copy back for the brothers later.

I set the book on my desk before I rolled rugs out of the way, exposing bare marble. No sense burning down the temple if my mad idea went wrong. I gathered everything I needed on the floor before sitting cross-legged next to the items.

Steeling myself, I open the bag with the grimoire. An alien feeling danced along my bare fingers. The same terrible feeling I had when I saw my first demon. Gritting my teeth, I pulled it free of the bag. An inaudible vibration went through it, almost a purr.

Despite the sick feeling in my gut from touching the book, I opened it and ripped out the first ten pages. The contaminated leather shivered against my skin, and what sounded like a high-pitched squeal of pain set my teeth on edge.

A horrible thought occurred. What if the leather wasn't from an animal, but the skin of a demon? What if it was still alive by some perverted method?

I quickly shoved the disturbing idea into a deep hole in my mind. If I couldn't stay focused, Balance only knew what kind of disaster I would make of this.

Placing the demon pages I'd taken on top of the first page of the Light spell book elicited another squeal, just as high-pitched, but not as loud. I placed the open tome on top of an old silk shirt in my lap. The material was commonly worn by those of high status in Jing. My assumption that it was resistant to demon influence might be a dangerous one, but I had nothing else to go on at the moment.

I debated on whether to return the grimoire to my safe hole before I started, but from the rate the cover of Kam's book was graying, I decided I'd best get my experiment over with. With thread and needle already to go, I quickly sewed the torn pages into the binding, after the glossary. Hopefully, it would appear that the original owner sought to hide their obscene work from the authorities. I bit the thread after I tied the last knot, and a sharp pain shot through my skull. The kind of pain I had when I'd eaten flavored mountain snow too fast.

I took several deep, slow breaths to get the ache to subside. And to make sure my actions hadn't left me susceptible to something from the grimoire's pages. After a long moment, I decided it was safe to continue.

Everything I'd done so far had been the easy tasks. The spreading gray along the Light book's original pages reassured me. I was on the right track if I didn't accidentally kill myself with this experiment.

Taking one of my older knives, I carefully carved the clerical shorthand symbols for "demon" and "magic" into the spine's leather. The work was painstaking and difficult because I had to feel what I was doing. It reminded me too much of temple lessons when I was a child.

Ironically, I was doing the very same things people who consorted with demons during the wars did to hide their grimoires. With everyone who had seen the book dead, imprisoned or one of my allies, no one I knew of could dispute the validity of the book.

I hoped anyway. The urge to make a childish gesture for good luck swept through me.

A little ash mixed with walnut ink smeared into the fresh cuts was my last task. I wiped off the excess paste and cleaned my hands on an old rag.

Once again, I had the feeling of someone peering over my shoulder even though I was alone. Maybe it was the ghost of Thalia. Maybe it was Balance Herself.

More likely, it was my imagination running rampant from the stress of this investigation and lack of sleep.

Inhaling deeply, I opened my mind to the fabric of time. This spell would cost me ten days of my natural life, but Luc was worth that small sacrifice. If I failed in my mad plan, we'd both be dead.

I reached out and plucked the requisite length of time forward in my own line. Knotted the loop I held to anchor me in the here and now. Snipped the thread.

A sharp pain thrummed in my chest. My heart didn't beat for ten counts. Another ache, duller than the first, as my heart resumed its rhythm.

Sucking in a harsh breath, I wrapped the thread around my masquerading tome. Knotting both ends to the book's now with the slightest of spaces between the ties. Another snip of a main thread. With a snap, the book's life extended into the past by ten days.

Magic dissipated, and I examined my handiwork. The pages and binding no longer held any hint of the familiar warm tingle of Light magic. Leather and paper both were the black that was an absence of color. Cold seeped into my flesh as I ran my fingers over the engraving on the spine.

I sent a silent prayer to the Twelve this insane plan would work. For an instant, I would have sworn I felt satisfaction from whatever peered over my shoulder.

Instead of Sivan shaking me or one of the wardens banging on my bedchamber door, I awoke to the feeling of someone watching me. A fox perched at the foot of my bed. It peered at me, not threatening in any way. A small pack lay beside its feet. The curve of its jaw seemed familiar. "Farrah?"

White light flared, and I quickly shielded my eyes. When it faded, the

Wildling second sat on my bed in her human form. She inclined her head. "Brother Jax and Sister Shi Hua send their greetings and give thanks for your attempt at warning them."

I had the distinct feeling of being mocked. "My attempt?"

"They suspected such a trap when Brother Luc's alleged captors rode for the Valley of the Lost. It made no sense to hide a hostage so far from Orrin."

I couldn't argue with Farrah's logic. "Was there anything else?"

"Magistrate DiCook passed on the place for the exchange to me. One of our brothers can take the form of an eagle. If there is any additional information, I can send it to Brother Jax, though he cautions against using that method unless absolutely necessary." She paused as if reluctant to bring up whatever request was on the verge of her tongue.

"Go ahead and ask," I said.

"Are you really going to trade the demon grimoire for Brother Luc?"

I hesitated. Lying now seemed the best course of action though I was loath to do so. If my allies believed I'd make the exchange, the more likely my foe would as well. "Yes."

She nibbled on her lower lip, as if to object, but she said no more.

To break the uncomfortable silence, I nodded toward the pack. "What did you bring me?"

She chuckled. "It is merely my human clothing, Justice. The citizens of Orrin would gossip if I left your bedchamber while naked." She waved a hand over her bare skin.

"The citizens of Orrin believe whichever story is the juiciest," I said sourly.

Another chuckle rippled from Farrah. "Very true. You are finally learning city ways."

"No." I shoved my bedcovers aside and swung my legs over the edge. "The outlying villages and farms can be just as rife with jealously and rumors."

"Those are the reasons I prefer the wild things," she said softly. "They aren't power hungry either."

For some reason, her comment disturbed me. "Is that how you see me?"

She snorted. "Hardly. You're more like a mother wolf running through the forest. You live. You love. You protect. And anyone foolish enough to invade your territory will pay dearly."

I wasn't sure how to respond to that statement either, so I rang the bell for Sivan. "Well, this wolf wants food before she tears into any interlopers."

My evening meal turned into a war council in the Balance receiving room after I truthspelled Jeremy concerning his legitimacy and loyalties as a priest of Light. Along with him were Little Bear, Tyra, DiCook, Marco dressed in Mat/Micah's robes, Farrah, Bertrice, Xander, Han, and surprisingly, Dragonfly brought Quan through the tunnels.

The Jing diplomat bowed. "Another message from Shi Hua. The same dozen men who captured Brother Luc are inside the manse where you are to meet tonight. He is with them. Eight additional men have joined the abductors. Your Wilding priests are watching the place."

One of his eyebrows rose. "They have a demon with them, Anthea. One hatched here from the Wildlings' observations. Since Shi Hua cannot approach too closely without it sensing her, she will meet you on the coastal trail three leagues north of the manse."

*Wonderful.* I resisted the urge to bury my face in my hands. My evening couldn't possibly become any better. Last fall, we discovered demons hatched in our plane of existence were weaker than their summoned counterparts, but no less dangerous.

"This doesn't change our plan," I said firmly.

DiCook frowned. "You're supposed to go alone, according to their message."

I laughed. "Except I have no doubt they assumed I would be stupid enough to bring the imposter priest with me to cover my backside." I waved at the duke. "So I will."

Marco shook his head. "That's assuming they really expect Mat to slit your throat once they have the grimoire."

Bertrice leaned forward. "You can't seriously be considering this trade.

We're better off destroying the book and marching en masse on the manse. Luc knows the stakes."

"And I know him," I said. "He's been collecting information about these fools while they have him. Your priority is still to get him out. Granted I want to get one of those bastards alive to question, but only *my* top priority has changed. I will be dealing with the demon now."

The ambassador crossed his arms. "With all due respect, Lady Justice, it took both Brother Luc and Brother Jeremy together with you to destroy the demon that had been secreted on my estate. Luc may not be in any condition to aid you, which leaves only Shi Hua."

"Then I need to go with you, Justice," Jeremy blurted.

"No." My hand smacked the tabletop for emphasis. "If this goes wrong, Orrin will need one Light priest alive."

DiCook snorted. "And what exactly is your concubine going to do, Ambassador?"

Quan's gaze flicked to me and back to the magistrate. "She's a registered talent. She can do quite a bit to assist the justice."

I shook my head. "Leave the demon to me. It's going to want the grimoire in order to summon its fellows to our plane. More so than these rogues want the grimoire."

Bertrice set aside her bean drink with a sharp *clink*. "So everything I did three decades ago was for nothing." Her bitter tone matched the scarlet heat of her face.

"No," I said softly. "I have no intention of throwing my life away. We may not be able to kill it through conventional means, but I can trap it." I didn't add that it meant trapping myself with it.

She threw up her hands. "And then what? You can't possibly hold it until the Reverend Father of Light sends reinforcements."

"And if I go with you—" Jeremy's tone was full of youthful earnestness.

"No." Again, I shook my head. "Han needs you here. Orrin needs you here. Just in case I am wrong about everything."

The chief brother of Conflict had been silent through the entire exchange, but the bass rumble of him clearing his throat drew everyone's attention. "Anthea, these people are vicious. You asked me to have a look at the bodies Bertrice's people brought back. For Gibb, there's no question that he had a clean death, but the other man—"

Han shook his head. "They started skinning him while he was alive. His pain is what fueled the shapeshifting spell as well as the trap. Thank the Twelve no one touched the corpse before it was salted."

"That's why I want you and Malven here in Orrin."

"You're still worried the city may be attacked," DiCook said.

"I don't know anything for sure." I inclined my head in Quan's direction. "The fact that they have one demon is news to me. They could have more with them."

Han shrugged. "Then we can only plan based on what we know." He cleared his throat again. "I went to visit Father Jerrod today. The staff at his temple said he was assisting you. Yet, I have not seen him."

I resisted the urge to rub my sweating palms on my thighs. "Yes, he helped with the questioning of Gerd. However, I have not seen him since he left this room."

Han cocked his head. "I don't need a truthspell to know when someone isn't telling me the whole story, young lady."

Part of me wanted to tell him the truth. I found I liked and trusted him. But the last thing I wanted was to drag another temple seat down with me.

Han's eyes widened. "For the love of the Twelve, you didn't stick him down in the gaol, did you, Anthea?"

The mixture of disgust and exasperation in his voice cut through my indecision. "I wouldn't put anyone in a cell unless he'd broken the law." I sounded like a petulant child, so I inhaled deeply before I added, "Jerrod's in a spare bedroom upstairs. He objects to my plan. I . . . wanted to give him a reasonable excuse in case—"

"Warrior's balls, woman! Bertrice and I aren't happy about your plan either. You going to lock us up, too?"

Little Bear and Tyra's hands immediately went to their swords. I raised my hand to stop them. The last thing I needed was my only allies fighting amongst themselves.

"Only if you two threaten to arrest me, Han."

The priest wiped a huge hand across his face. "By all the Warrior's names, do you think I'm that stupid? Especially with a demon running around. We can't be battling each other. And—" He waggled an index finger in my direction. "We can't be hiding anything from each other either. Anything else you want to tell us?"

I sighed. "Lady Alessa is upstairs under protective custody."

"And I fetched my wife down here while the justice napped to keep my sister company." Marco grimaced. "And to keep these murderers from deciding they need another hostage."

"Excuse me?" My attention flicked between the duke and my chief warden.

Little Bear finally said, "It was a reasonable precaution, Lady Justice. You told me to use my discretion in such matters."

His statement earned a howl of laughter from Han.

I scowled at my chief warden. "I would appreciate notice the next time my temple entertains the heir of Orrin."

My sour tone didn't faze Little Bear one bit. He simply nodded and said, "Yes, m'lady."

There was nothing else to say. Everyone rose and set about their respective tasks. Quan whispered something to Dragonfly before he approached me.

Tyra frowned and started to intercept him. I signaled her to hold back. Sharp displeasure issued from her, but she kept her distance.

The ambassador inclined his head. "I detect a measure of animosity toward me from your wardens, Justice."

I smiled. "It has more to do with the unintentional insult to their skills and training your concubine's late night visits engender, Ambassador."

His lips twitched, sending the beads at the ends of his moustache swinging. "A gift to assist you, Justice." He pulled a small package from his coat pocket and handed it to me.

I frowned at the feel of three round, hard items through the felt. "What—"

His hand covered mine. "Whatever you do, don't squeeze them too tightly. You'd lose your fingers. Translated in the trade tongue, they would be called 'flash bangs'. If you need a distraction, throw one at the ground as hard as you can."

I looked up at Quan. "Jing flash powder?"

He nodded. "Mixed in proportions with other ingredients to produce one bright flash and copious amounts of smoke. I don't recommend breathing it. And I don't know how it might affect your sight. We have neither the amount nor the time to test such matters."

The ambassador's gift provided a burst of inspiration. Or maybe Balance Herself decided to take an interest in my city and planted the thought in my head. I sorely hated to give credit to the imposter priest Micah, though he had ventured the original idea. "May I ask another favor?"

"Of course."

"Could you provide a measure of flash powder to collapse one of Orrin's tunnels?"

His body tensed. "You're not closing off the tunnel between the Green Lady and the Temple of Love, are you?"

"Why, Quan Po, I would never interfere with your . . . entertainments as long as they are legal." I smiled. "It would be one of the other tunnels. I have an idea on how to deal with the demon."

"Then our stores are at your disposal, Lady Justice."

"Thank you." I meant the words. And I became uncomfortably aware that the ambassador still held my hand.

"I've already informed Dragonfly and Han that my small household guard will assist in protecting Orrin, should such be necessary." He leaned closer, his breath warm against my ear. "Be careful in your escapade tonight, Anthea. I would miss our . . . sparring."

He released me, and a shiver ran through my body. The audacity of that man!

As if she knew what Quan had said, Dragonfly winked at me as she led him back to the tunnel entrance.

Through my bedchambers.

I gave myself a mental shake. None of the ambassador's innuendo would mean anything if I died tonight.

Which might actually happen since all I had was one insane plan of how to stop this new demon. And I could very well kill myself with my mad idea.

# *Chapter 24*

I loudly announced my name and Brother Mat's when Duke Marco and I rode out through Death's Gate at third evening. We had plenty of time to make the rendezvous before first night. The show we made was to allow Bertrice's disguised wardens to mark who paid attention to our departure.

We were well out of the peacekeepers' sight on the old coastal trail before we came upon the exit from the tunnel system. Farrah waited there in her vulpine form, her fluffy tail swishing with impatience.

Little Bear would follow from Government Gate, accompanied by Xander and a handful of other wardens along with DiCook and a half dozen peacekeepers. They would take the National Road, keeping my team's way back to the tunnels clear.

I prayed what little surprise we could muster would be sufficient. With Shi Hua and the Wildling priests joining us, I'd normally be confident with our numbers even against the renegades.

However, the demon made every strategy suspect.

I made note of the mulberry bushes that covered the entrance along with the fallen pine. Climbing off Nassa, I approached the dead wood. Faint lavender light emanated from the bark. If it was been any season other than winter, the tiny creatures wouldn't have been noticeable under the heat of growing plants.

Marco circled his steed around my horse. "What are you doing, m'lady?"

"Marking the path to make sure I know where the tunnel entrance is." I place my gloved hands on the log and removed them. Dark gray prints showed amidst the lavender glow.

"Do you really think the demon will follow you?" Marco said.

An evil smile tugged at my lips. "If it were just me, maybe not. But Shi Hua and I together will be too tempting of a target."

His horse's reins jingled as I remounted. "I hope you're right. Bringing the demon this close to Orrin unnerves me."

I didn't add that having another demon this near to the city made me anxious as well.

Farrah gave us a little yip of warning before Jax stepped out of the brush in his wolf form.

"You received the new plan from your eagle?" I asked.

He nodded, the human gesture incongruent with his canine form.

Shi Hua stepped forward from the other side of the trail. Instead of the usual temple-issued sword, fletching poked over her right shoulder and a short, recurved bow rested in her hand. "If I didn't know better, I'd say you switched to the Vintner's temple."

"I may be mad, but it would have been easier for all involved if you had consulted with me before you took off," I chided.

She laughed, a high, tinkling note. "But that defeats the purpose of not having a high priest to report to in a foreign land, Lady Justice."

Something was missing. Even with temple training, she couldn't match the Wildlings' pace, and it would be rude, not to mention unseemly, for her to ride one of them. "Where's your horse?"

More laughter. "Grazing with the renegades' mounts. Their counting skills leave something to be desired."

I held out my hand, and with a light leap, she mounted Nassa behind me. Since the renegades were expecting a member of Light to accompany me, it didn't matter if the demon sensed her power now. And I had to assume the imposter Micah was initiated somewhere, even if it wasn't Issura. A civilian with talent couldn't easily imitate certain aspects of the various priesthoods.

We continued south. Only glimpses of bright yellow-green fur through the hawthorn foliage told me the Wildlings paced our horses. I couldn't help examining the treetops as we rode. Demons had perched among the branches the first time I'd ever seen them. With a start, I realized Marco did the same.

"We've never talked in detail about how you were taken by DiRoy," I said softly.

"I had too many nightmares to want to discuss it," he murmured.

"Can demons fly?" Shi Hua's voice was as quiet as ours.

"No," the duke answered. "They swing from limb to limb among the tree tops. We humans never look up when we're fighting. We're used to someone on the ground with us. There's much our ancestors took for granted during the demon wars. I think they assumed certain things were such common knowledge it never occurred to them to record the information."

A wordless sound of acknowledgment vibrated against my back. "It explains a certain mandate at home I never understood."

"What's that?" I asked.

"All trees and bushes must be cut back a minimum of a league from the emperor's palace."

I laughed. "Someone recorded it. They should have stated why."

"Well, then. Let's use the demons tactics against them." Shi Hua slid off Nassa and disappeared amongst the dormant tree and bushes. The Wildlings split. The fox shadowed her while the wolf darted east toward the National Road. Probably toward Jax's bear priest who was still watching the manse.

"What is she—" Marco held up his hand. "No, don't tell me."

"I knew you'd make an excellent duke." I smiled at him.

Dragonfly had offered us talismans to prevent being truthspelled, but I didn't accept. I wouldn't subject Marco to torture if this stunt of mine didn't work. And Balance only knew if Micah had managed to get a message out to his compatriots about the counter spell.

The trees thinned ahead, and I resisted the urge to look up. Marco tugged his hood a little lower. All we had to do was stall until the demon was focused on me.

We entered the massive, unkempt grounds. The grass that had been knee-high on me last summer was flattened, a gray weave against the earth. Only faint blue-green at the roots showed the plants slept for the winter.

I had expected a sentry or two outside along the edges of the property, but I heard nothing except the distant crash of waves along the bluffs. There wasn't even the tell-tale glow of exposed skin. A glance at Marco confirmed he neither saw nor heard anything either.

If I had a demon at my side, maybe I would think I was invincible as well, and in no need of a sentry. Or maybe, Luc gave the renegades that much trouble.

We rode around the stone wall that originally protected the lady of the manor's garden, following the same path I had with the other priests only three nights ago. However, I expected the buzz along the back of my neck tonight, the same one from last summer. The demon was near, and it wasn't bothering to disguise its power.

I halted Nassa outside of the range where she had been disturbed the last time, and Marco reined beside me. Gambling that they believed Micah wouldn't break his impersonation of Brother Mat was an incredible risk, but we had very little to go on.

No, I had little to go on because of my desire for vengeance. I should have kept the imposter priest alive.

Faint glimmers of green and yellow appeared in the dark blue windows. Possibly archers. Marco and I would be easy targets if our assistance didn't arrive soon. And I didn't dare use silent speech in case I accidentally warned our opponents.

The main doors swung open. One man stepped out onto the portico. "Do you have it?"

I pushed back my hood. "Show me High Brother Luc first."

The man's dark chuckle made my fingers clench with the desire to run my sword through his heart. "He's having a little difficulty walking at the moment."

My throat hurt with the effort to keep my tone light. "Lady Alessa showed me the little gift you sent her. However, if he's not even alive, there's no reason to make the trade." I backed Nassa two steps. Marco followed my lead.

From inside the manse came a faint guttural syllable. Demon language. Marco tensed beside me, and his mount whickered. I prayed he didn't bolt.

"I guess there's no reason you can't see your lover."

The renegade's tone left a sick sensation in my stomach. It wasn't like I didn't know what they planned to do to all of us once they had the grimoire.

A moment later, two more men dragged a familiar figure to the portico and dropped him roughly on the flagstones. Luc grunted in pain when he landed. I tried not to wince at his injuries.

"Nice of you to come by," he growled. "I can see why you extolled the accommodations here, my love."

He was alive. My eyes stung. Whether with relief or empathy for his agony, I wasn't sure.

I pulled the false grimoire from my saddlebag, unwrapped the book from my old silk shirt, and threw it on the ground ahead of Nassa. "Here."

Another word in the demon language came from the manse. A feral grin spread on the man's face. "Kill her, Mat."

"Sorry, can't do that at the moment," Marco said, quite loudly. Instead of drawing the sword at his back, he spurred his horse forward. The skin, full of the poisoned oil he had held under his outer robe, fell from his hand, splashing over the contaminated cover of the false grimoire. He charged toward the manse.

I flicked a spark of magic at the oil-soaked leather, and it ignited with a *whoosh* of displaced air and brilliant heat. At my command, Nassa thundered after Marco's steed.

One of the renegades who had brought out Luc pulled his steel half out of his scabbard when gray feathers blossomed from his eye socket.

A screech of raw fury rent the night. A pure black form charged out the door and dived past our rush to the portico. Agonizing cold nipped my exposed skin in its wake. It ignored us.

Which was good because the abductor who'd spoken leapt from the railing and crashed into me, knocking us both to the ground. I rolled with the blow, hoping to land on top of him. It didn't work. We both landed on our sides, and we continued rolling as each of us tried to gain purchase.

Beyond Nassa, steel rang. I heard a muttered oath from Marco.

My opponent's fist struck my cheekbone. White shards exploded across my vision. In sheer desperation, I jammed my knee into his flesh. A high-pitched squeal rewarded me, and I broke free.

He climbed to his feet. We both drew swords. Before I could parry his blow, a shaggy shape flew past me. The man's scream turned into a gurgle when Jax tore open his throat.

Since Marco had blocked the door, one of the renegades smashed the shutters from a front window. With my free hand, I reached into my pocket and threw the hard, round object. The flash bang hit the man on the skull. His shout of pain at the powder burn left by Quan's gift abruptly shifted to coughing. The scent of smoke wafted across the yard, and my view of the renegade dulled.

An arrow whistled past my ear. I darted to my left and aimed a flash bang at another window with its shutters hanging at precarious angles. When the ball hit the rotting wood, it sparked before landing inside. Shouts arose, quickly followed by hacking coughs.

Another screech ripped the night air. I looked over my shoulder. The fire I started had been extinguished. The demon shredded the book in half and screeched again.

Balance help us, it had discovered my ruse.

Jax ducked his head, and the demon staggered back. It took another step toward us. Another ripple of energy from the wolf pushed the demon, but it dug its talons into the turf. Whatever the Wildling priest did only stalled the damn thing.

"Anthea!" Luc flew past me on Marco's borrowed horse.

Nassa galloped behind him. She slowed long enough for me to grasp her saddle and swing onto her back. I glanced behind me.

Thank the Twelve, Marco was still upright and struggling to keep his opponent boxed in the doorway. Jax ran toward him as more renegades tried to fight their way out of the manse. To my right, fire arrows from the wardens arched toward the roof.

So much for Xander getting Luc to safety.

*The old trail,* I said silently.

However, Luc was already headed in that direction. *Shi Hua told me.* He tried to block it, but I could feel the pain from his leg. I looked behind us, trusting Nassa to follow the path.

A third rider fell in behind us. *You definitely got the demon's attention, Justice.*

I'd laugh along with Shi Hua if I hadn't already seen what one of those creatures could do with its claws.

White light flared from the manse as its roof caught fire. Men shouted and bellowed. Mixed between were the higher-pitched war cries of women. Steel clanged. Above the cacophony was the shrieks of rage from the demon.

And those were getting closer rather than dropping away like the other noise.

I turned forward and kept my head low to Nassa's neck. Bright color dripped from Luc's stump, which worried me far more than the demon. If he bled out before we reached Orrin . . .

My heart caught in my throat. I couldn't think like that. Fear would paralyze me if it did.

Another shriek echoed through the trees behind us. Closer. Above us.

"Keep going!" Shi Hua shouted.

A check over my shoulder revealed her yanking on her horse's reins. "You can't!"

*I've no plans of dying today, Justice.* She whirled her mount in a tight turn, the arrow already nocked in her bow.

Magic tingled along my nerves. My protest clogged my throat when her shot hit the demon. I expected the demon to change so the steel tip and shaft passed through it, but her spell flared. The demon shrieked in pain. It started to fall until its talons dug into the tree's bark. Even I could see the pale yellow furrows scored along the trunk.

Shi Hua pivoted her mount in my direction. "Go!"

Nassa didn't need any encouragement on my part. She raced after the horse that carried Luc.

The demon let his fury be known to everything in the forest, and not just from its sounds. Anything that didn't flee from his approach was quickly covered in frost. Whenever that ice glaze started past me and reached for Luc, Shi Hua would turn and fire a magic-enhanced arrow at the creature. She had to have been blessed by the Twelve for she never missed.

But her efforts only slowed down the damned thing. We needed concentrated light balls to destroy the demon from more than one Light priest. It had taken two to kill the one hiding in the Jing embassy last fall, and that creature had been rather feeble, possibly a century old or more. I had no doubt that the demon chasing us was in its prime, and hardly weak even if it had been hatched on our plane.

*Last arrow!*

Another unearthly shriek of pain followed Shi Hua's warning.

*We'll never make it to Orrin.* Luc did his best to hide his flagging energy.

*So little faith, High Brother?* I mocked, but I was worried, too. The hard ball bouncing against my thigh gave me an idea. *Shi Hua, do flash bangs work against demons?*

Her bell-like laughter rang in my head. *With a little help.*

We slowed just enough for me to toss her the last flash bang. She muttered her spell, and launched it at the demon.

This time the creature howled as if it were burning alive. Maybe it was, but I didn't dare look. If we accidently rode past the tunnel, our trap was of no use.

I recognized our dead log just ahead, my handprints prominent in grey on top. *We're not going to the Death Gate. Count to three and rein to a stop.*

He did as I instructed. Green sweat dotted his face.

I leapt off Nassa as she slowed to a trot. "You need to dismount."

"Anthea," he hissed. The blood from his stump was no longer the occasional drip.

I swallowed my own fear. "We have help in the tunnels. Please, we have to."

His muscles corded beneath my grip as he swung his right leg around. We both tumbled to the ground despite my efforts to steady him. He clenched his jaw to keep from crying out.

Shi Hua's horse slid to a stop beside us. She quickly dismounted and slapped the beast's flank. At her shouted command, Nassa and the other two galloped for Orrin. Since they were temple-bred, they wouldn't stop until they reached Balance's courtyard.

It took both of us to get Luc upright.

"We don't have much time," Shi Hua whispered. "The demon will follow the blood trail."

"Tell me something I don't know," I said through gritted teeth. We struggled through the brush to the tunnel opening. Only a toddler could have passed upright through the entrance. Farrah had warned me.

"Let's set him down," I murmured since I didn't know how close the demon was. "I'll go through first."

As I crawled through the crevice, Shi Hua scuffed dirt and dead leaves over the bright red trail Luc had left. She couldn't do much, but I prayed it bought us a few precious moments.

I half-slid, half-tumbled down the sharp incline to the main floor of the tunnel. More bruises to add to my growing collection. Forcing myself upright, I called back, "Luc, crawl in on your back."

His Cantish curse reassured me that he hadn't lost too much blood. I grasped him under his shoulders and tugged. Once again, we tumbled to the ground. My body bore the brunt of our landing, but he couldn't suppress the cry of pain this time.

"I'm sorry," I whispered.

He panted and squeezed my knee.

"Coming through," Shi Hua said.

I dragged Luc away from the incline.

"Woman, you're going to kill me before the damn demon does," he muttered. I took his quips as a good sign he was still in this fight.

Amidst a mass of soil and gravel, Shi Hua rolled down the incline much as I had. A sharp crack indicated her bow was lost. She climbed to her feet and tossed the broken wood aside.

"Some of us need a little light," she muttered.

"What about the demon seeing it?" I asked.

"Doesn't matter if Brother Luc and I are tripping around down here." She murmured a word. Magic tickled my skin, but I couldn't see a difference.

Luc groaned. "That doesn't help."

Shi Hua crouched near his feet, well, foot and examined the wound. "Be grateful they cauterized the stump. You'd be dead by now."

"So my new friends kept telling me," he said dryly. "By the way, you two ladies are on the top of their list to assassinate."

"We know," Shi Hua and I said at the same time.

Without another word, I grabbed him under the shoulders, and she lifted his legs. I didn't remember him being this heavy as we shuffled down the corridor.

"We need to talk about lowering your food intake," I muttered.

"You're getting soft, sitting in a temple," he shot back.

Everyone was quiet for moment except for our collective labored breathing. My arms and back ached from the strain, but we didn't dare stop. In the distance came the sounds of stone hitting stone. Shi Hua and I picked up our pace, but in my heart, I knew I couldn't sustain it for long.

The guttural cry of the demon echoed through the tunnel. My lungs hurt worse than the hammering of my heart. We couldn't stop yet. If we did, we were dead, and Orrin would be at the demon and the renegades' mercy.

Out of the pale lavender light, I spotted the gray sigil we'd left, the Jing symbol for fire. "Almost there," I huffed.

"See . . . it." Shi Hua's face glowed with her exertions. The height of the tunnel increased. "Stop . . . here," she puffed out and lowered Luc's legs.

I didn't have a choice. I lowered his torso to the floor as well. "We'll be in the blast—"

She shook her head. "Give me your sword. I'll hold off the demon while you get him clear."

"I'm not leaving you!"

"Trust me, Anthea!" Claws on stone scrabbled near, emphasizing her point.

I yanked my sword from its scabbard and tossed it to her hilt first. She caught it, muttering a spell under her breath. The sharp buzz along my nerves felt like a hundred bumblebees had surrounded us at once.

"Come on," I said to Luc, reaching for him. His color had faded to a sickly green. My heart sank. He wasn't going to make it to the bend in the tunnel that would protect us.

The feeling of someone watching over my shoulder came back, along with the sensation of pushing. Whatever was guiding me was right. We'd come too damn far to lie down and die. I slung his arm around my neck, and he hopped on his remaining foot.

I focused on the bend ahead and ignored the screeching, the clang of steel on stone, the cry of pain. As I feared, Luc collapsed into dead weight several yards short of the bend. He dragged me down with him. My knees barked against hard stone, bringing tears to my eyes.

A glance back showed Shi Hua and the demon in a stand off. It had shredded her tunic and scarlet streaks showed through the tears. But her spell on my sword kept the creature at bay.

It spotted me as I pushed myself upright and hauled at Luc's body. In a flurry of motion, it knocked my sword out of Shi Hua's grip.

In response, brilliant flames spouted from her fingertips and blasted past the demon. Harsh staccato barks came from the creature. It could laugh all it wanted. Her aim was true. The wicks on the bags planted in the tunnel sparked to life behind the demon.

I dragged Luc, counting silently before we dropped and I covered him. Shi Hua sprinted toward us.

The world erupted into nothing but stone and sound.

# Chapter 25

I couldn't hear anything but ringing. No soft violet light either. Only the length of Luc's body under mine reassured me that we still existed.

Luc.

My fingers sought the pulse points of his throat. The thrum was uneven but still there. He erupted into coughing, but it was simply the dust in the air.

"I'm alive," he croaked.

"Anthea?" The feminine voice came from somewhere to my left. Orange fingers streaked with red laid near us.

I rose off of Luc as gently as I could. The motion left me dizzy, but after a moment, I crawled toward the priestess. Her left arm lay at an unnatural angle under a stone the size of a newborn. When I moved the stone, she bit off a cry. She had a multitude of cuts from the demon's claws and the flying debris. Running my hands over her, I could find no other injuries.

"The demon?" She coughed.

I peered through the settling dust. The lavender of the tunnel walls shone faintly through the gray.

And I saw something far darker than the stone and dust move.

Except . . .

I watched, and equally black fluid oozed and flowed over the stone. The liquid hissed over the pebbles, and they cracked and shattered, sharp little retorts in the tunnel. The demon shoved rocks aside, freeing itself.

Both members of the Temple of Light were down with major injuries.

Frankly, I wasn't in much better shape than Luc and Shi Hua. But the demon was injured, too. We might have a chance.

Slowly, painfully, I pushed myself to my feet. This idea was even more insane than my original plan and the secondary one put together. And the last time I'd tried this spell, I'd been healthy and had plenty of time to prepare.

This time all I had was brute force.

The demon rose on all fours. I no longer had a choice. And I'd been practicing this trick since the last demon we'd battled.

Sucking in a harsh breath and ignoring the urge to cough, I wrenched the strands of time apart around just the creature. The pain in my head was incredible, but I couldn't let go. The flow of demon's blood slowed, and the creature itself paused in mid-step.

"Luc. Shi Hua. It's still alive. I need light balls."

Additional magic tickled my nerves, but it was weak. Oh, so weak.

My entire body quivered under the strain of holding the demon suspended in time. The moment I lost control, it would rush us. I wouldn't be able to stop it.

One black forelimb inched forward.

"P-please," I hissed. "H-hurry."

Time snapped into motion. The ricochet of magic flung me backwards. My landing knocked the wind out of me.

"Now!" Luc shouted.

The balls flew and converged on the demon. It shrieked, but the sound was more anger than pain. Instead of burning, the faint scent of frying eggs filled the tunnel. The creature shook itself, and a cloud of ash joined the drifting dust.

It stalked forward, its intent clear.

And I was left with nothing but rocks.

I picked up a fist-sized stone and threw it. My projectile passed through the demon flesh and clattered against the others behind the creature.

Rage thrummed in my blood. Surviving everything I had for the last week, and I was about to die in a tunnel, eaten by a damn demon. I launched rock after rock at the thing. Some connected. Most didn't.

And worst of all, the damn thing was laughing at us again.

"Justice, down!"

I dropped at Jeremy's warning behind me. Magic sizzled past my skin.

The demon flew backward with a real cry of pain. More light balls whisked invisibly past me. This time the creature caught fire. I ducked my head against my shoulder as the flames became too bright to bear.

There was a final screech, then nothing.

Strong arms wrapped around me and lifted me upright. "Are you all right, Justice?"

I blinked. Jeremy's concerned face was inches from mine. "Luc and Shi Hua are hurt—"

"We've got them."

I looked around. Quan held his bodyguard while Master Aaron splinted her arm. On the other side of me, Master Devin and two healer journeywomen hovered over Luc.

"Can you walk, m'lady?" Jeremy's voice was soft as he attempted to preserve my dignity and support my bruised body at the same time.

"Yes. I would really like to not be underground any more." I took one step and everything dissolved into nothingness.

Once again, I awoke in a warm wooden room instead of my marble bedchambers at the Temple of Balance. My head ached abominably, as if someone had stabbed my brain with a dagger. A soft snort by my bedside drew my attention.

"About time you woke up." Gina rose and poured water from the pitcher on the bedside stand. "Need a drink?"

"Please." I sighed. "Then the privy."

Once she helped me with my needs and settled me back in bed, I said, "How long this time?"

She chuckled. "A little over a day, Justice."

I frowned. "Why aren't you over at Love?"

"Tyra's taken my watch over there. The priestesses prefer female wardens right now for some strange reason." Her attempted joke fell flat. She shook her head. "As long as it's her or me in charge, we're good."

"Meaning they only trust Balance wardens?"

Gina shrugged. "Since there's only five female wardens at Balance now, we've been working the Child and Death's female wardens and the Wildling priestesses into the shift rotation."

In other words, things were left out of the Love priestesses reports. Not that I had any great affection for their calling, but traumatized priestesses would not bring in the gold the Orrin temple needed.

"What about Shi Hua and Luc?"

"The Jing priestess is back at the embassy once they healed her arm."

Breath hissed between my teeth. "You know?"

"Everyone in the temples does." Gina chuckled again. "It's little hard to hide any Light talent when she's tossing it at a demon in an enclosed space in front of witnesses."

"And Luc?"

She was quiet for a long moment. "According to Devin, the chief brother will live. The healers had to take more of his leg."

I squeezed my eyes shut. What would the Reverend Father of Light do? Replace Luc and reassign him to a research position at the capital was the most likely choice.

After everything we went through to save him, everything I went through, and I'd never see him again.

"Did they capture any of Brother Luc's abductors?"

She shook her head. "Those not killed in the skirmish committed suicide. Except their leader, the skinwalker." She made a disgusted sound in the back of her throat. "That bastard managed to escape."

"Skinwalker?"

Another shrug. "A Diné legend. A sorcerer so powerful, it could take the form of whatever it killed and skinned. Also, Brother Jeremy recognized the skinwalker's victim by the drawing Lailani sketched from the Wildlings' description of the renegade. He was an instructor at the Standora Temple of Light named Brother Jon."

"How in the Twelve's names did a scholar from the home temple—" When I started to rise, my body abruptly reminded me why I was in a bed at the Healers Guild.

"We don't know, m'lady. Brother Jeremy has sent the news to the Reverend Father of Light and is waiting for the reply."

Nothing I could do about matters out of my hands. There were other things I needed to rectify though. "Could you send word to Balance? Have Little Bear release Father Jerrod and Lady Alessa."

Gina hesitated before she said, "Little Bear already did." She laughed. "Father Jerrod threatened to file charges, but—"

"High Brother Jax threatened to gut him?"

A bright grin filled Gina's face. "Actually, it was High Sister Mya of all people. The Ladies Katarina and Alessa were simply happy that the duke returned home relatively unscathed."

I sat up too fast, and my head pounded in response. "Relatively unscathed?"

"Cuts and bruises. Nothing that one of the journeymen couldn't heal in a few minutes, but the duke insisted they didn't. He said he needed some visible scars for the nobility to take him seriously as a leader."

Amused, I almost shook my head, but thought better of it at a wave of dizziness. "I pray to the Twelve none of his wounds become infected." I took a deep breath. "Now, can I please see Brother Luc, or are you under orders to tie me to the bed?"

My heart caught in my throat when I saw Luc lying on his own bed in a separate room of the Healers Guild. His coloring wasn't any better than when we had been fleeing the demon. Gina helped me to the chair at his side, then both she and the journeyman who'd been tending him left the room, quietly closing the door behind them.

His eyes flickered open, and he smiled. "So the healers weren't lying when they said you were still alive."

"No." I clasped his hand in mine. "I feared the same thing about you." I couldn't help glancing at the bandage stump on top of his blankets.

"Think you can love a crippled man." His humor was as self-deprecating as ever, but there was a bitter edge to his tone.

I squeezed his fingers. "You didn't have a problem with my unnatural eyes."

"That's—"

"No, it isn't different," I said fiercely.

He laughed softly. "We do make quite the pair."

A pair. Like my grandparents.

My throat wanted to seize, but I forced the words past the tightness. "There's something you need to know."

"Kam's dead," he said. "Master Devin told me."

"There's more." My fingers were cold against his warmth. This time, my throat refused to work.

"Anthea—"

"He's my grandfather."

A small smile tilted the corner of Luc's mouth. "I wondered if he would ever tell you."

I blinked rapidly. "You knew?"

"He was pretty drunk one night the month after my assignment to Orrin became official. I don't think he even remembered what he said because he never brought it up again." The smile faded. "Are you angry with me for not telling you? I thought it best that you learned the truth from him."

I shook my head. "I just don't want you to leave." I swiped at the tears that escaped.

"It won't be by choice," he said and squeezed my hand in return. "Let's wait until we hear from the capital before we panic."

I nodded and laid my head on his chest. His fingers stroked my loose hair.

He was right. No sense in fretting over things out of our control. But for the first time in my life, I truly worried about the future.

Worried about *our* future.

I wouldn't survive without him.

# *Chapter 26*

Two days later, the Reverend Mother of Balance arrived in Orrin with a full retinue plus extra wardens for Dragonfly. Around the same time, the Sea Peoples fleet docked in the harbor.

On the positive side, the islanders didn't get into much trouble since the Temple of Love was still closed. Nor did they go overboard on other entertainments. They seemed to respect Orrin's somber mood over the deaths of so many from the Temples.

On the other hand, the Reverend Mother did her best to disrupt my staff's routine. She and her party took over my chambers and the second floor of our temple. I found myself bunking with the female wardens. Gina and Tyra found the situation hysterically funny while the other three women were alternately nervous at the accommodations and appalled at the Reverend Mother's treatment of me.

The old biddy didn't even pause for refreshment. She questioned Donella and reviewed all our records before she bustled down to the Temple of Love.

She said nothing to me, so I held court as normal.

Well, as normal as the circumstances allowed. Poor Jeremy was run ragged because he was the only Light priest available. While Luc had been moved back to his quarters at the Temple of Light, the healers insisted he remain abed.

Unfortunately, that meant Jeremy kept nodding off during the court session.

Gerd remained in the gaol since the Reverend Mother had accepted my recusal on her case and would hear it. The old biddy couldn't even tell me herself. She passed the message through my embarrassed clerk. I did my best to reassure Donella that I didn't hold it against her, but my own irritation at the insult didn't help.

Ironically, criminal cases had dwindled to nothing between the ice storm, the increased street patrols, and the mourning of the Temples. Apparently, the entire city took my fear of a possible attack to heart and kept their sins in check.

I sentenced the hapless Bartholomew to fifteen lashes, five for each assault on Lady Alessa and Sister Gretchen. While I expected the duke and his family to observe today's trial, to my shock, Lady Alessa pleaded clemency for the former DiMara retainer.

"Why?" I glared at the noblewoman from my bench.

She lifted her chin. "Because I forgive him for his actions against me. He was well-intentioned, though misguided."

I tapped my fingers against the podium. "And what about the other charges?"

"Those are not transgressions against me, and therefore, I abide by your decision." She turned to the quivering man. "He needs to learn that raising a hand against someone in anger or jealousy is unacceptable if he is to work for me."

I blinked. Maybe the tunnel explosion had severely damaged my ears more than the persistent ringing. "I beg your pardon, Lady Alessa?"

She turned her attention back to me with a smile. "Forgive me, Lady Justice, but I'm assuming that there are no more claim challenges to my recent inheritance. If so, I'll need staff to maintain those properties."

My gaze fell on Bartholomew. "You have a choice. You can accept Lady Alessa's offer of service and receive only five lashes."

He opened his mouth, but I held up my hand. "I am still speaking."

His jaw shut with an audible *click*.

I jabbed my forefinger in his direction. "If you commit any more criminal acts, whether against Lady Alessa or anyone else, not only will I impose punishment for those charges, I will reinstate my original sentence of to-day." My hand brushed the pommel of my sword. "And you already know what I can do with a truthspell."

"Ah-ah understand, Lady Justice." His head bobbed. "Ah accept the lady's offer."

I leaned back in my chair. "Well, Lady Alessa, since you're here in court today, shall we complete the transfer of your properties?"

She curtsied. "Thank you, Lady Justice."

I woke Brother Jeremy long enough to truthspell her, and I went through the formal questions involved in the property transfer of the deceased. Once the formalities were observed and everything signed, I banged the pommel of my recovered sword on the podium. "Court is dismissed."

Just in time for the Reverend Mother to burst through the courtroom's main doors along with four of the wardens she had brought with her to Orrin. I resisted the urge to let my forehead fall to the podium surface.

"May I assist you, Reverend Mother?"

"A word with you, Chief Justice," she snapped, stamping her cane on the floor for emphasis. "Actually, more than one."

Everyone in the courtroom took that opportunity to flee, including Jeremy and my own staff.

*Traitors.*

When everyone was gone, she ordered. "The receiving room if you please, Anthea."

Not "your" receiving room. This did not bode well for our incipient conversation. Assuming I could get a word in edgewise.

My old irritation at the problems caused by my predecessor rose. If the Reverend Mother thought I'd meekly submit to whatever she planned to dish out, well . . .

The little glimmer of hope that she might cast me out of the order died a quick death inside me.

She took the arm of the warden to her right, and he guided her out of the courtroom. The warden to her left approached me and extended his elbow.

I held up my hand. "Thank you for the courtesy, Warden, but it isn't necessary."

His face glowed dimly beneath his cowl. "Forgive me, Chief Justice. I presumed."

I laughed. "As long as it doesn't take you months to relearn as it did my staff."

The retraining point may be moot, depending on the old biddy's mood. While our conversation may turn into a major battle, I would have my own words with the Reverend Mother about the Penelope situation.

Sivan was setting out refreshments as I entered *my* receiving room. Her attention flicked from the Reverend Mother to me and back again.

The old biddy waved away her warden escort once she found a chair. She sat with a muffled snort. "Quit flitting about like an ass-fucked bird, Sivan. Whatever food you didn't lick to offend me, I'm sure Anthea will spit on it."

I tried very hard not to laugh at Sivan's shocked expression. "Would you like me to piss in your tea while I'm at it, Reverend Mother?" I asked.

She hooked her cane over the chair back. "No, thank you. I'm sure you poured in enough of that Cantish pepper sauce you favor to upset my digestion for the rest of the winter." She cocked her head in the general direction of her wardens. "Get out, you carrion birds!"

The men didn't appear as surprised by her behavior as Sivan. I nodded to her, and she fled with the wardens. I remained standing, a petty maneuver on my part since she couldn't see me anyway.

"I swear you'll be the death of me, you sanctimonious little brat." Her hand darted unerringly to the apple tarts she loved.

"You had your chance to kick me out of the order, you conniving old biddy."

I reached for my tea and had taken a sip when she said, "You're just like your grandmother you know."

Tea spurted out my nose and mouth with my coughing fit. I quickly set aside the cup so I wouldn't break it. I might not-so-accidentally slash the Reverend Mother's throat with a shard. When I could breathe again, I said. "You already knew about Thalia and Kam, didn't you?"

"And their daughter, yes."

I stared at the Reverend Mother. "Why would you or your predecessor condone such a thing?"

She munched on a bite of her tart before she said, "What good would it have done, child?"

"It could have prevented a lot of heartache for one thing," I snapped.

Her little smile was almost . . . sorrowful. "Pull on one thread of time, Anthea, and what happens?"

"This isn't theoretical philosophy. You manipulated the Reverend Mother of Love to get Gerd the city seat after you knew what she'd done. What laws she violated. As a result of her machinations as chief sister, people are dead, including one of my own wardens. You're playing with lives here!" *With my life*, I wanted to say, but held my tongue. Better to take the high road.

The Reverend Mother sighed and tilted her head. "And sometimes leaving well enough alone is what saves many more lives in the long run."

I shook so hard in my anger that I thought I would fly apart. I started pacing in order to burn some of my emotions before I did something truly idiotic. "All the damage Gerd did destroyed those very people you claim you want to save."

The Reverend Mother raised her chin. "How do you balance those handful against the thousands lost in another demon invasion?"

"Demon invasion—"

My knees turned to jelly as what the Reverend Mother had been trying to tell me registered.

Or what she'd been trying not to tell me.

Dizziness spun the room. I felt as if I were truly blind again. My hand felt for the chair next to me and dropped into the seat before my legs totally gave out. "Seeing the future is only a theory . . ."

"No, it is . . . mathematics in a way. The probability of a copper landing on a side or its edge is easy to calculate because of the limited factors. Calculating the probabilities of life?" She laughed and shrugged. "That's a bit more difficult, but it can be done."

"But how . . ."

She waved a hand. "Those who try to foresee often are trying to circumvent the gods' will. It's another matter when Balance herself shows you things."

"She sent you a vision." My fingers tightened around the armrests until the wood dug painfully into my flesh.

"And my predecessor. The events in Orrin over the last seven months aren't coincidences. They are the prelude to another invasion."

"What does this invasion have to do with Thalia and Kam?"

She felt around the table until she found her napkin. Wiping her fingers, she sighed. "You know the ancient tales, Anthea. Love was the first child of Balance and Light."

Wrapping my mind around what the Reverend Mother said was equal to consuming more of Deborah's soma tears. Nothing made sense. "You're trying to recreate the scriptures through my grandparents? Are you insane?"

"Not me. I'm staying out of our Goddess's way."

"Staying out of the Goddess's way?" I could no longer stay still. Despite the healers' efforts, my muscles still ached from the poisoning and my abuse of them over the past week, but I rose and paced again anyway.

"That was the reason neither my predecessor nor I disciplined your grandmother. It's part of the reason why I've allowed your relationship with Luc to continue unchecked."

I paused in mid-step. For the first time in my life, true terror filled me. "Please," I whispered. "I beg of you. Don't punish him—"

She snorted, the derision obvious. "Nothing's going to happen to him. Nothing worse than what the poor boy has already suffered." She took another bite of her tart, deliberately driving me insane. "Or you for that matter. For some reason, the Goddess herself wants you both here. I may be a stubborn, ancient bitch, but I'm not stupid." She pointed a gnarled finger at me. "And you're just as mule-headed as Thalia and me put together. However, both you and Luc need to learn some discretion. I heard enough from the other temple seats. Kam's no longer here to cover your asses."

"B-b-but—" I sounded like an idiot, but I couldn't stop myself.

"Sit down, Anthea. Your damn pacing isn't going to help. I know Gerd started the original rumor. So do the rest of the Orrin seats." She grimaced. "But Jax knows about the two of you, and Han and Bertrice suspect it's true. So as I said, some discretion, please."

I resumed my seat. "And why did you chose not to hold Gerd's trial here like you did mine? That would have taken care of the problem with her lies. Truthspell her."

The old biddy cackled. "Because the queen wants to see her execution. Her Majesty is not happy about the recent events in Orrin."

A sense of unease stole over me. "Am I to be transferred?"

"Balance, no!" The Reverend Mother munched on the last bit of apple tart before she added, "In fact, the queen has requested your sentence be commuted."

My mouth gaped open. The Reverend Mother's statement simply didn't make sense. While the reigning monarch had the right to grant a pardon, the kings and queens rarely did so. And never over internal temple discipline.

"W-why?" I sounded like a fool to my own ears.

"Because I asked her to," the Reverend Mother said matter-of-factly.

I couldn't have been more surprised if pigs flew and birds rooted for truffles. There was no logic behind such a request except—

"You couldn't find another way to save face," I retorted.

She deliberately slurped her tea. "This isn't about saving face. It concerns legally freeing you to accompany Brother Luc to Tandor once he's recovered from his injuries since according to the law, even I cannot commute a sentence without new evidence."

"Recovered from his injuries?" My voice rose. "Those bastards chopped off his foot!"

"I spoke with your Masters Aaron and Devin. Clever fellows. They believe they have developed an interesting method to help your Light priest." She took another drink before she sat her cup and saucer aside with a loud *clink*.

She stared at me as if she could truly see me. "We need Luc, Anthea, loss of limb notwithstanding. With the disturbing revelations concerning the real Brother Mat's death and Gerd dealing in demon artifacts, the Reverend Father of Light and the Reverend Mother of Love must audit every member of their respective orders."

"So Luc won't have anyone but Jeremy for a while?" I said while I poured more tea into both of our cups. I had an excellent staff, but with the amount of trade coming through Orrin, Luc needed more than one junior priest at his disposal. Especially once the spring sailing season started. I'd help, but my mediation and negotiation skills left something to be desired.

She nodded sharply. "Exactly. And it's not just Light and Love, we are all having to do so. We cannot take the chance of one of these rebel bastards slipping through again."

A shudder ran through me. "That's why you're really here. To investigate my people."

"Actually, no." She smirked. "You're the only one of my priestesses I can truly rely upon, and the staff here have proved themselves when Penelope's affliction affected Orrin's day-to-day business."

"Are you sure about that?" The memory of my own temptation to betray the temples lay bitterly on my tongue. "None of us caught the imposter Mat before it was nearly too late."

Her mien turned quite serious. "Whoever is recruiting these renegades need women and men with temple skills, but who are also unflinchingly loyal to their cause and who will obey any order, including the command to kill oneself rather than to divulge information." She chuckled before continuing. "My dear, you question everything, even Balance herself, about your place in the world as well as everyone else's."

"But, Reverend Mother, if both Brother Luc and I are in Tandor—"

"Pish." She flicked a hand to wave away my question. "I've already had words with my counterpart in Jing about Luc's request to our respective Reverend Fathers of Light about this Shi Hua's temporary transfer. And a junior justice who's already been vetted by me is on her way. I trust your staff will assist her during your absence."

"I'm sure they will," I murmured. "But about Shi Hua, I wouldn't have requested the assistance if I'd known Brother Luc would be absent." If I gave voice to my suspicion that Shi Hua was actually spying in Issura on behalf of the Jing emperor, matters could become a lot worse. I trusted the Light priestess . . . to a point.

The Reverend Mother snorted again. It seemed to be her favorite method of expressing all her emotions. "Then let's pray your brothers are both smart enough to keep any truly sensitive material out of her hands."

Since I wasn't sure how to respond to her statement without digging myself a deeper hole, I remained silent.

Her fingers drifted over Deborah's pastries before she found what she was searching for. She took a hearty bite of another apple tart, smacking her lips.

"By the way, Justice Yanaba will be staying with you for additional training after your return. Assuming you don't find a way to get yourself killed in Tandor, my little death wish." The Reverend Mother cackled at her poor joke.

For once, I managed to keep my mouth shut over her pet name for me. "I have a few questions for you."

"Just a few?" She slurped more of her tea.

"You knew Justice Penelope was losing her faculties, and you did nothing."

She sniffed this time. "That's a statement, not a question."

"Why didn't you replace her?"

The Reverend Mother set aside both her tea and her half-eaten tart. "Because I needed you here, and you refused to take a permanent post without a battle. I am so tired of fighting with you, child." For the first time in my memory, she sounded as old as all the winters she had lived.

"Because the Goddess told you?" I asked softly. For once, I wasn't trying to be flippant or disrespectful.

"Because I don't have anyone willing to think for themselves." She sighed, a long, sad breath. "Did you know Thalia should have become the reverend mother of our order instead of me? But no, the damn bitch went and got herself killed. If I didn't know better, I'd think she did it on purpose."

"No, I didn't know that," I said quietly.

The Reverend Mother sighed again. "We've become so complacent over the last two generations. We no longer fear the demons. We look at our fellow humans as our rivals." She wiped a shaky hand across her mouth. "I fear for the future. The Book of Balance says our Goddess gave us a thousand years to prepare for the demons, but our own stupidity led us into a dark age for the second thousand."

I leaned forward and rested my elbows on my knees. "What does this have to do with Penelope?"

"Everything. Nothing." She reached for her tea and was about to spill it when I grabbed the cup and pressed it into her hand.

She took a quiet sip before she continued. "I believed in rules and tradition. Penelope was next in line for a seat when Thalia was killed. And she was the worst possible person to be assigned to Orrin. Neither the queen nor I had recourse to remove her because she always followed the letter of the law."

"But surely when both the Balance staff and High Brother Kam reported the degradation of her mental health, there was someone else in line."

"There was, but I didn't have the energy for a protracted war with you."

"A war?" I wanted to deny her words, but in a way, she was correct. "Why would I protest anyone you assigned? I'd be relieved."

"You were next in line."

Balance help me, she was right. I'd fought her for half a year when she added Orrin to my circuit, assuming she was lazy or she wanted to punish me.

I stared at the blood stains on my robes. "Does this mean you no longer believe in rules and tradition?"

"Some are necessary." She shook her head sadly. "Some not so much. We don't always remember why those rules are in place. Like why foliage is cut back from the palaces." She smirked and took a drink. Good to know she read at least one of my reports.

"So what does this all mean for us?" I reached for a pastry and picked at the sliced almonds on top, not really hungry but for something to do with my hands.

"The pardon means I need someone the queen and I trust to take a very close look at the Tandor temples."

"Not just Balance and Light?" I popped the nuts into my mouth.

"The reports I'm receiving from Chief Justice Elizabeth are . . . too perfect. Similar the ones I received from your Donella when Penelope lost her mind."

I mulled over the Reverend Mother's words while I chewed and swallowed. "But you're not getting reports from her staff of any additional problems."

"No."

"You do know that my pardon will vex some of the seats here?"

She chuckled. "I'd be very disappointed if a brainstorm took Gerd due to your pardon before I have the pleasure of executing her. But—" She took another sip of tea before continuing. "If I were you, I'd refrain from imprisoning any more of Orrin's seats."

"Unless they deserve it?"

"Unless they break the law," the Reverend Mother added firmly.

"And in the meantime, Luc and I are only investigating the temples in Tandor?"

"Impertinence doesn't become a chief justice, Anthea." But there was a slight smile on her craggy face. "Of course, you are to find this Ural DiSand and question him regarding his deal with Gerd. And this mysterious skinwalker who escaped as well, if you can."

Underneath her tone though, I could detect that she shared my own concern. As bad as things were in Orrin, matters in Tandor were far worse.

# *Chapter 27*

Sivan waited for me outside the receiving room once the Reverend Mother dismissed me. "We have another situation."

"Can it wait until after I visit Nathan at the Healers Guild?"

She smiled. "That's part of the situation. Master Aaron is here with Nathan and another girl." At my puzzled expression, she added, "The one Ambassador Quan sent to the healers."

In the madness of the last few days, I'd forgotten about the survivor of the Jing noble's fire. "Lead on."

I followed her to the kitchen. Nathan and a girl sat on stacked bags of flour, munching on apple tarts. Master Aaron simply tried to stay out of Deborah's way as she bustled about issuing orders and tarts equally.

She shoved a basket full of the treats into my hands and made shooing motions before I could say anything. "Ah don't care that the Reverend Mother is here. You can't keep using mah kitchen as your office!"

"My apologies, my lady." I bowed.

She snatched a bread paddle from its peg. "Don't think Ah won't take this to your backside, Anthea! Now, out!"

The children giggled and the adults snickered. I grinned as well and beckoned my guests. "Come with me if you want more." We trooped out to the garden and sat down on stone conversation benches near the fountain. I noticed the girl took the seat farthest from Master Aaron.

"Hello. I'm Anthea" I held out my hand to her.

She shied away from me and cowered close to Nathan, which I expected.

What I didn't expect was Nathan's words. "She's all right. She ain't like the other adults."

I lowered my hand. "What's your name?"

She trembled but said nothing.

"M'lady, this is Ming Wei," Nathan offered.

That statement brought me up short. "Are you from Jing, Ming Wei?" She nodded.

"Can we have some more tarts, Lady Justice?" Nathan indicated the basket I held. My staff must have coached him on his etiquette.

"Of course." I handed over the treats. He offered first choice to the girl, and she choose one of the almond pastries.

"Those are my favorite, too," I said softly.

"You don't stare at me," she blurted.

I blinked. "Why would I do such a rude thing to you?"

She bowed her head and remained silent.

"Because of her face, m'lady," Aaron said softly.

Then I realized why there was a slight differential between the left side of her face and the right. Scars. She had scars from the fire. "Well, I'm glad to know there are two of us in Orrin who aren't rude because I noticed you're not staring at my face either."

"I think your eyes are pretty," she said shyly. "Like poppies or roses. In Jing, red is the color of good luck." Her own color flared, and a wave of sadness rolled out from her.

"Lady Justice, can I show Nassa to Ming Wei?" Nathan said. If I didn't know better, I'd swear the boy knew when people around him were uncomfortable. He was determined to ameliorate the problem. Maybe I should arrange testing with Sister Mya.

Not that I would ever force him into temple life, but if he had talent he needed to be trained and registered.

For now though, he needed me to let him have a childhood. "Yes, you may."

The children tore off in the direction of the stables, their treats forgotten. "And don't get in Hogarth's way!" I called after them.

Master Aaron chuckled and reached for the basket. "That's the most animated I'd seen the girl since the Jing ambassador and his guards brought her to my doorstep. You could have warned me a little sooner."

"I seem to recall an ice storm the night I found out about her." I frowned and took an almond pastry from the proffered basket. "The ambassador didn't mention she was from Jing."

"He said you would question his motives concerning the girl if he kept her." Master Aaron stroked his beard. "His healers did as much as anyone could do concerning her injuries. There wasn't much else we could do."

"If she's from Jing she needs to be returned to her family." Fury swelled in my chest. Why did Quan insist on playing games?

"He told me her family sold her." From the ripple of anger in his voice, Master Aaron had deduced what had happened to the child. "She confided the same story to Nathan. Only our youngest female apprentice could tend to her, and only at your squire's insistence that the apprentice could be trusted. Given her circumstances, I understand why both an ambassador and an orphan boy think she's better off with you."

Under his analysis was an unspoken truth. With burn scars marring the girl's face, no one would take her without a sizeable dowry, an unfortunate fact in both Issura and Jing. But here at the temple, she could learn a trade. Maybe even learn to trust men again.

"Will she need additional care?" I asked.

"The important thing right now is plenty of exercise, especially to keep the scar tissue from causing her shoulder to seize." He chuckled. "I doubt if you'll have too much trouble with young Nathan egging her on. But those are just the physical effects. I've already sent word to High Sister Mya about Ming Wei's emotional problems."

I nodded. Mya would know far better than me how to deal with the girl. Then I asked Aaron the question I didn't want to know the answer to. "And Nathan?"

"He needs to eat mild foods for now." Master Aaron waggled a forefinger in my face. "None of that Cantish pepper sauce." He immediately turned serious. "His heart will need to be watched for the rest of his life. He may be short of breath on occasion. Any type of fighting is ill-advised."

Foreboding shivered across my skin, despite the unusually warm winter day. "If more demons come, I can't guarantee the last one."

"The rumors are true then? You killed another one just outside of the city walls?" He made a warding gesture against evil. How I wished defending our world against them were that easy.

Bitter laughter filled my throat. "Not me. Brother Jeremy saved us at the last moment."

"Still, that's three in less than a year." Worry tainted his voice. "It's been over a century."

"There were more than one summoned by Samael DiRoy, but yes, it is far too many."

Master Aaron stared at me for a long moment before he swore under his breath. "That's why someone poisoned our oil stock. They want everyone with talent, anyone who could oppose them, out of the way. Don't they understand what would happen by summoning demons? The temples and the guilds—"

"They know," I said softly. "They'd rather go down in a bloodbath than yield to what they view as a corrupt system. And if the demons eat us all, to them, it's what the human race deserves."

A familiar voice came from behind us. "If that's the case, your Reverend Mother has a head start." Magistrate DiCook dropped to the bench next to ours. He pulled one of the berry muffins from the basket.

Aaron stood. "It sounds like you two have other matters to discuss. Send a messenger if there are any problems with the children, Lady Justice."

I inclined my head. "Thank you for your assistance, Master Healer."

DiCook waited until Aaron had passed through the postern gate before he spoke. "Why didn't you tell me you'd discovered that my peacekeepers were accepting bribes?"

I swore under my breath. "I'm sorry, Malven. I meant to address the issue the next time we met."

He took a bite of his pastry, and slowly chewed and swallowed it before he spoke again. "I would have preferred it come from you rather than the Reverend Mother of Balance."

"How did she find out?"

"Sister Dragonfly," he said around another mouthful of muffin.

"Of course." I didn't know why I was surprised. The *berda* would overly share until she finally understood that she wasn't being held accountable for Gerd's crimes. "I apologize for not speaking to you sooner."

He shrugged. "We both need to learn to trust. It will work out, gods willing. You know I'm going to need someone to truthspell every single peacekeeper."

I groaned. "Brother Jeremy is already overtaxed—"

"I'd prefer you do it."

"Are you sure? You saw what happened with the spy Micah."

"Exactly. Your reputation will go farther than my threats of discipline. Consider it a favor I will owe you." He grinned. "As long as you don't leave me here alone with your Reverend Mother while you're having a grand time with High Brother Luc in Tandor."

I remained in the garden after Magistrate DiCook took his leave. The rare period of winter sunshine was too comforting to relinquish in the face of my mounting responsibilities. With my eyes closed, I sat on the bench, my face raised to the warmth, until someone cleared their throat.

Reluctantly, I opened my eyes. Brother Jax stood next to me, chewing on a pastry. He was naked, which meant he'd slipped into our compound in his animal form.

"I thought wolves preferred meat."

"Wolves prefer anything that tastes good," he mumbled around his mouthful. "I need to steal Deborah away from you. This apple tart is incredible."

"You need to switch temples if you're contemplating a career as a thief," I said lightly. "How may I serve you, High Brother?"

"It's how I can serve you." He sat on the bench next to me. "Two of my people found the bodies of the wagoner and his son not far from the Trill Bridge. It was the same place where Gretchen was—" His fists clenched and released. "There wasn't enough rain to wash away her scent in the grove they used."

"In other words, the renegades didn't have a specific target by placing her in that barrel."

Jax shook his head. "Magistrate DiCook told me about your rewind of the unloading. They made a point of putting the barrel with her body at the front so it would be opened soon. I agree with the magistrate that they hoped to steer you and DiCook at each other as a diversion from their true purpose of reclaiming the grimoire."

"It almost worked, too," I muttered.

He selected another pastry. From his closed eyes and ecstatic expression, the treats were beyond any other pleasure he'd experienced. When he finished it, he said, "Then you're ready."

"For what?"

He licked the crumbs from his fingers before he answered. "Your truth."

My laughter took on a hysterical edge. "I'm afraid you're too late. *Everybody* knows about Kam and Thalia's affair."

"Not theirs. Yours."

"I get enough word games from my own Reverend Mother, not to mention Ambassador Quan. Please, I beg you, no more."

"Nightmares are coming. You need to be in Orrin no matter how much you despise this place. You are the twist in the loom of Balance that will decide our fate."

I stared at the priest. We weren't friends. We were barely acquaintances. And yet, he was the one seat who didn't have some ulterior motive in this damn place. I trusted him because he brought Luc back to me. "If you mean another demon invasion has started, I agree on the nightmares portion, but for me to be the focus—"

He shook his head, blue and green locks flying. "No, our God says something far worse is coming. Out of the south."

The echo of the Reverend Mother's words ran over whatever hope I had that she was mistaken when she spoke of visions. I reached over and grasped his hand. "Balance was warned us of something similar."

He blew out a breath. "I would have told you sooner . . ."

"I wasn't ready. I know. Thank you for being patient."

The garden gate banged, and childish laughter followed.

I cleared my throat. "Not to be rude, but the girl was sold—"

White light flashed across my vision, and I found myself holding Jax's paw.

Nathan and Ming Wei raced around a turn in the garden path and slowed at the sight of a giant timber wolf sitting next to me. Their tentative approach made me laugh.

"It's all right. He's quite friendly."

Ming Wei peered around Nathan's shoulder. "Is that your dog?"

I released his paw. "You could say Jax belongs to everyone." The priest stuck his tongue out at me before giving the children a canine smile.

"Can we pet him?" Nathan asked.

"That's up to Jax," I said, suppressing my laughter.

The priest lowered his head for the children. After a few tentative touches, they gave him an enthusiastic rub down, which led to a game of tag between the three through Balance's garden.

I savored the moment. If Jax and the Reverend Mother were right, there was a great deal of heartache to come.

# *Chapter 28*

The next day were the funerals. After a brief consultation with Dragonfly and Luc, we had decided a joint ceremony was appropriate given the circumstances of the collective deaths. When we formally asked the Reverend Mother of Balance to officiate, she declined, stating we knew the deceased and she didn't.

Her comment added to the heap of guilt on my plate. I couldn't even say I truly knew my grandfather, much less the others.

Duke Marco and the magistrate surprised us by declaring a city-wide day of mourning. The square in front of Government House was packed with onlookers as we made the slow procession up Temple Street from Death.

High Sister Bertrice led the two riderless horses by their reins, the symbolic loss of the priest and priestess. The two-wheeled carts bearing the deceased followed, the horses guided by someone of appropriate rank within their respective temple.

Poor Jeremy had looked like he would cry when Luc informed him that he would escort Kam's body. But there was simply no possibility of Luc guiding a horse and walking at the same time. He was still becoming accustomed to the odd double canes that fitted to his arms. As the Reverend Mother had said, the healers cleverly contrived the contraptions.

Each of the Love priestesses escorted one of their fallen wardens. The priestesses had insisted, and no one could question their need to grieve or their sincerity. We would probably never know the full story of how the Love wardens were murdered. Gina still headed the replacement contingent from the warden academy at Dragonfly's request. The *berda* asked me to give the arrangement a month until she and the rest of her temple's personnel grew accustomed to the new wardens.

Instead of my chief warden escorting Aglaia's body, Tyra had begged for the honor. At his ready acquiescence, I vowed to keep a closer eye on the activities and proclivities of my staff.

"The entire city is wearing mourning clothes," Little Bear whispered in my ear as we walked.

I'd bowed to custom. He guided me, my hand clinging to his elbow. For once, I was glad of the support.

Behind us, Shi Hua escorted Luc, ready to assist though he didn't really need help at our slow pace. It was odd to see her in full Light regalia for the first time, but the clothing suited her.

Once each casket was set on its pyre and Bertrice said the appropriate rites, it was our place to speak of our loss. Dragonfly extolled Gretchen's bravery and generosity as well as those of the dead men and women who served Love. Luc talked of Gibbs and Kam's sacrifice in the name of duty.

Then it was my turn.

I stepped forward and scanned the sea of faces. Not even the furtive whispers of the children in the audience broke the silence.

"Gretchen. Gibbs. Kam. Aglaia." My throat burned before I finished reciting the names of the twelve Love wardens. "Remember those names. Especially Aglaia's. She died protecting the sisters of Love. Died protecting me.

"And that's a disgrace. Not on her part, but mine. As several of my wardens pointed out, I didn't bother to learn their names. I never learned Aglaia's until after she died. Six months and *I never bothered*. I didn't want to be here in Orrin."

The crowd rustled at my insulting statement.

"I was born here. In my pain, I clung to the bad memories of my childhood, and I forgot the good things about this city. The wonderful smell of Bakers Street in the morning. The laughter of the children. Magistrate

Malven DiCook who does his damnedest to protect all of you despite those of us who get in his way."

The crowd tittered, and the magistrate turned scarlet beneath his cap.

"Most of all, I forgot those who cared for me in my early years. Like High Sister Bertrice." I smiled at her before my attention return to the crowd. "Or Chief Justice Thalia and High Brother Kam."

Anticipation fluttered through the crowd. I realized then there was no use hiding or denying the truth. Doing so had caused nothing but pain.

"For those of you who haven't heard the rumor, yes, Thalia and Kam were my grandparents."

I didn't know what I expected, but total silence wasn't it.

"I learned the truth from Brother Kam on his deathbed. He kept telling me how much I was like my grandmother, but I'm not. Justice Thalia would have bothered to know the names of the wardens and staff in her service. All I can do is follow her example from now on.

"So I ask Balance to watch over Warden Aglaia and treat her much better than I ever did."

I sat amid total quiet. Bertrice gave the final benediction, and her priests lit the pyres.

Little Bear squeezed my shoulder as green smoke curled into the sky. Young Nathan handed me a kerchief. Only then did I realize I wept.

Turn the page for a sneak peek of the next Justice novel, *A Modicum of Truth.*

# A Modicum of Truth

(Excerpt © 2016, Suzan Harden)

I brushed past High Brother Luc's personal attendant Istaqa and laid the scroll I carried on the priest's desk. "The pardon arrived. It's official. I've been given leave to go south with you."

While Istaqa stood in the doorway and harrumphed in disgust, Luc took his time chewing whatever was in his mouth. A surreptitious sniff of the room revealed sweet pumpkin bread and eggs coated in Cantish hot sauce. The orange-warm items on his plate had bites missing. My empty stomach grumbled its delight of both aromas.

"Istaqa, the Chief Justice won't leave until you feed her. Also, please bring another pot of tea. And Anthea—"

I resisted the urge to sigh. Luc was determined to hold me to my oath at his predecessor's funeral to do a better job as Orrin's justice. I faced his attendant and bowed. "My apologies for my rudeness, Istaqa."

The man's second harrumph was slightly less disgusted than the first. He pivoted smartly on his heel and marched from the office.

"Sorry," I muttered.

"I'm impressed you remembered his name," Luc remarked.

I called him a Cantish name that questioned his parentage, though mine was far more scandalous than his. Especially since I'd recently learned his predecessor, High Brother Kam, was my maternal grandfather.

Scandalous since members of the Temple of Light took a vow of chastity. As did members of my own order.

Not that our vows had ever stopped Luc or I from indulging.

Luc chuckled. "I know you're excited about regaining your freedom, but you need to scale down the enthusiasm. Things are tenuous enough with Mother Bianca and Father Jerrod."

I winced. The two temple seats had sent letters of protest to the queen when they learned she planned to pardon me for my illegal execution of her cousin, Samael DiRoy. The priestess and priest seemed to forget I did it because DiRoy summoned demons in order to seize the throne. And Goddess only knew what else the little idiot had planned before I cut off his head.

It hadn't helped that I made Bianca and Jerrod look like fools when the plots and schemes of Gerd, the former High Sister of Love, came to light.

Balance help me, I couldn't even consider Gerd my mother anymore despite the fact the traitorous bitch had given birth to me.

"I imprisoned Jerrod for his own good. He will forgive me eventually." I snatched Luc's mug and took a drink. The overly sweet tea made me want to retch.

"You spit that back in my cup, and I'll throw you in the gaol myself."

I forced the mouthful down my throat and made a face at him while I set down the cup. "That's nearly pure honey. How can you stand drinking it?"

He slapped my hand as I reached for a slice of bread. "Serves you right for stealing someone else's tea. And it has medicine it to increase my blood flow. The honey masks the taste."

I tried not to stare at the stump propped on a padded stool. The stump where his left foot and ankle had been a month ago. Guilt squirmed in my mind. Luc had been abducted because Gerd had started the rumor we were having an affair. It was amusing how her spiteful gossip led everyone in the city to believe we *weren't* having an affair after she was arrested for treason.

Unfortunately, the renegades she dealt with and who believed her decided to hold Luc hostage against me and my office. Then they sent me proof.

"Stop it," Luc ordered.

"What?" I said, trying to act innocent.

"I can't stand that sad puppy expression you get when you look at me."

"It's my fault it didn't occur to me that the bitch was selling demon artifacts."

"And it's my fault I didn't realized that imposter Mat, Micah, whatever his birth name was, wasn't a true brother of Light," he growled.

"It's both of your faults that we are short-staffed at the moment." Istaqa set a tray in front me before he turned to Luc. "And once again, High Brother, I must protest. A woman as a member of the order of Light is highly inappropriate."

I gratefully sipped my plain black Jing tea, enjoying the fact I wasn't being lectured for once.

Luc sighed and leaned back in his chair. "What did Sister Shi Hua do this time?"

"She still insists on bathing with the men!"

I stifled a laugh at the attendant's mortified expression. Unlike the order of Light in Issura, Jing allowed both men and women to serve as clergy. Personally, I liked the woman. It had been my recommendation that the Jing priestess assist Luc while the Reverend Father audited all the temples of Light in Issura for additional imposters.

Luc appeared calm, but I could feel his irritation prickle along my psyche. "We don't have a separate facility for her. Not to mention she's used to joint accommodations in her homeland."

Istaqa's coloring creeped from orange to red. "This could turn into a scandal."

Luc crossed his arms. "Are you planning on sending her down to the public bath house? Because that would cause a scandal. It says my staff can't keep their vows, or their libidos, in check when we have a guest."

"B-b-but—" Istaqa turned to me for help.

I quickly shoved a huge bite of eggs rolled in flatbread into my mouth and gave him an innocent look. I'd done a great many ill-conceived things in my thirty-one winters, but I wasn't about to jump into the middle of this argument.

"There is no 'but' here, Istaqa," Luc ground out. "If neither you nor the rest of the staff can behave yourselves around Sister Shi Hua, I'll be happy to send the lot of you back to Standora for reassignment. And that's after she finishes kicking your asses."

The assistant's visage shaded from red to crimson. I wasn't sure if it was Luc's threat to send him back the main temple at the capital or that Luc reprimanded him in my presence.

Or maybe it was the fact that Shi Hua probably could take on the entire priesthood, wardens, and staff of Light and win.

"Yes, High Brother." Once again, Istaqa pivoted on his boot heel and stomped out of Luc's office. He slammed the door for good measure.

I finished chewing and swallowed. "Trouble?"

"Nothing you didn't start," Luc snapped.

His bad mood stung. "I was trying to help. With that damn audit and—" I shrugged. There was no judicious way to point out between the imposter who'd murdered the real Brother Mat, Kam's death during the battle to regain control of the Temple of Love, and Luc's own injury, poor Brother Jeremy had been run ragged until both the Issuran and Jing Reverend Fathers of Light agreed to Shi Hua's temporary transfer.

With my prodding and an assist from both nations' Reverend Mothers of Balance.

"I know. I'm sorry." Luc poured more tea into his mug and added a healthy dollop of honey. "With the current investigation into the infiltration—"

"Yes?" I prompted.

"This cannot leave my office."

I raised an eyebrow. *And how do you plan to stop Istaqa? He's listening outside your door.*

Luc sipped his tea before he grinned. *By using mind speech so he can't hear a blessed word.* He quickly sobered. *They found another infiltrator at the Temple of Light in Multnomah.*

A chill rippled across my skin. Part of me had hoped our situation here in Orrin was an isolated incident. *But that's in Pagonia.*

*And Tandor is on the border with Cant.*

Tandor. Our sister city to the south. All evidence pointed to our problems coming from there, but if Issura's northern neighbor also had been compromised . . .

*But our imposter was born on the island of New Thenos*, I countered

*And that's on the other side of the continent. I agree with Shi Hua. With the demon incidents here and in Jing, we may have stumbled across a worldwide conspiracy. Messages have gone out to the temples in other lands. Quietly.*

I couldn't suppress my shiver. Such a plot would explain why someone had hired the Assassins Guild to kill me. Thanks to my inept attempt to gain human eyesight, I was the only one who could see demons.

And once again, it made me wonder why Shi Hua was at the top of the Guild client's assassination wishlist. I was beginning to think it wasn't because she was a distance speaker of incredible power.

"You're worried about leaving Jeremy and Shi Hua here alone," I said, giving Istaqa something to gossip about.

"I'm more worried about my staff doing something incredibly idiotic," he started, using one of my favorite words. "Especially when it comes to Shi Hua."

"And this is what happens when they demand chastity from our orders," I grumbled. "I could have Gina guard her in the bathing room here if you want. Or she could use the facilities at Balance."

"Or I could petition the Issuran Reverend Father of Light to amend our order's criteria and allow admission of women."

I stared at Luc. "Do you think he'd actually consider such a proposal?"

Luc shrugged. "It all depends on what we find in Tandor when we ride down for the audit."

"And in the meantime?"

He grinned. "I'm looking forward to watching our Jing visitor wiping the cobblestones with anyone idiotic enough to lay an improper finger on her."

# Acknowledgments

Many thanks to the editor of the Sword and Sorceress anthologies, the incredible Elisabeth Waters, who took a chance on not one, but two, stories involving Justice Anthea and Brother Luc.

And even more thanks to the readers who sent me notes and e-mails, asking if I would ever do a full-length novel involving these characters. I'm glad you enjoy their adventures as much as I do, and yes, there's more on the way!

For more information or to be added to her mailing list, visit Suzan's website at www.suzanharden.com

# About the Author

**Suzan Harden** is a recovering attorney who writes fiction to regain her sanity. She currently lives in the Great Lakes region with a husband who believes writing is a practical career option and a kid who thinks she's too enamored with zombies.

www.ingramcontent.com/pod-product-compliance
Lightning Source LLC
Chambersburg PA
CBHW070435170726
48291CB00002B/520